KAARON WARREN

Walking the Tree

ANGRY
ROBOT

ANGRY ROBOT
A member of the Osprey Group

Lace Market House,
54-56 High Pavement,
Nottingham
NG1 1HW, UK

www.angryrobotbooks.com
Ghosts

Originally published in the UK by Angry Robot 2010
First American paperback printing 2011

ISBN 978-0-85766-043-5

Printed in the United States of America

9 8 7 6 5 4 3 2 1

For James, Mitchell and Nadia

Laburnum — OMBU — *Aloes*

The community of Ombu awoke to the sound of Leaffall. The soft early fall of leaves meant soon the Tree would let enough light through to dapple the sand and it would be time to choose the teachers.

Lillah's father began the selection process, collecting seawater in a large, leaf-lined wooden bowl. He covered this tightly with more leaves and tied it securely with a strong strip of bark. He placed the bowl in the roots, where the water drew strength from the Tree for ten days, after which enough sweet water had formed to wash the faces of the ten young women seeking testing.

Lillah collected the bowl then took it to the nine other girls up for selection. They sat in the moonlight and bathed each other's faces. The water would keep their skin honest, and in the morning, when they faced the fathers, only truth would be shown.

"This is nice," Lillah said. "You're gentle."

Melia laughed. "Lillah likes a woman's touch. She's going to be disappointed at the touch of a man."

The girls laughed, teasing and poking each other. Melia jumped up and spoke in a deep voice. "Are there any girls here who can match my virility? Any of you?"

"Oh, Melia," Thea said. "You will have some fun if they send you."

"They might send us all. You never know with the fathers."

"What are you saying about the fathers?" Melia's mother, Cynthia, came upon them. "The fathers are having a good rest in readiness for tomorrow. You would be sensible to do the same. Have you washed your faces?"

The girls nodded. Melia's mother's croaky voice made them listen, feel lucky. In her home Order of Parana, young people burned throats with an ember. When she whispered, the croakiness was not so awful, so she mostly whispered.

Whispering can be very strong.

"And the sap is prepared for the morning? Softening?"

Melia gave her mother a hug. "We are ready, as every group has been ready before us. We'll be fine. We are magnificent."

The girls giggled again and Melia's mother shook her head. "Bed, girls," she said. She was far more restrained than once she was. When she had first arrived she had been wilder. Life had tamed her. People said she had watched her own brother die in a terrible way. Sea monster? Deep black hole? Ghost cave? And that she had never recovered from this tragedy.

Lillah walked to her father's home, feeling her skin tingle on her cheeks. Living arrangements were fluid in the Order of Ombu. Lillah, Melia and Thea shared a house sometimes. Lillah otherwise shared a house with her father, or Logan and Magnolia. Melia shared with three, four, or five other young women. Thea lived with her brother Dickson and some of the young men. They treated her like a boy. But beds could shift. Lillah could wake to find Agara sleeping on the floor, or one of the children.

Lillah had moved in with her friends two years earlier, when she was nineteen. It seemed time to give her father space, and it was important to know the girls she would hopefully become teachers with; know what they were like to live with, so there would be less of a transition.

The sunlight dappled through. It was a wonderful time of year. Everyone was warmer without the constant shadow of the Tree. And with the shadow not constant, it seemed to the people that the sentinel nature of the Tree was at rest.

This enlivened the people. The sun on them in the daytime, the Treeshadow lessened. It seemed a good time for the teachers to be chosen and the school to leave. Time for the people to make their own decisions, not led by the nature of the Tree. Sometimes, in the wet season, water seeped up through the sand as far up as the roots of the Tree. Salty water, no good for growing food. Light bounced off the water and made the undergrowth seem brighter. Sand soft and warm and the sap running smooth from the Trunk, uncut, flowing uncalled for but precious down the Trunk.

Myrist, Lillah's father, speaking loudly over Leaffall, said, "Good you are here. Stay the night. I'll feed you and you will be full of energy for tomorrow. Though I may not be able to attend with you. I may not be able to watch the testing."

Lillah put her arm around him. "You have to be there! I will lose belief in myself otherwise."

"It will depend on Magnolia, Lillah. Her pains are starting to come through and if she is ready to give child tomorrow, I will be with her."

"I will be with her, too."

He shook his head. "No, Lillah. You will not be needed then. Afterwards, yes. But selection is all that matters to you tomorrow. You glow. You are beautiful," her father said.

Lillah felt beautiful and capable of all things. "I hope they will choose me for my looks, then. Is my dress finished?"

"A new dress is not going to get you a job as a teacher." Her father sounded tired: a deep bone weariness that seemed to come across men once their children were grown. His words were interrupted by a rain of leaves on the roof. The leaves had been dropping for six days now, and were stored to be used as plates, climbing shoes, buckets, spades, funnels, hats.

Lillah's father was right: the dress would not sway any opinions, not at this stage.

Lillah felt she had a good chance. She had passed the learning tests easily.

For the emotion test the fathers presented the girls with options. They told a story and the girls had to describe how the characters would be feeling.

"There was once an old woman who greatly treasured her shell collection. She would spend all day polishing and sorting it. She did not allow her husband to touch it. How do you think he felt?"

There was no correct answer, merely to have empathy for the man. So, bored, lonely, envious and annoyed were all acceptable. Lillah said, "Happy that his wife was happy," and was smiled at as an idealist.

It was much easier when the story was about the emotions of a child, because they had been children, could remember something of it. They had never been old.

Physically Lillah was as strong as or stronger than any of the others except Thea. She had always been a good eater and liked to be solid in her size. She had deep, secure, emotional ties. She loved her father, her brother and her brother's wife, Magnolia, and she would love their baby when it came. Fortunately there was no boy she pined for. Unlike two of the eligible girls, she had not fallen in love with a local boy.

Such a thing was doomed to failure. There could be no issue from the marriage. There had been babies born this way in the past. It was something Lillah remembered well from school: the preserved bodies of terribly deformed babies.

The physical tests were joyful: running, climbing, spinning. The monkeys leapt with them, screeching, getting caught under their feet. Erica hated them because they made her sneeze, and the crawling creatures on their skin she hated too.

Agara was the greatest at the water test. She loved to swim, and the salt didn't hurt her eyes. She could find the seaweed for their facial masks, the right kind that didn't cause burns, and she could dive down for it without a care. She liked to float on the water, letting herself drift, but others called her back, "Agara, you are going out too far." Agara's father worried more than most. He didn't care what any other girl did: only his own child was important.

He was a newcomer, having appeared near the ghost cave when he was fifteen. No family, no background. But it didn't matter. He was considered a gift for the new blood he brought. There were some who believed he came from the ghosts and would not go near him: Lillah did not like to get too close. She thought that sometimes she could see a mist around his shoulders, as if his Tree-ghosts were gathered there, talking to him.

They were tested on their cleverness, too, to see how they remembered their family background. Rham, one of the students, outdid the lot of them, muttering answers from behind a rock.

"Quiet, Rham! Let them do it themselves!"

Agara spoke a poem of the names in her lineage, making the past come to life. If selected, she would be given the Gift Poem to memorise.

Lillah talked of numbers, of how many in this Order and that, how many people would exist soon. Magnolia had helped her with this in the last weeks.

In the morning, the fathers gathered for the Talkings, where they would take each girl separately and ask many questions. Or none. Thea, Melia and Lillah waited in the small house they shared. Thea sat by the window, watching some children playing in the Tree roots and the women making the clay pots Ombu was famous for. Lillah and the others helped make the pots, too, when they weren't taking the time to be tested. "I wonder if they'll listen to us. Like us."

Melia snorted. "Thea, why are you thinking about this? We are in charge. It doesn't matter if they like us or not. Why don't you go and ask Dickson if he really intends to surprise us all when we leave. Try to find out what he is going to do."

Thea stood, nodding. "I can try. He likes me."

"You're his sister, Thea. Again, it doesn't matter if he likes you or not."

As Thea left, Melia rolled her eyes. "Part of me is hoping she is not selected for the school. Some time away from her would do me good."

"Who would you use as a slave then?" Lillah asked, smiling. She followed after Thea, knowing she needed to counteract her friend's cruel words.

"You're the only one who cares about me, Lillah," Thea said. "What will I do when you hate me like everyone else does?"

"I'll never hate you."

Thea had never been popular, but a tragic event a year earlier meant people distrusted her as well. Two children had drowned while in her care, and some said she did very little to save them.

Lillah's brother Logan poked his head in the door. "What are you doing here? Is it Magnolia?" Lillah asked, instantly alert. She placed a bowl of fruit on the table, taking a piece to eat.

Logan's brow furrowed at his wife's name. "She's very tired. She says she feels hot. She's ready for the baby to come. She's rambling about making pots and how she is letting us down."

"Who's with her?"

"Our father, and the Birthman. They aren't worried. They say she'll be fine." Logan sat on her bed.

"Get off my sulu," she said, pulling the long piece of patterned material, which she'd laid out on the bed, from under him. He moved to the table, sitting with his face in his hands. She wrapped her sulu around her waist, tucking the ends in and rolling the top down to keep it in place. She squatted to check there was room for movement.

"I still don't know if I'm ready to be a father."

Lillah threw her head back and laughed. Her soft dark hair tickled her back. She liked the feeling, liked to laugh that way. "It's too late to change your mind. You can't send a baby back." Logan looked very young, sitting at the table where they had whispered so many secrets, won and lost so many games. "You'll be a wonderful father. And I love Magnolia. She's a great woman. I'm glad she chose us."

Logan blinked. "Me. She chose me." Lillah, dressed now, took another sulu and draped it around her brother's neck. She pulled him close and kissed him gently on the mouth.

"Of course she did. She only had eyes for you."

The school system worked so well, she thought. Young women as teachers, walking around the Tree with their young charges. Five years, the walk took. They stopped in every community along the way, learning about the people, the food, the habits.

The young women sought partners along the way, engaged physically with any man they found attractive, until one man, one community, called too strongly for them to continue. The teacher would stay with that community, adopt it, and another young woman would take her place.

"You were both so beautiful to watch. I want that, too, Logan. That wonder you felt when you first saw each other."

"We still feel it. It hasn't faded. I wish that for you as well," Logan said. "That's what I came to say."

"And to escape the hard work! Get back to Magnolia. They need you."

The girls met to flatten their hair with the sap of the Tree. Lillah hated the smell of it and the feel of it. The hardness of it hurt her head. But this was meant to make them equal, to ensure one with beautiful hair did not influence the fathers. Those with ugly hair should have just as much of a chance at this stage. Of course, once the physical testing began, that could change.

Lillah sat next to Erica, who had thin, frizzy hair, which she kept tied back with thick grey twine. It irritated her face, wispy bits blowing into her eyes, feathery ends tickling her cheeks. They all sat in a circle on the beach. The sand was soft and warm and she could have easily slept. It was not like here everywhere, and Lillah had a moment of doubt about the journey. Should she leave? Or should she stay, where the sand was soft and warm?

At the end of the seawalk waited the fathers. They would decide between them who should go. Lillah was frightened of them: she knew they saw right to her soul, and would see her lying by the blackening of her blood. *Not that I've lied. Just that perhaps I smile more on the outside than the inside,* she thought.

She watched as Melia skipped back up the seawalk. She was gratified to see a tinge to Melia's face; reddened from too much sun, or from the questions the fathers had asked. Lillah and Melia were great friends and great rivals.

"How was it?" Erica asked as Melia stepped off the seawalk. For a moment she didn't speak, just stood clenching her toes in the sand.

"Hot," she said. She shook her head at further requests for information and sat in the circle again.

"Lillah. You're next," Aquifolia said. Aquifolia had no children of her own, so she had found a new position for herself, organising the teacher trials. She rarely took a lover. Her hair was like straw, her legs thick and pale like a root too soon exposed. She made it clear that she had sacrificed herself. Given her life so the girls would have an easy preparation for school is what she said, but truly she had only given up what she would never have. In the four Orders she had visited before stopping at Lillah's, she had found no affection. She was not happy. Lillah and Melia had discussed her choices. She'd stayed in Ombu for one man, Gutt, who had failed to impregnate her and then drowned. She frightened the other men and they wanted nothing to do with her.

Melia said, "In so many ways I pity her. She can't have children. She has no family."

"At least she is free to grow herself, do this job, become stronger. We will be mothers and not much else," Lillah said.

Melia shook her head. "You have a foolish view of being a mother. It expands you; it doesn't contract or confine you. Perhaps you should stay behind, if that's the way you feel. Don't go to school at all."

Lillah jumped up and ran to the seawalk. "I want this, I want this," she said. She wanted to go to school, she had to go. She rested a plate of sweets on her hip. She hoped they wouldn't get too sandy and regretted running out of the house, too lazy to find a cover for the food. She couldn't bounce lightly for fear of spilling it. Lillah was proud of her sweets knowledge. There was magic in her fingertips: she could roll a ball so perfect diners couldn't bear to bite.

"You should calm down," Erica said. "They don't like agitated teachers."

"Thank you for your advice, Erica. Of course you're right." Lillah couldn't stand being told what to do by Erica, who was as serious as she was beautiful. Melia and Lillah sometimes tried to tease her, but she had so little laughter in her it was not worth the effort.

She walked out onto the rough boards of the seawalk. She walked gently, toe to heel, knowing this was the way to avoid splinters. Her feet were tough from rock-walking, Tree-climbing, sea-walking, but even so, she would return to her place in the circle with at least a few sharp pieces of wood to remove.

The fathers sat fanning themselves at the end of the seawalk.

Melia's mother Cynthia sat watching on the shore, her feet thrust into the water. She had always been adventurous, from the moment she arrived in the Order. She had come from a place where the land stretched only a kilometre from beach to Trunk. The population was low and the people conservative, as if their small living space meant smaller minds. She always said her Order was dead; she had no intention of going back, neither would any other woman chosen as a teacher. Cynthia knew of just two teachers from other Orders who had chosen to stay in Parana but she guessed they would leave with homelust once their children were raised. The young women would leave as they always had. Only the males would stay, standing hopelessly looking up the beach for a mate.

The sun was strong out on the water and Lillah walked slowly, loving the warmth of it. It was so good to be warm. On days when most of the work was done, everybody liked to parade on the seawalk, sitting down, snoozing, catching up on some of the sunlight they missed under the Canopy.

Her feet felt sharp pains as splinters worked their way into her heels.

"Come on, Lillah, there are other girls to talk to," Melia's father called. "Let's speed it up, please."

I know that, I've just been sitting in a circle pretending to wish them luck for an hour, Lillah thought. She forced a smile on her face and knelt down before the fathers. "Hello," she said. The sun was in her eyes and she had to squint. She could feel the heat of it burning her, and knew she would look red for the physical judging in the evening. Lillah cursed herself for leaving her hat behind. She couldn't hold her plate of sweets and keep her hat safe from the wind, and she had chosen the sweets. Perhaps not such a good idea.

Suddenly, from land, came a terrible cry. Lillah instantly thought of someone crushed, trapped beneath a massive fallen Limb and legs crushed to jelly.

"It must be Magnolia," Thea's father said. "It's time." Lillah jumped up in shock. Her plate of sweets fell to the seawalk and shattered.

"Is she all right?" Lillah asked, realising as she spoke they couldn't possibly know.

"You run to find out, Lillah. Then come back to tell us." Lillah nodded and ran, not caring about the splinters now. She could work them out later with a long, thin bone needle, line them up like a score to show Magnolia how much she cared.

Lillah ran past the spectators, the pot makers and the young women waiting their turn. "What is it,

Lillah? What did they say?" she heard Erica call.

"Nothing yet, it's Magnolia," she shouted over her shoulder as she ran.

"I'll come with you," Melia said.

The shriek rang out again. Lillah felt her stomach clench and her legs falter. She did not want to see this. She did not like blood or pain. She had seen a man crushed by a Tree Limb, once, speared through the belly and anchored across the legs. The screams Lillah heard now equalled those of Araucari when that Tree Limb fell. This was worse, in fact. There was something very animalistic about it. Monkey-like.

Lillah and Melia ran.

As they approached Logan's house, Lillah stopped. She did not want to see. She wanted to go back to her interview, make them love her. Let them choose her as Number One, exclaim over her bonsai, score her highly for it and say how clever she was, how like the Tree it was. Let them lick their fingers to savour the last taste of her sweets. Let them say, "Lillah, we are unanimous in our decision."

The wails were much louder, now. Lillah could not imagine how her sister-in-law, a slight woman with delicate fingers, could make such a noise.

Lillah and Melia entered the house. It was smaller than their own, but much neater. Magnolia had been nesting in the six days before. Every surface sparkled. Everything had a place.

Magnolia roared.

"Oh, my, is she all right? Where's the Birthman? Can't he help?"

Lillah felt tears forming in her eyes. "Magnolia," she said. She knew she had to face this or run away forever. She stepped forward to the front door and pushed it open. She felt as if a wave of heat, miasmic heat, came pouring out. She choked.

Melia said, "I don't think they need me. I'll tell the others you'll be along."

Lillah heard "Nonononononon", and she ran then, knocking over a jug, ignoring the smash and the mess.

"Logan?" she called. "Magnolia?"

Her father opened the door to the bedroom and stepped out. Lillah gasped at his exhausted face, his slumped shoulders.

"Lillah," he said. "Your interview."

"They said I could come to find out about Magnolia. Is she okay? What's happened?"

Her father leaned one hand high on the door frame then rested his head against his straightened arm. "It's okay, Lillah. She's exhausted, but I think we're nearly there. We are into the second day. I wish I could take over for her. You want to take the suffering of the children."

"You look exhausted yourself. Can't you call someone to help?" Her father shook his head weakly. "The Birthman is here. He's doing all he can." He stood back and opened the door wide, so Lillah could see inside.

"I'm trapped, I'm caged," Magnolia wailed. Her eyes flicked open suddenly and Lillah jumped back. She thought Magnolia was going to sit up, point a finger, say "It is your fault", then collapse back on the bed.

"You're not trapped," Lillah said from the doorway, braving her sister-in-law.

"I'm trapped. There's no place to go but forward."

Lillah's father nodded. "Women always say strange things when they're in labour. Don't they?" He looked at the Birthman.

"The funniest things, some of them. Scream abuse at their men. Some of the things you hear! It's like they've been saving it up for their entire life, to spew out when no one will blame them."

Lillah stepped away and her father said, "Come on, we'll go out for a few blinks."

In the kitchen, Melia brewed tea. Lillah leaned forward and kissed her father. "I only hope I find a father-in-law as loving and accepting as you are to Magnolia. I wish I could stay here. Can't they send a husband to me? I don't mind waiting."

Tears came to Myrist's eyes. "You would not miss this journey for all the Bark on the Tree. It is a wonderful time. The learning, the joy. The hard work, too, they tell me, but the joy of guiding the children through their education…"

"I barely remember my teachers," Lillah said. The fresh water boiled, and they knocked at the bedroom door once, then again when there was no response.

"Magnolia? Logan?" she called quietly.

"Come in," Logan said. Lillah opened the door and entered, her father so close behind she could feel his heart beat.

There was blood in the room. The smell of it hung heavy, and the smell of waste, too. Magnolia lay slumped on the bed. The Birthman, Pittos, looked exhausted. He washed his hands, dried them on his apron. He was a very large man who almost filled the room. Lillah and the other children had loved him when they were little. Even as a young man he could carry six of them; one on his shoulders, one on his back, one under each arm and one clinging to each leg. He would stomp about, roaring and spinning like a giant salmon trying to shake off lice. When Rhizo had arrived, one of four teachers escorting ten children, she was light, like cobwebs, and she giggled like bird call. He fell in love with her and courted her with songs and playfulness. She fell in love with his joy of children.

Overcoming his tiredness, he smiled brightly at Lillah and Myrist as they entered the room.

"Myrist, I think we should change the sheets. Freshen up." Lillah's father nodded. Lillah helped change the blood-stained sheets while Logan held Magnolia, who was panting so quickly Lillah wondered she didn't faint.

"We're getting there, darling," the Birthman said. He stroked Magnolia's brow. "Some way to go, but we're getting there."

Magnolia opened her eyes wide as a new contraction rose within her. She rolled over onto her hands and knees and threw her head back. She roared. Logan rubbed her back, stroked her forehead.

"Is this normal?" he said. "Is she okay?" The Birthman nodded. "It's long, but she's fine, and so is the baby. We just need patience." He dipped a cloth into a bowl of dark-tinted water and gave it to Magnolia to suck. "This will help with the pain."

Magnolia sank back on her bed, eyes closed, then another contraction took her.

"Wonderful. That's just wonderful," Pittos said. He looked between Magnolia's legs and said, "This is good. That pain moved things along."

Logan sat, straight-backed, on the bed. Lillah could tell, even in these circumstances, he was presenting a face: a stoic, strong, loving face. He was that way; stoic, strong and loving, but he wanted everyone to know it, to think it of him.

Things moved quickly, then. Lillah kept back, watching Magnolia's face, knowing it was her but not recognising her at the same time.

There was a cry, a baby's cry and Pittos held a pink baby boy. He cleaned the child very carefully, with a soft, oiled cloth, smoothing him, cooing to him, creating a space of calm.

Somehow people crowded into the room, as if they sensed the moment had come. Someone said to Magnolia, "Don't be disappointed it's a boy.

More people have boys than girls, you know. You're normal."

Magnolia smiled. "Thanks." She saw Lillah stick her tongue out behind the woman's back and laughed. "I'll try to be happy."

"Do all these people need to be here?" Lillah said. The Birthman looked up, shook his head.

"Right, everybody, please, out," Lillah said. She pushed Morace, Pittos' red-headed son, roughly in the back. He clung to his father's legs, but Pittos shook him off. "We need firewood and food, we need the news spread, we need clean clothes and we need space. You've all been wonderful but it's time to go." Lillah had no idea if any of this was true but it didn't matter. The people nodded.

"Okay, Teacher," someone said, and they all laughed. Good to laugh when the danger is over.

Once the room had been emptied, it seemed cooler. All they could hear now was the retching breath of Magnolia. Each breath drawn in as if a battle was being fought, each breath released reluctantly, because it meant the battle would begin again.

Pittos bathed the baby. "You will do this next time, Logan," he said. "You need to be gentle but firm." He finished the bath and dried the baby carefully, then wrapped him in a light blanket, tucking his hands with their long fingernails inside.

"Help Magnolia to sit up," he said to Logan.

"What?" he said. He looked at her. "She's tired. She needs to lie down."

Pittos shook his head sharply. "It's the baby we need to think of at this moment. Nothing else is important. He needs to feed from her. This first feed is more important than all others to follow. There will never be a more important meal. He needs to feed now. If she dies before he drinks, he will miss out on much of what he will need to make him a strong man. Listen to me."

Logan started crying. "She just needs a rest. She needs to sleep."

Logan's father went to him and squeezed his shoulders.

"Your son needs to drink. Be a hard man, now, and help us."

Pittos rocked back and forwards toe-heel, murmuring in the baby's ear. The infant soothed, but his tiny lips smacked together and his eyes rolled.

Lillah, Logan and Myrist gently helped Magnolia into a seated position. They propped her up with the cushions and pillows stuffed with sand.

Magnolia said, "Dad?" Myrist squeezed her hand. "This is when you want your own family. But we are here. We will care for you."

Pittos knelt onto the bed and one-handedly arranged Magnolia until her breasts were exposed. He put two pillows on Magnolia's lap then lay the baby down. The baby began to whimper as he sniffed milk close by.

"Lift the baby up. Put both arms under the pillows and raise him," the Birthman said. He pulled back Magnolia's shoulders then grasped one aureole between two fingers.

"Okay. Let's hope he's a natural," he said. "Lift him so his face is close to the breast."

Logan, his face still, determined, raised his son. The baby snuffled at the nipple then opened his mouth wide.

"Put him on! That's it. Hang on." Pittos made a gentle flick at the baby's lips then settled back.

"That's okay," he said.

Magnolia winced, flinched, as the baby began to suckle.

Logan bent forward. "He's hurting her. This can't be right."

"It's all right, Logan," Magnolia said. Her eyes flicked open as the baby began to suck. Her other breast dripped a thin yellowish fluid.

"Lovely stuff. Perfect. That's so good for baby," Pittos said.

The very act of breastfeeding sent a signal to Magnolia's body, and she groaned suddenly as another contraction took her.

"Twin?" Logan said, confused. "Is she having another one?"

Pittos shook his head. "It's the placenta. This is perfect, exactly how it should be." Pittos held his hand up for silence and he helped Magnolia deliver the placenta, which he handed carefully to Myrist. "She's lost a lot of blood. We'll feed her half of this, save the rest for the Treeroots." The baby fed.

Magnolia was pale.

"This can't be helping her," Lillah said. The baby pulled his head off the breast and wailed.

"Quiet!" Pittos snapped. "You are disturbing him."

"Sorry," Lillah said.

The Birthman shook his head. "He's still hungry. Other side." They shifted him to feed on the other side. Lillah could see the depleted breast like an empty sac against Magnolia's chest.

The baby sucked until his eyelids closed and he fell asleep with his mouth still full of nipple. Magnolia sat up in bed, holding her baby, her eyes darting from side to side as if catching odd movement, which frightened her.

"We're lucky. It's rarely that easy," Pittos said.

Myrist nodded. "Neither of you took to it so easily. Both too headstrong. Your mother struggled and struggled to feed you. She was headstrong too."

"Are you saying my nephew is weak-willed?" Lillah asked.

Logan nodded. "It's started already. *In my day, things were like this*," he said. His voice was not quite up to the joke.

Pittos leaned over and popped the baby off the breast with a flick of his little finger.

"Hopefully he'll sleep now so we can deal with his mother. I've sent Tax out for spiderwebs but I thought he'd be back by now."

Logan laughed. "Tax. He's probably picking flowers for her as well. He's certain she really wanted to choose him for a husband."

"We need webs."

"I'll go," Lillah said. She ran away into the undergrowth around the Tree. She knew where the biggest spiders lived. They liked the darkest places, where Limbs grew low and roots grew high. The children didn't like these spots. Too dark and cold. They told each other the ghosts came out of the Tree here and stood watching the living. Lillah had seen this once, as a young girl. It still gave her the shivers to think about it. She had been playing with a pile of wood scraps, building a house for spiders, when she felt a soft breeze over her shoulder.

Standing there, breathing heavily, was a pale, tall man. He was naked, hairless. Lillah screamed, backed away, knocking over her spider house. "GHOST!" she screamed. He scurried back into the cave before anyone could reach her.

Lillah was always careful when collecting spiders, or wood from that place. She still told the children to beware, that ghosts could watch at any time and who knew what it was they wanted?

She rolled skeins of web around her fists. "Sorry, Madame," she said. The spider was as large as her kneecap. High in the next web a spider the size of her head, legs as fat as her fingers, watched her.

"Sorry, Madame Spider," Lillah said. "You can spin some more." While she kept her tone light,

Lillah knew she would scream if the spider landed on her. She didn't mind picking them up; she was in control that way. She loved the strength and intelligence of spiders and could watch, fascinated, for hours as they span their webs.

Her favourite spider legend was an old one. It was etched into the Tree so long ago those markings were long since disappeared up the Trunk of the Tree, but which was told so often, most people knew it by heart.

There was once a teacher who, tired of the noise of children, the chatter of the other teachers, went walking amongst the roots of the Tree. She was blessed as she walked because a massive Trunk fell and anchored her to the ground.

She called out for help until her throat was too dry to speak. She wanted to cry but knew she shouldn't waste the water.

Realising no one had missed her, or not trusting them to find her, she knew she had to throw the Tree Limb off herself. She managed to break a branch off, fit it under the large Limb and lever the Limb off her leg. Ignoring the excruciating pain, she twisted her leg free.

Once she dropped her lever, she collapsed. Blood poured from the huge gash in her thigh and she felt weak and very, very tired. She closed her eyes for second, then felt, above the pain, a tickle on her leg. Opening her eyes she saw an enormous spider.

She didn't scream. Something about the purpose-fulness of the spider calmed her.

The spider walked back and forth across the wound many hundreds of times, sometimes being washed off by the flow of blood. But the flow less-ened as the web thickened and eventually stopped.

Lillah, her arms full of webs, ran back to the house.

Magnolia was even paler, and there was a smell of vomit in the air.

"Here," Lillah said. Pittos threw back the covers and Lillah saw for the first time just how damaged Magnolia appeared to be.

Pittos unwound the webs from Lillah's wrists and thrust them up between Magnolia's legs.

"There were twenty-two people in here," Mag-nolia said. "How did they all fit?" Then she closed her eyes, still holding her baby.

"The baby will be fine," Logan said. "I won't take my eyes off him." Magnolia let go of her child but stared unblinking at him.

"More webs," the Birthman said.

Lillah did three more trips, each further afield. She knew where the spiders were because she stud-ied them, loved them.

Myrist took the placenta and carefully sliced it with his stone knife. Lillah and Logan took part of it and buried it in the roots of the Tree, while Myrist cooked the rest in tiny dice with onions.

"Don't cook all the goodness out," Pittos called.

"I think I would know that, since my own wife came to this Order with the tradition," Myrist said quietly, winking at Lillah.

He took the plate to Magnolia, resting it on her knees and feeding her piece by piece.

Logan stroked Magnolia's brow, kneeling on the bed beside her. He did not put any weight on her legs. Lillah watched him and thought him brave for not complaining. She could see blood soaking his pants where he knelt.

Lillah wanted to sit down and close her eyes. She knew her tiredness was nothing like that of Magnolia's, or Logan's, or Myrist's, or Pittos', but it was tiredness enough. She could not rest, though. She needed to return to the fathers, report back, give them the information they were waiting for. She didn't see how she could interview; in her exhaustion she would forget about her teacher face and be too honest. She dreaded the question: "Why do you want this job?" She was supposed to say, everyone said, "For the joy of watching the children blossom with knowledge, and for a chance to understand the Orders of the Tree through the eyes of an adult".

Her real answer, the honest one, was that all she thought about was sex; men; that she *could not wait* to lie with a man and feel him inside her.

That was not what they wanted to hear.

She picked up her bonsai and walked towards the beach. Only moments passed before word got out she was on the move.

"Is she all right? Baby? Boy or girl? Has he fed? Birthman gone? Are they sleeping?" Nobody liked a sick person. The sickness called Spikes made the ghosts in the Tree hungry. Any sick person knew how much your bones ached, how much weaker you became. The ghosts ate the bones of the sick, kept eating until the body was all flesh. The Spikes epidemic was not something people were proud of. Although Spikes had occurred hundreds of years earlier, people still knew that it passed from person to person, transported by the sick. They knew they did not want the population halved again. They did not want people to die. So they took precautions.

Lillah didn't know exactly what those precautions were; she only knew she did not want to sicken herself.

Magnolia didn't believe in this but that didn't mean it wasn't true.

Lillah stopped and spoke to every one who had a question for her. When she reached the beach, the circle of young women was gone. She peered to the end of the seawalk but in the dim light she couldn't tell if the fathers were there or not. There was a strange kind of light, evening with a storm coming. The heat had gone but the cold not yet risen. She felt as if she was caught between two worlds and that if she misstepped, she would stay in the wrong one.

There was a crack of lightning and Lillah stood on the sand, undecided, lost. She felt she needed to do the exact right thing, impress people with her choices, but couldn't think what they wanted to see.

"Lillah?" she heard. It was Melia. "Here you are at last. I got tired of waiting for Magnolia to give out that baby. The fathers are at the Tree Hall. They were wary of the storm."

The girls walked together. "Is Magnolia okay? And you?" Melia asked as they walked.

Lillah nodded. "I feel like I've been dreaming for days," she said. "You have to go see the baby. He's the most beautiful thing you've ever seen. Is the testing all over? Have I missed my chance?"

Melia shook her head. "Come on."

The smells of cooking as they walked made Lillah hungry. "My mother used to say we should cook food slowly and there's no rush if you start early enough. Her food always smelled so good."

Her stomach rumbled and she wished she'd grabbed fruit or bread from Logan's kitchen. She could picture the food on the table; Magnolia always had food ready. She was a wonderful hostess.

They reached the Tree Hall. The Tree Hall was low. The tallest in the Order had to stoop to enter, but could stand inside. There were doors at either end, but you entered through one, left by the other. Most of the Order could fit inside if they stood close together. Others would lean in through the windows. Lillah always tried to arrive late when the Order gathered here, to have a spot outside leaning in. It was so close inside, pressed together, thick, airless. The walls were curved, so all voices could be heard easily. It was very warm inside and people wore little clothing.

The other girls huddled outside the Tree Hall, and greeted Lillah with squeals and questions. Erica nodded and squeezed her hand.

Thea sat hunched over her bonsai, plucking at its leaves, grooming it until only bare twigs remained. She said in a low voice, "This is my last chance! I'll be twenty-five next birthday, and if I don't go now I'll never go."

"So go! What's the problem?"

"I just can't imagine how to like a man like that. It's terrifying."

What makes one person so shy and frightened, yet others so foolhardy? Lillah thought. "You don't have to do anything you don't want to," she said. "It is not set in wood that you have to be a teacher."

"I'm scared of leaving this home. What if others don't like me?"

"Haven't we always welcomed newcomers and teachers? That's how we'll be welcomed. Come with us and see. If you really can't bear it, you won't choose a mate and you'll walk home again."

Thea shook her head. "I have to be somewhere they don't know about the drowning. I have to start again, as me, not as the one who drowned the children."

Thea was called in to the fathers. Lillah, her head near the window, could hear most of the interview.

"I just don't know how I'll manage without Mother and Father. I'll never see them again," Thea told them.

"Thea, this is your obligation. The birth rate is low all around the Tree and you must play your part. There is no choice in the matter. If chosen, you will be with Lillah and Melia. Your home will be wherever you are with your friends and the children in your care. Then at last you will find a man to love and you will stop and have children of your own."

Thea was a very tall, solid woman. She sat uncomfortably on the floor, her knees pointing upwards. Her hair was long and she wore it in plaits, as if she wanted to cling on to childhood and not take on the responsibilities of an adult. "You have talent and strength to share," Erica's father said. "You are our strongest swimmer."

She loved to swim and was very fast. When someone spotted flotsam out at sea, often she didn't wait to see if it would come in to shore. She would swim out to it, rope around her waist to tow it back again. A carved plank of wood which once told a story but was now blurred. A pot with a strange sticky substance inside. A box with odd skin-like straps nobody wanted to touch.

"I would be happy to do that forever; swimming out to find treasures. I don't think I'll make a good mother."

The fathers sighed. "Any more reasons you shouldn't go?" one said.

Thea smiled. "I'm sure I can think of a dozen more." She looked hopeful; maybe they would let her stay behind. "Did you know I can't see very well? There's something wrong with my eyes. I'm not healthy enough to breed. I'm a defect. And I'm too big for a woman. We don't want that passed on."

The fathers were unmoved by her plea.

"You are the strongest, healthiest woman we've had in a long time. It is your duty to pass on those genes."

"There is no place for you here, now. You have to move on so another young woman can stay. This is how our world must work. We cannot have children born of two people close in geography or blood. You know that."

One of the other fathers had not yet spoken. He coughed now. "I am of the opinion that you are not a worthy teacher. You have shown us you are not capable of keeping children safe. You have, perhaps, shown us that you dislike children and do not think they deserve to be safe. I am of the opinion that you should stay here. It is our obligation to keep the flawed at home."

Thea sobbed. "No! I did all I could for those children! They drowned despite all I did to save them."

There was silence.

"You may go, Thea," Agara's father said.

Thea slumped. She crawled out of the Tree Hall, blubbering. Dickson and Tax, her brothers, hovering outside the circle, came to put their arms around her.

Lillah hoped she wouldn't take her depression along with her; it would make school very dull.

"Good luck," Melia said.

"Aren't you next?"

"They've spoken to me already." She shrugged. "It was okay. Terrifying, but okay. It's when they look at each other. I get nervous and start talking too much. Don't talk too much. Don't fill the blanks in. They know it all, anyway."

Lillah nodded. "All right." She stepped into the Tree Hall. With just the fathers inside it was a comfortable place to be. Usually there were too many people, too crowded, too close, not enough air. She hated that confinement, could feel it sucking the air from her blood.

The fathers sat drinking tea, talking. There was silence when Lillah entered.

"Well?" said one, after many blinks had passed. "We are waiting for the news. What of Magnolia and her baby?"

Lillah relaxed. They would try to frighten her, be aggressive, but all of it was a test. None of it was real. They were faking it to see how she would react. These men had fed her, bathed her, tended her wounds, comforted her.

"It's a baby boy, he's fine, he's already fed."

The men murmured and smiled at this news. A baby who did not take that first feed would be trouble for the Order. Especially a male baby.

Lillah felt pleased for Magnolia that she and her baby had managed this first thing. Male babies who fed poorly were considered unhealthy and not expected to lead long or fulfilling lives.

"And Magnolia? The bleeding?"

Lillah nodded. "When I left the bleeding had stopped and she was sleeping."

"Her cheeks? What colour were her cheeks?"

"Pink. Quite pink when I left." The murmurs again, and laughter. Lillah felt a sense of ownership, pride, as if as messenger she owned, had created, the good news. "She seems frightened, though. Nervous."

Agara's father, a strong-voiced, kind man said, "So many of our babies die in the first day. She doesn't want her baby to die. Now, Lillah, we have a report about your behaviour."

He is so arrogant. He is trying to frighten me, Lillah thought. Let them explain. Don't apologise or speak before I know what they're talking about. Is this about shouting at my father? Did they hear that Dickson tried to kiss me? Or is it about throwing away scraps of food because I'm too lazy to mince and compost them? Any of the small things she did in a day could be up for discussion.

Lillah let the silence sit, until Thea's father laughed.

"You're certainly good at holding your tongue when you want to," he said. "That is a talent, Lillah, which may help you in the future. You must be careful not to silence your true self, though. So many of us ignore our inner voices in trying to please those around us, and we can lose our individuality. I would hate to see you lose your character, Lillah. You must pick a partner with whom you can be your true self, but also a man strong enough to speak the truth himself. It will be very easy to choose somebody who worships you; you will find this wherever you go. You don't want to be a precious stone, untouchable, Lillah. You want to be a leader and you will be a great leader if you find a strong partner who is not frightened to tell you when you are wrong."

Lillah had to strain to concentrate because the words meant to her that she had been selected, even without the interview.

"Thank you," Lillah said at last. "Thank you. I will not ignore what you say. But can I choose someone handsome?"

The fathers laughed. "All want a handsome man, Lillah," Tilla said. "What will you seek beyond that? Do you have anything to you beyond what we see before us?"

Lillah felt tears prick her eyes. Tilla was an old man, his children grown, and a good friend to her. He made her laugh, helped her view the world honestly. Why was he being cruel to her now?

Dickson entered the hall and walked to the fathers.

"You should not be here, Dickson. This is not your place."

"I have a report to give. Pittos has asked me to come."

He spoke with the fathers as Lillah watched, her heart beating. She felt sure he was not saying anything good about her.

He stepped away, pursed his lips at Lillah, and left the hall.

The fathers conferred.

Then Tilla rose, took her hand. "Lillah, we have learnt a lot more about you from the way you handled yourself in your sister-in-law's birthing room than we would ever learn from hearing what you think we want to hear."

Lillah's eyes opened wider and she looked at the fathers. She felt guilty; she had underestimated them. They were not ego-driven at all; they were full of the spirit of the Order.

"I hope I didn't offend anyone when I asked them to leave Magnolia's room," Lillah said. "But there was no air, and it was too hot. They needed to go. There was too much pity, they thought she was going to die and wanted to be the first to offer sympathies and hold the poor motherless baby."

"You were right. You did it beautifully." Melia's father stood up and drew her into a hug. "The young men need to pass their judgements next. We will discuss placings tomorrow and the circle will meet at dawn on the day after that."

Lillah joined her friends in the small home they shared. "Do you think we will all be chosen? Melia, of course you are a teacher."

"So long as the young men approve," Melia said, smiling.

Lillah span around joyfully. Her skirt flared out from her thighs then softly rested back. Her skin felt so sensitive, so ready for touch.

Lillah wondered if Magnolia had felt this elation when chosen as a teacher in her own Order.

The girls giggled as they prepared for the young men. They wore the lightest of their clothes, shirts carefully woven from strands of leaves. They coloured their nipples, showing them off. Men associated good breasts with good mothering.

The community gathered by the Tree Hall, resting from work and looking forward to the show. The young men, keen for their chance to be the centre of attention, preened and strutted, making people laugh. Then Melia's father called, "The girls are ready. Everybody sit."

A seriousness dropped over them all. This was one of the moments that identified a group. Who would they send? Would they send the right teachers, keep the right girls at home?

The girls knew how important this was and were excited by it as well. Melia went first, walking through the young men, staring them in the eyes and smiling as she had never smiled at them before. The others followed; Lillah found it hard not to laugh. It felt ridiculous. The young men enjoyed it, though. They liked to feel they had some power. They felt that if they sent their best women away, other men would send their best women to them.

It was hard to take these young men seriously at first. They had grown up together, played games together. But Lillah found herself aroused by the process. Her nipples hardened as the young men stared at her, and she raised her arms and swayed. Catching Dickson's eye brought her back to reality.

This was the only time they would act as seducers. As they travelled, it would be up to the men to seduce them.

The young men left to talk together in their home, a low, neat shelter they shared at times. The young women, exhilarated, danced around in the shallow, warm puddles of low tide. Melia draped seaweed on her head and tossed it around like long hair. Thea stepped clumsily about, wanting to join in but not knowing how. Even Erica, her wispy hair loose, danced and span.

Agara's father called to them. "Girls, we are preparing to feast around Logan's house to welcome the baby and I imagine your help is needed over there. You go now, Lillah. Your cooking will help your father."

Lillah knew her cooking skills outshone the other girls. Her mother had been a famed cook.

Thea caught up with her. "Can I come and see the baby?"

They ran together.

Logan swept the veranda surrounding the place. He whistled, dancing with the broom. Lillah watched him, her heart filled with air at his happiness. His love for Magnolia, his joy at not losing her.

"Hey, Daddy!" Lillah said. Logan saw her and dropped the broom. He ran to her, picked her up and span her around. Thea looked at the floor.

"Isn't it wonderful?" he said. "I can't believe it. Just the matter of a few cups of blood. A few cups of blood more and I would have lost her."

Lillah squeezed him. "We're very lucky," she said. They heard voices: the people were arriving with dishes to share.

Magnolia slept. Her breath was less ragged and the baby was beginning to wriggle in his small wooden cradle. Lillah's father had made the cradle for Logan and Lillah to sleep in when they were born; it was very precious to them. Carved from one large piece of wood, he had spent the whole of Olea's pregnancy making it, carving pictures and stories. Many babies since had used the cot. As Lillah helped her father clean it in preparation for Logan's baby, he had spoken of how dear she had looked sleeping in it.

"Hungry again," Pittos said, back in attendance after a break. He smiled over the baby. "He can wait a while this time. Lillah, I need you to run out for me again. We need fallen bark. Dry stuff, if you can find it."

Magnolia began to stir as the baby whimpered. "Is he okay?" Magnolia asked. "Don't tell me. You will take him anyway, but I don't want to know."

"What is she saying?" Lillah felt nervous of Magnolia's weak tone.

"In some Orders they take a malformed baby and hang it off the Tree as a warning against love with someone too close in your line. We don't do that here, Magnolia. We accept deformities as part of growth. But your baby is perfect. I have not seen a boy so lovely in many years. Sturdy legs, strong voice, good will. You have done well."

"And a baby's death is part of growth as well?" Magnolia said. She kept count of them, the numbers. She liked numbers.

Magnolia started to twist in her bed, crying out. Logan came to stand beside her, his arms drooped, his fingers flicking as if he wanted to do something but couldn't think of the right thing.

The baby began to cry more loudly.

"Some Bark, Lillah," Myrist said.

Lillah found a bowlful and carried it back to Pittos, who shredded it in the bowl then squeezed a musky oil over it. He placed the bowl in a corner.

"It will send a good smell into the air and absorb the bad ones," Pittos said. "And now I must take my leave. My wife wants me home."

Borag, one of the youngest children who would travel with the school, stood waiting in the kitchen. Lillah banged ingredients onto the bench to make a healthy soup.

"I'm busy, Borag. I can't talk to you right now."

"I want to watch you cook," the child said, leaning on the bench.

The two built the soup. It smelled good and rich. Logan came down, sniffing. "This will cure a blind bird," he said, smiling. He kissed his sister. "Thank you, Lillah. You should get back to your testing."

"I can always go next year," she said, but they both knew she wanted to go now, get away, begin.

"A kiss for you, Borag? Our new cook?" Borag squealed and ran.

"When will the soup be ready? They are arriving, and hungry," Logan said. "But wait... are you selected? Are you a teacher?"

"They haven't told us yet. We are waiting for the young men's assessment. Do you think I will be?"

"I think they laughed in your foolish face and told you to clean the seawalk for the rest of your life."

Lillah hit him.

"Of course you'll be chosen. How could they say no to you?"

"I hope you're right. Has anyone collected plates?"

"We have plenty stored from the last Leaffall. But fresh ones would be nice. You always find the largest leaves. Good, dark green ones."

Chattering, excited laughter came to them as the villagers arrived. Lillah and Logan went outside to greet and seat them around the house on the veranda the villagers had all helped to build. There were five hundred people in Ombu, living in many houses. They brought bowls, pots, baskets of food. Someone brought tomatoes, small, red and juicy, and they ate them whole or threw them in the pot with fish and the greens that sprouted at the edge of the sand.

The coconut bowls were passed and each person scooped their portion from the cooking pot. More pots came out, with ground vegetables, crushed berries, birds' eggs, and people ate their fill.

Logan moved from one person to the next, thanking them, loving the attention.

That evening, word of the teacher rankings went around. "You are all beautiful. Erica is the most beautiful, then Lillah. Agara is clever with memory and the water. Melia is good with movement. Thea is beautiful but too shy. She is strong and a good swimmer. We have chosen to believe that she did all she could to save the drowned children and that she did not let them die. We recommend all those as teachers. Others are not selected." One of the five girls not chosen began to cry but the others accepted the news. One of these, Ruta, a girl Lillah expected to be chosen, stood tall, congratulating the teachers, comforting the others.

Agara's father spoke to Ruta. "Will you accept the position of trader?"

Ruta nodded.

Logan kissed Lillah. "You must go in and tell Magnolia and Dad."

She walked inside and upstairs. "Dad?" she called through the door.

"Come in," he said faintly. His voice sounded tired but not distraught. Lillah burst into the room. "I'm in! I'm in! They didn't even interview me they like me so much!"

"Shh!" her father said, though kindly. "They're both asleep. I was just cleaning up. I'll come out now. Tell me everything."

Lillah held her father's arm and told him all that had been said. Her father squeezed her tight. "I'm so proud of you. Not surprised, of course. But proud."

With one more check of Magnolia and the baby, he walked outside with Lillah to join the others around the Tale-teller.

"You must enjoy each moment of the Tree. Never be angry at it. It will not be with us forever." There was a murmur as this familiar tale began. Annan, their Tale-teller, had a smooth, enticing voice, lulling you to believe all he said. Lillah loved to listen to him, and tried to mimic his voice when she told stories.

"In the very centre of the Tree there is a fire. A slow, slow fire, burning the Old Tree like the sand smoothes the rock. This fire started many hundreds of years ago, and it is why the Tree feels warm to the touch sometimes when you think it shouldn't. The Tree is being destroyed from the inside out. One morning all we'll hear is a creaking, a massive creaking, then a crashing so loud we won't be able to talk, to say goodbye, we'll just lie down and let the Trunk crush us." Red salt was passed around and sprinkled on root vegetables.

Annan, the Tale-teller shivered. "No one knows how close the fire is, but we know it's burning. We can hear the crackle of it sometimes, can't we, if we press our ears up close to the Trunk." Lillah had done this many times as a child. Word would go out that you could hear the crackle and the children would run to listen.

Dickson snorted. "I won't be lying down, I'll be running to the sea. If I swim past the shade cast by the Canopy, I won't be crushed."

"You don't actually believe this story, do you?" his friend said. Dickson lost his cockiness. "No!" he said. "Of course not. I'm just saying what I would do if it did happen. I wouldn't lie down, that's all."

"No one's going to lie down," the friend said.

Dickson thumped his chest. "Not me. Imagine what it would be like to live without the Tree.

There'd be sunlight for most of the day. And we'd be able to see across the land." They loved the Tree, adored it without question, but they also loved the sun, and the Tree so often took all the sun from them.

"No one can see that far."

Annan, annoyed at their chatter, said, "You try living without the Tree for a day, see how you go. No fire, no medicine, nothing. No shelter. No rain water storage. This Tree keeps us alive and you know it. Even hanging our sick dead from a Limb is, to me, dangerous. What if the illness leaches out into the Tree?" He pointed to the hanging Limb. On the Trunk, very high, Lillah could see symbols and words, the names of those who died in the great Spikes epidemic. "We lost so many to the Spikes epidemic and still the chance of it is with us."

At the mention, Lillah instinctively felt her shoulder blades. No growth.

The Tale-teller, Annan, said, "I charge you teachers with caring for your bodies and ensuring you catch child only when you choose to. In this way we preserve our place around the Tree."

Erica said, "I can't understand why we're so scared of babies. We've hardly got any people."

"We don't want lots of people. This is the perfect amount for our world to work, for us to stay alive." The Tale-teller shook his head. "You should know this by now."

Thea said, "Imagine if there were too many of us. Everyone would fight for a place to live, and many would be closer to the Trunk than they'd like."

Dickson stood like Annan, strong and confident. "Oh, Great Tree, grant me my every wish because I am your humble servant. I will do your bidding, oh Tree. Oh, Tree, tell me your wish." There were shocked chuckles around him. He leapt off the balcony and jumped up to grab a low-lying Limb. "Ah," he said, when he had climbed up and was settled on a branch. Then he lowered his pants and pissed against the Trunk.

There was laughter and shocked gasps. Annan shook his head. "You are a man without worth."

"Rude! You are so rude!" Lillah said. Dickson jumped down beside her with his pants still about his ankles.

"And you wonder why men can't be teachers." She squeezed her eyes shut. "Dreadful thing. We don't want to see it. Put it away."

"You'll be seeing a lot of this, soon, Lillah. Better get used to it." Dickson waved his penis at her and she spluttered into laughter.

"I hope there will be none like you where I'm going. Though I'm not encouraged by the ones I hear about. You are all crazy. You should live inside the Tree, not under it." Lillah stood up. "I am going to check on my nephew," she said.

Lillah found Magnolia sitting up in a chair near the window, breast feeding her baby, wincing.

"Does it hurt?"

"A bit. It's getting better. I just have to be patient. The village would never forgive me if I didn't feed him this way. I want to be a good mother, not a bad one."

"You're lucky it doesn't hurt too much, then." They sat together, watching the village eat, drink and dance.

"This makes everyone very happy, doesn't it?" Lillah said.

"This will be you one day," Magnolia told her. She stood up, still feeding. "I'm so tired."

"I'll help you to bed."

When the food was eaten and the debris cleared away, people began to walk around the house, talking as they went, crossing paths. They walked this way and that, whichever way they liked. The hum of voices rose to match the thrum of the ocean. Lillah walked with them, almost asleep on her feet. In this way they welcomed the baby, kept him safe in a circle.

Lillah tried to make the most of her time at home. She would miss her family so much and she wanted to be there to help. Two days before school would depart, Logan and Magnolia went out for a walk, although the wind was high and the monkeys on a screech. Magnolia said she would scream if she didn't get some sun. Lillah said, "Let me take the baby for a while. I won't see him forever. I want to get to know him."

"He's a month old, Lillah. He doesn't really have anything to get to know."

"That's what you think." Lillah spent the next hour carrying the baby around her childhood house, telling him everything.

"Now, they don't know this but this hat was left behind by a school teacher and I never told anyone. Of course, I can't wear it because people would ask me where I got it from. I'm too embarrassed to say. I would have sent it with a messenger long ago, but I didn't so there you go. Now, this clear stone was found by my mother before she left.

"This picture I painted after a glorious dream. Can you imagine living in the clouds like that?"

Lillah closed her eyes and tried to memorise her home with her other senses. She knew how it looked: two rooms downstairs, two up. One bedroom she had shared with her brother until his marriage; now she slept there again, some nights, wanting to spend more time with her father before school left.

Her father's bedroom, much smaller. His clothes were stacked in outboards, the cupboards built outside the walls of the house, wooden doors flat with the walls. The large bed almost filled the room. It was made of the same wood as the floor and Lillah imagined it had grown there, a complicated mesh of limbs twisting into the family bed. The baby slept in her arms and she didn't think she had ever seen anything so peaceful.

Her old bedroom smelled damp. It was the room closest to the Tree, so it got no sunlight. It never really dried out. To the touch it was also damp. Not so her fingers would get wet, but if she was pressed hard against the wall, held there while being kissed, the damp would penetrate her shirt at the shoulder blades, her skirt at the buttocks. She used to keep her clothes folded under the bed.

Her father's room caught more of the sun so it was brighter. The smell there was of him, an aged liquid long gone yellow. The smell was a combination of the leaves in the forest by the Tree, when they have lain on the forest floor and have almost turned to sludge, mixed with the perfume of the head-like flowers that grew in the next Order and could be dried and crushed for the scent. Her mother had loved this perfume more than she did the sea.

Downstairs was the kitchen and storage room, kept cool with thick walls of wood, Bark, mud and sap. They kept their food here. Lillah's mother once had a complex system of rotation, where the new food was placed behind the old. To Lillah, this meant she never ate food absolutely fresh. It was always a day, a few days old. The fruit browned, the bread covered with mould. She swore that when she ran a house she would eat the freshest food first and throw old food onto the compost, for the roots of the Tree to enjoy. Still, she couldn't bring herself to completely ignore her mother's teaching.

Then there was the gathering room, with its woven rug on the floor. The rug scratched you if you sat on it; its bark and leaf weave was so harsh it left marks on your buttocks and the backs of your thighs. You had to shift positions many times so the discomfort could be spread about.

"Don't fidget," her mother had snapped at her when she was just three or so. Maybe four; at no age to be forced to sit still like that. Her mother was telling a story about school; the time she was a teacher. How she chose to stay in Ombu, what food she missed.

And she liked full attention. Otherwise tears would come to her eyes and she'd say, "I'll go tell it to the Tree." Lillah had shrugged. That didn't sound like a bad thing. She often saw the grownups lined up whispering, whispering: secrets and confessions they could never speak aloud.

The houses in Ombu were built to fit; no wasted space. Enough room above the head so they didn't feel like they were in a woodcave. They liked to feel the air above them.

The kitchen was the best room in the house. Everybody made it a place to be happy in. Doors opening out to the sea, though Lillah's mother used to keep hers closed, to keep the salt air out of her food, she said. "You want to know the secret of my great success? No salt in my cooking. Salt kills other flavours. Without it the other flavours can grow and exaggerate themselves until you can identify the taste individually."

The kitchen smelled of bread and raw vegetables. It smelled of things growing. The bench felt smooth, worn to a satin from years of work. Lillah's father had sanded the wood when her mother caught child, picking up handfuls of sand and rubbing for hours of every day. People wondered aloud at his patience and dedication; in private they wondered at his obsession. Once the bench was finished, people brought him objects to work on: chairs, chopping boards, cradles. He sanded the cradle Logan and Lillah slept in, *rock rock rock rock*. It was solid, stories carved into the feet and the sides. It took a long time to carve and sand, all those tiny crevices, but he did it, sitting patiently on the beach and humming in time to the waves.

Lillah sat with the baby as he dozed. She closed her eyes, letting memory take her, letting it drift her and transport her.

Lillah thought back to when Magnolia's school had arrived at Ombu.

Lillah was nineteen and word came ahead that the Number Taker was coming, travelling with the school from his own Order, Torreyas. The Number Taker always came from Torreyas, receiving training in numbers above all else. The Number Takers were known to like things ordered. They usually wore broad-brimmed hats because they didn't like to look up; the Tree with its branches and leaves was far too chaotic to make them feel comfortable.

The children at school with the Number Taker became well versed in counting, because everything was tallied.

If there were no dwellings to count, or people, or animals, it would be stones on the beach, piled into tens and counted in thousands.

The arrival of the Number Taker always brought great excitement. It was so rare a man travelled and stopped to visit. The women who had missed out on being teachers looked at the Number Taker as a potential husband. Word would be sent ahead about his looks and manner.

This one was coming with eight teachers and fifteen children, a huge parade. Word was he liked to laugh. He wanted to be amused. And that the school teachers with him were beautiful.

Logan carried on with his business: fishing and collecting the wood. He pretended he had no interest in the teachers, that he wanted to remain single and have to worry about no one but himself.

"Why should I take on a dependant? I'm perfectly happy with you and our parents demanding things from me."

"So why have you taken your shirt off, then? Not trying to get browner in the sun out there?" Lillah said. She cupped saltwater in her palms and flicked it at his back. The droplets hung on the pale hairs there and he shivered.

"Right!" he said. He put down his net and picked up a wooden bucket. Lillah squealed as he scooped it full.

"Children!" their mother had called. "Stop playing and get moving. Come on, they'll be here soon." They could see her shaking her head on the shore.

"You see? If I get married, no one will call me a child anymore. I'll have to be a man."

"There is nothing manly about you," Lillah said. "Nor will there ever be." They grinned at each other. Logan went back to catching fish.

"They won't be here for three days, though," Logan said. "We'll need to keep the fish in the water basket."

He lowered the fish into a basket kept anchored on the shore, then dropped it under the water. The fish swam frantically, banging against the walls of the basket, able to breathe but not able to escape.

Lillah felt breathless for them. How awful, to be locked in a cage in the water. She grimaced. "The poor creatures. It must be terrible to be trapped like that, still able to breathe but not able to swim away. Or even move very much. It must be awful."

"We have to keep the fish fresh, Lillah. We don't want to poison the Number Taker."

They both widened their eyes at the very idea.

"I'd better go back and see what Mother needs," Lillah said. "I hope she doesn't let hopelessness take over. Her knees go weak and that's all she can think about."

Lillah walked back to shore, feeling excitement in her heart. She hoped Logan's future wife was coming. Someone fun, clever, to keep him thinking and not let him turn into a mess of a man, flesh with eyes, like so many of them once they'd fulfilled their parental seeding.

She reached her parents' house and entered. She smelled baking bread and wondered how her mother would keep it fresh for three days. She found Olea with her head on the kitchen bench, surrounded by flour.

"Mother! What's wrong?" Olea lifted her head and Lillah snorted with laughter before she could stop herself. Olea's tears left runnels in the flour on her cheeks.

"It's not funny, Lillah. It's a disaster. The Number Taker's favourite sweet is semolina balls soaked through with cardamom and I can't find the main ingredient."

"Someone'll have some cardamom, Mother. If no one here does, I'll run to the market and get it. You keep going with your other arrangements."

"I can't do it, I just can't manage," Olea banged her head on the bench. Lillah stood beside her and stroked her back. "Mother, you've cooked for dozens before. You're famous for your cooking, not just here but in Aloes and Laburnum, too. People take your recipes away with them."

"But what if they don't this time? What if I fail this time, make everyone sick at the thought of my food? It would be better if I wasn't known. Then they wouldn't have any expectations, be looking at me to fail."

"Nobody wants you to fail and you won't. I'll find you what you need then we'll do it together. Is there anything else you haven't got?"

Olea named a few things and Lillah nodded.

"Don't take a long time. No chatting or news spreading today. Hurry hurry hurry," Olea said. She wiped away her tears and got flour in her eyes. Lillah smothered a laugh.

"It's all very well for you to laugh. You didn't grow up in the same Order I did. I would be beaten for failure, there. They hate success and envy it, yet they punished failure with great cruelty. If it wasn't for your uncle, I don't know that I would have survived. Yet he was Outcast, because my cruel mother didn't feed him from the breast."

Lillah didn't really believe Olea, who loved to dramatise things.

Lillah went out of the house leaving her mother blinded, dabbing at her eyes with a cloth.

It was nightfall before Lillah returned from knocking at every door in the community. She was laden with prizes of all kinds, treasures.

Dried fish, slow salted and delicious. Dried berries, very rare. Small cakes you could fit in your mouth all at once. The cardamom her mother needed.

She hoped it would help to relax Olea. She was glad she'd found all the ingredients on Ombu. She didn't want to run to the market between Ombu and Laburnum because it was far away and the walk stony, until you reached the market where seaweed washed up to the sand. Closer to Laburnum, seaweed covered the sand. Seaweed always came to the beach in Laburnum. Lillah and her friends were sure that was why Laburnum was known for the perfume they made. They needed to cover up the smell.

Only in a powerful wind did the smell reach Ombu. At those times people felt lucky to live in Ombu, not Laburnum.

Although the time alone, walking six days to market and back again would have been nice, her mother could not have borne the time. Lillah reminded herself to talk to the trader, ask for some spices on his next trip.

The Number Taker's group was spotted on the horizon at dawn.

"They're here! The school!" shouted one of the children. The arrival of new people lifted them all. The Tree Hall had been cleaned to perfection, and colourful material draped about to make the room look welcoming. The single men had washed and scrubbed, scraped away hair, pulled on their best clothes. Even Logan had done it, "out of respect for the Number Taker", though he winked at Lillah as he said it. At the very least he would have sex with one of the teachers. All the men knew they had a good chance of sex, and their voices were louder, talking over one another, and they wrestled, physically unable to keep still.

The women laughed at them, though kindly. The men all worked hard and deserved some release. This was the natural way of things.

The single men had all arranged places they could go to be alone with an interested teacher. Some had arranged bedrooms, sending roommates to sleep elsewhere. Others had warm woodcaves, prepared with rugs, candles, sweet treats.

Lillah watched it all and fantasised about the day she, too, would be welcomed like a queen.

"They're coming! They're coming!" the children yelled on the run, racing along the beach to greet the schoolchildren, wanting them now to come into the village to show them toys, hideouts, climbing places, swimming spots.

The adults were more restrained, but all gathered on the beach to greet the Number Taker and the teachers.

"He's very tall," whispered one girl. They squinted. He did seem very tall. Too tall.

"No, he's got a teacher on his shoulders," someone shouted, and they laughed, all of them, joyful at the joke of the Number Taker carrying a teacher.

"How many teachers with them?" called Thea's oldest brother, Tax.

"Too many for you to manage!" a father said.

"Here's one, running for me. She can't wait," Tax said, pushing his way forward.

The teacher ran towards him, arms out.

"Civilisation! Hooray!" she said, and the crowd surrounded her, all chattering at once and offering her sustenance. The other teachers followed more sedately.

Lillah watched the Number Taker. "He seems to be struggling," she called. Logan turned to look, squinted, then ran along the beach.

The Number Taker fell to his knees as Logan approached, grappling with the young woman riding on his shoulders. Logan dashed forward and grabbed her. He held her in his arms as the Number Taker rose, then they walked together, Logan carrying the teacher, towards the crowd.

The crowd moved forward to greet the Number Taker, take him in, look after him.

Lillah ran to find a blanket then laid it down so Logan could place the teacher on it.

"Thank you," the teacher said. She winced. "I cut my foot on a sea urchin." Lillah glanced at the foot and could see it was swollen and discoloured.

The Birthman stood over them. "The Number Taker said we had an injury here," he said. "Wouldn't take any refreshment until he knew you were okay."

"He's very kind," the teacher said.

"This is our Birthman, Pittos. We call him Mr Miracles."

The Birthman blushed. He was a shy, red-faced man whose wife had just lost their sixth child. She had Morace, a lively child, ninety-six moons old. They had failed to have more.

"I'm Lillah, and this is my brother Logan."

"I'm Magnolia," the teacher said. She held out her hand and Logan took it. He sat beside her, still holding the hand.

"Thank you for carrying me," she whispered. Logan leant close to hear and she kissed his cheek. He said nothing.

"He's a bit shy," Lillah said, dropping on to the blanket beside them. The Birthman cleared his throat.

"It's too crowded here for me to work. Lillah, go get some juice for our patient. Logan, you can stay and hold her hand. This may hurt." Logan squeezed his face up.

"Not you, me!" Magnolia said.

The Birthman removed the spines and cleaned the wound

"Thank you, Birthman," Magnolia said. Her cheeks were flushed from the pain. Logan took a washcloth and ran to the water to soak it. He came back and gently stroked her cheeks and forehead with the coolness.

Her skirt had worked its way up to her thighs. When Lillah came back with the juice, she saw Tax lying a short way down the beach, angling his head and grinning at what he thought he could see.

"Shoo, Tax," Lillah said. "Shoo, fly. Go find a rock pool to put your head in."

Magnolia laughed and fixed her skirt. "Don't worry, I've seen worse than him."

The three sat on the blanket and laughed and talked until a messenger came for Lillah.

"Your Mother's crying on the front step," he said.

"Oh, rubbish," Lillah said, rolling her eyes. "I'd better go help. She's preparing the feast single-handed, according to her."

"I'll help, too," Magnolia said. She lumbered into a standing position and tested her heel by putting her full weight on it. She winced slightly. "It's fine," she said. "If you could help me up there then I'll sit to chop or roll or whatever," she said.

Magnolia walked between Lillah and Logan. They exchanged smiles behind her back, nods.

Magnolia and Lillah had met twice before. When Magnolia's school walked through Ombu, Lillah was nine and about to leave for school herself, Magnolia eleven. Logan was eleven, walking the Tree, at school. Lillah hated him being away. She was sad, even as an adult, about those years they could have shared. Lillah's school walked through Magnolia's Order when Lillah was eleven and Magnolia thirteen, and just returned from her five years away. They both remembered that meeting very clearly. Magnolia had been very kind to Lillah, finding her sweets to eat when she felt sad and left out.

Magnolia was good with numbers and Logan watched, bemused, as she made the figures show who had been what age at what time.

The feast was a great success. In the end every-one helped with the cooking and the serving, even the Number Taker who took great delight in cutting the bread into perfect slices.

"Look at that!" he'd say after each piece. "Perfect!"

"Is that how they slice it in Torreyas?" one of the women asked.

"I barely know how they do things in Torreyas, I'm there so rarely." He tipped his broad-brimmed hat back, leaving a shiny forehead.

The men in particular listened to his every word. A man who travelled was such a rarity, and from the way he spoke, they could see why. 'Who would want a life like that?' the men said to each other. 'Never at home. Always away. How could you know who you are?'

Lillah and Magnolia had screeched with laughter at the sight of Tax the swaggering so-called heart-throb of the village (not Logan. There was no swagger about Logan). Leaving his trousers to sag loosely below his hips, showing pubic bush combed with twigs, the fashion of the day amongst some. Leaving tiny twigs amongst the curls. Lillah had turned away, her shoulders shaking at the foolish-ness of him. Magnolia had joined her, laughing too. Two teachers were fooled by Tax, though; they fought for his affections. Lillah, Melia and Agara watched the women snarl at each other with fixed smiles. One managed to spill hot food on the other but that plan backfired: Tax took her away to clean her up.

"We'll never be like that, will we?" Agara said.

"Certainly not over someone like Tax," Melia said. "A fool from a foolish family."

Thea sat at a distance, but her shoulders flinched.

"She heard that," Lillah said, whispering.

"I don't care," Melia said, whispering so loudly she may as well have been talking.

With all that, all the fighting and fuss, neither woman chose to stay. Tax's charms were short-lived. At least he was clear in his base intentions, Lillah thought. One thing in his favour.

The teachers paired off with young men for the night, everyone else stayed up shouting and singing until well past the very dark. Lillah missed Logan's presence but was thrilled he was with Magnolia. At one stage he came back for more Bark wine, his eyes bleary by firelight, his hair mussed. He raised his eyebrows at Lillah and grinned, a very happy man.

Six days later, when the Number-Taker's school prepared to move on, Magnolia announced that she would stay, if she was accepted. Logan turned cartwheels till his face was red and Olea took Magnolia in a tight hold. "You are family," she said. "I will thank the Number-Taker for bringing you to us."

Thea watched as the group left. Lillah tried to be kind to her out of pity; her only friends were her brothers Tax and Dickson. "Did you like those teachers?" Lillah asked.

"I will stop with them if I ever go to school. I will stop where the numbers are."

Olea was kind to Magnolia but it was clear she was unhappy.

"Logan has someone now. What am I for?" she said to her husband Myrist.

"Lillah will need help preparing for school."

"School. What good did school ever do?"

"We would not have met and made our children if you had not taught with your school."

"Again, I say, what good did school ever do?"

Myrist shook his head and turned to Lillah. "I don't know what is wrong with your mother's tongue, but she doesn't speak for me."

Lillah had seen this in her mother long before anyone else did.

"Your brother is so important. I left my brother Legum behind to teach school, and then I heard word that he disappeared. Our brothers are the most stable relationship we have. Our love for lovers comes and goes. We tire of them. Our brothers will always love us, and we will never forget them. I wish I knew Legum was safe." She touched her ear. "He listens. All the disappeared listen."

Soon after this Olea went walking and did not return. Sometimes Lillah woke in darkness and felt as if Olea was there, watching, but the dark room showed her nothing.

● ● ●

The baby began to mewl and she realised she had been lost in memories, not seeing the present. Lillah kissed her nephew's head. That seemed so long ago, and now she would be travelling, seeking love, preparing for motherhood herself.

Thea joined her as the baby began to grizzle. "Shall we bathe him?" she said. "Babies like to bathe." So they filled a large bowl with water and carefully undressed the tiny thing.

Thea held him, lowered him slowly into the water. Lillah turned to collect a soft sponge.

"Careful!" she said. Thea had let the baby's shoulder slip back and his face was almost underwater.

"So small," Thea whispered.

Lillah talked and cuddled him as she dressed him and was sad to pass him back when his parents returned. Magnolia checked him all over for marks and smiled nervously. "I'm sorry, Lillah. You're not like the others, I know."

"What others?"

Magnolia held the baby close. "Everybody."

Logan kissed the crown of her head. "All mothers worry terribly. You are safe here."

Wind began to howl around them and Magnolia pulled her child even closer. The noise of the Tree increased.

"Does it have to make so much noise?" Magnolia said, covering her baby's ears with a blanket.

"It'll be okay," Logan said. "It'll pass."

Some of the more frightened amongst them packed up containers of food and warm clothing and made camp at the base of the Tree. This was the safest place when the leaves were being shed. There were stories from other Orders of people being killed by a massive Leaf. It had never happened in Lillah's Order. The Leaves of the Tree had a varied nature and size. Some could be used for plates, others to insulate walls, and there were the huge leaves, the dangerous ones.

The school would leave after the arrival of the next messenger. It was good to go out fully informed, and he would bring news from Laburnum that might be useful to them as they travelled.

He came late in the night, and his news was not important enough to wake them. In the morning they gathered to hear word of a new batch of perfume being completed, and of a school on the way containing a child who could scream so loudly the cups would shatter.

"None of our children will behave like that," Lillah said. "Ours will be a joy to look after, and the messengers will run ahead shouting, 'Oh, you should see these children! These children are the most beautiful you've ever seen.'"

"Why do you always have to be the best, Lillah? Sometimes we can just be, you know. We don't have to be known as the best school ever."

"You may not, Melia, but I do. You ask your questions; I'll be proud of what I do."

The messenger was sent back with the clay pots Lillah's Order specialised in, to hold the perfume. In the next Order, where they made jasmine oil, the pots were well respected too.

The night before they left, the Order gathered for a party. The celebration turned rowdy. Raucous laughter, shocking stories. Lillah felt light-headed. Queasy. She walked away from the group to give herself some space.

"Who's there? Who is it?" she heard.

"It's me, Tilla. It's Lillah. Your rhyming friend."

The Bark of the Tree was very dark, mottled in places. Sometimes Bark shed like dried flakes of skin from the scalp. Tilla's face, old and lined, reminded her of the bark.

"Good. Come and tell me what's going on."

Lillah had not forgotten how poorly he had treated her in the Tree Hall, but she walked towards his voice, squinting in the moonlight. She found him sitting on a jutting rock, his fat walking stick resting beside him, his old legs dangling down.

"However did you get up there, Tilla? You can't manage to fish or wash, but you can climb onto a giant rock."

Tilla snickered. The sound gave Lillah the giggles. Most people laughed loudly, mouths wide open. "I am the watcher, looking out for secrets. I climb where I can. What's going on over there?"

"Why don't you come and see?"

"Hah! Expect me to talk to those fools?"

"You'll have to talk to somebody some time."

"I'm talking to you, aren't I?"

"Yes, but Tilla, I'm leaving tomorrow. I'm going away with the school."

Tilla choked and Lillah stepped closer, thinking he had swallowed a night bug.

"Tilla? Are you all right?"

He was crying. Tears trickled down his old face and he didn't wipe them away.

"Why do they send our best to die?"

"I won't die. I'll find my partner. I'll send news back with the school."

"They won't be back. They never come back. Haven't you noticed? They go away to die." Lillah realised that was why he had been so hard on her earlier, in her teacher interview.

"Oh, my Tree Lord, Tilla," she said. "You went yourself. Don't you remember?"

"I remember a strange dream a long time ago, that's all."

He gazed out to sea. "The shore gets smaller every year. I can see it. Every year the Trunk gets thicker and thicker. It won't be long before the beach is gone altogether. The pot my ancestor buried for my inheritance is covered, now, by the Tree. I'll never get to it."

He looked up the Tree. "There's stories up there long forgotten. Lost. No lesson learnt."

"You still remember a lot of it. And the younger men are learning it. Some of our people tried living in the Tree, you know. Many years ago. But it went wrong, very wrong. They could not put their babies down, you know. Not even to sleep. This is not the way a person should be. A person needs to sleep alone at times."

He scrabbled in his pocket. "Here," he said. "Tell them to bury this with you. At least they'll know where you came from."

He handed her a flat rock. She could feel that it was etched but couldn't see the design.

"Look at it tomorrow," he said. "Go now, I'm tired."

"Will you tell me just one story? One I can share with the children on a lonely night between Orders?"

"I'm tired." But he smiled at her; he loved to tell stories. "I'll tell you about a time when the canopy was not so vast. When we could stand at the water's edge and receive sun all the time, not just when there has been Leaffall. Every year we lose more sunlight as the Tree grows and casts more shadow."

"Tell me the story."

"This is the story of your uncle. Your father's brother. We were dear friends."

"He doesn't talk about his brother."

"He misses him too greatly."

"I know that he floated out to sea on a large piece of Bark he found shed from the Tree. I never knew him; he sailed before I was born. He said he was seeking the other side of the world, but he never returned. The Order believed he'd been taken by the sea monster. I think that could be true. My mother said they looked out to sea sometimes, hoping to see him returning to them."

"You have exploration in your blood, Lillah."

"Why would he do such a thing?"

"He wanted to know. He wanted to see what else there was, if it was an alternative to living on this island. He knew that the Tree was growing and he had a different sense of vision to most people. He knew that in ten generations, the land would be gone and other homes would need to be found. He believed there was another place to live on land; although not the Island of Spirits."

"How could he know such a thing? No one knows where it is but that doesn't mean it isn't there."

"He did not believe that is where the spirit went after death."

"So what did he do?"

"We had no idea he was about to take to the water. A school had just left and he had made love to three of the teachers. None stayed; they were only from Bayonet, two Orders away, and they were not ready to settle. These women talked a lot about children, of ten children each, of building Order. There were arguments around the talkfire, most believing that keeping our population low is the way to keep ourselves safe from disease. These women did not agree, nor did they care. It was not the most amusing evening.

"Your uncle was furious with them for their lack of understanding, and he said that he would find a way to avoid sharing the land with them. That was when he made the plan to enter the sea."

"He had a plan?"

"He was very organised! He took food, drink, clothing, implements. If anyone could survive, it would be him."

"Yet he never returned."

"No. Some say it is because he was sucked into the Tree on his little vessel, and that in there are ghosts who live on our blood. They use our blood to fill their veins. Your uncle is ghost food."

Lillah looked at him, horrified. "This is not a story to tell to children."

"It is your story, Lillah. There is no lesson in it. Your father will not tell you, but it is your history."

Lillah thought she had too many lost relatives.

"Can I help you down from your rock, Tilla?"

"NO! Just go away," he snapped. She climbed up and hugged him quickly. His hard body stiffened then relaxed. "Find someone else to talk to, okay?" she said.

He grunted, and she walked away.

It was only on celebration nights they stayed up past dark. Other times it was early to bed. Early up in the morning. Lillah wondered if other Orders slept differently.

She didn't join the others in drinking sap wine. She needed to keep her head clear for the morning. The first couple of days were the hardest, she'd been told. The third day was painful as the muscles screamed, and they usually rested on that day.

"It's not meant to be tortuous," Aquifolia told them. "Pain is okay in small doses but no one can think when they are hurting. Stop when you need to. There is nothing weak about it."

Lillah woke early on her first day of school and thought, "Sometime soon I am going to have sex." She lay in bed for a while, imagining what her lovers would look like. Not so different from the men in her Order. The only real difference was that she could sleep with them.

She sat up, dizzy. She had not slept well in the night; the anticipation of leaving on her first day of school proved fertile ground for imaginings.

"Lillah. Come on. Breakfast with the family." Her brother spoke through the door, then knocked and pushed it open. He poked his head in. His eyes were puffy. He looked like he hadn't slept well, either. "Come on, Lillah. We won't see you for many years. Until you get homelust and come back to us."

"That's if I meet the man of my dreams," she said. She and Logan exchanged glances, not quite of longing, nor of regret, but a mixture of both. "I'll pack my bags then come to join you."

"Breakfast first. Father has prepared a feast."

Lillah nodded. "He's going to be lonely. Without me."

"He'll have plenty to do with the baby. He's a great help to us."

Lillah shook her head. "Don't let that be his existence. Promise me? He is more than grandfather. Make sure he travels to the markets sometimes, sees others his own age. Make sure he has a hobby, not just holding your child."

"Yes, yes," Logan said. "Come on, eat, then I have to get back to Magnolia and the baby."

They walked together outside. Their father had set up a picnic amongst the roots of the Tree. Eggs, sliced boiled cassava, diced salted fish. He waited impatiently.

"Sit down, sit down, hurry up. We need to eat. Magnolia needs us. That baby won't let her sleep."

"Why don't we take breakfast to her?" Lillah said, piling egg and fish onto cassava. "Let's eat while she's feeding the baby."

Lillah's father made himself a pile of food, too. "All right. I can't concentrate, thinking of what's going on."

Already the wrens were hopping about pecking up crumbs, and the ants were lining up for their feast.

"I think we'll let nature have the rest," her father said. He rose, dusted his lap.

They heard a distant wail. Logan dropped his food and ran.

"It always sounds worse when it's your own," Myrist said. "I'm sure the baby's fine." Nevertheless, they walked quickly. Myrist spoke, out of breath with the exertion. Lillah didn't feel it in the least. Training for school was intense.

"Now, Lillah, you have a very exciting and challenging time ahead of you. The things you'll see will stay with you forever. We forget a lot of our schooling; the knowledge is there without us remembering exactly where it came from. But when you do the trip, as an adult, it is with you. You have the power to leave your name on many places in the Tree. You will see many people, meet many men. Not all you meet will love you. Some will want to hurt you. Be careful of those people. There are killers about. You have heard the stories from other teachers. Killers to be wary of."

They reached the house. Logan fixed a drink for Magnolia. He said, "Should I be listening to this?"

"You've just become a father. That's your great adventure."

"It wasn't enough for our mother. Why will I be any different?"

Lillah poked him. Her brother was a genius at turning the attention to himself.

"Um, you two can talk about fatherhood once I'm gone. I want to hear Dad's true confessions."

"I don't really have any true confessions. It's nice to see the children your mother taught grown up and starting to have children of their own. I remember every last one of them as children. Cleaned them up. I remember what they wouldn't eat. Helped me with you two a lot. You know, understanding how each child likes different dinners."

"Mother always made the best dinners, didn't she?" Logan said.

"Your mother was very clever. You're a good cook too."

"Come on, Dad, tell more about what I should know. Teach me everything now. I can take it. Tell us about Mother's lovers," Lillah said.

"You don't really want to hear that, I'm sure."

"Come on, Dad. I'm not squeamish."

"I'm squeamish. I'll just say this; you are in control. You have the power. Never say yes to anyone you dislike, and approach anyone you do like. Compatibility is obvious, even from the first kiss. Sometimes you'll kiss a man and your stomach will heave. Truly. I don't know if it's a smell they release, or a chemical reaction between the two of you, but it will be obvious. Some say it's because there is an unknown blood connection, that like blood abhors the smell of like blood. These ones you will push away."

Lillah nodded. "Thea can't stand the smell of Dickson. Is that what you mean? So did you know when you kissed Mother?"

"I did. All other thoughts left my mind and I knew this was it."

Logan said, "You should ask about our Uncle Legum along the way. Perhaps he was washed up along the coast." He touched his ear.

"I'll ask everywhere. Mother used to say he was so distraught when father married her he sailed out to sea on a huge piece of bark."

"I thought she said he swam out?"

"She told it differently every time."

"Our stories change by the hour, don't they? Each new thing that happens to us changes the things that have happened to us before. Now I am a father, all my past experience seems different."

Lillah took his hand. "You are a serious man now, Logan."

"You'll understand what I mean before too long, Lillah. You will change."

"Not me. I am who I am and that is set."

They shared their breakfast with Magnolia. "Magnolia? Sorry, Magnolia?" Lillah whispered. "I'm going to school soon. Do you have a message for your people? I know we'll reach them. I'm looking forward to meeting them. Is there anything you want me to give them?"

Magnolia opened her eyes a slit and waved her arm. "Logan?" she said. He jumped up.

"I forgot. It's here. Somewhere. Wait there." He left the room and they could hear him thumping and swearing around the house. Magnolia and Lillah exchanged glances.

Logan came back into the room carrying a small hessian bag. He held it up. "Got it!" he said. "She's so organised. She packed this long ago, Lillah."

"How heavy is it?"

Logan passed it to her. "Not very."

Lillah took it, weighing it in her hands. "I should be able to carry that."

Magnolia sat up, breastfeeding. It still hurt her sometimes, and Logan hated to watch. Magnolia said, "If I don't breastfeed him he'll be treated differently. Logan, now bring the parcel I've saved from the Number Taker."

He returned with a roll of paperbark. "Is this it?"

"That's it. Lillah, I have here writing-bark. The Number Taker gave this piece to me, hoping that I would begin to map the country. Map the island, Botanica. I didn't do it, though. I was too eager to play and I didn't take it seriously. Will you take on the job? Will you mark the map?"

Lillah took the paper. She had never felt the stuff before and she liked it. Her fingers itched to begin.

"I will do it, Magnolia. I will try, at least." She would map, Lillah decided. She would keep track of all she saw, of how each Order differed. She would try to understand, to contain, the Orders of the Tree.

Myrist joined them, saying, "If you're taking gifts, please, you'll be passing through your mother's Order. You'll see her. She left for her walk two years ago; she would be there long by now. Give

her my love, and give her this as well. You know
we found each other when I went walking with my
school, don't you? We knew then that we would
find each other again."

He handed her a beautifully carved necklace, one
piece of wood crafted into links.

"It's beautiful."

Her father began to cry softly. "I wish she hadn't
gone for the walk home. I wish she'd stayed."

"I wish she'd stayed also. She was a wonderful
person."

"She still is, Lillah. You better go make your
preparations. You will need to begin your bath."

They entered Logan's kitchen, and for a few
blinks they worked, cleaning and tidying. Lillah
touched the things lingeringly; the pots, the uten-
sils, the containers. She would not see these things
again, most likely. She would take on another's
household items. There was no room to take it with
her. A few select items. Not the clay pot that had
been in her father's family for generations. That she
would miss the most. It would not be possible to
carry one with her. The smallest crack would ren-
der it useless as a cooking vessel. Some of the pots
were very old, had been used over many years.

"Your mother used to say the only thing she felt
sorry about was the women friends she made and
had to say goodbye to. You can only communicate
for so long using the messenger, then people move
on, get busy."

"I will always send messages back," Lillah said. "I will map the Tree, too. I will map the shape of Botanica."

"She learnt about food on her journey. From her home Order, Rhado, she brought knowledge of how to grill meat and keep it tender. In Bayonet they taught her how to grind nuts and coat a piece of fish. In Chrondus she discovered the secret of stuffing fruit into more fruit and poaching it in honey."

"Now I'm hungry again," Lillah said.

"I've got some lovely fruit drying out there. The taste of the sun will warm you when you're on the dark side of the Tree. You will need to keep your wits about you. Don't be fooled by a pretty face and an easy wit. You dabble and play as much as you like, my dear, so long as it is your choice. Never let anyone decide for you; always follow your own instincts and desires. And stay clean. Wash yourself often. Use the wood soap. It will keep you healthy. And never make do. There will be someone for you, and if you make do you might miss him. And... I have so much to tell you." Her father breathed heavily, too many words.

Lillah felt sudden sharp pain at leaving him.

"Will you be all right? You seem sad."

Logan put his arm around Myrist. "I am here, Lillah. It isn't all up to you."

Lillah smiled. "You are a good brother."

Lillah almost leapt away from the house, as if the tie that kept her there had been released. She felt free, unburdened, young.

The feeling did not last long. She was summoned by the Birthman.

"My wife needs to speak to you. It's about Morace."

Lillah did not like being too close to Rhizo, Morace's mother, but she tried to conceal her distaste from Morace. It would not do to have him think his mother frightened people. He was unconscious of smell and her look.

Lillah breathed through her mouth in the small room. For some reason (probably Rhizo, it was the sort of thing she would do) they kept fresh air and light out of their home. Windows tightly shut, covered with the sort of thick material not often seen. Blanket material, precious for keeping people warm at night. The beeswax candles were bright, casting sharp, strange shadows at all hours. Lillah hated to feel enclosed.

Morace's mother sat in a wooden chair, smiling. She said, "He's got his bag packed. All the things you need for a night away from mother." Lillah stared at her, mouth open. The parents were supposed to prepare the children so the tears could flow before school began. There would always be tears as school left; Lillah remembered crying herself. Melia had not cried and thus set herself up as the strong one.

"Morace, why don't you go out and choose your smoothstone, now. Something to make you think of home. You'll know it when you pick it up. It will sit in your hand and calm you," Lillah said. She smiled at the echo of her father's words of comfort about choosing a mate.

Morace jumped up, excited. His hair was plastered to his head, greasy. His mother didn't let him swim in the ocean. She thought it would make him sick. Lillah couldn't wait to see the boy swimming, bathing. He would be more popular once he was clean.

"Morace!" his mother said. "A kiss!" He came back and kissed her on the cheek. "I'll only be gone for a few blinks, Mother," he said.

She sighed as he left. "I'm still not sure we should send him," she said. "I think I can teach him just as well at home." Lillah looked around at the closed-off room.

She said, "He'll learn nothing here." As the words came out, she realised they were terribly harsh. "I'm sorry. But school is so vast. Physically, it gives them the basis to be strong adults. And he would never learn all he will learn about the Orders of the Tree, and our history, sitting here protected by you. It's one of the things that keep us peaceful, the understanding of the children of other cultures. It is a leap of faith to send our children out. We understand that. A sacrifice of those years with your child for the good of Botanica. So that children will grow up knowing people everywhere, and will be less inclined to plan hurt against people they have known."

The mother blinked. Her face reddened, and Lillah felt frightened. This woman was, after all, a mother, albeit a seemingly weak one. Lillah stood up. "I'm sorry I made you angry," she said. "But if you expect him to marry, he needs to go away to school. No girl would choose a boy without experience of the Tree. That's just how it is."

Rhizo stood up. She stepped over to Lillah and took hold of her wrist. She leaned close and Lillah tried not to recoil from the smell of her breath.

"I'm going to tell you something, Lillah. This is a deathly, deathly secret. Can I trust you?"

Lillah nodded, but she wasn't sure. Already she was thinking of how she would tell Melia this story.

"Everyone thinks we smell because we don't wash," Rhizo said. Lillah laughed in embarrassment, then covered her mouth.

"Sorry," she said.

Rhizo smiled. It lifted her face for just a moment. "I know that's what people think, and I don't care. I want them to think that, Lillah. Because it keeps them from seeing the truth."

The woman sat down again. "Bring us tea," she called. Her husband Pittos, the Birthman, stepped into the room. Strange how shy he seemed when he wasn't working.

From the day they married, he had quietened. Rhizo came from an Order where people liked to be quiet, which made the whole Order quieter. People said she had married him for his loudness, but then hated him for it. He had learnt to speak in a whisper.

"Tea and something sweet," he said. Lillah thought he was the kind of man she wanted to choose. Though she wouldn't quieten him.

"Yes, nice," Rhizo said. "I'm going to tell Lillah."

"Are you sure?"

She nodded. "I can trust you, can't I, Lillah? I would tell the fathers, but they are not the ones going with him."

"So you will send him?" Lillah said.

"Well, I have to. If he's got any chance. I can't keep him here."

"So what's the secret?" Lillah said. Rhizo closed her eyes. "I think I'm sick, Lillah. Very sick. I have terrible pain, now, in my lungs and my stomach. Nothing will help it. I've tried jasmine in all its forms, camomile; I've tried everything I ever heard about, anything the teachers brought with them. I don't know if it's Spikes, if it's catching. The others aren't sick. It's just I'm worried. If I die when Morace is away, what will happen to him? If they decide I am contagious. What will they do?"

Lillah had some idea but she hated to be the one to say it. There had been three sick children passing through Ombu, in her memory.

These children did not continue with the school. They were treated.

They disappeared.

"But if he stays with you he might get sick."

"If he goes with you and I get sicker, they will be after him. They will watch him for the slightest sign. Lillah, I'm telling you because I want you to care for him. Keep him well."

"I can care for him like I will the other children. But I can't stop him from getting sick."

"You can hide his illness from the others. Particularly those of the Order you are in."

"You can't fool the Tree, Rhizo. The ghosts. I can't do anything about that. Once he sickens, the ghosts will start to eat his bones."

Rhizo squeezed her eyes. Squeezed a tight smile. "You are a great believer, Lillah. As you say, you can't affect that. You can affect the people around you, though. If news comes that I have died…keep him safe. I will try to pay the messengers not to bring true news of me. Please, Lillah. Please. I will give you everything I have. My smoothstone; I will give you that."

"I don't need you to give me anything." The older a stone, the smoother it was, the more value it had.

"Take it anyway," said the mother. "Take anything. You deserve the earth if you will keep him safe."

"I need to think," Lillah said.

"I don't want Morace to know how sick I am. I don't want him to worry."

"He'll have to know eventually."

"I know, but if he's away from me when it happens, the distance will help. It will give him time to get used to it. It won't seem real until he gets back home."

Lillah stood up and went to hug Rhizo. "I can't believe how brave you are," she said.

"I guess I am brave."

"Is there anything for now? Anything you want?"

Rhizo sighed. "You know what I miss? The smell of the leaves. I'm so closed in no smell reaches. Could you bring me some leaves? I don't want to ask my husband. I don't want him to know how much I miss outside, or he would make me go out."

"Why don't you go out?"

Rhizo started to speak. Her eyes shifted slightly as she thought, and Lillah wondered what it was she was hiding.

"I don't want people to know I'm sick," she said. "It is so different here. Where I'm from, we were worshipped by the people in the next Order. Worshipped! Can you imagine? Here I am nothing."

Lillah felt too inexperienced to see beyond the words. "I'll get some leaves," she said. "A sackful, different colours."

Outside, Morace and some of the children waited. Rham, with big eyes and a quiet tongue, saw all. She nodded at Lillah. "Will he be coming?

I hope he comes. He is good to talk to." She had a small carved wooden puzzle only she could solve; she carried it everywhere.

"You will have plenty of children to talk to along the way."

"But many of them are so dull. I like the bright ones. I'd rather talk to grown ups."

As she collected the leaves, it dawned upon Lillah what Rhizo was asking her to do. Risk every Order they visited. Take Spikes with them, perhaps. Leave each Order sick, all to keep one child from treatment.

Lillah returned with her leaves. "I'm sorry, Rhizo. I don't think I can do such a thing. This is not how we are brought up to think."

"No. No. You're right. I shouldn't ask you. But I did ask you for a reason. I thought you knew; I thought your father would have told you."

"Told me what?"

"I have held him back from school these last two years until you became a teacher. I know the others think it is because I cannot bear to let him go. That is true. But there is another reason. It is something most people are not concerned about, but that my husband," here, she lowered her voice and looked in the direction of the room Pittos sat in, "does not know. He is an unusual man in that he suffers great anger if I am not his alone."

"I am confused. What is this to do with my decision?"

"Morace is your half-brother, Lillah. My husband could not give me a child, so I went to your father. Morace is your family. You have to look after him."

Lillah walked to her father, who fished at the water's edge.

"I have been talking to Rhizo," she said.

"I thought she might talk to you. I wondered if she would call upon you."

"I wonder why you didn't say anything. I have always liked Morace and would have cared for him anyway, but I wonder he wasn't part of our family."

"Rhizo is a very odd woman. She was more bothered by the process than anyone else I have met." He put down his fishing pole. "I'm sorry not to have told you. I would have, at some stage."

"It doesn't matter." It was odd, though, to realise there had been a secret for ten years.

"I think perhaps you should not tell the other teachers. We do not want them judging your teaching or his learning because of your relationship."

"You're right. We will keep the secret."

Lillah's best friend, Melia, emerged from the water. Her hair was wet, slicked back, shiny as a seal's. Her skin glowed with good health and her body was brown. She was a sun worshipper, always had been. When she was too young to understand about cycles and shade she would cry in the days of darkness.

Lillah and Melia had been to school together; had learnt about the sun and the Treeshadow, how when part of the country was in shade, the other part saw the sun. They were good days, though lonely without their families.

This time, they were adults. Adults seeking a partner.

Lillah felt the blood rush between her legs. She had no fear that she would be nervous. She wanted this. The only hard part would be concentrating on the children.

"Lillah! You'd better hurry and bathe. We'll be leaving soon."

"Can I borrow your soap? I forgot mine."

"Of course. Here. Hair soap, too. Your hair is looking greasy. You want to look your best when we set out. Make the boys ache to think of you leaving."

"I doubt they will ache," Lillah said. "Laugh, perhaps, at us dressed as adults. Teachers."

"I suppose. Anyway, the others have bathed already. You're the last."

"I was talking to my father. I'll bathe then I'll visit Magnolia. You know, she seems to have forgotten how much that baby hurt. I don't think I ever want a baby. It hurts too much."

"I've heard there's places you can go where it doesn't hurt so much. They give you things to take the pain away. My sister sent back word. I think its one of the reasons she picked her husband. And there's another reason. I'll tell you at school."

Melia winked. Lillah winked back. The things they would talk about on the trip! Melia's sister Ulma had sent messages with every passing school, full of stories of marriage and love making, what a man did, what he said.

Lillah ran into the water. It was cold; bumps rose on her arms and legs. She dived into a low wave, letting the salt fill her eyes, her pores. She felt the tingle of it cleaning her. She stripped off her wrap and used it to clean under her arms, her neck, behind her ears, between her legs. Out here in the water it was easy to pretend nobody else existed; that there was no beloved sister-in-law; no magnificent nephew; no father preparing for the loneliness of losing a daughter, no crocodile of children, eight, nine and ten years old, all of them, these children waiting for Lillah and the four other teachers to lead them around the Tree. It was a five year journey. Lillah had begun hers as a nine year old and come back educated. It would be interesting to experience it again as an adult, through adult eyes.

Though truth be told, Lillah at twenty-one did not feel much more experienced or knowledgeable than at fourteen, when wearily, too full of information to speak, they had arrived back in their own town.

She walked out of the water and wrapped her sulu around. It clung to her wet body so she pulled another over the top. Here, in her own Order, she needed to show prudishness. Once away with the school and so long as the children were safely under the attention of other adults, she could be what she wanted to be. Lillah finished bathing and dressed carefully. She gazed out to sea and fancied she saw a glimmer of an island out there. She turned around once, looked again. Nothing. Her heart calmed and she relaxed. To see the island of the spirits twice meant death to someone in the Order.

She knew that Annan, the Tale-teller, would be at work by the Tree and she wanted to be witness to it.

He smiled when he saw her. "None of the others take an interest but you, Lillah. You like to see the words being spoken, hear them for yourself."

"I'm just checking to make sure you get it right. Can't have you telling the Tree the wrong information." She smiled at him. She would miss Annan in an odd way; he was the Tale-teller, yet he rarely spoke beyond Telling the Tree. He knew all, though, saw all, kept it to himself, and the Tree.

"Many times you have stood with me and helped me remember the days, the moments worth recording."

Lillah bent her head to rest it on his shoulder. He was a short man, not much taller than she was. He was getting stouter in his old age. He knew the history so well he recited it in his dreams.

He leaned into the Tree and put his mouth to a small smooth hole in the Trunk. He spoke the names of the teachers and children leaving, and he spoke of the birth of Logan's baby. Lillah felt satisfied hearing the words, as if now nothing would be lost to her memory.

"Everything is cyclical," he said. This was one of his favourite sayings.

The Tale-teller or his allotted helpers were the only ones allowed to tell the Tree. It was important that the information was correct. There was a time when nobody wanted to take on the responsibility of Tale-teller, so everyone just spoke whatever information they thought important or interesting. Unfortunately, not everyone took it seriously: one young man kept a tally of the teachers he slept with, including names and crude drawings he etched into the Trunk. This information was not relevant and it did not speak to inheritance. He did not impregnate anybody and many of the names were invented.

Also, people forgot to tell the Tree on the day of events and would do it months later, sometimes forgetting precise times. The Tree sickened, stopped giving fruit, and after it was decided to vote for a teller from the citizens, the position was filled once again.

It was an offence punishable with caging to tear Bark or Limbs from the Tree. Enough timber dropped to fill their needs.

Lillah felt a hand creep into hers. Logan. He didn't know the stories of the Tree as well as she did. He had to memorise what Lillah told him to; it was like she could see the actual words.

"Come to bother me?"

Logan dropped her hand. "Is this how you want to leave? Leaving me to feel bad? Inadequate?"

"Inadequate? Be glad you weren't chosen to carry the bags. Now that would be a shameful thing." They both glanced at the teller's feet. His son sat there, back against the Tree, feet resting on a root.

As the teller stepped forward to tell further news to the Tree, he tripped over his son's ankles.

"Blast it! Move! Away from the Tree!" he shouted. The poor boy shrugged, stood up, sauntered away, as if he had not been spoken to like an idiot.

"He shows no interest unless there's a crowd," the teller said. The boy's large head seemed too big for his body. His fingers were long and bony, almost tapered; Lillah had seen him scooping the guts out of a fish then almost shucking the flesh from the bones. She imagined his fingers like knives. He didn't need tools, she thought. He could use his fingers to cut story into wood.

Logan strapped on shoes to climb the Tree. "These feel awful."

Lillah and the other teachers had memorised three generations of births and deaths. They remembered the time they lost six men, out building an extension to the seawalk when it collapsed. No one could reach them to rescue them, and it was devastating to the Order to watch them inching closer and closer, but never reaching shore.

They knew that one Order remembered the story of Spikes, which killed so many of them.

Annan said, "The others will join us?"

"Yes. Should I gather them now?"

"I'll send my son," Annan said, and he kicked the boy to action.

Before long, the rest of the teachers gathered to hear the telling of their lifelines. Many others came, too; this was a recital they enjoyed.

Annan closed his eyes and murmured. Lillah knew he was apologising to the Tree for the intrusion.

Then he began. He was not as great a performer as some she had heard of. Maybe Dickson, if chosen to take the aging man's place, would enjoy the performance aspect more. Dickson was a natural show-off and scene-stealer. His classic story was that moments after Thea was born and everybody was cooing over her, he pulled his pants down and defecated on their mother's bed.

Anything for attention. Dickson would enjoy being the teller, but it wouldn't be enough. He wanted everyone around the Tree to know his name. He wanted to appear in the voices in every place.

Annan finished his recital but the people stayed gathered, chattering and amusing each other.

Dickson was bad tempered at Thea and Lillah's leaving. He would not admit it, but he would miss them terribly. Thea was the only person who'd listen to him, who found him interesting.

"Dickson," someone said, perhaps trying to cheer him up. "I see a drawing of your mother here." The person pointed to a pile of faeces left at the base of the Tree. One of the children would be punished for it.

"Cover it up," Lillah said. "Don't joke about it. Cover it up."

"There's no other evidence of his mother. His parentage. I thought this must be it."

The joke was cruel and not funny.

Dickson ran to the rope. "I'll climb it and you'll see my line. You'll see where I'm from."

He climbed the nearest rope, then reached out for the rope before it. The young men loved to climb, and the women, too. The children were up in the branches all the time, feeling tall, proud, strong.

Dickson tugged at the rope, testing it. He heard creaking. He did not have the courage to climb further up the ropes, so he pulled down his pants and pissed on the people below. The crowd shouted. "Dickson! You fool!"

"Dickson's climbing the Tree!" the call went out, and many in the Order laughed. There had never been a self-death at Ombu, through teachers who arrived from other Orders had experienced this loss and didn't find it a reason to joke.

Lillah noticed Morace standing quietly to the side.

There was a large fissure in the Tree nearby. Morace had always been fascinated by it.

He stood there, arms stretched up, hands holding the sides of the fissure on either side. He leaned in, sniffing the air in there.

"Morace!" Thea screamed. She ran forward and pulled at him. "Don't go inside! There's ghosts in there!" He threw her arm off.

"Don't touch me," he said.

Zygo stood beside him. "Don't touch him, Thea."

Some of the other children watched, terrified.

"He nearly went in!"

"My grandmother's in there. And she drowned and got eaten by crabs, so you could see her insides," Zygo said.

Borag squealed. "Don't go in! He's too curious. Doesn't he know how dangerous curiosity can be?"

"Come on, Morace. There's something I want to show you," Lillah said.

Morace reluctantly let go of the Trunk. "I like the way it smells in there. Different to the way it smells out here."

Lillah took his hand and led him towards the beach. He slowed as the brush cleared then balked altogether. Inwardly, Lillah cursed a mother who would cause her child to be frightened of open spaces.

"It's okay," she said. "Look." She pointed along the beach, and Araucari, the man who had lost the use of his legs, waved.

"Help me," Araucari had whimpered. "Help me." The men had worked together, ten of them heaving at the wood.

"It seems to weigh more when it falls," grumbled one of the men.

"Be quiet and keep lifting. If we don't free him soon he will die."

"What use will he be without legs?" muttered the man, a jealous, lazy type who had never attracted a wife. "He won't be able to find food, or build. What could he do?"

Someone said, "He can remember, and think. This one is our puzzle solver. Remember when a child disappeared from one of the visiting schools? We all thought she'd drowned, but he remembered her talking about the sun, how she wanted to be close to the sun. We found her on our highest reachable branch. Remember? Someone had to climb up and coax her down with the promise of sweets. He listens, this man. Even more now that he will be inactive."

"He's a very handy man. Now heave." They threw off the wood and one of the women wrapped the sodden bandages she had prepared as a compress around his legs while he panted and showed them the whites of his eyes. They pulled the stick from his stomach and saw the wound was shallower than they had thought.

"We need to draw out the poison. This needs to be changed every hour if he is to live." If he died, he would receive a hero's burial, full of worship. Dying by being crushed by falling wood is considered worthy. It hadn't happened in Lillah's lifetime, but etched into the Tree Trunk was a depiction of a man under a huge branch, with a ray of sunlight directed into his face.

Araucari did survive. Now he mostly ate food that slipped through his body easily: seaweed, cooked to sludge. Lots of liquids. He was known for a certain smell and had no chance of ever finding a wife.

His legs were never useful again, and you knew where he had been by the drag marks in the sand or dirt. His arm muscles had grown massive and the skin on his hands calloused, thick. He could pick up a red-hot ember and toss it from palm to palm, without feeling a thing. He could pluck food out of the pot and let it cool before passing it around. And he was very kind to the children. He knew he frightened them, so made sure his smile was mild. He did not hand out sweets to them. "I don't want to trick people to like me," he said. There had been a number of disappointed schoolteachers who hadn't realised the extent of his disablement. He would never be a father, and could only morally marry a barren woman.

"Araucari's made something for you. Come on. He can't come to us. I'll lead you. Close your eyes if you like."

Morace did, squeezed his eyes shut and trusted Lillah to lead him.

They reached Araucari and Lillah nodded to him. He handed Lillah a hat and she placed it carefully on Morace's head.

"Open your eyes," she said.

Morace opened one eye, then the other. He gasped. The hat had three flaps; two concealing the world on either side, the third cutting the view in front to just a few metres.

Morace stepped forward on the sand, then took another few steps. He turned to face the man, grinning broadly.

"I can pretend I don't have a face with this hat. People will think I am a hat on a body."

Araucari chuckled. "We understand each other, Morace. I was once like you: afraid of open spaces. I liked my small house, my small room. People could not see me there, and they would not laugh at my legs, my weakness. If they made me come out, I would stand with my nose to the dark, dark, mottled Bark of the Tree. I would breathe it in. We had a school walk through who brought a drink they had made with the Bark and I liked that, too;

one drink and your brain was quiet, you had no more thoughts until waking. But it hurt the next day and it was three, four days before you could start thinking again. That is no way to be.

"Then another school came through, and one of the young boys was like me. I watched a lot because the teachers had no interest in me. That was okay; I understood. Although they did not realise I could bring pleasure to them. They didn't know that."

Lillah felt her cheeks blush, and she looked at Araucari's long fingers, her thoughts going elsewhere.

"This young boy was not happy on the walk. He did not like school. We sat and talked and we thought that the world was too big for us, that we did not like to see the world all at once. We liked small views, things we could understand one by one. So together we made a hat each. This is mine."

"I haven't seen you wear it," Morace said. He did not take the hat off.

"No, I don't need it anymore. I am no longer scared of the world. That will be you, too, by the time you return."

Morace smiled. "By the time I return I will have eyes at the back of my head and on top of my ears, so I can see the world all at once."

Araucari squeezed his shoulders. "You will come back a well-worthy child. I will miss you and your jokes, Morace."

Lillah squeezed Araucari. He was a good, good man.

"Dickson seems even more agitated than usual," Myrist said quietly.

"I think he was hoping Thea would choose to stay with him. But she cannot live with her brother forever. He thinks no one else will choose him."

"And he sees that as whose fault?" Myrist said.

Lillah nodded. "I know. He doesn't see what sort of person he is. He thinks he's fine the way he is."

They heard screaming and ran to see Dickson spinning a child so fast all was a blur.

"Dickson!" Myrist shouted. "You'll hurt that child."

"I told him," Erica said, her hands on her hips. "I told him again and again. He doesn't listen."

Dickson stopped, panting. "Will I? I didn't realise you could tell the future."

He let the child slip to the ground.

"More?" the child said, and those watching laughed.

Dickson hopped about, unable to keep still. His mouth pursed into a whistle, he waved his arms to try to get Lillah's attention.

"Come on, Lillah, I want to show you something."

"I've already seen it, thanks," she said. "I've seen it plenty and I don't need to be reminded of what it looks like." She tied her hair back in a plaited vine and set up a bowl of hot, salty water. She bent over the steamy bowl. She closed her eyes and let the heat absorb her. Her face began to sweat and it was harder to breath; the steam hurt her lungs.

"I don't know why you're doing that. You're already beautiful," Dickson said.

Lillah lifted her head up, feigning annoyance but glad of the excuse to stop steaming her face.

"Dickson, you are the most self-centred, dreary person I know. Can't you leave me alone for just one minute?" He shook his head and danced from foot to foot.

"It's important for the future of our Order," he said. He tossed his head; hair was always in his eyes. She sighed, dried her face in a soft cloth and stood up. He took her hand and she was surprised at the comfort of it. Not too soft but not callused, his hand was firm as it held hers.

He led her down over the rocks and to a small rock pool.

"There," he said. He squatted down and tugged her down, too. In the rock pool there were small, perfect pieces of shell, colourful and glowing in the water. "I want you to tell my future bride that I will make a necklace for her. I'll collect these until she arrives, then I'll string them for her. No one can find shells the way I do. I've got the nose."

Lillah made no comment on his nose, which was long and fat, with a blob on the end that was almost penis-like. Thea's nose was similar; she hated it.

Lillah ran her fingers through his shells, admiring their differences. "You should share the shells. Unfair otherwise."

"Oh, I'll share," he said, but he turned his head away and flapped his hand at her. When he turned back his eyes were teary, and Lillah wasn't sure if it was the salt air or something else.

"Send me someone beautiful in your place, Lillah. Someone worthy of my love." He rotated his hips and kissed his lips at her.

"I'll try," Lillah said. She imagined there would be one like him in every Order they stopped at.

"I need to get back, Dickson. Don't go telling everybody we did anything, all right?"

He shrugged. "I never lie. Don't you think it would be better the first time with someone who knows you, cares about you? I would never forget it."

"That's the problem. You'd never forget, always think you have a hold on me, that I would remember you with affection and come back to you. It will only lead to disappointment. There's a school arriving tomorrow or the next day. There will be your partner amongst them. Your perfect girl. And if not that school, then the next. If my brother can win a girl, then you certainly can." Lillah winced as she spoke, knowing these words would not comfort him. His mouth turned down and he stepped away from her.

"You know your brother used trickery to win Magnolia. Tax says so." It seemed so odd that Thea could have two such awful brothers.

"I wouldn't call it trickery. Kindness, I would say."

"He pretended to be kind just to get her interested."

"He wasn't pretending. He is kind. Maybe you will need a few tricks, though," Lillah said. "Come on. I think they are eating cake. I don't want to miss out."

"I'm not coming. I don't want to see those people."

Lillah wondered what he was up to. She followed him to the Trunk of the Tree, and heard him whispering into its Bark, "This is the teller Dickson. Today I had sex with both Lillah and Melia, because they wished me to seed them before they left. This was my duty for the day."

Lillah waited until he was gone, then whispered over his tell, "No, he didn't."

As the moment for departure approached, Lillah felt as if she was awakening, that she was in that moment just before, that moment when defences are down and a different, internal reality takes over. This is the time Lillah felt frightened. Sometimes she tried to fight it, other times she gave in to the randomness of it. There was a sense of green, and a sense of big. This bigness filled her brain to the very edges. The bigness took all the space, till there was room for nothing but bigness. And the bigness was green. This green filling was frightening because she had no control over it. It wasn't like the times they drank too much sap wine; those times the body was uncontrollable, but the brain didn't care. This bigness filled her and she just had to let it be.

The whole Order came out to the water. Excitement filled the air with noise: eating, collecting messages for people, last-minute conversations about important things. The pot thrower lined up pot after pot, although he was not completely happy with the clay.

"Too dry. It misses something."

Lillah gave her childhood doll, Treesa, to one of the little girls too young for school, who hugged it to her chest. No point leaving it, no point taking it. She would make a new doll for any child she had; this doll should stay here.

Myrist cleared his throat three times but didn't speak.

"What is it, Myrist? If you have something to say, now is the time. Any messages you send after me will be lost in translation, you know that."

"I know I shouldn't worry. I want you to be careful, though. Be observant. Watch everyone and everything carefully. Don't let a racing pulse lead you to make a wrong choice. Look at the surroundings. Notice everything. Some Orders appear to be friendly but beneath there lies anger and fear."

"I'll be able to tell," Lillah said.

"Some Orders will try to terrify you into making the choice they want you to make. Some places will show you the consequences of a wrong choice."

Lillah's brother chimed in, "Nasty little babies, twisted and in pain. Dead babies." He kissed his own baby on the head.

A shout went up, signifying a catch of crab. Logan held out his baby for someone to take. "They'll be an age yet, bringing it in. They don't need you," Lillah said. "Sit with me and talk for longer. What about what we've been talking about, our message?"

Logan smiled. "Do you think it will work?"

"It's worth a try."

"All right. When you've been gone two years, I'll send you a message. You send it back to me as you hear it. And we'll see!"

"We'll see how clever our messengers are. How much information is changed by the sending. They won't believe us, but it's worth a try, don't you think?"

In an informal ceremony around talkfire, but an important one, all the women whose birth Orders were elsewhere around the Tree came one by one with gifts for the teachers to deliver. Lillah found it hard to remember. It was Agara who had the good memory; she took the poem to heart.

There were painted leaves for Parana, coloured sand for Arborvitae and shells for Sargassum.

Thea sat apart, plucking out her hair, peeling her dry skin. She held her bonsai on her lap. Agara's father approached her and said, "You understand we must only send the best? It is our responsibility, to keep us strong."

"I'm not strong," said Thea. She rose above them, then, towering high and clenching her fist.

Melia's father tapped his temple. "Not in here, you aren't, Thea," he said. "But you can learn that from the other teachers and all you meet."

Thea threw down her bonsai and ran. The others girls stared at the mess, the precious dirt, the denuded branches.

"Somebody clean it up," Melia's father snapped.

Dickson and Lillah followed Thea. "I will send you a message so you know I am thinking of you, sister."

They drew her back to the farewellfire. Tilla was shouting at them: "Don't know where you think you're going. No one can walk around the Tree. No one. Can't be done."

The Order laughed. "But you did it!" Lillah said. "You went to school."

"I never did."

Somehow the old man had forgotten every leaving. For him, the world began and ended only as far as he could see.

Lillah would meet others like him on her travels.

"But what about people who leave in this direction and come back in that, five years later?"

"Liars. All of them. Don't ask me why. I don't know how liars think."

Lillah stood ready, the children who were about to travel with her running at her feet, the noise of them lively and setting an edge to her nerves.

There were no tears. The leaving of the school was accepted because it had always been that way. Women and children left. Children came back; women sometimes did, many years later.

"You know if you just keep walking you'll get there eventually. There is no way to get lost. Keep the Tree to your right shoulder and just keep walking," Erica's father said.

"We send our best away! Why do we send our best away?" Dickson said.

Pittos put his hand on Dickson's shoulder. "Because the best are sent to us. That is the way it works."

"And the best are the ones who deserve to find a place with fresh water," Melia said. She hated salt water.

Aquifolia gave Lillah a message for her home Order. It was a bundle of twigs, marked and etched. It would be difficult to carry and Lillah wondered if she would get away without delivering it. She'd rather throw it into the scrub before too long passed. She also handed them a pouch of dried moss. "Take a small pinch of this every morning after you take a lover. It will stop you from catching child. The most important thing is to see my mother. Everybody wants to see her. She has no time for her own children, but she will find time for you."

Lillah thought it would be hard to have a mother so sought after.

"She'll tell you your future by reading your burn scars. Fire is cleansing."

Everybody had at least one burn scar. Worship and fearfulness of the fire somehow led to a lack of wariness. Some people had more scars than others. Aquifolia reached behind her and the ember she had was still red. She thrust into onto Lillah's forearm.

Lillah recoiled, too shocked to scream. "Run to the water," Aquifolia said. "The water will take the heat from you."

"You *burnt* me," Lillah said. She wanted to take a stick and thrust it into the woman's eye.

"You will thank me when you meet my mother."

"See you children in five years," Logan said.

"Make sure my nephew knows who I am, where to find me when he goes to school. I'll look for a child who looks like you. Our strong family features."

Rhizo had asked Lillah not to share the secret with anybody, but Logan should know he had a brother.

"Walk the seawalk with me, Logan."

They walked closely together, shoulder to shoulder, and she told him about Morace, and Rhizo and the illness.

"She shouldn't ask you to do this. I never liked that woman. If he's sick, he's sick."

"But he's our brother."

"And this is our Order. Our world." He paused. Looked back at shore. "Brother, huh? So my son has an uncle?"

They walked back together, joining the others.

Magnolia held him from behind. "You find a good man like your brother. You will have to look hard. You watch out for the men in Douglas. I grew up with them as my neighbours and I thought that's what neighbouring men were like. You watch out for them. Learn from them, too, though. Learn to appreciate a good man." Logan and Magnolia let tears fall. Lillah tried to remember her school years, walking through Douglas. She did not think badly of the place, but knew that their teachers would likely have protected them carefully.

Magnolia said, "Say goodlove to my brother, Ebena. You'll like him. He makes me laugh."

Tax, much settled now, waved goodbye, his family around him.

The children's long fingernails were cut. "You are big people now." They stared at their odd-looking hands. "My fingers are shorter!" Rham said.

The teller Annan stood by and told his tales. "When walking the Tree you follow in a noble tradition, you walking women. The Tree is bigger than the land space and you walk the Tree. The first woman walked, too, seeding the ground and seeding the Tree, changing its nature from place to place as she walked. She taught all women about bloodline and she began the telling of the Tree. She left us messages of the dangers, and this is why we don't all walk. Men stay behind to care for the Order, keep it safe and keep it happy. They die of old age, as men should. The women walk and with this walking comes danger. Sometimes a teacher is lost and sometimes a student, but to die as you walk is a very great thing."

Borag came to stand by the water.

"What are you eating, Borag?"

"Bread sprinkled with cinnamon." She ate it with great passion; even a simple piece of bread could excite her.

"You will learn to control your joy in food when we are given food you dislike."

"Not a food exists I won't like."

"We'll see."

Lillah looked out to sea. If her mother was there, they would have looked out together. It was a thing they did, very early on, when talking about the dangers of the world. Her uncle, too, long gone out there.

In her mapping, Lillah told the Tree: *Home of brother too much to say will need this to come from another teacher who does not know us so well.*

Here, the Tree grows berries sweet and bitter. The leaves are dark, the Bark is dry.

Ombu — ALOES — *Ailanthus*

It was an easy day's walk, their first one. They knew the terrain, had met and traded with people from Aloes partway. It was a six day walk to the market meeting place, then the same back again. They were allowed to travel to market with the trader as they neared teacher age. This to prepare them for the physicality of the walk and so they would be heading for something familiar, not completely unknown. This market was one of the closest between communities, Lillah knew. In some places, they would walk for thirty days, or ninety, with no sign of another human being, just the Tree and the birds to keep them company.

The burn Aquifolia had given Lillah itched and wept. She tried to keep it clean but sand worked its way into everything. She knew she'd be scarred: the skin rubbed off as she walked.

They could smell the moisture in the air and knew that rain would soon come. There was a high wind blowing which frightened Morace and some of the other children. Lillah hoped they would reach the Order Aloes before the real wind started. They would be prepared for it there and have places to shelter.

The Tree Trunk wept red sap, sticky stuff which the children rolled into balls. The teachers turned away, pretended not to notice. They did not care as much as the older people did; didn't think it disrespectful to play with the sap.

Rutu, the trader, came with them as far as the market, carrying the clay pots which would be traded or filled with jasmine oil and returned to Ombu. She liked to complain each morning as they rose with the sun and began the work soon after the morning meal.

"Where do you get your energy? You won't have it in a few months, I guarantee that. You'll need your sleep just like I do. You'll dread the rising of the sun."

Lillah shrugged. "We'll see," she said. She knew Rutu was speaking lines spoken by traders before her. A trader was supposed to be world-weary and wise, and even though this girl was a year younger than Lillah, she would play her role perfectly.

Rutu was glad to be going this far, and Lillah wondered if she had it in her to just keep going, stay with them and pretend she'd been selected.

"It's a shame you have to go back, Rutu. You would make a good teacher."

"The fathers decided otherwise. They know that the position of trader brings with it great privilege. A bad trade could end good relations with neighbours, and it could leave an Order poor for future trades. Much as I want to come with you, I am happy with my position."

"I'll be sorry to say goodbye to you, Rutu. I'm glad you're trader, though. You will experience so much more that way than if you were stuck in Ombu."

Rutu nodded. "Thank you, Lillah. You will do well on your journey."

"If I can find the patience. This man is so slow."

The market holder seemed to take an age filling the jars and sorting out his products.

"I'm happy for the walk to be slow. I like being away from home," Rutu said. "I like to walk."

Too soon the jars were filled for Ombu, and she loaded them onto her pack and said her goodbyes. It was a strangely low key farewell, after the fuss made leaving Ombu.

"Why don't you sleep one more night here?" Melia said.

"I don't like much to sleep the night in the market. Ghosts are at their most powerful here. Their most envious. They will steal my hair, steal my thoughts. I prefer to walk."

Lillah was disappointed: she'd wanted to see some rebellion from Rutu. An attempt, at least, to stay with the school. Lillah would have supported her, argued her case. But she left quietly, no back-ward glance.

The children whispered together. "Is it true?" Rham asked Melia. "Is it so dangerous to sleep at the market?"

Melia nodded her head. "That is what is said. You know that the trader before Rutu used to tell stories of other traders, ones he knew in his youth, before the lessons were learned. He said that they did not ever have children, the ones who slept in the market. He said that no market holder has ever had a child, and that most of them talk in short sentences with no real meaning. It is a risky job to take."

"We can sleep further around, though," Lillah assured them. "There will be no danger there."

They all assessed the market holder. He was bald, it was true. And his eyes seemed paler than most; as if they could see a short distance only.

Melia bounced around, chatting with the children, telling them jokes which made them squeal with laughter. The children ran ahead and splashed in the water until the teachers caught up, or they lagged behind collecting shells and pebbles. Morace hung back, watching them. Lillah gave him a small push on the shoulder. "Go on, Morace. You can join them."

"I don't know what to do."

"They don't either, Morace. They are just playing. Making it up as they go along." He caught up with the children but did not join them in their whooping and screaming.

"Not a very disciplined first day," Erica said. Melia and Lillah exchanged glances and laughed. Lillah threw away the sticks Aquifolia had asked her to deliver, dropped her pack and cartwheeled up the beach, making the children scream with delight.

Melia carried her things and passed them to her when she was done. "What about the sticks?"

"Oh, my Tree Lord, leave them. I'm not going to carry them all the way for a woman like that. She burnt me. I already have Magnolia's bag to deliver."

"How you suffer," Melia said.

Agara plunged into the water, shocking them, then stepped out dripping to speak her poem, the one listing the gifts and the places they needed to go.

We carry a bonsai Tree to offer in welcomefire to Aloes.
We carry shells for Osage from Ombu.
We carry a bowl for Cedrelas.
We carry a necklace from Myrist to Olea in Rhado.
We carry sticks for Sargassum.
We carry a bag of secrecy for Torreyas.
We carry painted leaves for Parana.
We carry coloured sand for Arborvitae.

"I'll pick up some sticks when we get close to Sargassum, if I am still travelling. Or someone will." Lillah and Melia walked behind the group so the breeze carried their words away.

"Do you think he will be waiting?" Melia said. The messenger to the market from Aloes last time was a handsome young man who had asked Lillah when she would become a teacher. "I'll be waiting," he'd said. Lillah had told him he would be her first stop.

Lillah nodded. "I hope so. I hope he's up to it."

"There's been one school through since then. Hopefully he's been practising."

"Oh, no! Do you think he'll think I'm foolish? Useless? Inexperienced? What if I don't know what to do?"

"They say it's very natural, so long as you don't think too hard about it."

"I can't help thinking. That's who I am."

When they stopped for a rest, the teachers lifted their skirts and rubbed sand gently onto their thighs, knees and shins.

"What are you doing?" the children asked.

"Just smoothing our legs," Melia said. The children shook their heads and ran to play in the waves. The ways of the teachers were mysterious.

"But why?" Rham said.

"You don't need to know everything, Rham," Lillah said. Sometimes the questions were too much for her.

Lillah and Melia remembered the Order Aloes from when they walked with school. The people smelt very different to their own people, that sickly smell of jasmine distilled. The flowers grew where

Lillah lived, but not in vast quantities.

None of the children had been here before and were excited at the prospect of a feast and, perhaps, gifts. They lifted their tired legs and ran.

Morace stayed by Lillah's side.

"Mother says these people will hit me if I let them," he said. "I don't think I'll let them."

"I'm not sure where your mother heard about that, but it's not true. They won't hit you," Lillah said, though she exchanged a glance with Melia. Their fathers had warned them: "On the first three nights all will appear perfect. On the second three nights you will be dear friends. On the third three nights they will begin to tire of your presence, and by the twelfth night you will see them for what they really are. This is true for every Order you'll meet. That's why you will stay twenty-eight days. After twenty-eight days you will know and accept who the people are."

"Here, let's look at what message Tilla has for me on the stone." She pulled it out of her pocket and held it in her palm. He had etched a horizon line which seemed to enter the stone and go on into eternity. Path without end. No return.

"Foolish old man," Lillah said.

"He doesn't think we're coming back, does he?"

"He is a know-nothing. How many schools has he seen return in his lifetime? Many dozens."

Lillah dug a hole in the sand with her heel, dropped the stone in and covered it up.

Morace giggled. "He'll be mad."

"He'll never know."

Morace held up his smoothstone, a very old one from his father. "Should I bury this, too?"

"No! The smoothstones are past and future, all possibility. Not nasty like that thing." She flipped her head. "You keep your stone. Where is the one you found?"

"I didn't find one. Father gave me this one instead."

"We will find you one as well. It is important to select your own smoothstone. Part of your growing."

They could smell the Jasmine as they approached early in the evening. They walked along a path lined either side with small david-saplings.

"Welcome to Aloes," a beautiful woman with reddened skin said. She smiled.

The man Lillah had thought about for many months was waiting for her, leaping up and down. "You're here! You're here!"

Lillah looked at him and thought, Dickson. He has as little grace as Dickson. He took her hand and tried to lead her away. He said aloud, "No one leaves here unsatisfied!" but someone said "Let's let everyone settle in first." The woman with reddened skin said to Lillah, "No one wanted him at the last school so he can't contain himself."

Lillah felt all desire leave her, and felt terribly disappointed by it. She no longer wanted this man.

Were there others here she would find attractive?

Lillah saw another familiar face. "Look, Melia, it's that teacher from Chrondus. Do you remember? Corma. She told us those great stories. Creepy stories."

Melia looked. "The ones about that killer? What he'd done? I guess she stopped here. She looks as if she has caught child, doesn't she?"

"What killer?" Thea asked. "What did she mean by that? Why didn't she tell me?"

"You were probably swimming, Thea. You would rather swim than talk. We have not seen it, but some will take the life of others without a thought."

Thea said, "Never."

Erica snorted. "You say that, Thea. Yet you swim with children without the slightest thought of their safety."

"That was not my fault, Erica. Nobody says it was my fault."

"You think so?"

"We are not talking about that, now," Lillah said. "That is in the past."

"You can't forget the past simply because you don't like what sits there, Lillah," Erica said.

Lillah said, "Do you remember the nightmares we had after she told us those stories? I'm sure that's her. Corma. She must have decided to stay. Her school is long gone."

Lillah approached the teacher. They had enjoyed her company.

"Corma, it's me. Lillah. From Ombu. You came through with your school. I thought you might even stay with us."

Corma was red-cheeked. She nodded. "I nearly did stay. I hated the walking. Awful. I won't be walking home, ever." She rested her hands on her belly. Lillah looked down.

"Have you caught child?"

Corma smiled. "Yes, I have. But they didn't tell me something beforehand. Well, two things. The Jasmine is so powerful that it's dangerous to women who have caught child. They don't tell you that. And they are going to send me away to have the baby. They have no knowledge of childbirth here. They have no Birthman!"

"You know, I remember women from here coming to us to see our Birthman. Is that why? I never really wondered."

"They either go to your Order or to Ailanthus," said Corma. "My husband, Hippocast, wants to go to Ailanthus, because he's heard about the nut fish they make there. He thinks with his belly, that man. I want to stay here. I don't want to walk any further."

Melia said, "It's very nice here. Very neat."

"They are very neat here. Very clean. Have you seen inside their homes? They spend a lot of the day cleaning. They don't achieve much else, but their houses are clean."

"I love the shells lined up along the paths. And the bowls decorated with shells."

Corma nodded. "It's like magic at night. It's one of the reasons I chose to stay."

"We heard about the paths," Lillah said.

"They are beautiful. It's taken time, but there they are." And she was right. That night the shells glowed gently, leading the way to homes and woodcaves. In one of the kitchens, the welcomeschool dinner cooked. Four huge pots containing a wonderful-smelling stew.

Borag came to Lillah. "Do you smell that? Can we watch it being cooked?"

"Let's go."

Hand in hand they walked to the kitchen, where the cooks welcomed them, happy to talk about their work.

"Slow cooked food is the best," the cook said. "There's no room for panic, it's done anytime between now and then. Nothing overcooks or spoils and you eat when you are ready to eat. The wind will not come this dayseason. We can work on our food without rushing for safety."

"And the smell," Lillah said. She breathed deeply. It was good, rich and meaty with an undertone of flowers. There was an undertone of flowers everywhere in this Order, even out on the water.

"We know that everything in food has a match," the cook said. "In the ground this is true, and also in the pot."

The welcoming feast that night began with a bathing session. One of the men said, "We know that some Orders have sea sponges wash up to their shore. Have you heard of this? They soak up water and you can carry them filled." The Order sighed as if this was a treasure they would love to have.

Next came a demonstration of the bonsai Trees by the young girls. The girls set their tiny Trees out to show the school.

"When are we going to eat?" Borag said. Melia handed her some dried fruit to nibble.

"Their bonsai are not very good," Thea whispered. Her fingers twitched.

"You leave them alone. No Leaf plucking. They have their Trees the way they want their Trees. I can't believe you're feeling lonely for a tiny Tree when you sit beneath our great one."

Thea said, "I can't believe you're not missing your bonsai. How do you forget it like that?"

"Don't frown, Thea. You won't be chosen if you frown."

"Everyone's chosen if they want to be, Lillah. I know that. You know that. Don't try to make me nervous."

Lillah sniffed deeply at the meat, trying to get beyond the jasmine to the food. Ensure it wasn't bad.

The local woman took Jasmine oil and seaweed fresh from the sea and ground them together to make a paste.

"This firms the skin, keeps it smooth," they said. The teachers sat while the stuff was plastered on their faces. Lillah could feel it stinging and imagined it drawing out the poisons of the walk.

Everybody laughed; Morace sat at the end, waiting for his mask. "Stop being a fool," Erica snapped at him.

They sat within a circle of the glowing shells. These ones were very small, lined up by the hundreds, a work of art.

"There was once a time when the Tree had no room at its roots. People lived like maggots, writhing over one another, crowded and hungry. They lost interest in the Tree, forgot to leave sacrifices or to worship it, and the Tree grew angry. The Tree's anger burns from within. You know the Tree feels fury when the Trunk is hot to the touch. When the Trunk is cool, the Tree is placated.

"The Tree was not placated at this time. The Trunk burnt hot, so hot that when a man touched it, he burned to the wrist. His head was so hot his eyeballs melted, and those who touched him burned, those who touched them burned. Their foreheads burned so hot they made the sea boil when they tried to cool in it. A monster filled the Tree and that was it.

"Spikes spread quickly and no one knew how to cure it. Soon there were bodies floating out to sea on rafts by the day. Sent to the sea monster to eat. The empty rafts drifted back to our shores, but they were changed. Somehow the sea monster ate the bodies and changed the rafts."

As the fire burned the cook stepped forward and back ritualistically, respecting the fire. Jasmine brewed tea was passed around. Lillah found it bitter and horrible, but she drank it. Jasmine rice to go with a fish stew, and that tasted good. Agara offered the bonsai Tree as apology for any small wrong they might do, any small misunderstanding. She received a jar of Jasmine oil in return.

They ate very late. Most of the children had been given their bowls already and were fast asleep. There came a sudden great splashing from the sea, as if a huge wave had descended. The adults paused, waiting for it to subside.

Thea began to cry. "I don't want to hear that here. We hear it at our place and it frightens me."

"Does anyone know what it is?" Lillah asked.

They tutted her. "We do not wonder. Wondering is dangerous. Things just are as they are and do not be curious."

The man Lillah had thought would be her first lover was sitting at Thea's feet, massaging them. He didn't pursue Lillah. It seemed he liked an easy win; did not like to battle for it. Thea looked terrified. A quiet man with deep brown eyes the same colour as the Trunk attended to Lillah, bringing her more tea, which she refused, then some fermented tea that warmed her and made her smile at him.

"You feel warm and good because there is an element in the tea that affects the way your blood feels. Our bodies are affected by everything we take into them."

The men around him laughed. "We call him Brother Answer. He cannot simply accept. He needs to know why."

Thea plucked in the air at imaginary leaves.

"What is she doing?"

"Her bonsai. She misses it."

"My name is Bursen," he said. He smiled at Lillah in such a way, as if she was special. "Are you tired still? How many days did you walk?"

His questions calmed her, and they spoke about walking and the moon, how pleasant it was to walk by moonlight. How different the moonlight was from the sunlight muted through the trees. His voice was deep and soft and he looked at her intently as they spoke. He didn't try to touch her, as she had seen over-eager men do, didn't push her or pull her or try to force her to do anything. She felt comfortable and happy. He brought her food and only then, once she had eaten, and rested, and relaxed, did he gently take her hand and begin to stroke the fingertips. He stroked her wrist so gently she barely felt it, but it sent a flutter through her, a heartbeat.

Erica bent over her belly, taken with moon pains. Lillah felt sorry for her: this was not a good time for the bleed. One of the women took some jasmine cream to her and began to rub it into her stomach with gentle yet firm circular movements. Erica closed her eyes, too much in pain to protest.

After a while, she opened her eyes.

"It worked. The pain is far less now. Thank you." The woman led her away to make her comfortable somewhere and to make it clear the men would not select her in this condition.

Melia sat by a pale young man, taken by his silence, his grace. He did not respond to her, though, and she didn't have the experience to deal with such a thing.

She shifted closer to him, but two of the locals, tall, young women, came over and lifted her away.

She threw their hands off and stood, fists clenched. "Who do you think you are, to lift me away?"

"He is not for you. He is a newcomer. He is for us."

Agara stepped in. "The girls of Ombu treated my father like this when he arrived. No wonder he's so arrogant."

The local women came with a small bowl of liquid. "Leaves from the base. Squeezed and squeezed. A drop in your eyes will make them bright and desirable."

A drop in their own eyes and it was that way, colours more powerful, whites like the new moon.

When the feast was over, a delicious meal flavoured with red salt, Lillah's heart began to beat faster. She had seen this moment so many times at home, when the teachers and the young men disappeared to rooms or woodcaves, or amongst the roots of the Trees. She'd anticipated it but she was terrified. The teachers quickly gathered to speak their family Trees, ensure enough disconnection. They spoke of parentage and ancestry going back four generations. Bursen listened, eyes closed, nodding, when Lillah spoke.

They had seen it happen more than once in Ombu. If there was a shared grandparent, the union could not take place. A shared great-grandparent and the fathers would make the decision.

"It's okay," Bursen said. He took her hand and led her to the cave.

"I've heard there are some caves so deep you could enter the Tree," Lillah said.

"Not this cave. This cave is warm with the fire of the sun."

He led her inside. The smell of jasmine was overpowering, and Lillah knew she would never use the stuff again. The closeness of his cave took her breath. Small.

She said, "Your cave is very nice, but what about the ghosts? Can't they see us?"

"Do you believe in the ghosts? That they are in the Tree?"

"Doesn't everyone believe it in some way?"

"I don't believe it. Many of the others here do, but I don't believe it. Why would the ghosts stay in the Tree?"

"But what about the bones going missing? The bodies? What about the things we find that can only have come from within the Tree?"

"Those mysteries I can't explain."

"Some say the Tree is full of the dead. I've seen them myself. They don't know the difference between alive and dead. "

He closed her eyes with the palm of his hand, warm palm against her skin and for some reason he didn't smell of jasmine, he smelt more of salt, and a deep honey smell she couldn't understand. He drew her down to the floor and she opened her eyes.

His smell was so rich it made her dizzy.

"No one leaves here unsatisfied," he said. Somehow when he said it, it didn't disgust her.

They heard a scream. Thea. Lillah ran out to check on her. It was the agitated young man: he thought he had won her over and was trying to drag her into his cave.

"There's lovely pictures in here. Of the jasmine flowers, so nice, come inside, I did it myself," he shouted, his voice cracking.

Bursen walked over and handed him a clay pot.

"Use the jasmine oil," he said. "Rub it on your fingers and let her smell them. Run her fingers through her hair. We've been through this."

Thea quietened at his voice. The eager boy dipped his fingers into the pot and rubbed his hands together. He gently touched Thea's cheek and she turned to allow her face to be cupped in his hand.

"That's better," Bursen said. "Now, into the cave, you two. You'll be fine."

Lillah wondered suddenly if she should be acting as Thea was, nervous and shy. But she couldn't do it. She was too excited.

Bursen led her back into the cave. It was very dark in there now; no moonlight entered to shine.

"Touch and smell are the most important senses," he said. "And taste. We don't need to see each other. In fact without vision it changes. Becomes a different sensation."

She tried to keep her burn scar covered with her sleeve but he didn't seem to care.

His experience made it good for Lillah. He was kind and gentle, in no hurry. He showed her how to shift positions until she was both comfortable and stimulated. He taught her how to kiss without spit dribbling down her chin. He removed himself from her at the last minute and spilled his seed outside, amongst the roots of the Tree.

"That's how we do things here," he said.

Then he covered her with a blanket and let her sleep.

In the morning Lillah fumbled in her little pouch for the moss. She had always wondered what it tasted like. It was not for general consumption; women who took it when they didn't need to, who lied about having slept with a man the night before, were known as moss-munchers. Any kind of liar could be called a moss-muncher.

"Are you taking it?" Bursen said. She popped some in her mouth and began to chew.

"My choice," she said. This man was not ready for children; neither was she. "I've only just started on my journey."

"I don't spill inside you, though. You won't have a child."

"Still, this is my precaution to take."

She felt nauseous in the day, but that was good. The moss was working. Her lover took some to study; he was curious as to how it worked.

Lillah looked up at the canopy, which covered the sand most of the time, leaving dappled warm patches. She felt peaceful, complete and capable.

"Why did you sleep so long? We didn't know what to do," she heard. It was Morace, squatting among the roots.

"You knew where I was. You could have come to find me."

"I did. I did come." Morace drew a snake in the dirt, refusing to catch her eye. Bursen came out, placed a gentle hand on her shoulder. Kissed her cheek, kissed her ear. She felt her breath, his breath, and she took his hand to lead him into the cave, but Thea came over, shuddering. "Why did I get stuck with him?" She plucked at her hair. "He's got a nasty sore on his heel, from stepping on a sharp shell or coral. I don't like the look of it."

"I haven't noticed," Lillah said.

"He has it covered up. He doesn't want them to see."

Thea hadn't noticed the children nearby.

"He's got Spikesfoot! He's got Spikesfoot!" they sang.

"Don't tell," Thea said, but the children looked at her as if she had asked them to dive into the ocean and swim far away. They ran off, and Thea jumped to her feet. "Should I warn him?"

"About what? He's got a sore foot. What will they do?"

Thea shook her head. "You are so caught up in your own world, you can't see outside it."

Soon a group of people gathered in front of Thea's lover's cave. It was a quiet group; no words were needed.

Thea's lover came out. Someone bent to inspect his foot.

"I scraped it on a shell," he said.

"It's Spikesfoot," the person said. The group walked with him at the centre to the roots of the Tree. The roots here were very broad and tall and he could stand between them, one hand on a root on either side.

A ruth-stripling was pulled from the Tree and the Bark removed. Two men held him still as another used the ruth-stripling to beat his legs a dozen times, until blood beaded behind his knees and soaked the weapon. Then he was led to the water, where he rolled in the salt of it, shouting.

The ruth-stripling was thrust into the Tree.

"Take Spikes from us," they said. "Let the internal fire take it." Lillah wondered at the sense of sending disease into the Tree rather than out to sea.

"But that will draw the ghosts out," Lillah said. "That will make them know there is a weak man ready to be taken."

Bursen shook his head. "Only if the illness will kill him anyway. It's a form of sacrifice. An indication of honesty. And the Tree purifies all as the sea cannot."

Lillah put her arm around Morace. If word got out his mother was ill... She needed to keep him safe.

They took the children down to the sea to bathe. Zygo stripped naked as he ran, and he wheeled and turned like a swimming fish.

"I've only just realised. They don't have a sea-walk here," Lillah said.

"They rarely go beyond thigh level."

They looked far out to sea, to the line where the sky met the water.

The people didn't stir until the sun was high in the sky. It was odd to wander the Order with most of them asleep. She bent to look at the shells that lit their way at night. They seemed dull, lustreless in the sunlight and she admired the ingenuity with which they had been laid in the path to light the dark night way. Lillah went back to bed and slept some more. Bursen reached for her in a lazy manner, barely raising a sweat. She laughed at him, saying, "Let's wait until your energy returns, la?" and he closed his eyes, unprotesting.

"Wake up, Lillah," Bursen said. She didn't want to wake up. She was enjoying a pleasant dream of climbing the Tree, finding small gifts in the branches and throwing them down to the children below.

"You'll want to join in. We're picking the flowers tonight. You're here on a very good day. We only collect in full moonlight."

Then there was stirring from the home of Corma, the teacher who had caught child.

There was a groaning noise. A whimpering.

"She refuses to go. She refuses, as she has all along," said the expectant father. "She won't listen to sense. I said I would go with her. But she wants to stay."

Someone whispered to Lillah and Melia, "She thinks it's a myth. Untrue. That jasmine oil is safe for women who have caught child. Would you risk your child's life to prove such a point? Not many would."

Moans again.

"Her baby isn't due yet?" Lillah asked.

He shook his head. "The smell is upsetting her. If you're not born to it, it can be intense."

"True. But she smelt it many times before. What worries her this time?"

"Jasmine oil excites the senses. It is an oil of sensuality. But overuse can lead to bad things. Because it can take away minor pain, some use it to take away major pain, and that is never a good thing. When we make it, even those used to the smell can be carried away by it."

"Can we watch it being made?"

"Of course. We would be honoured."

The teachers gathered the children for the next lesson. Erica rose from a comfortable bed. The pain was gone and she was ready to join the group.

"I learned about this when my school passed through. I was only eight," Lillah said.

"You can learn something of it now, but every skill requires deep and abiding knowledge in order to teach it," one of the young men standing next to Bursen said.

They picked flowers for a long time, mounds and baskets full.

The smell of the flowers was too rich, too thick, and it made Lillah's stomach clench. She worried that something bad might be covered by the smell.

The flowers were collected in mounds.

The men stripped naked and ran down to the sea, where they rolled in the water and rubbed sand to clean the dirt off. They walked dripping up to the oil press.

Someone handed Bursen a young switch, cut from the Tree.

He lifted the switch and with a flick, hit himself

on the back. He flinched, lifted the switch, flicked it again. Agara's lover joined him.

Both men did this until their skin was reddened, with small cuts in places. The people seemed unconcerned they might be frightening the children. The Order's children were clearly not bothered by it.

"I told you they would beat us," Morace said. Lillah hushed him.

One of the fathers said, "We need to be very pure to make the oil. The oil cures Spikes, so there can be no infection amongst the creators."

"Any contamination can make Spikes come," someone said. In Lillah's Order they had talked of Spikes. They understood that it had happened quickly, that one sick child meant two, meant four, and therefore sick children should be isolated until they are well. If they didn't get well, they should be treated.

Lillah felt her cheeks redden at the sight of those reddened backs.

Thick reddish brown oil drooled from the lip of the jug. A broadening puddle of it formed, flecked with impurities dropped from the Tree and blown from the sand.

It went unnoticed by the rite-makers, although wasted oil would not make them popular. They would cover it with dirt; hide it to prevent panic.

The Order liked their oil pure – the oil makers pure as well. They were proud of the fact they had never lost a citizen, but sending their women away to give birth elsewhere skewed this number, as did their encouragement to old people to "take the walk": women to their original Orders, men out to sea.

An unfair arrangement, Lillah thought. Bursen stepped around lightly on his toes, watching the procedure carefully.

"This is very specialised knowledge," he said. Behind him trailed two young men, watching everything.

They would take over one day, if they could keep up, prove themselves. It was very competitive, to be the smartest man in the Order.

"They need to understand how everything they do has a reaction, so they must do the right thing. If I push a child, he falls over, and his mother will beat me. If I use the wrong flower in perfume, it will smell like rot from the bottom of the sea. You cannot guess these things; you must know them."

Lillah admired Bursen, her lover, for his cleverness. He thought to the next step, did not merely accept.

"Everything we take, everything we do, everything we combine, has an effect," he said. His assistant yawned.

"They don't like my talk." He took Lillah's hand, a bottle of fresh oil in the other.

"I like it," she said.

"You will learn more than most on your journey, then."

His assistant said, "I'm glad I don't have to travel elsewhere. I like to be where I know."

Bursen nodded. "It's good to be a man."

Lillah knew many men feared 'elsewhere', and was glad to have the curiosity to walk.

He took her to the water's edge, where small deposits of salt lay. "I have heard there are places where red salt lines the shore. I believe that salt with this oil, rubbed into the skin, will make the flesh strong and pure."

Lillah smiled. "How did you get your position? You are very young."

"I fought long and hard and had the desire from a childhood spent at work. I passed many tests. Those young men will have no chance. There's another, very young, just back from school. I plan to take him as my apprentice. I believe he will be successful."

Lillah watched the talkfire for a while. It was a wild one, but they didn't seem concerned. Later, though, when the wood seemed alive it was so hot, one of the logs rolled off and into a pile of cloth. It burst into flames in high, hot tongue.

"The fire!" Lillah shouted, her heart pounded. The other teachers panicked also, knocking things over as the fire spread.

Calmly, the apprentices fetched water and put out the fire.

The majority of the jars of jasmine oil were set aside. "Will you trade these at market with Ombu?"

Melia asked. Ombu's main trade was Jasmine oil with Aloes and perfume with Laburnum, so they could make themselves smell nice.

"No, those are for Ailanthus. We owe them for the birthings of the last year."

It was strange. Lillah's father had been right: people were very different when you got to know them. The contrast of the welcoming party, full of joy, and the rare glimpses that Lillah had had, on rare previous visits, were different to the way the people were. The purity of them, the devotion to cleanliness. They wouldn't drink water if there were impurities in it. They used polished wood plates and discarded any with cracks. They passed the plates, each person touching their lips as they did so.

"Why do you touch your lips each time?" Melia asked. She always wanted to know answers. The man next to her said, "It is to give thanks to the Tree for the flavour the wood brings to the food."

They nodded. Yet, when Melia questioned them further, another said, "It is to wipe Spikes from our lips. Take the disease away." They nodded at that, too.

"Which is it?" Melia said. Their vagueness frustrated her.

"It is to remind ourselves that food is the essence of life. We do not take the food for granted," said one woman, and they nodded again. Lillah touched Melia's arm. Leave it, now.

Mugs of tea were passed out, ceremonial tea for strength and happiness. Lillah was used to the taste of Jasmine, now, and it didn't seem so strange to her.

They drank the tea.

On their final night, they bathed in the sea, using salt to rub off the oil. Fresh water only for drinking, much to Melia's disgust. The teachers were used to the intensity of the smell by now. The children gathered to rub their scalps with jasmine, thread flowers through their hair.

The Order gathered to farewell them. By now they avoided Melia: they thought she asked too many questions.

A david-sapling was planted along the path by which they had entered.

"That's for my baby," Corma said. "They plant a david-sapling for every one of us who leave. Some of those are for teachers. They plant a david-sapling a year after the teacher has left. Some of these david-saplings are there for babies who never existed, or who died, but they don't seem to see that. I think it's bad luck. I don't like it. I wish we could pull it up or something, but I don't want to risk offending them."

"Try not to worry about it. You're going to an Order where they understand childbirth. A better place. You may not even come back." Lillah helped her stand.

"They'll make me come back. You know that. There are other men here who have said they'll be fathers."

She stretched in the sunlight. Lillah saw her belly as her shirt lifted up; broad, brown, stretched, it looked uncomfortable.

Behind her a father appeared. "It's well past time. It will take you too long to reach Ailanthus if you don't leave soon. You don't want to birth in the sand, do you?"

"She is testing her resolve," Melia said.

"What is the point?" Lillah said.

"You are one of the wise teachers," the father said. "Some teachers are wise. Not all. Some are chosen for strength, health, beauty or humour. You, I think, are wise."

Lillah laughed, choosing not to be insulted.

The last night with her lover was odd. Lillah wasn't sure if she should be thanking him, or gifting him, and she realised this was something they hadn't been taught.

He said, "You don't need to give me a gift. I'm sad you're leaving. I would have liked you to stay."

"I would like to give birth in the place I choose as my home."

"Yes. Then let's not talk with our mouths any more."

As they left, they were each given a small jar of

Jasmine cream for the pain of childbirth and of menstruation.

Erica took hers greedily and asked for another. It was hard for Lillah to understand; she had never suffered that pain and always thought Erica was making a fuss for attention. The reaction of the women here showed her that this pain was a thing many women suffered.

The teller stood by the Tree, whispering events passed. Lillah wanted to know what he was saying, have the chance to tell the Tree what really happened. Could she do that in another Order?

As the school departed, there were no tears, not even from Morace. The children were excited to move on. Erica was so grateful for the pain cream she hugged everybody and smiled, rare behaviour for her.

Corma and Hippocast stepped into place behind them. "Do you mind if we walk with you?"

"Of course not. You are both walking?"

"I am allowed as far as the next Order to see Corma safely there. Then I must come back," Hippocast said. He ran forward to walk with the children.

"You don't need him to keep you safe. What are they thinking?"

"He begged them to come and I think it's very nice of him," she said, turning her back.

"Of course, of course, if you want him with you that's different! He seems to be a good man. They are all good men."

As they walked, Lillah asked Corma to talk more about the jail in her home Order. "Are there others? We don't hear much about the jails."

"I believe there are others, though I haven't seen any. They are modelled on ours, though."

"And is it only people from your Order locked in one?"

"No. I think they take people from along the Tree."

"Tell me about it again."

"Why? It's horrible."

"I know. But sometimes I like to hear about the horrible."

"They are small cages dangling over the water. They float, so that the criminal's feet, or some part of his body, are always in the water. They are given some food but they mostly catch fish and eat it raw. The only thing for them to do is to catch fish and watch the Order. It is a terrible punishment. They are isolated and lonely. They get sick from eating so much raw fish. Sometimes they get belly Spikes and then they have to be treated."

"It sounds awful. But they do get to spend more time in the sun out there. That would help the sadness. And there has never been a fish with Spikes. We have not known one."

"Nor have we. You will never be in a cage, don't worry."

"Do you ever feel like swimming out to talk to one of them?"

"Never. Who would do such a thing? One thing I've heard about Ailanthus is they know how to stop the bleeding."

Lillah, while startled by the quick change of subject, said, "Magnolia bled all over the place. I collected an armful of spiderwebs and we stopped the bleeding with that."

"You can't take the webs from spiders. Haven't you heard the story? A man was climbing the Tree to steal some tender shoots. He swept aside a giant spiderweb, that had caught in his fingers. He didn't care; he pushed more out of the way.

"He stole the shoots, then tried to climb down.

"He slipped and fell; this a man so surefooted he ran on the rock pools at tide down never slipping, as we all did.

"The spiderwebs caught him. Hooray, you think. But no. They caught him around the neck in a stranglehold and no one could climb up to reach him. There he stayed.

And he grew two extra arms, so he dangled like a giant spider until he rotted and fell to the roots."

She ate some nuts. "You don't touch spiderwebs. Too much bad luck."

• • •

In her mapping, Lillah told the Tree: *Jasmine smelling far too much, clever oiling from the flower, clever thinking brain using fear of spiderwebs, danger for those who have caught child.*

Here, the Tree grows Jasmine, the leaves are dark and the Bark is oily.

Aloes — AILANTHUS — *Cedrelas*

The trader from Aloes travelled with them, laden with jars of jasmine oil.

"I'm not sure what you will make of the market we share with Ailanthus. The market holder is odd. He camps by the roots of the Tree, waiting for market time. He does nothing else. I am glad to be the trader, though. This walk, fifteen days, this is a good walk."

The market was better built than the one between Ombu and Aloes. The market holder collected driftwood in his waiting time. He stained it orange by scraping some of the bright moss off the long Limbs bent towards the sun.

He built shelves into the natural crevices of the trunk and here he stood goods of all kinds. Lillah recognised some of Ombu's jars, but it seemed he had items from everywhere in Botanica.

Sea sponges, decorated plates, painted nutshells, necklaces, hair clips, perfect shells. The teachers and the children cooed over the treasures.

The market holder and the trader did their business, then he leant back against the Tree, knees spread wide, his sulu tucked between his thighs. He smelled very sweet, not such as jasmine, but clean and fruity.

"You live here all the time?" Melia asked.

"Too many things to transport now. And I can't leave these things out for the monkeys."

"Or the ghosts," Thea said.

"There are no ghosts here. Not in this place. That's why I chose it."

Thea pointed at a fissure beside him. "What about in there? That looks like a ghost cave to me."

He turned. "No ghosts, teacher. You are safe here. Would you like to stay with me? It's a lonely life but a fine one."

He smiled, his teeth large and blunt. Lillah was not sure if he was joking. "You are too old for any of us to choose you, market man," Thea said. "You are old and ugly and dull."

Her anger surprised everyone. The market holder turned his mouth down. "I would like someone to stay with me."

"You would soon tire of a companion," Lillah said.

"Yes. You're right."

Melia spoke to him, more questions and more, while the others looked at his goods.

Morace stood by the fissure, arms stretched up,

hands holding the sides of it. He leaned in, sniffing the air in there.

"Morace!" Thea shouted. "Leave that alone. Leave the ghosts alone, you stupid child."

"There are no ghosts," the market holder said.

Borag squealed. "Don't go in! The ghosts will take you and put a ghost child in your place."

Zygo rolled his eyes into his head and walked stiffly, his arms out, towards Morace. "I am dead-but-walking," he said. "I will steal your heart and feed it to the fishes. I will eat your mother and your father and I will spit their bones out all polished and white."

Morace screamed. "Keep away from me!"

The children were agitated. Tired. The teachers were warned this would happen once the excitement faded. "Does everyone have their smoothstones?" Erica called out. "Hold them in your hands, take comfort from them. Touching the smoothstone is stroking your mother's cheeks, being lifted by your father."

"I don't have mine!" Borag said. Her voice was high with anxiety, disconnected somehow. "I dropped it!"

"Maybe you put it in your bag. Or someone else picked it up."

"Why would someone else pick it up?" Zygo said.

Yet when they searched the bags, there it was in Zygo's things.

"Somebody put it there!" he said.

The teachers felt panic, unhappiness around the children.

"Let's move on," Lillah said.

"There are crabs ahead," the market holder said. "Too many for me to eat. Where you see the Tree hanging low in the water, you will find too many crabs to eat. They like rocks or limbs to crawl on. They don't mind bones, either. These are the tastiest crabs you will ever eat. They love to be eaten. They crawl along the sand with their claws and with their tiny voices they call out, 'eat me'!"

The children leapt about with excitement, mimicking the talking crabs. Morace and Rham made them all laugh with their play; two crabs fighting over an old fish-head. Lillah smiled at the market holder, impressed at his knowledge of children and their humour.

He said, "You know how good crabs are? Did you know that the ones which eat humans still taste like humans, they say."

Corma nodded as if she knew all there was to know.

"How do you know how humans taste?" Rham asked, and the other children laughed at this. Lillah kissed her head, thanking her.

"All right, let's pack up and look out for crabs as we walk," Lillah said. They waved goodbye to the market holder. Corma's husband Hippocast had exchanged a shell he'd found for a necklace of seeds; Corma looked happier than before.

The children ran ahead, finding the crabs. Zygo found the most, draping them around his body and dancing, ignoring the pain of their nippers. They cooked up a feast.

Having Corma and Hippocast with them changed the nature of the walk. The children loved having Hippocast along, because he never tired of playing the games they loved to play. He was nervous to be away from home so he laughed and joked most of the time to take his mind off his fear, and it was hard to be serious with him around. It was hot, most days, so hot they tried to walk in the shade of the Tree, dunking themselves in the water whenever they paused to eat or rest.

After a while, Lillah began to tire of the constant chatter and laughter, and to need some time alone. She held back; when Melia raised her eyebrows questioningly, she shook her head and waved Melia on.

She could think alone. Not that there was much to think about, but she had taken her first lover, made her first new friend, and managed to keep the children alive so far, so there were some things.

Her father had heard of Ailanthus, and their prowess at cooking. He'd said, "Your mother would have stopped there if she could. She envied an Order that worshipped food like these ones do."

"But we liked her cooking."

"It wasn't enough for her. She wanted it to be worshipped."

So Lillah looked forward to this Order, but was nervous as well. What if they expected her to have some knowledge? What if she couldn't tell the difference between their food and that of the two other Orders she'd eaten in?

She caught up with the school. They were tired and ready for a break, but she knew they could make the next Order by nightfall if they hurried. It was a worthwhile effort: they were all tired of sleeping out of doors.

The sun was setting over the Tree when they arrived. The first thing they saw was a hand-built rock pool, which sat on a part of the sand where the sun reached most of the time. It was filled with rainwater, they were told later, which was collected in carved wooden bowls and poured through cloth to keep it pure.

"Look at it," Melia said. "Clear. Clean. Imagine what it tastes like." She bent down and paddled a finger in the water. Tasted it. "It's okay. When I find a place with good, fresh water, that's where I'm staying."

Three young women came up to them, children running at their feet. "Welcome to Ailanthus. We are happy to have you here, aren't we, children?" The children cheered and laughed and they began to chase each other around the adults' legs.

There was far less fanfare on arrival in this Order. Everybody was busy, gathering nuts, cooking,

preparing the feast. Corma was taken to the Birthman so he could see her shape. Her husband,
Hippocast, was collected by the young men. "I'm
supposed to go straight home," he said.

"You cannot leave your wife with child. She
needs you here. You need to look after her," he was
told.

Borag watched the cooks; saw how the root vegetables they grew were pale pinkish in colour,
perhaps from growing near the flowers. The flowers
growing here produced a sweet sticky substance.

A woman came up from the water, a large fish flapping in her arms. She ran with it, heavy feet almost
tripping in haste.

She knelt down and let the fish wriggle into the
fresh water pool.

"He won't like it. But you watch. In a day, maybe
two he'll puff like this." She opened her mouth and
breathed out heavily. "And he won't taste so salty."
The teachers gathered the children and the woman
taught them about the saltiness of the fish, how to
lessen the salt for a better flavour.

The children knelt by the pool and watched the
fish.

"Does the salt come into the water?" Rham, the
cleverest student, asked. She fiddled with her
wooden puzzle.

"Yes, it will cloud the water so that we can't use
it. We empty the water, fill a new rockpool with

fresh. It's hard work but worth it for the good fish we cook."

Rham became obsessed with catching the moment the fish breathed out, and with the changes in the fish as the hours passed. Morace kept her company while he could, but crept away at times.

"He's flopping about!" Rham called. "Come and see."

So Lillah was there when the fish opened his mouth and puffed out a cloud of salt which floated then dissolved as they watched.

Once the fish released its salt, it was killed in the water, a quick slash across its gills.

"It needs to die quickly or the skin will toughen," the cook said. "It needs to think it is alive until it is dead."

While the fish eyes were still ,flickering, it was scaled and washed, gutted and beheaded. The head was thrown into a large pot for a soup.

The fish was rolled in the sticky flower pulp, then in crushed nuts. Then it was wrapped in large leaves and thrust into the fire.

"This will crispen the skin while keeping the flesh soft."

"Those pots are huge. How did you make them?" Borag asked.

"We understand the fire. We find the metal on the beach; everybody does. But we know about the fire, and the heat, and we build the metal into the pots. That is why we are the greatest cooks along the Tree. We make these pots big to remember the people who used to live. The tall as a Tree people. If we forget them, they will be angry with the child-birthing."

To make a sauce, the cook used nut oil, a dark brown, highly scented oil which did not burn easily.

The children lost interest in the process after a while and just wanted to eat. The Order's children showed them how to gather the nuts that fell, nibble up the left over bits and crumbs, while the grownups shooed them away. They compared their smoothstones; the Order's children were nervous to show theirs, saying that it meant bad luck for a stranger to see your stone.

"Where are your bonsai?" Thea asked the young women.

There were exchanged glances. "We don't follow the bonsai here. We feel it is taming the Tree and should not be done. Don't you think you can damage the Tree that way?"

Thea shook her head in a way which meant, I never thought of it that way, and will never do so.

After the welcomefire, where the jasmine oil was exchanged for nut oil, they talked about fire as the cook gave them further instruction.

"Listen. You know the sound a fire makes. You know how hot it is by the way it sizzles and crackles. Now we put the bread on."

The cook threw little round rolls of dough into a square pot on the fire and shook it in a frenetic motion until they darkened.

"Every part of the Tree is edible if you cook it right."

The bread was perfect with the nut fish. Lillah soaked up the last of the wonderful sauce with it. She felt very full, not ill. She felt so well and great she wanted to climb to the top of the Tree and shout.

There was more food, though: sweet things and salty, things fried in the nut oil and served in great mounds.

Borag and Lillah watched, taking it all in.

"Not everyone will share their knowledge," Lillah said.

"Knowledge not shared is wasted," the cook said. "I am happy to have people listen to me and to pass on this food."

The teller told the story of an old man who loved to eat the tender flesh of babies. He deep fried them whole and crunched them, bones and all.

"They still hear him. They say he's inside the Tree, crunch crunch, you can hear sometimes." The teller took a piece of fish, cooked with all its bones, and crunched it, swallowing it dramatically, eyes rolling.

"They say his brother took to the sea, fishing out water babies all salty and sweet. They say if the brother ever comes to land, just his foot on the sand will turn the grains to poison along the Tree and all children will die a throat-parched death."

He touched his ears as they all did, to honour the missing.

Thea swam for seaweed, and they used that to soothe tired feet and sore muscles. Thea sat watching, refusing treatment.

"Thank you for the seaweed," one of the men said.

Thea said, "There would have been more if any of the children helped to collect it."

The men were larger here. Fleshier. They seemed to breathe more loudly, but they were busy, active all the time. They made the teachers laugh with their antics.

Corma, feeling for kicks in her belly, watched it all, sighing sometimes. Hippocast sat with her, brought her treats and told her happy stories. She felt her stomach more frantically, stopped, looked at him. "My baby isn't kicking."

They roused the Birthman and he looked at her carefully. "It's ready to come. Sleeping, ready to come. We must prepare."

Lillah found all of the men attractive. There was one with curly, wild hair, and she wondered what it would feel like to get her fingers tangled in it.

He noticed her smiling at him, and jumped up with a sweet for her. She shook her head, so full of food she couldn't have any more. He popped it into his own mouth and led her off to show her the kitchen in his small house in the roots of the Tree. A small monkey sat on the roof, chittering. It watched her carefully.

"Is that your wife?" Lillah said. "She looks angry."

He shook his head. "That is not my wife." He didn't smile when he said this, and Lillah lost some interest in him. A man without humour was not so attractive.

"You don't use the caves here?"

"No! Never! It's dangerous inside the Tree. Once a teller stepped in there to speak more closely to the Tree and he was never seen again. We found a clump of his hair three days later; that's all. It was stuck in a clump of sap and we knew this meant that the Tree is blood and flesh and bone inside. We like the Treehouses. They are warmer. Who would sleep inside the Tree?"

"You have no courage. I would sleep in the Tree." This from another man, one Lillah hadn't noticed before. He was grey about the temples, although he didn't seem old.

"Don't listen to him. He's gone grey with terror, can't you see? From stepping inside the Tree."

"There's a place where the Tree whispers. You can sit and listen if you like. If you close your eyes, you can almost make out the words sometimes," the grey man said.

"Is it the ghosts?" Lillah asked.

"I think it's people living on the other side of the Tree. I think the island is around, not along, and that if we tunnelled through the Tree we'd be able to visit each other." Lillah looked at the grey-haired man with admiration. His thoughtfulness reminded her of the sensitive market holder.

The curly haired man said, "He knows that if he tunnels through the Tree he'll kill it, so his crazy theory will never be disproved."

The grey-haired man said, "Sometimes I whisper back. Tell them things I don't want people to know."

Lillah chose him. At least he was brave, and curious.

"I try to scratch the words as I hear them," he said. She saw his walls were a mess, scratched lines lifting squares of Bark away. There was nothing readable. "In other homes, they press coral in to make shapes and patterns. That is all it is though; patterns. There is no meaning."

He stopped to listen, standing still, unblinking. It frightened her; she felt if she collapsed to the floor in a faint he wouldn't even notice.

She took off her shirt and began massaging her nipples, rubbing them roughly and enjoying the all-over tingle when they hardened. This he noticed; took one of her nipples in his mouth.

His sucking was too loud, almost squeaky. Lillah wondered how she could get away from here.

Could she just push him away and say no? But her body took over and she desired sex after all. It's very addictive, she thought.

Afterwards, she said, "Aren't you more afraid of the sea than the Tree? Of what dwells in the sea, what lies beyond the sea?"

"That's not our business. The Tree is our business. We think nothing of monsters of the deep here."

He had a second small room in his house, walls lined with metal, and the floor was hard, too, striped through with metal and tough on the feet.

"You are clever with metal, all right."

He nodded. "We have to be. We are taming the Tree by not being so reliant on it. The Tree grows each year, towards water. Stealing our land sliver by sliver."

Lillah found this adversarial relationship with the Tree odd, and wondered if other Orders she'd visit would have a similar attitude. They carved symbols into the Trunk, things she didn't understand.

They were sorry to leave Ailanthus. The food was wonderful, and they would miss that flavour, but they took bowls of nuts with them and they knew the method. They hoped they could cook for themselves.

Corma sat sulking on a rock as they prepared for the next walk. She said, "Do you know how many babies die here? Have you seen the bones?"

"Of course more babies die here. More babies are born. Can't you understand that? Just as many die in Ombu. You said yourself they are experts at this. They know how to stem the blood."

"They'd better not use spiderwebs. That's all. I don't want those on me."

"No, I asked. They use shredded coconut fibre. You'll be fine. You're eating better than you've ever eaten. You'll be fine."

"Go climb the Tree, Lillah, I won't be fine. I'll never remember all their rules."

"They need rules to bring luck. Babies take luck. You need to follow them because your baby will take luck."

Lillah's grey-haired lover said, "We need a lot of extra luck. We have more babies and babies need all the luck they can get." His father, who had looked at Lillah in an unpleasant way, said, "Babies steal the luck." He didn't like the children; the teachers had warned their charges to keep away from him.

"Some men are never chosen, and that makes them angry and bitter," Melia said.

"I was chosen. How else would I have a son, you monstrous fool?"

Lillah's lover pulled his father away and Lillah put her hand on Melia's shoulder.

As they left, one of the women came up and tried to press a gift upon them. "Take this for my brother," she said. "I miss him so terribly."

It was a beautiful ring, carved from the bone of a large fish.

"We can't do that. We are not chartered to take gifts from anywhere but our own Order."

"How can it hurt? How can it be wrong?"

"We cannot risk the bad luck it might bring," Lillah said, knowing that would make sense to the woman.

After she'd gone, Melia said, "Why do they think we should cart their foolish gifts for years for them? We can't carry everything."

"Thank goodness for rules," Lillah said.

They were fully half a day away when Morace noticed he wasn't wearing his hat. Every minute that went by made Lillah happy; he was learning to do without it.

He couldn't breathe, though, once he noticed, and he blinked his eyes to clear the tears.

"My hat, Lillah. I've left my hat."

The temptation for cruelty was great; she could justify it as being in his best interests. She pulled the hat from her backpack though. It was up to him and she didn't want the guilt of taking the hat from him.

"I saw it as we were leaving."

The look he gave her was one of pure adoration.

They were further along, another one meal's walk, when a young boy caught up with them. He shook with exhaustion, his hair wet with sweat.

"What is it?" Morace said. "Why are you running after us?"

Agara gave the boy some water and the children put down mats for him to lie on.

It took him blinks but he was young and healthy. "It's that girl, Corma, you brought her with you. She's having her baby but it is not going well."

"You have your Birthman."

"No, they have sent me because it is going very badly. The girl is screaming and fighting, she says they are killing her baby."

"Where is the husband?"

"He has gone to sleep like this." The boy stood, then rolled his eyes back and collapsed to the ground.

"Sometimes people sleep when they don't want to be awake. He sleeps like a sea snake, my mother said. They want you to come back and help."

"I'll go. Agara, will you come too? The rest can camp here until we get back," Lillah said.

"I'll go," Thea said. "The children will be sad without Agara."

"Not sad without me?" Lillah said. Thea did not understand how cruel her words could be. How foolish she was.

It was a good spot to stop. The leaves were quite light overhead and the sand wide. There were rock-pools with small silver fish, easy to catch using a shirt.

Lillah and Thea couldn't keep up with the boy

once he'd regained his puff. He didn't answer any of their questions and it became a game with them.

"Is there a band of snakes living around your ankles?"

"Is your father a good cook or does he make you eat your sand raw?"

"How many leaves does it take to make left-over plates for evening meal?"

Thea and Lillah thought they were funny, but the boy ran faster until he left them behind.

"I guess he's not ready for school," Thea said.

It was strange to be walking in the other direction for so long. The horizon looked wrong, at a strange angle, making Lillah felt dizzy.

As they approached, one of the fathers, a long scratch on his cheek, ran towards them.

"A ghost has taken her. More than one, perhaps. We don't know if one has taken her child. She calls for you."

"She's not from Ombu," Lillah said. "Not from where we are from."

"Still, she calls."

Lillah and Thea both knew that women in birth can seem possessed. They heard a low moaning, almost like the seawalk after a long rain, drying out in the sun.

They entered the room and were sickened by the smell. Vomit and shit, and always jasmine, the jasmine oil over the stench of everything else.

Corma saw them and moaned softly. "They are trying to kill me."

"They are not."

"I am dying."

"No, no you're not," but the Birthman behind her, holding her shoulders steady to guide her, nodded his head.

"You moss-muncher. You liar," Corma screamed.

Lillah walked to the bed and held her hand. Her pulse was irregular and weak.

"Is the baby coming?"

"No baby," the Birthman said. "There will be no baby. There will be flesh and bone for the Tree."

One of the children ran in carrying a turtle.

"You see? This will hold your child's soul. It will drift safely over the sea to the Island of Spirits."

He placed the turtle beneath the sheets, between Corma's legs.

"He will snap up the soul."

"Aren't you going to help her birth?" Hippocast said, woken from his faint.

"Of course. Water, you. And ask the women for some soft cloth."

Lillah went out, but put her hand on Thea's shoulder. Stay. She did not like the way the Birthman behaved, how sad he seemed.

She went out and spoke to the people there. One woman humphed, a furious noise. "Wasted on a failure. Our good materials. This one will die. It is clear in her blood beating, and the colour of her."

"Why do they send us the weak ones? This place is for the healthy."

Lillah looked at their faces. They liked healthy births, easy ones.

"She won't fail."

"She already has."

Lillah went back inside, feeling numb and helpless.

Thea sat by the bed. Her large hands twitched, plucking imaginary leaves.

Corma was void, empty, her head forward, shoulders slumped, hands untouched. The sheets were red with blood.

Hippocast wailed, "Why didn't you staunch it? This is what you do."

"The ghosts had her. There was nothing I could do."

"The ghosts didn't have her. She's healthy and strong. If you'd helped she would have been all right."

The Birthman said, "No. The baby was taken some time ago. You know what happens to an old bird. Dead in the roots. You've seen it. Smelt it. This is what poisoned her. I let her bleed hoping to release the poison, but it was too late."

"What about my baby?"

"He will not be saved."

"How do you know it's a boy?"

"Only boys kill their mother."

Lillah wept with Hippocast. He shook with it.

"Cut her open!" he shouted. "Take my baby out so at least I can know his face."

The Birthman nodded. He took a sharp knife and sliced Corma across the belly.

"My sweet Tree Lord," he whispered. "My sweet, sweet Tree Lord."

They heard a baby cry.

"It… is a boy. He lives."

They stayed with Hippocast overnight, but Lillah knew they could not remain for much longer. She said to Thea, "We must go now. We can do nothing for the baby."

"Can Hippocast care for him? Perhaps I should stay with him."

"That really isn't up to us," knowing that Hippocast would not want Thea.

The Birthman said, "This baby was born dead and yet his limbs moved as if filled with a sea serpent, a frightening sight."

"Do you think perhaps the baby was alive all along, then?" Lillah said. The Birthman didn't comment.

"I wonder what would have happened if the baby was born malformed. Corma spent so much time in Jasmine before agreeing to leave. Do you think she knew, as she died, that it was her own fault? That she caused her own death and almost killed her baby? And she would have thought her baby dead as she died. That's what she would have died believing."

"Be quiet, Thea. You speak poison."

As they prepared to leave for the second time, Lillah's grey-haired lover came to her and held her. "Perhaps you are meant to stay with me. Perhaps this tragedy needed to happen to bring us together again."

He kissed her hard and passionately, but she didn't like it. She was sad to be so attracted to his mind, and his words, but not his body.

"I'm sorry. It's not time for me to stay. I liked being with you." She kissed him. She left.

In her mapping, Lillah told the Tree: *Birthman Birthman more than one, rules for safety rules for luck, fish in water puffing out salt, fish in nut coat.*

Here, the Tree grows soft nuts. The leaves are soft and the Bark pale and tender.

Ailanthus — CEDRELAS — *Rhado*

There was no market day between Ailanthus and Cedrelas. Morace was disappointed. The stall lay empty, leaf-covered. Lillah wondered what this said about the people of Cedrelas. It was a long, eight week walk between the two Orders.

Lillah remembered her mother talking about Cedrelas and the stuffed fruit dish they were famous for.

"That's where I should have continued to," Olea used to say when Lillah was young. "I should have kept walking till I got there. I had forgotten how much I loved that fruit when I went through with my school as a child. I thought to myself then; this is where I will stay. But I forgot, and I ended up in Ombu."

She didn't seem to realise how cruel she was being.

"But then I wouldn't be here," Lillah said. "I'd be there, and my life would be different." Lillah was fourteen and questioning the choices life brought.

"I would be with my own people. I would be happier amongst the cooks. They don't appreciate my food here. I'm considered a nuisance. I know this. I know this for sure."

But Lillah knew her mother liked to be the best cook, the one others turned to for advice.

Her father had whispered to Lillah before she left for school, "Your mother might be there, at Cedrelas. She might have stopped there, rather than walk all the way home to Rhado. Be prepared to see her."

So as they approached, Lillah felt her heart beating faster, and tears forming at the very thought of seeing her mother. She missed her, although it was not the way they were supposed to feel about their mothers. They were supposed to let them go, send them away without any guilt, set them free. Lillah was hot and sweaty and wished for rain, although during the wet season she tired of rain so easily.

"My mother might be here," she said to Melia.

"And if she's not here, then she'll be in the next Order. That's hers, isn't it?"

"It is."

They could hear the shouts and laughter as they approached.

"I think they started the feast without us. Listen to them!"

There was no one to greet them, and when they reached the central meeting place, they saw the whole Order gathered, drinking from large shells.

"Aha! You're here!" shouted one, and everyone cheered.

"Spikesbringers are here!" and they cheered again. The teachers would find these people hard to understand for some time. They seemed to laugh at things not funny, be angry at things not worth worrying about. Why would they cheer the deforming Spikes? Lillah restrained herself from looking at Morace. They couldn't possibly know yet. News hadn't come from home about Rhizo and her health.

"Too serious! Here, have some of our special drink." The teachers were handed shells, and the children, too.

Lillah sipped hers. It tasted like fruit juice, almost, but with a spiciness to it, a tang. It made her feel dizzy.

"We add a tiny drop of sap, you know. You will smell it in your sweat for days. This is a special treat."

When they heard that the school was from Ombu, they said, "Ah, you do the semolina balls with cardamom."

"You've heard of our semolina balls?" Lillah asked. "How did you hear of it?"

"A woman walking home made it for us. It was delicious."

"So she didn't stay? I think that was my mother."

"She stayed a while, but she wanted to keep moving. She was a wonderful cook."

"Lillah's her daughter. She knows," Melia said.

So Lillah cooked the balls for them, and they were pleased indeed.

"I'm sorry your mother's not here. She'll be in the next place, for sure. But now, we need to feed our visitors," they said, and the men set off to catch the dinner.

As the men worked, drawing in the nets full of fish, the teachers watched. There were some crabs amongst the catch; these creatures were thrown into boiling water by an old man, summoned to do the job.

"He touches no one but himself," someone said. "So he can touch the crabs when they are alive."

Borag watched carefully. "They have different colours to the ones we have eaten. How do they taste?"

The old man scratched at his arse, his underarms, and Borag held her stomach. "He makes me feel ill."

"Hey," Thea said, holding out her arms. Borag ignored her.

Agara poured a cup of lemon water. "This will help, Borag."

Borag swallowed it. "He's such a disgusting old man."

Thea held her arms out to Borag again, who didn't move.

"Better?" Agara asked. Borag nodded, and ran to nestle in Agara's arms. Thea stood, arms still open, inviting, ignored. Lillah saw anger in her face. Anger at the rejection.

"He's got a very nice back. That one," Melia said, pointing to a man with long thick hair who worked tirelessly, sharing glances like the other men did, tossing jokes around like balls of fluff.

He didn't look at the teachers though; an odd thing. It was as if he barely noticed they were there.

For Melia, that meant a challenge. She liked the ones who weren't so forward; the ones who didn't fall at her feet. "Who is that?" she asked a young girl.

"That's Phyto. Don't worry about him."

Lillah took a walk under the Tree, wanting to find where the spiders sat. It had become routine for her to find the spiders as they settled into each community, just in case. The handsome man, Phyto, joined her. "You like to explore?" he asked. His voice was deep and strong. She nodded.

"I do, too," he said. "I like to walk the Tree, also. It helps me to think. Sometimes I feel as if I could touch the Trunk and gain all knowledge, know the truth of whether the Tree grew from a stake, a david, thrust through the heart of the first man, or did it grow from a seed dropped by a bird from far away."

Lillah listened to him speaking his thoughts aloud. He didn't try to stroke her, kiss her. He didn't look at her in the usual way.

"Are you the teller?" she asked.

"No. I wish I was. Ours is lazy and thick-tongued. Very poor with speech."

Later, after the men had bathed, they gathered for welcomefire, where nut oil was exchanged for fruit wine. More fruit wine was swallowed. And more.

"Where's that blond man? The handsome one," Melia said.

"His name is Phyto. Interesting man. He showed me some of their Tree carvings," Lillah said. "Though they seem prouder of their craft. Seaweed woven into patterns to hold plants and hang off a Tree Limb."

"I think I will go and find him," Thea said. "I'll see if he will talk to me differently."

Melia looked angrily at her. "I saw him first."

"Leave him be. He'll join us when he's ready. He's not so good with big groups," one of the men said.

Melia filled her cup with wine and took another. "Maybe I'll go make a small group, then."

One of the others grabbed her leg.

"Stay with me instead. You'll have no luck with him. No luck at all. You need one of these for luck with him."

He pulled aside his shorts to show his penis, which rested fatly against the base of his thigh.

"You say he doesn't have one? How sad for him," Melia said.

"Sad for him but not for me," he said. He gave Melia more fruit wine, and she threw back her head and swallowed the lot.

Agara was louder than they had ever seen her, screeching with laughter and leaping about the place. She looked beautiful, Lillah thought. Rested, red-cheeked and thrilled to be alive.

The lively night time people were very different in the day. Lazy, sleepy, they slouched around the place kicking over the remains of unfinished projects: half-built fires, one wall of a home, part of a pot. All begun with enthusiasm, then discarded.

At night, they lifted again, and put on a hilarious performance for the visitors.

In it, the monkeys were the kings, and they ruled the Order. Everybody dropped to the floor with laughter, though Lillah realised the more fruit drink she had, the funnier it all was. Morace joined in, and was the funniest of the lot.

After they had been there three days, Agara collected the other teachers together to give them some news. "I've decided to stay. I like it here; they rest a lot, and they aren't strict, and they're so happy all the time. And I don't want to walk anymore. I'm tired of the walking. I like them here."

Lillah, Thea, Melia and Erica leapt up with joy. "Our first one! Our first one gone!"

It was a strange feeling. Like the first time they'd realised they were women, at the first moon bleed. It meant they were grown, now. Serious. That they had to make decisions that would change their lives.

The wedding feast was set; it would happen before the school left, on Oldnew Day, the day between the old year and the new when anything is possible.

Agara stood on the shore, looking along the coastline.

"I wonder what's ahead," she said. Lillah squatted and ran her hands through the sand.

"Could be anything. Are you sure you want to stay?"

"I like it here. Like the pace. And the fruit." She shaded her eyes and squinted, as if to see beyond the rocks far in the distance.

Thea sat quietly. She seemed angry to Lillah. "Is everything all right, Thea?"

"I wanted to choose this place."

"But why? You've had no physical connection here."

"That's all that's important to you, isn't it? That's because you have nothing to forget in your past. You can live with your history. I like the forgetting of this place. When I drink that fruit wine, it's like my actions never took place. My family is not what it is. I do not look or act the way I do. When I'm here I can be happy."

"You can't stay in that state forever," Lillah said. Sometimes Thea wearied her to the point of disgust.

Agara reddened her cheeks with red salt dissolved in sap. She rubbed a sea urchin against her lips until they looked swollen.

They heard calls behind them and turned to see most of the Order gathered. They held an armful of twigs and sticks. The stronger amongst them carried or dragged large branches to build the weddingfire. Agara's chosen mate came and took her hand.

The dress of painted Bark had been softened in lemon juice and painted with signs of love and children. Agara's dress showed her lineage: mother, father, beyond.

Her betrothed had spiders in the great reaching branches of the Tree on his shirt. They promised to adore the Tree and allow each other freedom of movement.

"The Tree came from man, grew from a davidstake thrust through his heart. We should always treat the Tree with the respect we would give the man."

This ceremony was not important in other Orders they'd visited. Many partnerships were made without it.

Here, they liked the idea of holding onto an ancient tradition they barely understood. They knew it came from the ancestors: they had heard their grandparents telling stories about their own grandparents.

The teller sat down and told them a tale. "There was always a Tree sitting here but there were not always people. The Tree was here a very long time, roots deep to get to water, branches long, twisting up to get to sun. It seemed the branches grew together, like they were lonely for the touch of another, and soon they grew into the shape of a woman.

"The rain fell for many days, one hundred or more, and when the sun came at last she started to bounce to set herself free from the Tree.

"'You'll hurt yourself when you land,' the Tree whispered. 'Wait until my leaves drop and drift down with them.'

"The woman wasn't waiting, though. Too much to do, too many things. So she shook and trembled till the branch holding her tight cracked, and she tumbled to the floor in a mess and all.

"The Tree covered her with leaves and she slept through two seasons. She woke up hungry, thirsty, lonely. When she rose, she saw in the shape of her body in the sand a stone the size of her hand. She had no bruises or marks from this stone, because it was smooth and flat. She didn't know if her body had pressed it that way but she picked it up and carried it with her."

The children pulled out their own smoothstones, wondering at the history, the age of them. Zygo, who had interrupted all the way through with comments to make the children laugh, gave them a push, to try to knock out their stones. Morace said, "Zygo, no one wants you to play this game. I will fill your mouth with stones if you don't stop."

Zygo span around a dozen times, dizzying himself. "Ah, now I can see you!" he said. "You are such a weak man I need to spin my eyes in order to see you."

"Listen to the story," Thea hissed.

"So she ate fruit and drank its juice, then she set off, walking to find a mate. That's why we walk around the Tree. Because it's always been done."

Someone bent down and selected a switch. Agara stepped back, thinking she was about to be purified like they'd seen in Aloes.

"This ruth-stripling represents the first woman and the spirit of her adventure," they said.

The audience stood rapt, loving every word. One woman stood slumped sideways, and the child at her breast sat high in her arms, stretching her nipple until it popped loose.

The teller asked for tales from the teachers. "The visitor brings new stories to the group. These are welcomed". At least on the surface, Lillah thought. They did not like it if stories contradicted their own.

Melia told a story that made the teachers laugh, so full it was with familiar detail of their home.

The locals enjoyed it; Melia told a story well. They didn't laugh, though. It was the familiar that

made the teachers laugh. The laughter of homesickness.

Lillah told the story of Araucari, the man who
was trapped by the Tree and survived. It impressed
them, that someone would have the spirit to live
on after such an event. She loved to tell stories, to
keep the attention like that.

Then the drinking began. Lillah could never remember, later, how she'd managed to get
undressed even. She certainly didn't remember sex
with anyone, and was hard pressed to understand
how the men could manage it. She had a vague
memory of morning, of the sun coming up before
she went to bed. She remembered taking her
morning-after moss. And she knew that Agara had
kissed all the men in the Order, confirming her intention to treat them as equals, to consider them all
husband. The locals tipped wine into the water but
Lillah was beyond caring why.

When she woke, Lillah felt ill. Her head ached and
she felt as if her stomach was in her mouth. She
roused herself when she heard a timid knock at her
door.

"Lillah? None of the other teachers will get up.
The children are sick."

Lillah dragged herself up, feeling dizzy. She
opened the door and squinted into the sunlight. It
was one of the Order women, looking healthy and
bright.

"You are not used to the fruit wine. You drank too much. Many newcomers do. And all of the men. Plus you didn't make offering to the sea monster. He likes the flavour, you know." The woman passed her some water. "In the water is a squeeze of fruit. You will find it good to help you."

Lillah drank it, and it did make her feel a bit better.

"The children?"

"I'm afraid they took the fruit wine as well. No one noticed as we were concentrating on our own enjoyment. It won't hurt them. They feel very sorry for themselves, though."

Lillah and the woman took water and juice to the children, and mopped their brows with water. Morace was so pale he seemed to disappear.

She felt an empathy for the children, more affection than she'd felt till now.

"*This* is sick," he whispered loudly.

Lillah shook her head quickly at him.

The celebrations and storytellings went on for two days.

Agara's replacement was chosen, a pleasant girl called Gingko, and they spent many hours in lesson; Agara teaching Gingko the poem of gifts.

We carry shells for Osage from Ombu.
We carry a necklace from Myrist to Olea in Rhado.
We carry sticks for Sargassum.
We carry a parcel of secrecy for Torreyas.

We carry painted leaves for Parana.
We carry coloured sand for Arborvitae.

Phyto did not take a lover, managing to avoid both
Thea and Melia. Lillah wondered if he yearned for
elsewhere.

She asked her lover, a bouncy, almost sexless
man himself, about him.

"Is it true he has no penis?"

Her lover laughed. "They say that because he
never takes a lover. We do not dare to say it to his
face, though."

The young men here liked to prove their bravery
by dancing in the shallows, taunting the sea monster. Those who lost a toe or a finger were the
bravest of them all.

Lillah's lover had all his fingers and toes.

Lillah remembered the talk she had had with Phyto
and was interested to find out more about him and
his choices.

"What is it, Phyto? Are you deformed in some
way?"

He laughed. "I know that's what they say about
me. But I do not find any woman desirable. I simply
don't. I think it would be dishonest of me to pretend. It is men I find attractive. Men I think about.
But I have no hope of such a thing."

Lillah thought for a while. "You know, we've
heard that the people in Osage are like you. A

messenger came back not long ago, saying that the men were with men, the women with women."

"I had not heard that." He spoke quietly.

"You should go there. You'd be much happier."

"I'm not a teacher."

Agara had joined them. She said, "He should go. Why not? He should go. It's too hard for him to live without passion."

"He'll have to stay hidden in most places until we're sure the Orders don't mind men travelling. He'll be jailed, otherwise. Hobbled. We've seen those men. Ones who try to travel."

So it was decided. Phyto would travel with them. He was sorry to leave his home Order, but he knew he needed to seek out love, or lust, seek out what the rest of them had so easily.

In her mapping, Lillah told the Tree: stuffed fruit eating wild fruit drinking my mother not here and all are happy quiet in sunlight not at night problems forgotten and never solved.

Here, the Tree grows sweet fruit that ferments. The Leaves are mottled and the Bark marked with dark spots. The ground lies dark and damp beneath the Tree.

Cedrelas — RHADO — *Thallo*

Phyto helped carry bags and loved to talk to the children. He could listen to their chatter for hours; the teachers loved him for that. He kept them going through the long days of walking. A messenger passed them without stopping, running at a steady pace; it exhausted Lillah just to watch him.

The first test of how his presence as a travelling man would be taken by society came when they reached the Cedrelas/Rhado market after three weeks' walk. Those from Cedrelas who knew him were not concerned. Those from Rhado assumed he was trading and were also not concerned. It was a busy market, lively with jokes and laughter, people not rushing to get back to their Order.

Lillah had only distant memories of travelling to Rhado during her school trip. She remembered it was her special place; the place her mother came from. She had slept in the bed her mother had as a young girl, and saw the stones that had been set into the wall before her mother left as a teacher.

Things had changed since then. Many women had left, travelling as teachers or taking the long walk home.

Lillah remembered a friend she'd made here, a girl called Nyssa. Lillah was ten. Nyssa was seven. Then Nyssa went through Ombu when Nyssa was thirteen and Lillah was fifteen. Lillah had been home for a year, school like a dream in her past.

They had laughed so hard, so long, the others were annoyed. Strange to find a friend so quickly, and one you knew would be gone in only days.

They found a smoothstone each and exchanged them, so they would not forget each other.

Lillah had long since lost hers, but she would never forget Nyssa.

Lillah felt an ache from her heels, up the back of her legs. Each step was a jolt and her head thumped with it. Magnolia's hessian bag wasn't heavy but she felt as if it weighed her down.

"I'm almost frightened about seeing Mother and her family again. What if they hate me now I'm grown? Mother always said they didn't like her much. They thought she was too different. What if they think I'm a failure, or ugly? What if they think I'm not her daughter, that I've been switched for a ghost from inside the Tree?"

"What were they like when <u>we</u> walked through with school?" Melia asked. "I don't remember."

"They were kind. But I was a child, then. They don't judge children. They think children are unformed. I'm a teacher now."

"It'll be all right," Melia said. "It's nice to go home. Think how we've been when a daughter comes to us."

"But why is this supposed to be home and not Ombu? Ombu is where I was born, where I've spent my life."

"Ombu has changed already, Lillah. You know that. Just by us leaving, it's different."

They could see a small crowd gathering on the beach up ahead.

"Can you see your mother? I can barely remember what she looks like," Melia said.

"I can't see her yet. She will be fixing a meal, knowing her." Lillah looked at the children straggling behind. "I hope they enjoy themselves here. It wasn't so much fun at the last place, when we got sick."

"It's not always about fun," Erica said. "It's about learning. Meeting people. Finding understanding." She had not yet slept in anyone's cavity.

"There are my people, here," Lillah said. "You might find someone you like."

Erica blushed. "Time enough for that. Time enough." They heard a shout. Morace had fallen again, pulling Zygo down with him. "You're a pain, Morace. You hurt my arm that time," Zygo said. They liked Morace, most of them. He was funny.

Morace had sand down his front and he limped. Suddenly aware she'd barely spoken to him in two Orders, Lillah took his arm and helped him walk.

"How are you?" she said. His arm felt very thin, like a twig covered with sun-warmed Leaves.

"I'm all right. I've started thinking about Mother. How do you think she is? Is she all right?"

"We'll get news of her if anything happens."

"Yes, but whatever it is will be long over by the time we get the news."

Phyto carried children on his shoulders and told them stories, exciting tales of adventure and bravery.

He pointed at a giant seabird overhead. "That one? Was once a human. All seabirds are. They are attracted to the smell of human beings. The giant seabirds catch and eat people. They like little children."

He whispered to Lillah, "And get the taste for human flesh. But the children don't need to know that."

She shook her head.

There was a smell in the air Lillah didn't like. Sap gone sour or something, she didn't know.

"I can't smell it," Phyto said.

"Perhaps it's a woman thing."

"I can't smell it either," Erica said. "It's because these are your cousins. You can't lie with them."

Phyto patted Lillah's shoulder. "Good luck, Lillah. I'll wait near the trunk and walk past the Order at night. See you at the other side. Unless you decide to stay here."

"I can't stay here," she said. "Why don't you come with us this time?"

"Maybe next time."

The group was quiet as they approached Rhado. A tall woman stood alone, her legs spread, her arms crossed. Her hair was piled high on her head. She didn't smile or walk forward to greet them.

"They hate me already," Lillah said.

"It'll be okay," Melia said.

"Which of you is Olea's daughter?" the woman said when they reached her. Other locals came up behind the woman and stood silently.

"I am." Lillah stepped forward. She peered through the crowd, looking for her mother, wanting to be held in her arms. She felt tears come at the thought of being held by her mother; she hadn't realised until that moment how much she missed her physically. She touched the necklace her father had given her.

The woman grabbed Lillah's shoulder and span her roughly. "We heard you were coming."

"My father sent this necklace for Olea."

"She is not here. We will take it for you, if you like. It is better here than travelling. And we'll give you one in return. This is precious; I hope that you are worthy of it." The woman hung a string of shells around her neck. It was scratchy and ugly.

"I'm sorry, but I will keep the wooden necklace my father made. It is for my mother. He would not be happy if I didn't give it to her."

"You won't find her." The woman squeezed her chin. "You look like her. And already you are behaving like her. We're not interested in having people here who aren't Order-minded. Who aren't willing to put in a day's work for a day's meal."

"No, no, I'm not like that." Lillah was confused. "I don't understand why my mother isn't here."

"She was here. Was. Walked all that way then we weren't good enough for her. How she imagines she will find a better place I do not know. We have not found one because one does not exist. We do not want people like that here, anyway." The woman snorted. "I am your auntie. Simarou. I walked home and here I'll stay. You'll stay with me. Don't follow your mother out to sea or wherever it was she went. We think she went to sea. Just like her brother-in-law, Legum." She touched her ear. "They say he disappeared, without a goodbye. I don't know what the ignorant people in other Orders know, but we know that those who disappear are watching us, listening to us, and that they get very angry if we don't think of them.

"Legum," she touched her ear, "sailed out to sea on a huge piece of Bark and has never been seen since. Some say that he sank to the ocean floor and built a home there. Some say he lost his flesh from hunger and floated into the air. Some say he is still on his raft, eating fish and shouting with loneliness. We will never know and we do not care for his rejection. Olea did not fit in. It was like she was found as a baby in the roots of the Tree; that she was sent from inside. They didn't want her in there so they sent her to us. You may find the spirit island as you walk. I don't know where it is and I don't know anyone who's found it. But on that island, if you sleep, you will dream of the dead. Your mother may be dead and she will come to you. Your ancestors will come."

Lillah knew she would not be seeking any such thing. She was glad she had not allowed them to take her father's necklace. He had meant it for Olea, not this place.

The smell of the food cooking made Lillah's mouth water. She wanted to watch, to learn from these people who had taught Olea how to cook, but they didn't seem welcoming. They seemed to find the process upsetting, and they shouted to each other, abused each other, seeking perfection.

"That is so like my mother," she said to Melia. Melia smiled.

"Wonderful food, but you pay in tears for it," she said.

"I'm not like that, am I?"

"You? The day you cook a feast for this many people, perhaps you will be. When you cook for us; no, you are not like that."

Borag stood just behind her. "Why are they fighting?"

"Sometimes you can be too proud of your food."

The fire-tenderers, too, seemed overly proud of their work. The flame changed for each dish and the cooking plate.

The food was delicious. Fish cooked in coconut milk, greens diced with soft vegetables, flat bread salty and sweetish. The coconut milk had a wonderful, smoky flavour to it. They heated smoothstones in the fire then, using two sticks, lifted and dropped them into the milk, which boiled briefly and instantly.

The plates, clay here rather than leaf, were crushed and then stamped beneath the feet, a shouting, thumping roar of an event that took Lillah by surprise.

"Every six days we do this," her aunt said. "New plates made of old ones ground to dust. We'll soak the dust and dry it, make a nice glaze. Each glaze becomes stronger and better. Until the glaze becomes so good we no longer need to crush the plates, then we start all over again. I like to think the food improves with the aging of the plates, as if the memory of each good meal is absorbed into the next good meal. After a birth we will mix in the placenta to give life to the clay. We place dry leaves in some plates, but those are for a special feast."

"I like the way you cook your fish."

"Everyone eats their fish differently. Some like it shredded finely, others like big, barely cooked steaks. We like it with the coconut milk, but we also like it cooked hard in a fire. We like ours minced and marinaded, also. We like to eat food that has absorbed flavour; taken on the flavour as its own."

The welcomefire saw the fruit wine exchanged for a plate, crushed and remade six times, then the Order walked out onto the beach and took to the seawalk. They liked it out there, it seemed. The warmth of the sun reached them, and, they said, helped digestion.

"So your mother cooked well? Looked after you? And your father is a good man?" her aunt asked.

Lillah nodded. She realised they wanted to hear no negatives.

"She's lucky she knew a good man from bad. Her brother helped her to see that. He was a good man." Her aunt shook her head.

"My uncle?"

"Yes. He would have loved to meet you, I'm sure. You are so like your mother. But there was a terrible accident. Terrible. We think it was the punishment of the Tree because your mother was never as she should have been. She always thought more of herself than others did. We think the Tree punished her by taking her dear brother."

"But how was he taken? She never said."

"She never knew. He was taken at Leaffall. It was

punishment for her behaviour. You should protect your own brother by not behaving as she did."

Then food again: some strange kind of meat, cooked with onions. Lillah didn't like it; it reminded her of the placenta cooked when Magnolia's baby was born.

"We cook our placenta like this in my Order," she said. She felt uncomfortable in the silence that followed. "My mother taught our Order how to cook the placenta into a decent meal. She was well-liked because of that. And your Order was very well-thought of."

"Well, that's good. It is a recipe to be shared." Lillah didn't believe the speaker supported her own words.

"So you cook the placenta? How surprising and original," said one of the women, and they laughed. One hissed in Lillah's ear, "That is our tradition, teacher. If your mother told you about it, it's because she stole it from here."

Lillah touched the wooden necklace around her neck. She was glad she had kept it from these people. She wanted to walk away with something still left of Olea's memory that wasn't tainted.

Lillah watched Melia and the other teachers testing out the men, and she couldn't understand how they found them attractive.

"They smell funny, don't you think?" she said.

"You always find your relatives have a strange smell. It's a warning off, in case your memory of the chain is flawed. It shows you how certain it is you should not have children with those closely related to you," Melia said.

"This one in particular you go nowhere near," Lillah's aunt told her. "He is your cousin, and flawed. He should not be touched by anybody." Lillah would not have considered the poor young man anyway. "He is flawed. If his father hadn't been well-respected he would have been placed in the Tree at birth to have his bones sucked dry. Those bones stolen by the ghosts inside."

He was a charming boy, though, funny and thoughtful, and Lillah enjoyed spending time with him knowing they wouldn't mate. She wouldn't take any of these men: all of them too close to her. Morace joined them and the three talked of the mysteries of family and birthright.

Thea came and took Lillah's flawed cousin's hand. He did not refuse.

Later, as the other teachers left for their evening's enjoyment, Lillah's aunt tried again to convince her to stay, to take her mother's place. "You don't need to be a mother," she said. "Your duty is to us, to take her place because there is a gap now."

Lillah had no desire to stay with these people, but a small part of her felt the guilt of her mother's sin of desertion. She walked, digging her heels into the sand and feeling the sharpness of the grains bite in, considering all she would be giving up to salve her conscience.

Lillah saw the lump on the ground and could not begin to understand what it was. She hadn't seen a damaged human before.

She thought of placenta, first. A great mound of it, a whale mother huge and spent in the water, her placenta washed up, for surely only water could support a mother of that size.

Then it shivered.

Lillah stepped closer, though fear made her move slowly.

It was blood. To see blood is to see injury, death, childbirth with its own inherent risks. Lillah knew it was a fluid better kept in the body.

"Hello?" she said, woefully inadequate, but she could think of nothing else.

Just a small whimpering breath; a release. It brought to mind the salty fish, the way its last breath had been so gentle yet so definite.

The mound shifted as it breathed and Lillah saw it was her cousin with the missing toe.

"Who did this?" she whispered. It was clearly not one person. This violence came from many.

She ran to the Tree, touched her forehead to the Bark in apology, and tore a piece away. She caught the running sap in the torn Bark and carried it, two-handed, back to the boy. She dribbled some in his mouth. But he wouldn't swallow.

"Borag? Spider webs," she called. The girl ran to help. Zygo watched, tossing a stone up and down.

"What happened to him? Did he make a joke and no one laughed?"

"Zygo, help with the spiderwebs."

He was dead, though. The blood no longer pulsed from his many wounds.

Lillah ran to the Order, distraught, calling for punishment, but they talked her down. "He was flawed and he thought he could behave as if he wasn't," said one man.

"You seem to be flawed yourself," Lillah said. She touched his belly. The skin there was raised, pink, furry. He usually kept it covered; she lifted his shirt to show it.

"This is my family sign," he said, hunching away from her. "It isn't a flaw."

Her aunt told Lillah, "In the next Order, Thallo, they would punish such a man. Your mother, Lillah. This is her fault. She brought a curse on the family. She didn't fit. She did the wrong thing."

"I cannot believe this violence is not to be punished. If it had been a woman beaten like that? A teacher, or a mother, what then?"

"Then, if she wasn't flawed, there would be great punishment. That is a very great sin." Lillah felt the Tree growing down on her, closing her in. People around her, too close. She pushed away gently, knowing the fuss would cause attention and she

didn't want attention. She walked away, not knowing where to go.

When she returned, someone said to her, "Don't
be a moss-muncher about this. Don't tell stories
that aren't true."

Lillah saw her students crying and worried. The
other teachers gathered around them, comforting,
but she knew she had to lift herself. Pandana, her
favourite teacher, had done this many times.

It had made her mind up, though: there was no
way she would consider staying in an Order such
as this one. She felt no loyalty, no love. How could
they allow a violent death, welcome it?

The Tale-teller spoke about the death. The way
he told it was twisted to justify the actions, which
made Lillah realise all tales could be told to suit the
teller.

The teller, so tall Lillah reached only his elbow,
stood on his toes to tell the Tree. Stretching up to a
small carved hole, his arms stretched even higher,
grasping a knot hole, a protruding bump, caressing
these things as he whispered.

Lillah stood close to him, desperate to hear his
words. How would he tell such a thing? She knew
how the Annan, Tale-teller in Ombu would tell it.
He would tell the truth. He would find the culprit
and tell the truth.

The teller here said, "Your own teacher told us
something to strike fear. Hear all the facts before

you judge. Your own teacher, who went to that boy's bed. She said he showed her a sharp knife. Said he would cut the toes from the men, women and children in the Order so he would no longer be different."

"Is that true, Thea? He really said that to you? He said nothing like it to me," Lillah said.

Thea nodded, her eyes wide.

"She's lying," Melia said.

"She always lies," Rham said.

Thea turned and ran.

"She does always lie, Lillah. She is your friend, but she is a liar," Gingko, Agara's replacement, said.

"What would you know, Gingko? You don't know her well. You didn't grow up with her."

"It doesn't take long to get to know someone like that."

They gathered up the boy's body and carried it to the Tree, where one of the stronger men climbed the Tree and threw down a vine tied to a branch. They dragged him up, tied him securely. They steadied him so he wouldn't swing; rhythmic movement like that could bring his ghost to life and they didn't want a vengeful ghost about.

Below they gathered hard wood twigs, saved in a cave. The smoke would purify the body and the air around it.

As the school prepared for departure (the children waiting up the beach, tired of this place, sickened by it) the aunt and the uncles surrounded Lillah.

They pressed softened leaves into her hand.

"Walk with one in your shoe, and your future home will be clear."

"The leaves feel very soft."

"We soak them in seaweed oil. It makes them last longer. You must wear it till it disintegrates, and you will know when it's time to stop. We must be the ones to choose, to control the Orders of the Tree. This is how the human race will survive. Women think first. Men act first, when it comes to teachers."

They said nothing of the dead boy. When Lillah tried to talk of him, they hushed her. "Gone now, gone away," in sweet, comforting tones, touching their ears.

Lillah held the leaves in her hand, choosing not to put them in her shoe. She did not believe anything these people said.

In her mapping, Lillah told the Tree: *My mother from here and fine, fine cooks, though people die and no one cares they think if they are flawed then death is a reward.*

Here, the Tree grows coconuts. The leaves are soft, almost pink and lie thick around the base. The Bark sheds here like loose flakes of skin.

Rhado — THALLO — *Parana*

"I was so scared," Lillah told Phyto when he met them. He held her, listened to the story. "Seeing the violence done to this boy, and the way they didn't care. The way they looked at me when I cared."

"Where does fear come from? It isn't a thing you feel unless you are in danger. And the first time you feel it, it would be milder, I think."

"It started for me fearing Magnolia's dying in childbirth."

They walked twenty-five days.

Lillah felt for the first time that she had a purpose beyond school, beyond saving Morace, beyond sex. She knew why her mother had left Rhado: the people there were cruel and destructive. She wanted to walk quickly now, find her mother, sit down to talk about Rhado. How little it had changed, perhaps. And to thank Olea for not passing on that mood, that style. For protecting Lillah from the cruelty of mind.

They walked on.

Walked on.

The rain hurt their scalps with its intensity, and shards of lightning flashed through the Tree. The children complained and cried and the teachers were no better. Phyto stayed positive, helped them settle each night, watched the food to make sure they had enough and that it was cooked well before the children were hungry.

A messenger came up behind them. He was slower than usual in the rain, and they offered him food and a warm drink. He shook his head. He knew that he was not allowed to stop along the way to share meals with schools. He fed himself or he did not eat at all. Phyto talked to him about travelling, and the loneliness of it. "At least you can speak to all you meet," Phyto said.

"No, I can't. I don't talk to those I meet as I travel. In the communities they talk to me only about my messages. Nothing else."

"I wish I could go into Thallo with the school in a few days. I am tired of the deep loneliness I feel, waiting for them each time."

The messenger nodded. "I understand."

The light was dulled by the rain and it seemed as if the world was blurred, dark.

With her tired eyes, Lillah at first thought she was seeing a rock in the shape of a person. "Look at that," she said, pointing.

"There's another one there," Morace said, and they saw more, human-shaped rocks posed on the sand. Zygo jumped up and down. "More! I see more!"

When one of the rocks shifted, they screamed.

"They're alive! They came to life!" screamed Rham. Melia walked towards the rocks, calling back, "Let me see what they are. Wait here."

She neared one of the rocks and it rose and opened its arms to her. She hesitated, then allowed herself to be embraced.

She ran back to the group panting. "It's okay, they're people. They're painted with clay."

The rocks began to move towards them and the children screamed and hid behind the teachers. "Let's meet these people," Lillah said.

The teachers struggled forward, the children hanging around their legs.

The people walked stiffly, carefully. Their skin was smooth and pale with the clay and they looked young, not yet teacher age. As they stepped closer, though, Lillah could see wrinkles in the clay, and she wondered at their magic, that they made themselves look so young by plastering their faces.

"Welcome to Thallo." A broad man, his clay darker than the others, held out his hand.

Lillah took the arm extended and stepped into the embrace.

The other men were naked and smooth. They had thick clay cases over their penises and they walked carefully in order not to crack them. They hung back, away from the women, as if frightened of being noticed.

"We're very happy you are here," said one.

Welcomefire was held; the plate exchanged for a pot of paint colours. Then food was given, and drink. The school felt welcomed and wanted. They were led to the seawalk, where the whole village walked.

"I hope it's strong enough to hold us," Melia muttered.

There was an older woman with clay paint on her face, so Lillah and Melia did not recognise her at first. She took their hands and squeezed, saying, "Ah, my girls. My girls. You are grown and teachers yourselves now. You are beautiful, even without clay face."

Lillah said, "Your voice is familiar," and the woman laughed. She knelt on the seawalk and bent down to scoop salt water in her cupped palms. She washed her face clean of clay and looked up at them. It was Pandana, their favourite teacher. They had never forgotten her. She was a tall and beautiful woman who spoke in a loud, strong voice and whose laugh could be heard around corners.

"Pandana!" they said together, and fell upon her with such force they almost pushed her into the water. Lillah felt a splinter probing her knee but she ignored it.

"This is where you stopped?" Lillah said.

Pandana said, "I liked these people." She showed them her home and pointed out her three children.

"You have a beautiful necklace, Lillah. Who carved it? Perhaps you shouldn't wear it while you are here. They think here that having the sap touch your skin is dangerous. That it will take all your strength, and the strength of anyone close by. Perhaps you should keep it in your carryall."

Lillah, not wanting to cause trouble, took off the necklace her father had entrusted to her and stowed it.

Pandana walked with a limp. Lillah wondered how she'd been injured but didn't ask: there was too much else to talk about.

"You know, there is word of your Uncle Legum here. They talk of a man at sea who went out alive and never came back. These people here say he has made friends with the sea monster. You should not confess he is related to you." She touched her ear.

"I'm glad you are here to tell us all of these rules, Pandana," Lillah said.

"I can see why you would have chosen here. The men are beautiful. It will be hard to choose one," Melia said. She stood high on her toes, stretching her legs out.

"They are very good to look at. Good workers, too. Hard workers. All in this Order are. You should observe the women. Our skills here are remarkable."

She took them to meet a woman who was dyeing cloth.

The mother had three buckets of dye, changing the colour of pale cloth.

"Where do the colours come from?" Melia asked.

"The red is from Bark, but only the Bark where the sap has oozed and softened in the damp.

"The green comes from the leaves, but only those which grow black-green higher up the Tree.

"The brown comes from twigs, but only those gone dark with age."

"Those are beautiful colours."

"They're for the feast tomorrow night. We like to dress up. There'll be wonderful music, too. Oh, my Tree Lord, I love the music."

There was no music in Ombu, apart from the sound of rain drops, the flow of water down the Tree, the rhythmic pounding of roots for paste.

Lillah watched two identical children playing apart from the others. It took her a while to realise there were two; each time she looked up she thought it was one child, until she saw them together.

Twins. A multiple birth. Their mother sat to the side, working clay into intricate boxes. She mixed ground, dried seaweed into the clay and Lillah thought, That's so clever! It will bind the clay and keep it stronger.

No one spoke to this woman. The two children stumbled and fell a lot, rose without tears. The mother ignored the falls, which was odd in this Order. Mostly the children barely shed a tear before an adult lifted them for comfort, a sweetness popped into the mouth for distraction.

Lillah walked over to the woman. "Those boxes look very sturdy," she said. "What do you keep in them?"

The woman looked up and smiled. "Berries or seajewels. Stones. Teeth. People keep different things." The boy fell again, this time gashing his head on a rock. This time the mother dropped the box she was working on and ran to staunch the blood.

"It doesn't stop once it starts," she called. The cloth she held against her son's head turned crimson, so Lillah ran into the leaves around the Trunk seeking spiderwebs.

Most places she identified a web soon after arrival, just in case, but she had been distracted by the beautiful, quiet men in clay.

She found webs a hundred steps away and wound them carefully and quickly onto a twig she broke off. She noticed odd drawings in the Trunk and vowed to come back once the boy's bleeding had stopped. The limbs here were oddly smooth, the larger ones reminding her of a man's leg, with tapered ankles. There were small bones (fingers?) hanging from the toes. Lillah wondered why the ghosts had not taken these bones.

The mother watched Lillah gently press the webs onto the boy's forehead. The bleeding stopped and the mother gasped.

"I had heard of this but had never tried it. I took bleeding as another punishment. Born as two, that's what. My punishment for a bad choice."

"Why were they allowed to live?"

"They were left out on the Trunk but they survived the night. It was decided that they were not meant to die, and they have been protected ever since. I am to do nothing but watch them. Nothing. But if I had not agreed to this, we all would have been treated. You have a bad baby, you are treated as if you have Spikes. I chose a man too close to me. This is not a good place to stay, for all its beauty."

Lillah walked back to the place she had seen odd drawings. It smelled unpleasant there. The drawings frightened her. They told the story of a killing labour of birth, the woman torn apart. A man stood beside her, and the artist had cleverly drawn him so it was clear he was related to the woman.

The artist worked as she watched. She marvelled at his gentle touch. He used a flattened bone to mix his paint and a sharpened one to draw his pictures.

"There was once a box of painting things washed up. There were wooden sticks with soft hair at the end of them, and bright colours you have never seen."

"I bet the pictures didn't last, though. I imagine they disappeared with sun and time."

"They did. That's true."

There was a mess of a baby painted in the trunk at the man's feet, limbs twisted, eyes pupil-less.

There were other babies depicted, too, deformed. Unable to live.

Lillah heard a peck peck and looked up to see a white bird at something in the high branches. She couldn't see, so climbed a branch up, then another.

It was the almost-pecked clean skeleton of a baby. Above it hung another and above that, more.

Lillah fell backwards in her horror, and landed hard on her tail bone. The bird flew away.

Olea's words came back to her. "Be observant."

"Not too hard to observe that," Lillah muttered. No wonder they had an obsession with lineage. Dead births told of wrong matings. These men must be very poor sires. She noticed a small cavity she had missed before. Inside lay the skeleton of what looked like a tiny baby. There was only a torso and head; no limbs. Someone had made a bed for it; sewn a tiny mattress, stuffed a tiny pillow. There were dried flowers, and nuts, and a small, hard ball of sap. Carving on the walls showed birds on the wing, stars. Lillah felt sorry for person who had built this shrine. She stepped back, not wanting to see any more.

Pandana stood there. She took Lillah's wrist between her forefinger and thumb and squeezed.

"Did you touch anything?"

Lillah shook her head. Pandana squinted at her, then stepped over to the cavity. She stared in, then reached up and made a minor adjustment. "The men here are no use, for all their good looks," she said. "It is best to let them be the last. They are even more useless when they are old."

"Maybe the Tree ate their man-bones," Lillah said, and the two women shared their first adult laugh.

Pandana had many children living with her. The parents could work harder for the Order that way. Morace and the other children of Ombu were urged to join the crowd but they felt overwhelmed. Lillah and the other teachers found they had a child holding each hand most of the day.

The feast took place as the sun began to set, out on the seawalk. Men played music, dropping heavy, tethered items into the water rhythmically, restfully. Lillah thought she could get used to this place; Pandana was there, the music was good. There was the cleanliness, though, and the obsession with deformity.

The food was sea-based, and very tasty, served in the most highly polished coconut shells Lillah had seen. The men served it to them, and Lillah saw that the women would sometimes pinch their legs, their arms, scratch at them with little sticks. Lillah noticed they ate every scrap, and even the bones they tossed into a pot to be boiled later for stock. Lillah wondered why the men were treated badly here. Did it all come down to the lack of ability to catch child?

"They do not waste here. They come from a different type of land than yours, Lillah. You come from a place of great privilege, plenty of land, set back from the water. You are on the sunny side of the island. Your needs are met so much more easily when your land provides." Pandana sucked on a bone, and limped over to the pot to drop it in.

"I hadn't thought about it until we travelled. I always thought everybody had the same sort of place to live as I did."

"No. No. Not at all."

The musicians began a different kind of music, a great clanging of metal that hurt the ears.

"It's the parade," Pandana said. "The Cautionary Parade. You should have seen it before you stopped at the last place, but it seems you didn't need it."

"Need what?"

"The reason not to mate with your relatives," Pandana said. "Shhh."

Along the seawalk came children carrying thin earthenware pots. They held these out to the visitors to see; the school children started crying to see it. Lillah stepped forward. "What are you showing them? Let me see." She was angry; she trusted every Order not to hurt her charges, upset them needlessly.

In the pots were the babies who should never have been born. Who had died at birth, or been exposed. The ones who could not expect to live at all. Babies swollen up, or with too many limbs, or not enough. Babies distorted by bulges and splits; the sight made Lillah sick.

"Now, the recital," announced one of the fathers. The teachers stood up and recited their family Trees. The young men did, too; while this was a habit in other Orders, here it appeared to be a way to entertain. They did it with flair, humour, music.

"We take the list very seriously, as you can imagine," Pandana said. "So many deformities. But that doesn't mean we can't enjoy it. People listen more carefully this way."

The young men were very handsome, though Lillah thought perhaps she was more forgiving and needy after the last Order, where to her they had smelt strange and were very unattractive.

"I don't like it here," Morace whispered to Lillah. She looked at him, annoyed. The thought had crossed her mind to stay here. She loved being with Pandana. But she couldn't leave Morace. He was weaker, now, and she needed to keep him safe.

The Tale-teller watched all, nodding. He seemed so sleepy Lillah wondered how he'd manage to remember everything well enough to tell it.

In a deep, carved bowl rested roots, the ones which grew up pale and broke off to rest on the earth.

Lillah picked one up, even though she knew that in most Orders, it was considered the same as touching a ghost.

The root was like a miniature naked person, limbs and groin, arms raised, small twisted face.

Lillah picked another up; it was the same. She could see why this food was taboo in most places.

The children's smoothstones here were carved with distorted figures, which Lillah thought was wrong. The stones were supposed to give comfort, not cause fear. Dead babies are to be forgotten, not thought about it. In Ombu, they would be grieving too often.

The man Lillah chose to be her lover was so attentive and delightful, after a very pleasant evening her skin was smooth. Fine sandpaper as their skin rubbed together. Lillah had noticed there were no old men in the Order. "What happens to your old men?"

"They like to walk the sea." Lillah's lover took her hand and led her to a place in the Bark. Depicted there was a man with weights around his ankles, the list of his offspring beside him.

"They walk into the sea when they lose their beauty," he said. He bent and kissed her lips softly.

She said, "That could never happen to you." He smiled; she had said the right thing.

He gave her some red salt and showed her how to dissolve it in water to make a face wash. She loved the smoothness of her skin afterwards; so did he. He reminded her of the market holder they had met so soon after leaving Ombu. Understanding, thoughtful.

Lillah wondered why Pandana had so little respect for the men here. She had caught child, at least. But others hadn't. Perhaps that was it.

During school, on the long walk, Pandana had kept them alert, always asking questions. She wanted them to think, to analyse, to understand. She did not seem to want to answer questions now, though. Lillah asked her about the men and why they were treated badly, but they began to talk about the school they had shared and about Lillah's return to Ombu at the end of it.

The parents had been waiting; parents who knew them in an instant, despite the five years that had passed. Lillah had barely recognised her mother; in her mind's eye she had a beautiful glow, like the sun behind the Tree sometimes, almost like the branches were on fire.

In reality the woman standing there, arms outstretched, eyes only for Lillah, looked old and grey. There was nothing glowing about her at all, in fact she could barely make her mouth work well enough to say "Lillah!" Lillah felt nervous, seeing this woman.

The woman's fingers clutched at air, like a snapping crab. "Lillah! Lillah!" she said. Lillah turned away. She was only fourteen, and had lived in the company of her nine schoolmates for five years. The people of the other Orders welcomed them, but not with the same neediness.

Her brother, Logan, had come running out, past the scary, needy parents. He looked the same, just older, more handsome.

Lillah clutched the hand of Pandana, her favourite teacher.

"Who's that?" Pandana said, quietly for a change.

"It's my brother. He's bigger than me," Lillah said. She stood behind Pandana's shoulder.

Pandana had taken the place of the teacher from another Order, who stopped in Osage to marry Pandana's brother. Pandana was happy to go; she was bored in her Order and desperate for new experiences. She had been with them for less than a year, but Lillah loved her more than any other teacher.

"How much bigger?" Pandana said.

"Two years. He's two years older."

"Sixteen." Pandana turned, sighing. "Too young." She squatted amongst the children, her legs in the short skirt squashing fatly. Muscly.

"Now, my students, you're home. You've learned so much but now you're home. No more walking, no more travelling. This is where you'll stop."

"But what about you, Pandana? Are you going to stay with us?"

"I will walk the children ready for school until I find my place."

The families were holding back, not wanting to frighten the children any more. Pandana stood up.

"Now," she said. "Who belongs to these children? Who belongs to Melia? Who belongs to Lillah?"

Parents stepped forward to claim their children. They carried gifts: perfect shells, sweet dried fruit in woven baskets, dolls made of leaves, delicately painted bowls, to welcome them, distract them from the strangeness of it all.

Lillah's parents and Logan stepped forward for her. Logan picked her up and span her around. "You're back, you little pest. Back to annoy me." He put her down and rubbed noses with her.

"This is your brother? I thought you said he was stinky and ugly," Pandana said. Lillah giggled, then squealed as Logan began to chase her.

Pandana and Lillah's mother watched them, smiling. Pandana said, "He's a handsome boy."

Lillah's mother looked at her quickly. "He is. A boy, I mean."

Pandana smiled. "It's okay. I'm sorry. That sounded wrong. I do love your daughter, though. I've become very attached. It seems like a nice Order." Lillah's mother took her hand. "Come to the house. I'll get you a drink."

They walked to the house. Lillah came running out. "Mother! Mother! My bed is just the same! Look!" She waved her favourite childhood doll, made of Bark and leaves. Treesa.

"Got it back into place just in time," her mother whispered to Pandana. The two women smiled. Lillah threw herself into her mother's arms.

"I missed you," she said. "I cried every night." Her mother glanced at Pandana, who shook her head, smiling.

Later, during the welcomehome feast, Pandana leapt and danced to the music.

"I wish we had someone for her," Lillah's mother said. "All our men are married and our boys are too young. She would have been lovely to keep."

Melia's mother said, "It's a shame she can't just stay. But it's a lot to ask. We can't expect her to give up the chance of her own family. Can we?"

"She's got that desperation about her. Some of them find that off-putting."

And Pandana had chosen Thallo, with its lovely men and frightening ways.

Lillah could see that everyone listened to Pandana. She shone with wisdom. Lillah felt envious, wishing people would look to her like that, that she could be so wise and understanding. How to get that way? She was too selfish and she knew it.

Lillah ran down to the water's edge. Her tail bone ached from sitting and she wanted the smell of salt in her nostrils.

When she felt clean again, Lillah sat and thought about what she'd seen, the awful display of babies. The children played in a deep, dug out pool. Gingko watched them, trying to join in, but they yawned widely at her, bored with her ideas. They didn't seem too bothered by what they'd seen and Lillah wondered if they would be different once the school walk was finished.

Pandana came and sat beside her.

"What made you decide to stay here, Pandana?"

"The last school through here had eight teachers and six students," Pandana said.

Lillah looked at her. She stared out to sea, barely blinking. So she doesn't want to talk about it, Lillah thought.

"That would make caring for the students easier. But there would be more fights amongst the teachers, I imagine. Fights over the men and competition for who is the leader."

"You don't seem to have that much in your little group."

"We're lucky. Melia and I are the greatest of friends. Thea is in awe of both of us and would never stand up to us. Erica is more of a battle, but even with her we greatly respect each other."

"That's good. I'm proud of the way you handle yourself. You remind me of your mother."

"Did she ever come through here, Pandana? I thought I would find her in Rhado, but she didn't stay."

"She didn't make herself known to us."

Lillah felt so good with her old teacher, and so enamoured of her lover, she said, "I could stay here.

It has a lot of strange things, but it's the people that matter, isn't it? You, and my lover. And the water is warm here. And I like your seawalk."

Pandana was quiet for a while.

"You don't want me to stay?"

She took Lillah's hand and led her away from the Tree. In the branches, a man squatted, watching, waiting for secrets. "I'd be a very bad person if I allowed you to stay here. In fact, I'm going to tell you something that will cause me great trouble. I want you to leave now. Right now. Gather the children and the other teachers and go, before this evening's feast."

"But it looks so delightful! Everybody is dressing in brightest colours."

"Yes. It looks beautiful. But Lillah, you have to leave. They want one of you to stay, so you have to leave."

"But I might like to stay."

Pandana blinked at her. "Have you noticed my limp?"

"Of course."

"And the fact that most of the other women limp here too?"

"I did, I guess. I didn't think about it, though."

"At the feast tonight, they will break the legs of one of you. That's what they do to keep you here."

"Is that what happened to you? Why didn't your school take you with them?"

"How could they? I had two broken legs. I couldn't walk. It took many months until I could even drag myself along."

Lillah was suddenly terrified.

"Come with us now. Come now."

"I can't. I have my children."

"They can come too."

"They're too young, Lillah. When they go to school, I'll walk. That's not too long. And it isn't so bad here. But I don't want you to be trapped. I want you to walk on."

Lillah hugged her, crying. "Is there anything else we should be wary of? Some have warned us of the men of Douglas."

Pandana nodded. "I have heard that they are not what they seem. I was not with you when you travelled through, and I stopped here. I did not reach that community."

"We will have to judge for ourselves. I can barely remember Douglas myself." Lillah had a thought. "Tell me about Osage. The men there. What are they like?"

Pandana smiled. "Our men are kind and gentle. They make loving husbands and fathers, and they also love each other very dearly. If any of you wished to stop there, you would be most welcome, but you would need to know that the men will prefer to be with each other in the night time."

Then Lillah gathered her school. It was a testament to the way they communicated that there was no argument: they packed up and left.

• • •

In her mapping, Lillah told the Tree: *Pandana broken legs, fish so good you eat too much trap the teachers let them go.*

Here, the Tree grows cruel pictures, awful babies and pawpaw. The leaves are blood red and the Bark weeps.

·

Thallo — PARANA — *Torreyas*

Phyto greeted them boisterously. "You're early! I was lonely! You've been gone so long."

"Lillah made us leave," Borag said. "She made us miss a feast."

"I'm sorry, Borag. But they wanted a teacher to stay and none of us chose to. That might have upset them."

"More than running away?" Melia said. But she nodded; she knew all was not right at Thallo.

"The market will be open in twelve days if you want to see it. We'll need to walk quickly," Phyto said.

Zygo groaned. "I don't want to walk quickly. I'm tired and hungry."

"Let's see how we go."

They didn't reach the market in time, but did pass two limping women returning to Thallo.

"Didn't like our handsome men? Must be something wrong with you all," one woman said. She looked Phyto up and down. "He's not one of ours."

"He is not yours to worry about," Erica said.

They walked on, thirty days along the water.

The Tree here had roots right to the water's edge, thick and high. Someone had cut a doorway through.

"Look at it!" Zygo said. He ran his hands over the smooth entrance. "It must have taken hundreds of moons."

"Sharp shells or rocks? Did they scrape and scrape day by day?" Rham said. "Or was it already here, formed by the waves?"

It was terrifying to walk through the doorway. They felt as if they were moving to another world, as if they might not be able to breathe on the other side. They were certain they would not come out alive.

The school felt hot and nervous as it neared Parana. Melia had warned them that it would be about questions, questions, questions on questions. Every answer would spark more questions.

"Aren't you looking forward to meeting your family?" Erica asked her.

"I'm looking forward to getting rid of this bundle."

Melia had been carrying the beautifully painted leaves since she left home. Her mother cried as she left, to think of Melia's uncles opening the gifts. Remembering how much she loved them.

"And unless things have changed, you know their attitude to sex."

Melia's mother had warned them before they left, saying that the women here were brought up to believe that sex was a thing to be despised, an ugly, dangerous killing thing. "Why do you think I was so happy to leave?" she said.

Lillah felt no clarity, no realisation that here was the place.

They were met on approach by a woman dressed in drab-coloured clothes. It was a stark contrast to the place they had just run from, and the drabness of it made Lillah feel safe, as if in this place there would be no trickery, no broken legs or captives.

"Welcome," the woman said quietly. She looked the teachers in the face and then said, "Melia? You are one of us?" but she was looking at Thea.

"I'm Melia."

The woman nodded. "Your mother has explained that we think differently here? You understand that you are not here to seek sexual partners, but to discover your heritage and perhaps learn something? Perhaps decide to stay for the Order, not just one man."

The teachers tried not to giggle. It was too serious, and they must give a good impression to the children.

"My mother sent me with gifts for her brothers," Melia said. The woman nodded. "Of course she did."

• • •

The night was clear and warm, the food was very good, but the mood was very quiet. Welcomefire saw an exchange of the pot of paints for a bag of tea leaves. Lillah realised why it was so quiet: children.

There were very few children here, and no babies.

There were few young men.

"Where are your young people?"

"We do not catch child as often as others do. Most of our children are at school. They will return soon. Tomorrow or the next day. Soon."

The teachers exchanged looks. It was bad luck to run into another school.

"So, Melia, your mother is well?"

"Yes. I think she'll do the walk soon. At least, she was thinking about it. She's very happy at Ombu, though. Especially when the other mothers walk, and she's left there alone with the men."

Melia and Lillah laughed at this, but the Order didn't.

"Wild, like her mother," one of the old men muttered.

Lillah, thinking to take the attention from Melia, said, "Do you get many women walking through? Older women?"

"Some. They don't always stop."

"Do you remember a woman who was very good with food? She would have been proud, perhaps to the point you tired of her."

"I remember someone like that. It was a while ago. She stopped here for a day or so only. She did not seem to know where she was going."

Later, Melia paced restlessly about and the movement made Lillah feel agitated.

"What's the matter?"

"This is my blood. This sluggish, baby-less Order. This is mine."

They watched as one of the men walked by, his shoulders slumped. He didn't brighten to see them, as most men did.

"It's peaceful here," Lillah said. "And I like the way they have built carved Bark into their homes."

"They are peaceful because they know the Order is dying. And they're just giving up. The Trunk thickens by a fingernail every year here. They leave the carvings because they think nothing else will be left."

"Everywhere the Trunk is thickening, isn't it?"

"Here more than anywhere. They are being squeezed out."

"They sound sick," Morace said. "They make me feel sick. Their voices are scratchy."

"I wish I didn't say that about Mother. Poor Mother. I didn't mean to make her look bad. I've said that in other places and they've laughed and agreed."

It struck Lillah again how lucky she had been, growing up. The space they had, the distance from the Tree to the sea, was fortunate indeed.

Here, where Melia's mother had grown up, the distance was no more than five hundred steps and she felt that every wave could creep over the sand and reach her toes.

It was the first time Lillah had seen people actively resenting the Tree, hating it. They spent their leisure time tearing strips of it off, hacking into it, trying to make more space.

"Are they allowed to do that? Doesn't someone stop them? Damaging the Tree there could damage it all along."

They watched the piles of Bark form. Lillah thought the Tree was bleeding: she could see reddish sap. The sight made her ill, and angry.

"Don't you know that some people believe the sap will give them eternal life? If you took some your Order would live forever," Melia said. They disgusted her.

An old man, his hair the pale grey of the under-Bark of the Tree in places, said, "The first woman floated in from the great sea as a child. We still have the remnant of the wood she floated on; it is very different to that of the Tree. It is light, soft, and it floats very well. We do not know the origin of that wood, though we have asked many questions about it.

"She was a small child, not yet ready for children herself. She arrived with her eyes bound, one leg tied to the wood so that she would not fall off. She had a basket of fruit beside her, but that was almost empty. She said she has the memory of eating fruit and nothing else. That was all she remembered.

"She did not land in this place. She landed not far away, though, and after untying herself she began to walk. Each place she stopped, she defecated, ate and slept, and we see the remnants of her walk now. She was seeking a place like home, and that she didn't find. There were seeds in her shit, seeds she spread around the Tree.

"She finally entered the Tree, when she saw a large cavity she could step into. There she found one man, a young man, lonely, pale and without the power of speech. They grew to maturity together, and they began the walk again. In each place they had a child, and another, and they stayed with those children until they reached maturity. Then they moved on.

"Each child was different, born of different blood, because each time the man stepped into the Tree he was transformed. All men are one man, one man is all men, all children from the first woman. That is the story of the first woman." They began to sing, beautiful music, far sweeter than Lillah had heard before.

"The teller is so old," Lillah whispered.

"He is a newcomer. Appeared amongst us as a young man. He never chose to take a teacher. He has no children."

"Do you know, in the last Order we saw a parade of the children born to brother and sister? They say

that it should be avoided no matter what or deformities will be born."

"They say, we say. The first woman and her lover
were not brother and sister. Each new blood makes
a change."

They threw huge, dry leaves onto the talkfire and
the heat was intense. The fire smelt like food,
cooked meat, perhaps, or the soft scent of coconut
milk scalded.

Lillah felt the fire against her back, although she
was a long way from it. She turned to see a young
girl staring at her.

"You're very red. Are you hot?"

The girl shook her head. "I'm all right."

It was hard to understand what she was saying: the girl had swallowed a burning ember as
a challenge and her throat would always be
scarred.

The girl tugged at Lillah's hand. "Come to watch
the deepfoodfire. They want you there."

"I'll come soon," Lillah said. She felt uncomfortable in this place even if it was where Melia's
mother came from. There was no joy here; the people distrusted a smile.

The girl dragged her to a campfire away from the
main buildings.

"We acknowledge the fire because of the great
gifts given us by our ancestor. He was famous for
harnessing the power of hot stone, giving the way
of cooking to the islands.

"He could warm his hands between his thighs, then hold a stone until it burned white hot.

"He found no one honourable enough to learn before he died, drowned when the sea monster sucked his limbs off so he couldn't save himself.

"The magic of heat was lost for many years."

The men had been working since the sun rose. "Some Orders will dig the hole in the days before cooking. This is inviting bad luck. Ghosts love holes; they will jump in and burrow down like a wood-worm. Then, when you begin to cook they will burrow into your food. If ever you've tasted food that is ashen, you've eaten a ghost.

"You can salt your oven to keep them away. We will always sprinkle a light layer, not so much as to affect the cooking. We like to dig our hole on the day. The men will dig the hole flat as a smooth-stone and deep, then sprinkle the salt, lay the tinderwood and dry leaves, then the stones. Once the tinderwood is alight, they will layer the heavy wood and let it burn until it is white hot. Mean-while, we wrap the fish and the root vegetables in wet leaves, and we tie them with vine to keep them together.

"When the fire is ready, we place the food on the hot wood, then cover the pit back in.

"Time to rest, swim, talk. Long time. Then uncover it and you have the good food. Some Orders use the surface. This is pure laziness. The hole needs to be deep and flat. Some Orders think sacrifice must be made for the food to be good, but we believe the animals themselves are the sacrifice."

Borag listened to this with such attention, Lillah wondered if she was breathing.

The men looked on the verge of tears. Not one of them seemed capable of seduction. They talked, asked questions, in their gritty voices. But that did not seduce.

"Do we still sleep with them, simply because we feel sorry for them?" Lillah said.

"Don't ask me. They're my relatives. I don't have to touch them," Melia said.

Thea said, "I do feel sorry for them. I doubt spending the night with me will fix them."

"True."

The idea of being with one of these men did not appeal in any way. Lillah imagined their skin dry under their clothing, she imagined it flaking off, peeling away like the Bark on the Tree peeled away.

After a while the men rose and they began to throw a coconut to each other, further and further, shouting. Zygo joined in, leaping around with them, fighting for the power of the coconut. They seemed happy and full of energy for that little time, then it lifted off them again and they collapsed, panting, leaving Zygo standing, triumphant.

• • •

Around the talkfire the youngest sat. There were
not many. Babies were scarce in this place. The old,
sad men couldn't attract the teachers. Only those
like Thea, Lillah thought cruelly, who wouldn't be
welcome elsewhere. Morace, Borag, Zygo and
Rham sat watching. They sat closely together, forming a wall. They drew back from the fire, all of them
frightened of it.

One boy stood before the fire, his head tilted
back. He held a burning ember tied on a string of
wet seaweed.

"Don't do that," Lillah said. The girl shook her
head.

"He has to do it. His voice is too gentle. Sweet.
Who will love him like that?"

"I don't want to see it, then."

"But he likes you. He wants you in his cave."

"I'm not attracted to him."

"You will be."

The boy, held up by friends on either side, lowered the ember into his mouth. He gagged, and his
friends let him fall to the ground. One reached
down and pulled the ember free. He gave it to the
damaged boy.

"Would you like it?" the boy croaked, holding it
out to Lillah.

There was a moment when she could have taken
the ember from him. Closed herself off to feeling
and done it for his sake, to make him feel like a
better person.

She didn't, though. She couldn't.

"I don't understand why you would do such a thing."

"No, you wouldn't. You have not burnt your throat. We learn humility through the burning; we learn not to question, not to speak too loud, not to shout. Fire is cleansing. You may not ever learn such a thing and I feel pity for you with that." Lillah saw Gingko looking and decided to show her a lesson. She leaned over to the boy, kissed his cheek, stroked his cheek. Gingko leapt into action, as Lillah knew she would, and walked slowly over to the boy. She spoke in a quiet, croaking voice, and she threw her hair back, exposed her throat.

Lillah slipped away, smiling to herself. Gingko had stolen something from her she didn't want; that was good. She heard her name being called; Morace. She ignored him. She thought, The children are together. They can look after themselves for a short while. Leave me alone. She wanted to shout this at them. She wanted time to think without their questions and their neediness.

Lillah backed away from the fire and walked to the water's edge. Melia was there. Crying, her face wet, her legs wet with sea water.

"You're a mess, Melia."

Melia smiled. "This place is so awful. My mother spoke about her life here only very rarely and I can see why. They are so dull and empty, living off imagined stories of the past, hurting themselves to prove something meaningless. I haven't dared ask them about my uncle. They are so hateful."

Melia rubbed her face, rubbing sand into her cheeks. "I miss her. I want to tell her I understand why she hated this place. She told me they questioned but she lied. They ask nothing, know nothing."

"At least you know where she is. At least you got to say goodbye to her."

They tossed a coconut to and fro.

Lillah said, "Those raspy voices are so irritating. Your mum's voice is not as bad compared to them."

Melia looked back along the beach.

"If she started walking after we left she'll be here, soon. Will she get here before we leave?"

"She might hurry to say goodbye again. Or she might want to come here as herself, not as your mother."

"We'll see."

"When will you give your uncles the painted leaves your mother sent?"

"The time has not been right. I feel as if they do not deserve such things. I'm worried they'll throw them in the fire and use the flames to burn themselves."

"Perhaps that's what she intended, Melia. You need to give them the leaves."

They were summoned: two women walked across the sand, their annoyance clear.

"You are going to miss the Tree telling and you have not woven your seating mats. Even the children have done theirs."

"Perhaps they could make ours then, if they are not busy," Melia said, smiling.

"You will make your own mat."

They were shown to the rushfire, where coconut leaves softened in boiling water.

Melia carefully plaited coconut leaves, working on a small mat. "Lucky I've got a small bottom," she said. "If Aquifolia was here she'd be weaving for days."

"I can help you," Morace said. Lillah and Melia exchanged glances. They thought that Morace was a little in love with Melia.

The teller took Melia and Lillah to the base of the Tree, a barren area with odd, rusty mud that stuck to the feet.

"You see where your uncle hung swinging, Melia? His blood dripped down and turned all this to waste."

"Hung swinging?"

"He was not happy on the ground, that man. He felt things that shouldn't be felt. He liked his sister far too much. Your mother didn't want to leave but she was forced to go. This was not the place for her."

"She never told me her brother died."

"She doesn't know. He took the climb after she left."

Melia choked, coughing on something bitter in her mouth.

"What will happen if she returns?"

"She will be welcomed. There is no reason for her to be treated badly."

There were other pictures, further up. Tall women, very tall, twice the size of Lillah. Lillah climbed the Tree to see their faces. Tongues sticking out, the rough Bark made them seemed scarred.

She didn't want Melia to see these pictures. They were not truth. They were nightmare.

The messenger came. He was a lazy boy, slow and languid in his words. He brought good news and bad; there was no difference in his voice when he told the two.

"I have news from Ombu. Araucari, he of the useless legs and the useless appendage, will marry Aquifolia, who sent you on your way as she sends all teachers. She will give birth soon, they say. They say that his appendage is not so useless, because no other man will take to her."

"Agara, now of Cedrelas, has had one child, a boy, and the Order say he is the strongest born in many generations. Does anyone have news to share?"

"Tell my father I have the necklace still and it is protecting me. He needn't worry anymore," Lillah said. Mention of Aquifolia, who had been so bossy, who had deliberately burnt Lillah, made her irritable. The woman had the glory and really did nothing for it.

Lillah didn't know where Melia was and couldn't bear to look for her. She was so sad, so angry about where she came from, and Lillah didn't know what to do.

Lillah woke the next morning sure she was being punished for abandoning her best friend. Her womb ached in a terrible way, and she knew her bleeding was about to start. She had not had such pain before and she understood now what Agara went through each month.

One of Melia's uncles came to see her with a tea infusion, saying quietly, "This will help the pain."

It sent Lillah back to sleep, and when she awoke the pain was gone.

"What was that tea you gave me? Can we take some with us?"

"You can. I'll give you a large pouch of it. The leaves the Tree produces here give us this tea when dried and crushed. I don't know about elsewhere. It's a good tea. You take it in small doses for the pain, unless you have caught child. This tea is not good for a growing baby. It causes damage. Those babies will be born but must be left out to the Tree. The burden of them on any Order would not be worthwhile."

"LEAFFALL!" It was the loudest cry they had heard, and it sent them into a panic. They looked up, and the leaves were shaking like they were having a fit. In every place the variation of leaf was vast. Some were the size of plates, some could be used for painting, some were so big and so sharp-edged they could cause great damage.

The rustling intensified slowly, so that when the leaves started to fall there had been some warning. Most of the Order pressed under the Tree, though Lillah thought it made more sense to be near the shore, out of range.

"It's safer here," a man said. He pressed her gently up against the Trunk. He had an unpleasant smell about him. Not unwashed but as if his insides were not right and were exuding. Lillah did not regret not choosing him, or any of them, in the night.

Gingko, emerging from her lover's cave triumphant, her hair a mess, her eyes half-closed from lack of sleep, walked forward. She wanted to swim; rinse clean. No one saw her, and she didn't notice Leaffall.

She heard it, too late; a sheath of leaves, sharp-edged, huge, floated down, back and forth, slicing, ready to slice. Too late she stepped away, and she was cut to shreds.

When Leaffall ceased, everyone emerged to check for damage. Some of the houses had been hit, causing small damage.

It was Rham who found Gingko's body. It was a terrifying sight and she screamed until the teachers ran to find their bloodied fellow on the ground.

Lillah screamed, and the other teachers ran forward, lifting the leaves off, stepping back as Gingko's blood slicked out.

"Keep the children back," Lillah shouted, waving her arm. They should know death but not like this. This was too horrible.

But the children pushed forward, not stopped by any of the Order.

"This will teach them to be wary of Leaffall," one of Melia's uncles said.

They covered Gingko's body, weeping gently. They wept, but they exchanged glances: *We are glad it isn't Agara. We are glad it isn't one of us. This wasn't a good teacher. She did not deserve to die, but we are glad it is her and not one of us.*

"It's quick when the blood runs out," Melia said, trying to find comfort. "And it makes you sleepy."

Gingko's lover knelt in her blood and stared in disbelief. He thought she would stay with him, but not like this.

The children chattered, so unaffected by the death that Lillah worried for their souls.

"We barely knew her and she was cruel to us," Morace said. "She carried a sharp stick to scratch us if we didn't listen to her."

"She didn't do that."

"She did. Look." He showed her long, deep marks in his arm. Lillah felt sick to her stomach at how badly they had served the children. "We will be better teachers from now on."

"You know the only bad thing about losing Gingko like this?" Melia said. "She didn't pass on the poem of the gifts."

"We know it. It's fine. We remember each gift. We heard the poem often enough." There would be no news of Gingko.

The messenger would tell her home Order, but there would be nothing beyond.

Gingko was washed and dressed in leaves stitched together.

The teller stood over her body. "This woman gave her life to the Tree, to the Tree's desires. We cannot judge the Tree for the lives it takes, the Tree knows all. We will not give the Tree the best of this woman; what remains after the deepfire pit."

In what seemed to Lillah a very wrong ritual, they dug a deep pit and built it the same way they would build a food fire.

It was far away from the Order, though.

Gingko's body was placed in the pit over the stones then covered. "That fire will burn for many months. It will not go out while any of her remains. You needn't worry. We will care for her."

A new teacher was chosen. She was a happy girl, much happier than those of her Order, and she made the children laugh. Rubica loved to run ahead with them and roll in the sand when there was a dune. Her cheeks reddened with it and she was very pretty.

The children were happy with the choice.

The other teachers taught her the poem of the gifts:

We carry shells for Osage from Ombu.
We carry a necklace from Myrist to Olea in Rhado.
We carry sticks for Sargassum.
We carry a parcel of secrecy for Torreyas.
We carried painted leaves for Parana.
We carry coloured sand for Arborvitae.

The teller said, "We have not received those painted leaves. Why have you waited? Do you despise us so much? Will you remember us so sadly?"

Melia took the leaves. "These are for my uncles from my mother. She sends them with love."

One of the uncles came to take them. "You should not have waited until this sad time. Now these leaves lose their meaning. Your mother would not be proud of you."

"I am not proud of myself," Melia said, and she turned and ran away.

Lillah followed her.

"We aren't going to wait for them to dig up Gingko are we?" Melia said. "I want to get out of here. I haven't had a man in months." They both knew her desire to leave had nothing to do with men.

"I think we should go soon. We have seen enough of this place."

"Watch out for the perfect men," whispered the uncles as they left. The women nodded. "Perfect men are not to be trusted. You watch out for them."

These women grew herbs. Lillah knew the men pissed on them, went outside and pissed their frustration onto the herbs. It made the herbs grow well.

They gave Melia some herbs that made her dream vividly while awake. She said it would help her want to stay alive.

Suddenly they were alone. Not to be waved farewell.

"The school has returned! They are coming!" Far in the distance the Parana school returning after five years.

The teachers hurried their charges along. It was the greatest misfortune to meet another school.

"Things will be wild tonight in celebration. As wild as this Order can get."

"And hard for long after that."

It was hard adjusting to life after school. Having to keep still, do daily chores, see few new people. The older children in particular often disrupted the peace in their frustration.

In her mapping, Lillah told the Tree: *Parana is a small beach big Tree long seawalk no children place of quiet and reflection. And pain tea. And death by Leaf-fall.*

She drew the curve into her map.

Here, the Tree grows herbs to help in many ways. The leaves are large and deadly, the Bark peels like old skin, the ground so soft it feels like rot.

Parana — TORREYAS — *Douglas*

Phyto said, "Where's Gingko?"

"Killed in Leaffall."

"She didn't take cover? I heard the shake of it and walked to sea."

"She didn't notice. It was awful, Phyto. The children saw it. They will be always careful, at least. We now have Rubica with us. We like her."

"Hello, Rubica. I'm Phyto. I am the guide between Orders. Without me this school would collapse."

Lillah laughed and Rubica too. "Do you sleep with us?" Rubica said. "Can I practise on you?"

"You won't need practise, dear," he said.

Rubica walked well. She seemed to see it as a test and would not complain through the sixty days of solid walking. She talked with Morace, Borag and Rham, and she played games with Zygo until he was exhausted.

A messenger passed them, running quickly. How he did so, day after day, for more than sixty days was a topic for much discussion as they walked.

Thea giggled more nervously than usual as they approached Torreyas. As the home of the Number Taker, Torreyas held a position of some importance. Lillah was glad to be reaching this place; at last she could get rid of Magnolia's hessian bag. She was tired of carrying it.

Children met them, dozens of children, and they were led to see the books. These books were precious, the only ones along the Tree.

Thea could not wait to meet the Number Taker. "Is he here? When will we see him?"

"You are lucky. He is here. You may not find him in a happy mood, though."

The Number Taker greeted them kindly, but with great weariness. "I am a lonely man, and tired; no sooner do I arrive home than I need to leave again, counting and walking, knowing all."

"We are often moving towards, ahead or behind you. How do you count the teachers and students?" Melia asked.

"The schools are not counted. The numbers are only for those in one place," he said.

Melia bent over the book, fascinated. "You can see every Order here," she said. "All counted. Do they show you the lines? I mean of parenthood? Do they show you the bloodlines?"

Sunlight filled the room and Lillah thought they had built in a very sensible place to catch the sun like that. The light here was paler then it was in Ombu.

It didn't burn as much when you stood out in it.

"We do show the bloodlines. You tell us where you are from and we will tell you where else you came from."

"We come from Ombu. One of your teachers stopped there. Magnolia. She married my brother. You carried her on your shoulders as you entered our Order."

"I don't remember her. Too many girls. Too many boys. How am I to count them all?"

Thea stood and watched. There was a twist to her lips as if she wanted to speak but didn't know what to say.

Rubica handed over the pain-killing tea at welcomefire and received a red bead necklace. Melia was not impressed with it: they had seen these beads in other Orders. The welcomefire was supposed to offer something unique from the Order.

Rubica said, "I think it's beautiful and obviously means something to them. We should be thankful."

She is so different from Gingko, Lillah thought, and wondered briefly what was happening to Gingko's body.

Lillah saw them eyeing her wooden necklace and wished she'd thought to put it into her carryall. Most places envied it and she needed to be careful.

The meal was served in rough clay bowls inlaid with shells.

• • •

After the ceremony, the one for Oldnew Day began. It was simple here, as it was in Ombu. The Order walked together to the water's edge and washed their smoothstones clean. Any dropped in the water meant bad luck, so they held on tight and washed.

There were more people in this Order than any they had been to. This place was closest to being a ruling capital, and they had some say in how the criminals were treated and disposed of.

Here, the dwellings were different. They had seen the occasional home like these; most Orders had at least one, even if it was only small and housed the toilet. Built of flattened wood, painstakingly painted white, with square windows and smooth floors, they were remnants of homes from a time long ago. No one knew when they were built, nor could imagine how. Yet they stood, sturdy, ugly, out of place. The houses were well-built and solid. Lined up and accounted for. Lillah didn't feel she could wander into one as you would elsewhere, welcomed in. There was even a small house where you could exchange smoothstones or other treasures for cooked goods, good leaves, bowls: anything you would like to find easily. It was like the markets between Orders but more organised.

Lillah looked at the faces around her and could easily pick out which was Magnolia's mother, and

Ebena, her brother. Her sister was gone, settled in an Order somewhere.

Lillah took the hessian bag from her pack and handed it to Magnolia's mother.

"I've carried this for almost two years and I am glad to give it to you. Your daughter was very clear I should give it to you." It was good to pass on the responsibility. Magnolia's mother sat with her knees spread wide, an enormous sack of sea pipis beside her. Her thumbs were so strong she could crush the shells with a pinch. She scooped out the meat with the longer fingernail on her little finger and sucked it up.

She ate dozens, and Lillah felt ill standing beside her.

"What's inside the bag?" Magnolia's mother said, lifting the bag and feeling the weight of it in her palm.

"I haven't looked. It's for you."

Magnolia's mother wiped her hands on her skirt and undid the bag.

Inside was a small clay ball with three holes in it.

Magnolia's mother turned it over in her fingers. Sniffed at it. Closed her eyes.

Lillah felt uncomfortable standing there and began to edge away.

"Stop!" the woman said. She lifted the clay ball. "Why would my daughter send her child's soul to me? Is she fearful for its life?"

"I… don't know. She has no need to fear."

"Are you sure?"

Lillah suddenly thought of the number of children who died in Ombu. They had not seen such numbers in other places. Parana had many skeletons but that was a collection of many years.

"Yes. Yes, I'm sure," she said. There was no point telling the woman otherwise.

"I am not sure. My daughter is not sure."

"My brother is a good man. They love each other."

"That's something."

Magnolia's mother tucked the clay ball into a fold of material at her feet.

"Thank you. I will keep this safe. If her baby dies, at least his soul will be with me."

"Perhaps she is scared if her baby gets sick the ghosts inside the Tree will eat his bones," Lillah said.

"Why do you believe such a nonsense?" Nobody in Magnolia's Order seemed to believe that the ghosts ate the bones of sick people. Lillah couldn't understand that.

"You're frightening our guest," Magnolia's brother, Ebena said. He took Lillah's hand. He was so like Magnolia, and Lillah felt a very strong attraction to him. She knew what it meant; that her small and secret desire for Magnolia (secret even to herself) was something she may be able to satisfy by loving with her brother.

He led her to the seawalk. It was empty, this time of day: people busy, people sleeping. He seemed awkward, as if he didn't know what to say.

Lillah said, "Come, we'll talk. A good conversation is like a whispering Tree." She told him that Magnolia sent him goodlove.

"What was she like as a child?"

"She was fun to be with, but wanted all the attention. She liked to be with the boys rather than the girls, but she was popular with the girls."

He tripped over a piece of wood and stumbled, dragging Lillah down with him.

"I'm clumsy. Is she still clumsy? She was very clumsy when she was here."

They sat at the end of the seawalk and Lillah talked about Magnolia and the baby. She told him about Logan, what a good man he was, how funny, and how happy he and Magnolia were. How she did not find an interest in the other men, but was happy with Logan.

"That's good news. She has found a place to be herself."

Lillah wondered if Logan had remembered to send the message they discussed. It was around now he was supposed to send it by messenger. She wouldn't receive it for a long time; it would take that long for the messengers to catch up with them.

At the feast, this story was told. "In the very centre of the Tree there is a fire. This is a slow fire, that singes the Tree, smoothing it like long-time water.

How long ago this fire started we do not know, but the Tree feels warm to the touch sometimes because of it. This warmth is destroying our Tree. One day there will be a terrible, bone-shaking noise. We will have enough time to say goodbye, to thank the Tree, and we will sink to the sand and allow the Tree to crush us."

The Tale-teller shivered. "Deep inside the fire burns. We don't know how far away. Can you hear it? Crackle, crackle, if we listen closely. Listen." He whispered comfort to the Tree, cool, kind words to keep it happy.

Lillah had listened like this many times as a child. Word would go out that you could hear the crackle and the children would run to listen. In Ombu they believed there was a massive insect inside, a giant termite, nibbling away at the flesh of the Tree. They said if you scraped your shin on the Bark, left any skerrick of yourself behind, the insect would come for you. Once he'd had a taste of you he'd come to gobble you up.

Morace sat close to her, shivering. She said, "Are you cold? Frightened?"

He shook his head. "I can't stop it. My body shakes without any reason."

She put her arm around him tightly. "Don't let them know. Don't show them." He rarely showed signs of weakness and they both knew that once a community noticed anything wrong, they would act quickly.

The young women were attractive here, though not as connected to thought as others had been. Melia said to the other teachers, "Do you think there is someone here for Dickson? He doesn't like them too smart. Should we tell them he is making a necklace and see if they go running to find him?"

Thea pushed Melia roughly. "You shouldn't talk about Dickson like that."

Melia snorted. "Just because he is your brother you can't always support him. I would not expect any woman with brains to spend more than a night with him."

Lillah washed her face with red salt before joining Ebena. He had Magnolia's laugh. It was lower, deeper, but he laughed in the same way, head thrown back, tears in his eyes. He laughed at the same things. He and Lillah spent many hours on the beach, talking about Magnolia and the baby. About Logan.

"You'd like him. I wish you could meet. You'd get on very well."

"If he's like you I would. Though I wouldn't want to do this to him." He leaned over and kissed her. His lips were firm on hers, and she lifted her hand to grasp his hair.

"Ow."

"Sorry."

"Gentle with me." They kissed again, and the

thought crossed her mind that he was so like Magnolia he could be her twin, and that this was not a bad thing.

It surprised her, to realise how much she admired Magnolia.

She liked being in this place, and she knew that if it wasn't for Morace, she would perhaps choose to stay. She wondered what it would be like in the wet; places changed a lot with the seasons, she imagined. The kiss made her sleepy, made her eyes sink closed.

"Show me where you sleep," she whispered.

They walked silently, words done now. He took her to one of the flatwood homes. Inside smelt bland, old.

"You live here alone?"

"Some of the other young men are here, too. They are out fishing. They want to impress you teachers."

"We are already impressed."

She stretched up to kiss him again. His arms around her tightly, she bent backwards under the pressure of his kiss returned.

He led her to a bed upstairs but tripped along the way, dragging her down. They collapsed, laughing, and crawled to the room.

The lovemaking was fun. It was not the most passionate, but it was joyful and satisfying. Afterwards they found more words and they talked, fingers interlaced.

Later, Lillah heard her name being called by the children. "Come see, Lillah! Lillah! There are dolphins in the water!"

Lillah and Ebena dressed. She liked that he wasn't annoyed by the children. In fact, he was very good with them. He played games with them, throwing a coconut from child to child, trying to get it into a hole dug in the sand. One small child with skinny legs, knees that didn't work, watched from the side until Ebena carried him on his shoulders.

"Why is he so weak? He seems a nice child," Melia asked.

"His mother died when he was born. He received no milk," Ebena said.

"Poor little thing." In most Orders, a child was treated differently if his mother died. Some said only boy children lost their mothers, but Lillah had never quite believed that.

A messenger arrived, with news from Ombu. The children were healthy, and a new teacher had stopped in the Order. Agara, now of Cedrelas, had another baby. Also, Morace's mother had caught child, despite her great age.

Morace looked shocked, but Lillah knew that this was a code from Rhizo, to say that she was ailing. She was telling the Order she had caught child and too old to do so, hoping they would avoid her for fear of causing the baby's death.

"That's exciting news," Melia said. "A brother or a sister for you at last." She smiled at Lillah, one of her unpleasant, knowing smiles. Morace smiled back, but Lillah could see his gums in it; a forced, frightened smile. She whispered to him, "It will be okay. Don't worry. Your mother has it all planned."

"But she's sick, Lillah. She may die soon."

"You will have to be prepared for that. You have known since we began that she will die, Morace. That can't be changed no matter what we do."

"What about if I talk to the ghosts? Perhaps they will save her. Perhaps they have a body she can use. Perhaps they can cure what's wrong with her."

Lillah looked at him, horrified. "Don't you talk that way! Don't think about the ghosts like that. They will do nothing for you but damage you and steal from you. They will force you into such pain you will never think again. Don't you understand this? Morace, they will not save your mother."

He nodded, but she knew he wasn't listening. "You keep away from the ghost caves." He nodded again, and he walked away.

Melia, who had been watching from afar, said, "Everything all right? He doesn't seem happy to have a brother or a sister."

"He likes to be the only child."

"And perhaps he is worried that his mother will eat the baby."

"Melia!" Lillah laughed. "You are a cruel woman." Lillah had barely seen Melia, who had not joined the feast or other Order events. "Are you okay?"

"The giant birds are our friends," Melia said. Lillah saw her fingers were stained with green. She had been tasting some of the herbs the women of Parana had given her.

"You shouldn't take so much of that herb. It stops you thinking properly."

"You don't seem to remember I learned my uncle killed himself. I don't want to remember either. I'm trying to forget."

Ebena laughed. "Lots of people go crazy when they first find the herb. She'll be okay."

He's thoughtful, Lillah thought. Beautiful. Funny. Could I be happy here?

"Are you thinking of staying, Lillah? I think it would be good." Ebena seemed able to read her thoughts.

"I need to think."

Lillah went to sit against the Tree, hard sharp bark against her back. The thought of stopping appealed in many ways, but she was still learning. There was much to observe, to know. And there was Morace. She had promised to care for him, though it was an unfair promise Rhizo had extracted.

Melia, her eyes clearer now, joined her.

"Are you thinking of staying?"

Lillah nodded. "There is no 'knowing', though. No certainty. Do we really find that? That absolute certainty?"

Melia shrugged. "Most settled teachers say yes. That there is a place exactly right, and that you'll know it when you see it."

"Then this isn't it. But I do like it here."

"Thea does, too. I don't think they want her, though."

"Too smart for the other women here."

Melia gave Lillah one of her looks. "Yes, it could be."

The days passed so easily Lillah felt she was in a dream. Then Ebena asked her if she would like to look at the numbers. The books.

"What is listed there?"

"Everything. How many people are in each community. Who passes through here."

"Passes through? Would there be names? Descriptions?"

"There is usually a record of where the person came from. The number taker likes things to be even."

"I would like to see them. I wonder if there will be a line for my mother. I think she passed through here."

It was there. "Olea, late of Ombu."

"It doesn't say where she was going."

Ebena looked at her strangely. "Where would she be going but around?"

"I don't know. I just don't know when she will stop."

"You don't need to know, Lillah. You should stay here. Some day a messenger will bring you her story and you will feel satisfied."

Lillah knew this was not enough. She needed knowledge. She needed it as most people needed air and food. She had to know.

Lillah told Ebena she could not stay. "I feel there is something important for me ahead. Something I must do."

He kissed her. Tears. She thought, Oh, have I missed it? Is this it, and I missed it because I think too hard?

"I'm glad my sister is with your brother," he said quietly.

Morace came up to them, tugged at her skirt. "Come on, Lillah, time to go."

"Stay with me and make babies," Ebena whispered.

Lillah pulled back. "I don't know if I want babies," she said.

As they left, Magnolia's mother warned them of what lay ahead. What sort of men lived in Douglas.

"If you conserve your energy, walk at shadow night, you could miss them altogether. Walk through and camp in the roots a half day's walk past. Then you won't need to meet those men and their sisters, because there is nothing to be gained there. Nothing for the children to learn. All they know is the weather, and we know that ourselves.

They know the weather and the animals and the insects, they can predict the rain and know shadow night as no other. But it isn't worth it."

"Knowledge is always worth sacrifice," Melia said.

"There are things you can do to ward off the ghosts you will encounter on the walk to Douglas. You sing as loudly as you can, without tune. Walk loudly to scare away the ghosts. Chew nuts to keep a crunching noise in your ears. If you can't hear the ghosts, they will not be able to enter your head."

Morace was reluctant to leave. Zygo had been bored here but Morace liked it, and sulked most of the walking to the next Order.

Lillah told him, "Zygo, we will need you on our side in this next place. You know what we've been told about the men. We will need to be together and figure it out together."

In her mapping, Lillah told the Tree: *Magnolia's home will she return numbers here everything counted the Number Taker comes and goes and leaves a counted home behind.*

Here, the Tree grows nuts for the brain. The leaves are small and the Bark hard.

Torreyas — DOUGLAS — *Sequoia*

Lillah caught up with Thea, who was stamping on ahead.

"You always said you'd stay there," Lillah said. "Ever since we were children and we came through. I remember when Magnolia stopped at Ombu and you told her you would take her place in Torreyas."

"It wasn't for me. The place was too big. I didn't remember it being so big."

Phyto waited in the roots of the Tree and ran down to join them.

"Was that a good Order? Did they like you?"

The children chattered at once to tell him their stories. In between, the teachers spoke of the warning they'd received about Douglas and the way there.

Melia said, "They told us there is a whole section up ahead where no Order sits. It is always dark and there is a smell of mould about it. People say if you spend the night there, you will wake up without a soul. Some people say this happened to the men of Douglas. They slept the night as a rite of passage and lost their souls."

Melia loved to tell ghost stories.

Erica said, "Don't you think the children are frightened enough?"

"Fear is not a bad thing. It makes us cautious and thoughtful. Part of our journey is to stop in every place. We can't let the voices of others stop us."

The children were quiet. Some of them shivered and they pulled extra layers of clothes on to cover themselves. It was raining, and would likely continue to rain. Cold. Phyto tried to cheer them with stories to make them laugh.

As they walked along, it felt like moonlight although the morning was fresh.

Melia spoke in a loud voice. She had swallowed some of the herb. Lillah tried to quieten her but she would not be shushed. "All time departs in this time of the world. The sand seems smooth, but they say that footprints will appear out of nowhere. Whatever you do, don't stand in these footprints. They belong to the long dead, chained to earth for their sins. If you let one small part of your body touch where their foot has trod, you will have to take their place."

Morace sat on the sand drawing patterns with the edge of his smoothstone, tired and not willing to go on. He looked back the way they had come. "Look!" he said. "Someone's coming!"

Lillah and Melia squinted to see. "Probably an old woman on the walk back home. If she catches up to us we'll give her some food and ask her for her stories. It's probably a walking woman."

The teachers knew about these women: Lillah's mother was one. They passed through Ombu on occasion. These women cared for their children and their adopted Order, using every last square of energy while they were needed, then slumping, hollowed out, when the need was over. Homesickness would come to them, the desire to return to their place of origin. They were the ones who travelled, either with the school, helping with food and bedtime, keeping busy, or alone, stumbling away quickly, without looking back. Often they would go after the husband's death: men died more easily than women, sooner, and with greater acceptance. Women were made strong by the long school walk, the job of schoolteacher, the choosing of a mate. Women seemed to digest the hard work. Many were left widows. If there were no grandchildren the decision was easy.

"Do you think it's your mother, Melia?"

"It could be."

The market they passed was decrepit. Closed. Some mouldy woven baskets sat in a clump, some with the remnants of fish and some with crafted small things.

"This market doesn't seem to be running. Someone should do something about it," Morace said.

"It is so far, the distance between the communities here. I think eighty days' walk at least. That is too far to travel to market."

"I would make a market people would travel a full year to visit."

They walked later into the night than usual. They talked about their options. Phyto thought they should just keep moving, forget about learning about the weather, forget about stopping at this Order.

Melia said, "We have an obligation to stop everywhere. We are supposed to meet all types, know them all. The children need to know that not all people are good. And who knows, perhaps the people of Torreyas have some bone to pick with these men, and they don't like them. Perhaps they are perfectly fine people. We should decide for ourselves." It was a sharp night, making their vision further-reaching.

Melia looked back. "There's definitely someone coming. There, in the distance. Closer than last night."

"We'll sleep tonight and see if she is closer tomorrow. If it's a messenger they won't rest. If it's a walking woman, if it's your mother, she will catch us eventually."

At the approach to Douglas, Lillah said, "Let's cover up. They're expecting us, and they know what we're here for, but let's make it clear the choice is ours, not theirs."

"Let's just walk past," Thea said.

"No," Melia said. "I want to know what they know. It's knowledge that should be shared. And you know they dive for sea sponges here. We could fill our bags with them."

"Phyto, you should walk in the night, past the Order and onwards. Meet us at the other side. We don't want them seeing you. Be even more careful than usual."

"I want to be with you. You may need help. I want to protect the children."

"You can come for us if we don't get a message to you in a few days." Although they were reluctant to enter Douglas, after such a long time walking they were happy to see it on the approach. Lillah felt no clarity as they neared the Order. This was not the place she would find her love, if her relatives were to be believed.

The school walked closely together, pressing up to make a mass. Rham, in front, said, "What is that?" and it was a long length of bones, stretched out, picked clean. There was a scurry of red on it, crabs at work, gorging.

The children ran to the Tree screaming, to hug the Trunk, the normalcy of it.

They walked closer, and heard a hissing sound coming from the overhanging Tree limbs. A growling sound, a yip, a high pitched noise as well. Looking up, they saw men in the Trees, sitting on the branches and walking along wooden pathways built up there.

"Do they live in the Trees?" Rham asked.

"It looks like they spend a lot of time up there," Melia said. "Or perhaps that's their watcher, protecting their secrets."

The leaves were huge, the size of a food plate. They were the palest green Lillah had seen. One of the men dropped down from the branches. He smiled broadly, and Lillah thought, He doesn't seem too bad. Very nice looking.

"Welcome to Douglas. We're very happy to have you and hope we will be able to learn from each other."

The other men dropped down carrying garlands of flowers for the teachers, small carved boxes for the children. Melia and Lillah exchanged glances. *All right so far.*

They were led to welcomefire, where Rubica gave over the red beads with an apology. "These came in trade. We are sorry."

"This is not your apology to make. The people of Torreyas are not known for their generosity. They are too busy counting."

In return she received a bracelet carved of delicate bird bones.

"Feel free to roam where you please. Our Order is yours."

The men left to fish and prepare the feast. The women, quiet till now, welcomed the teachers in their own way.

One of the women said, "Perhaps the only place you shouldn't go is the bachelor house." The men here shared homes, the women in their own places.

Built amongst the roots, reaching above and beyond the lower limbs, this house was full of small rooms.

"We don't know what is in there. It is not a place for women to go. It leaves the men their freedom," one woman said, and whispered, "But freedom goes both ways." The teachers wandered into other houses, admiring shell spoons delicately carved.

The men welcomed them to the feast with singing so beautiful it brought tears to Lillah's eyes. They stood, united. She thought, They couldn't sing like this if they were bad people.

"Here," Melia said. "Have some of my herbs. You won't feel so worried then."

Lillah shook her head. "I like to see what's happening in this world, not one imagined."

Afterwards, Zygo joined them in a game, much rougher than any they'd seen, but he held his own. He came to Lillah bloodied; worried. He said, "These men... their voices are the best part of them. That is not how the game is played anywhere else we've been."

The men were deep out in the water, diving for sea sponges, and it was something indeed to watch.

They came up with sponges in their fists, their brown skin gleaming, their hair slicked back, their voices proud.

"Nice," Melia said. "They do not seem to be the awful men they are reputed to be."

Lillah tried to look at the men as if she knew nothing about them, and wondered if she would have found one attractive if she hadn't been warned off them.

Their voices were beautiful, and some were wonderful to look at. But there were other elements. Sadness, which made their voices flat and their faces depressing to look at. Desperation, which made them laugh when nothing was funny, hold your hand far longer than was comfortable and stare at you. This made them hard to look at.

Some had eyes the same green as the Leaves.

There were two older women of the Order not gone on the old woman walk. They were quiet, tired.

"These are our boys. I feel like we need to keep them safe." She spoke with her eyes shut and Lillah wondered if she was protecting others from the men.

"We feel so guilty, but all of us had the same trouble."

"What trouble?"

"We couldn't feed them from here." The woman squeezed her soft, flaccid breasts. "We took chance from their side and made them weaker men. It might have been different if we'd had girls."

"Many places we've been are like this one."

For a moment the woman's shoulders lifted. "All sons are like ours?"

"No. No. I mean that many Orders have more sons than daughters. Don't you remember from your time at school?"

"I remember nothing but here. This is all I need to know."

Lillah thought, You need to forget how other people live so this seems normal. She said, "Do you have many old women walk through? Do any want to stay?"

"Stay here? No. No."

"My mother…" Lillah said. "My mother I think walked through. She liked to cook. She was very good at it. Do you remember her?"

"A lot of them don't even pass through here, Lillah. I don't know why." But the women exchanged glances and Lillah saw that they knew very well why.

"She was not a frightened woman. She was never scared of a new experience or of people who behave differently."

"I don't remember her. You should not let such a thing bother you. Nobody else does."

The Tale-teller's voice was deep and melodic as he told the story of the creeping ivy.

"You see how we do not cut the ivy here? It grows wild; it holds the Tree up; it is strong enough

to support a man. We do this because it contains
the souls of every child who ever died while being
bad. That is most children; most children are bad
until they learn how to be good. You, and you and
you: if you died now, the ivy would reach down,
lift your body up, and draw you into its folds. It
would slowly suck the flesh from your bones,
slowly drink your blood, until you were nothing
but soul. Then it would fold your soul into a small
square and tuck it into a Leaf, where it would use
everything you ever loved or knew to help draw
the next child in. You would know you were doing
this but you wouldn't be able to stop it; you see a
child behaving badly and you want to scream 'Stop
before the ivy takes you', but you won't be able to."

The children were crying quietly. Morace had his
arm around Rham, and Borag and Zygo clung together also. Lillah said, "I think that's enough. The
children go to the island of the spirits like everyone
else, their spirits carried by a turtle or a crab."

"You have to earn a place there on the Island,"
one man said, and he covered her mouth, held
hands around her throat so she couldn't breathe.
"This story will not hurt them. It is a lesson they
need to learn."

"Don't you know how the Tree came to be? Are
you big enough to hear it? Are your teachers brave
enough? Because once you've heard the true story,
you'll never be able to return to a time before you
knew."

The children breathed hard, hoping the teachers would let them hear it.

"It's just a story," Morace whispered. "Can we hear it?"

"It's not just a story. It will take a place inside your head, reside there until you drop to bone on the ground."

"I don't think it's a good idea," Lillah said, but the children squalled, *Please, please*, and the man began to tell them the story.

He had them hold tightly onto the Tree limbs so they didn't fall out, bare-skinned.

"You want to feel that roughness. Feel the bite of it, the snap of it. You live beneath the Tree and walk around it, without looking at the detail of it.

"If you could see your skin with the eye of a fly, see it close and huge, your skin would look like this Bark."

He dug his fingernails under a piece and lifted it up. He sniffed it, then turned it over and showed them the insects underneath. "You would think that would hurt," he said. "To have those insects under your skin. But we do have them, crawling beneath the surface. Can you feel a slight bump on your arm? That's most likely a crawling creature, working its way to your heart. There are many different insects in Botanica. So many you could not count them. Each has a purpose but no ambition. They are happy that way, agreed?" He took Lillah's hand. Kissed it. His lips were warm and thick and despite her revulsion at his words, Lillah felt her blood move faster.

"There are insects that roll shit out of the sand. Some who use Tree mould to build nests. Others plant eggs in the joints of the Tree and the egg sacs strengthen the limbs."

While he was talking, Lillah was interested. Melia, too, listened open-mouthed at this new information.

"My heart hurts," Morace said. Lillah took his hand, hushed him.

"So long ago that no one remembers, the people who lived here were as tall as ten women. There was no Tree then. Instead there was a massive drinkwater that the people could drink from and be refreshed. They washed in the sea, laid waste there too. They kept the drinkwater clean, and they lived together in one Order. There was no school and no long walk. The land was their home and they shared it.

"Then a flock of birds arrived at the drinkwater. These were birds forty times the size of the ones we know. The people watched them land and drink and wondered if they would make good eating.

"They caught one and roasted it, then sliced it open.

"Inside was a sight to make them ill. They knew even then how our bones sat; they tied their dead to deep-seated stakes on the sand and let the saltwater and sand turn body to bone.

"This bird inside was one bone. Smooth, like the water on a still day or the sand before a soul has trod on it.

"The flesh smelt good, though, so they ate, and cooked another and ate that, too. Then a terrible thirst took them, so great they drank with their faces in the drinkwater till they couldn't move. Then they drank more, and more, until one by one they tipped into the drinkwater and drowned.

"Now, usually, when the body dies the bones stop growing. Not with our ancestors. Bones broke through flesh. Bone grew up, out, bones met and melded."

He folded his fingers together. "Bones formed a Tree. This Tree. Deep in the Tree, if ever you should go there, is the last remaining spring, the last drinkwater from that time. We have an outlet here; the water you drank tonight came from there."

His whispery voice gave Lillah the shudders. The whisper was like a shadow of his real voice: the dark, thick, quiet whispering you hear in the moment before sleep. The voice of doubt, bitterness and regret.

Lillah found Melia. "We should leave here sooner rather than later. The children are frightened. Especially the girls. Have you seen the way they look at the girls?"

"Have you seen the way the women look at us? It's like they think we're going to steal something.

I need another day or two to get this information. They know a lot about the insects of the Tree."

"Is any of it information we couldn't have gathered ourselves? If we put it together?"

"They've put it together, Lillah, that's the thing. It's about connections. From a flower to a bee to certain plants around the Tree. They know so much about how each affects the other."

"But why do we care? It doesn't affect us. We know when it rains, when it's dry. We know so far which plant grows where."

"It's information, that's all. They know beforehand of things that might be coming. They told me that when spider webs fly, it will soon be dry. If spiders are about in the daytime, rain is coming."

"You already knew that, Melia. This is not new knowledge. You observed all of this yourself."

"But the slugs, the slugs come out when it's going to rain. And the chrysalids; if they're on the slender branches, there will be fair weather."

"Let's leave in the morning. I'm worried about Thea. I think she likes it here."

There were ladders along the Tree, and Lillah, the other teachers and the children climbed up to a deep curve in the Tree, with branches upper and lower, so they could gather and talk.

The men joined them. Broad shouldered, with big bones and broad smiles. One sat beside Lillah in the Tree. They called him the Tale-teller but he didn't act like any teller she'd known.

He lifted her necklace. "Where did you get this?" He squinted. "It is beautifully carved. I've never seen anything like it. This is very nice. What will you take for it?"

"I can't give it away."

"Yes, you can. You can get nothing for it or something for it. Up to you."

"I will think," Lillah said, to give herself time. "You would do well at market. You are a deal maker."

"We don't care for trading. We like to use our own resources."

Lillah wondered if that was true, or if perhaps the neighbouring Orders did not like to trade with them.

After the children were asleep, the men spoke to the women differently, their voices thick and their words sexual. They thought that fear would bring the women to them, but not one of the teachers could bear to touch the lips or any other part of these good looking but cruel men.

"I'm tired. I'm too upset to be thinking about making love," Lillah said. The Tale-teller's face wrinkled angrily.

"You have no choice. You are a teacher. This is what you do. It's what you do and all you're good for. You destroy those children by protecting them from the truth and you give them no weaponry to survive the world."

"We don't need weaponry to survive the world."

"Of course you do." He stood up to leave. Lillah saw him adjusting his crotch.

"Where are you going?"

"If you won't oblige I'll go visit one of the little girls. One night with me and she'll climb the Tree."

He was so large, so strong. She thought of the other women; if they attacked him, they may succeed. But he was not alone: two other men stepped up beside him.

"How goes it?"

"I'm thinking a visit to the little ones. You?"

"These teachers are cold as the sea base."

"What is it you like?" Lillah said. She felt a sick desperation, as if this was the moment she became a real teacher. The sacrifice for the children. She would never doubt herself after this.

"We like quiet women who will scream like the Tree in the wind when we are taking them."

"I'm not too quiet," she said.

"But you will scream," one man said. His voice was soft, a whisper of the ocean waves. Lillah was not sure she heard the menace in his voice. Then he stepped forward and grasped her wrists. "So skinny. Like the smallest Tree root. Delicate."

"Like a flower, do you think?" she said.

"Come and see my cave. I've decorated it just for you, with flowers and insects."

"You do love insects, don't you?"

"Yes, I do." For a moment she thought she had imagined his threats, had dreamt his aggression.

Then he took her wrist roughly and she knew she needed to go with him, to keep him away from Rham and the other girls.

Inside his cave, along the roots of the Tree, she saw a cry for help. Pictures of a weeping man, bloodied body parts, children in a pile, a great pile of dead children depicted on his wall. If there was a spirit cave, where your dreams would welcome the dead, this was surely it.

She backed away but he took her wrists and held on so hard it hurt.

"You want me to visit the little girls? Or will you do as you're told? I'm big. Little girls don't always recover from a visit from me."

He dropped his clothing and he was big. Men along the Tree boasted of their size but this man was big. His penis was thick and tall, and the tip was reddened.

"You see?" he said softly. He pushed her backward. "Take it, would you? Stop talking."

Lillah squeezed her eyes. She was unprepared so it hurt. She was tense and frightened. She was glad this was not her first time, that she knew men, had known good and gentle men.

He was not as rough as he could be and when he was done he lay beside her with a smile on his face to make her feel as if she could say, "Why do you act around women this way? Don't you know how other men act? They have teachers go to them willingly because they are attractive people."

"We are not other men, and we find willingness dull. This would swing low if I had a woman want it."

He flicked his penis. "No more talking now. Tomorrow night you'll be with my brother. He's not as gentle as I am."

Lillah waited until he was asleep and left his cave. She found Melia by the water's edge, tear-streaked.

"I seem to cry a lot at the moment," she said.

"I think we should leave tomorrow."

"Will they let us? Do you really think they'll let us?" Melia said. "They will want us to stay until they tire of us. The children too."

"No, they won't leave the girls, will they? I'm sure of it. I could walk to Phyto, get him to come and help us," Lillah said.

"He couldn't beat them." Melia splashed water on her face.

"They know so much and yet they are so cruel."

"Knowledge makes you cruel," Melia said. "Come on, we'd better get back to the men."

"Mine wasn't as rough once he got going."

"Mine was."

Lillah returned to his cave and settled for sleep. She was not woken by the children. Odd. Most nights at least one of the children woke up needing something.

In the morning, Lillah spoke to Erica and Rubica. The other women had been crying, too, and Lillah said, "We did what we had to do for the children. We obviously did it well because the children are happy this morning."

One of the women of the Order joined them. "Our men are different."

"Not in a good way."

She shook her head. "They will not let you go until you offer some kind of sacrifice."

"Where is Thea?"

"With Melia somewhere. I haven't seen her."

The men mostly slept in the limbs of the Tree, but the children found it too frightening, fearing they would fall out once asleep. The children had terrible nightmares, Treedreams. The worst kind.

Morace said, "You wake up from a Tree nightmare and the Tree looms over you. You know you will never lose the fear."

"Is this another bad place? Why do we have to run so much?" Rham said. Lillah had asked them; they had woken, they said, but didn't get out of bed.

Are they growing up? Don't need us anymore?

"We'll stay longer at the next place. Don't you miss Phyto? We want to see him."

"Yes!"

At breakfast the men ate alone, leaving the women to serve themselves. "They'll be all over us again tonight," Erica muttered. "Oh, Thea."

Lillah looked up as Thea entered the food area.

"Thea!"

Her face was cut, her hair in a rat's nest.

"Thea! What happened? Are you all right? I'll call in their Birthman."

"Shh," Thea said, but the men ignored them anyway. "No! I don't want to see him. I'm all right." She took a sip of water, then wiped more over her face. She looked up at Lillah and smiled.

"I've found the place I belong."

"You can't stay here! They're unkind and cruel."

"That's what I deserve. I deserve to be treated like this."

She laid her hands in her lap.

"Did one of them take you by force?" Lillah whispered. Thea shook her head, but a small smile lifted her lips.

"Thea?"

"Three of them. Three of them. I saw inside the bachelor house." Her eyes were wide, unfocussed.

"What was it like?"

Thea shook her head. "Not for you to know, Lillah." And then she cried.

"Thea, you don't deserve it. What happened in Ombu was an accident, and it's time for you to stop punishing yourself for it."

"I'm a good swimmer. I should have saved those children."

"You were frightened of the sea monster. You couldn't possibly have gone out there. And you couldn't have saved more than one, anyway."

"At least it would have been one."

"You can't stay here, Thea. They'll kill you."

"Maybe I deserve to die. We can die anywhere. Gingko died so easily."

"At the very least you need to help me protect the children."

"I can't, Lillah. Perhaps I can help to protect the women here, make them stronger."

"That's not why you're staying. You're staying because you think the punishment will absolve you from guilt."

Thea plucked at her hair.

"You know you can leave whenever you want. Walk home. No decision is final."

As the man who had taken her in the night approached, Lillah recoiled. He twisted his face at her. "At least we are honest. Other men are the same. All men are the same. They conceal it. At least we are clear about what we want."

"I'll give you my beads. The ones you admire. Would you like that? You can have them."

The man took the beads; ran them through his fingers. Ran them over his lips.

"We will take them."

One young girl, who could be a teacher if a school was ever created from here, whispered to them, "Shadow night is a time we find frightening. Things aren't shadowed at night unless the moon is very bright. Long shadow night. Spirits at work, released by the shadows. You never step into a shadow; shadow walking is a risky business.

"These men shadow walk because they have given up on a good life. They've given in to their dark side; they don't nurture or create. Dark places are not for us."

Lillah wondered if it was jealousy or truth that lead her words.

The men went to their work out at sea, and the teachers and children slipped away. No ceremony. Thea couldn't bear to say goodbye, knowing how disgusted they were in her but she sent someone to take her place: Tamarica, the young girl who had tried to warn them about the men.

In her mapping, Lillah told the Tree: *The stories are true about these men; they are bred cool but dive for sea sponges. They say they tell true stories but is it truth to terrify us? Do we need to know such truth? And why do they want to steal what would be freely given?*

Here, the Tree grows bitter fruit and rich, perfumed flowers. The leaves are pale green and huge, the Bark run through with more insects than I can count.

Douglas — SEQUOIA — *Alga*

Lillah could barely talk to Melia. She felt so confused about losing Thea to such a place she did not want to talk to anyone, but the girl who took her place, Tamarica, bounced around, so thrilled to have escaped she couldn't contain herself.

"This is so good. So good! I love to walk. I could walk forever if I was allowed to. I like to run but I won't get too far ahead. We have to stay with the children, don't we? Do we have to stay with the children all the time? They seem really cute. I like them. I'm not used to children but I like them. Isn't it good it's stopped raining?"

Lillah threw a desperate glance at Erica who stepped up kindly. "Let's meet some of the children. You can chat to them as we walk. There's also somebody else who joins us on the walk. I think it's seventy days to Alga, isn't it?"

Phyto waved from ahead.

"It's a man," Tamarica said, stopping.

"The men you know are unusual," Erica said. "Most men are good to know."

Phyto ran up to join them. Erica introduced him to Tamarica and he embraced her, a welcome she seemed to find confronting. She sank into it, though. Lillah saw her shoulders relax.

Morace seemed angry, and finally he said to Lillah, "Why are you being so mean to Melia? It wasn't her fault. You should be nice to her."

They found the market after thirty-five days, only by accident. Rham, cross at other children for laughing at her when she spent too long investigating a rockpool, walked near the Tree rather than along the shore line. Lillah could see her in the distance, kept her in sight.

She came running down to the group, calling, "The market is here! Open!"

There was excitement at the news. Lillah wondered what would be on display. It was a large structure, with shuttered windows. The teachers gathered items to barter and walked up to the market. It seemed quiet; certainly there were no bargainers gathered.

"Is anyone there?" Phyto asked. Melia and Rham went forward. Rham stuck her head through an open small window.

"There's someone asleep here!" she called back. The children ran up to look and the teachers followed.

Inside, a large man with long, tangled hair slept on a bed of leaves and feathers. Flat on his back, his legs and arms spread, his hair filling much space around his head, he breathed deeply, his huge stomach rising and falling.

The children began to giggle and he stirred. They ran, screaming, "The whale is awake! The whale will eat us!"

Phyto called through, "Hello! Are you there?"

The man leapt up with far more agility than the teachers imagined he would have.

"Where did you come from? I'm closing up. Market is done."

Phyto said, "You seem to have nothing to swap here. What sort of market are you running?"

The man stepped outside, squinting in the light. He opened a storage box and pulled out some coconut straps which he ate himself without offering to share.

"People took it. All gone."

"People?"

"Every time I fall asleep more of it disappears."

"Why don't you go home, then? Or stay awake?"

"I can't go home. I have nothing. I stay here until someone comes to get me."

"This is an easy life then."

"It's a hard, lonely life."

"We will leave you to it, then."

"Don't tell them. I will get more things for the market."

Phyto shook his shoulder. "We won't talk of you at all."

As they walked away, Phyto said, "He must like it here or he wouldn't stay."

Morace said, "If that were my market, I would hire a boy to watch while I slept. Then nothing would be stolen. And when I was awake the boy could sleep, or he could collect more items for me to sell. I would never have a market with empty shelves like that."

They walked on, Rham sticking with them this time.

"Will you talk to me now, or is all talking done?" Melia said after a day's silence.

"I'm sorry, Melia. It just seems so awful, to leave her there."

"Of course. But she's made her choice. She's picked her Order."

"We wouldn't have even gone there if it wasn't for you and your curiosity about the weather. That doesn't help anyone. Anyway, why should I speak to you? You think I'm a giant piece of fruit or something. When you are out of your brain."

"I've finished those leaves. All I see is dull, flat truth now."

"Is that really what you think of your world? I think you're selfish. Your own knowledge is more important than anything else."

"That's true. That really is true. But I won't take the blame for this. We are obliged to visit each

Order, regardless of the sort of people they are. That is how the school works. If Thea's guilt kept her there, that is her choice. You know that you were the only one who refused to see what she was. What she has done. What she may do again in the future. You didn't see it because you were blinded to the bad in her, because you forced her to come on the school. You couldn't stand to be wrong. You are as selfish as I am, in your own way."

Rubica came forward. "Tamarica is happy talking to Morace about the tide, now. She says that there are bone collectors in the next Order. That most teachers are scared to walk in."

"We've heard about those. But they leave living people alone. We have nothing to fear."

Phyto said, "You can't skip quickly through another Order. This one will be fine, I'm sure."

Birds circled overhead, huge ones. Tamarica said, "We usually shelter under some leaves when they fly over. These children are quite big, but those birds have picked up children that size in their claws and flown away."

"Children, gather," Lillah shouted. "Come on. Let's rest under the Tree." The children ran so fast Morace and Rham fell over, laughing.

They sheltered under the Tree as the birds circled them.

"They don't come to land very often. The fish must be low in supply, or swimming deep in the water."

The birds caught monkeys in their sharp claws and flew out to sea. "They will stay away now," Tamarica said.

Still, they spent the night close to the Trunk, feeling safer there.

As they moved along, the sand became very fine. It clung to their shins and sparkled when the sun hit it.

This Order sent a delegation to meet them. "It's nice to be welcomed," Tamarica said. Three young men stripped to the waist, their skin golden brown and shining. The light on the water, the sky itself, seemed golden, smacked through with a burnished red that made Lillah think of roasted pepper.

"It's like oil," Tamarica whispered. "Don't you think? They're covered with it."

"I hope there are more than three of them. Three won't be enough for all of us," Melia said, and the teachers laughed. One of the men carried a large clay bowl.

Lillah stepped forward and nodded.

The men bowed their heads in welcome. The carrier placed the clay bowl in the sand. Lillah saw sea sponges floating in clear water.

The tallest man picked up a sponge and squeezed away the excess water. He took Lillah's hand, squeezing her fingers gently.

"This will refresh you," he said. He sponged her face so gently her eyelids fluttered closed. The water was warm and had a rich, flowery smell to it.

"Sap. Life-giving. Very precious."

Other men approached with bowls until each teacher had an attendant. The children ran ahead to the Order, ready to explore a new place. "Can you believe the difference from the men of Douglas?" Tamarica said.

A massive pebble break stood at the tide line. It was three times the height of the tallest man, and stretched as far as they could see.

"I've never seen one that big before," Melia said. She bent down to pick up a pebble. "This must have been forming since the Tree was a david-sapling."

"We built it ourselves, mostly," one of the men said. The rest nodded proudly. "We gather every pebble washed up between here and there," he pointed to a rock pile further down the beach, "and soon we have a wall like this."

"But why? You could use the pebbles to build shelters."

"This is to keep the sea monster away. He lives just out there. You don't know; you haven't had him eat your people."

Lillah noticed there was no seawalk.

"He's a very angry monster. He came from the air and he can't escape the sea, now, so he's angry and wants to punish us. This pebble break lets him know we are in control, we rule the land. He can't get us."

Along the high tide line, they had lined up large bird and fish skulls.

"Bodies are laid out for the birds until bones are picked clean. Bones line the tide line. Then the ghosts steal the bones and we are done with it.

"We line the pebble wall with bones to stop people talking their secrets. We have learned the hard way that speaking secrets is not good. The sea monster will use the secret against you. He gets angry if we take anything from the water. Only that which he gives us can be taken. A caught fish is full of poison."

They used dried grass stalks, woven into mats, to sit on, and they used these mats to shield their view from the sea as well.

"Do you trade these with Douglas?" Melia asked. "We noticed the market didn't seem too vibrant."

"We don't like trading with them even though they are fair traders. They don't like to be cheated and will see a cheat where none exists."

"Does anyone really cheat them?"

"It makes them very angry."

The sand was damp here, cold to sit on. It was good for building, though, and these people had made an art of sandcastles. Beautiful, intricate things, some of them so big you could crawl through the rooms. Lillah felt nervous doing so: she didn't like the walls of sand around her. Hated to think of them collapsing onto her face, breathing grains of sand in.

This was a very serious Order. A new baby, born as they arrived, came without fanfare or fuss. Lillah liked it; the calmness of the baby's appearance took away some of the fears. The mother carried the baby around the village showing him off. The father followed her, a large green coconut in his hands. The mother would sip from it when she was thirsty.

The baby's fingernails were as long as its small fingers. "A strong one. Nice long nails to hang on so he never slipped out."

"And scratch up the poor mother inside."

There was one man Lillah was attracted to, a sandy-haired, tall man with tiny downy hairs covering his body. Because the sand here was damper, heavier, it didn't cling to the body like it did in some places. His name was Sapin. Her heart beat quickly and she wondered if this was it. She had felt physical responses to men before, but not this heart-thumping change.

He had not been here when she came through with her school because he was travelling with his. She'd heard stories of people finding a match at age nine or twelve, and that match surviving. Her own parents met that way, they'd told her.

As they gathered for the evening meal, the Order built a tall sandhouse, as tall as Morace. The sand was so damp it set. On the walls they drew incredibly beautiful pictures, depicting the sea monster as something immense and powerful. Sapin was the main artist.

Lillah sat down with Sapin and showed him her map.

"You see how badly I draw. Can you fix it for me?"

"What is it?"

"It's our world. On paper. As I travel I mark it down."

Sapin cried, looking at it. "This is our world," he said. He picked up a twig and laid it over her drawing of the centre of the Tree.

"All you need to show is the stick to be our Tree."

At the feast, welcomefire saw the swapping of the bird bone bracelet for a metal plate. The feast was all plant and animal, no seafood. Tamarica laughed loudly, danced around the men, enjoyed the smiles. "I feel so free. I feel as if I can be myself and not worry about being hurt."

"Who would hurt you?" one of the men asked. He stroked her hair, her cheek, tender sweet. Lillah told them about the men of Douglas.

"They took you by force? And made one of you stay?"

Lillah and Melia exchanged glances. Melia said, "Yes. But Thea did stay willingly. We can't say otherwise."

Tamarica said, "I didn't realise that wasn't the way other men behaved. I didn't know it. I couldn't stop it."

"No one expected you to stop it. It's not your responsibility. And you're away now. You're with us. You can meet the good men of the Tree."

"We have heard this many times before. We do

trade with them sometimes, of course, share news. They treat us well. They never show an interest in the women of this Order," one woman said.

"They are smart enough not to damage the relationship, I suppose. What can we do about them? We were warned on our journey, but they are hard to avoid. You don't believe what these men will be like, because you haven't met men like them before."

"So what is there to do? These men should be punished."

"It is not our place to tell other Orders how to behave. They may come here and find our behaviour offensive. We can punish those within our own Order for breaking the Way, but not those in others. People from such a community will be flawed. These people have no judgement."

Lillah comforted Tamarica, pulling her in, head on shoulder. Tamarica smelt good, like a salty stew. "Not you, Tamarica. You are a good person and you will grow beyond your community."

A flock of the terrifying birds flew overhead. One dropped a great chunk of fish, and the people ran to pick it up. The cook wrapped it in leaves and tossed it into the fire. It cooked quickly and was rolled out of the flames with two long sticks.

"You'll eat that fish?" Melia said.

"It's from the land."

Melia sniffed at the fish. "It doesn't smell right to me."

Borag, who had already taken a mouthful, spat the fish to the ground. She sniffed as well. "Not right," she said. "Too long out of the water. If it was salted it would be better."

There were vegetables and greens, too, and they settled to their food. One of the women told them a story.

"The Tree was so small once that children could leap over it. As it got higher, people held competitions to see who could jump it. Eventually no one could. Can you imagine jumping this Tree?"

They looked up. You could not see the top of the Tree; you could not see the end of the Trunk.

"It sprang from a seed in the belly of a woman who lived here long before memory began. She came from the stars, flew down and landed, but she died. The animals (there were large animals, then. More monkeys than there are now, bigger ones) buried her, because they knew the stink a dead body could bring. In her belly was a seed from the stars, and this is where our Tree came from."

"Look at these plates," Lillah said. "Aren't they beautiful?" Someone had painted them all, edged them with delicate flowers and stars.

"Deep in the water is the metal house. We don't go down to it, but when we need metal we will send out a sacrifice and some metal will come to us. We are fortunate in that. This metal sometimes washes up elsewhere as well. It is a very generous monster. He likes us because we do not forget him.

But we never travel alone. No matter how much he likes us and our gifts, he can't resist a person alone. We do everything in a group. It is hard to think of being alone."

Lillah had noticed there didn't seem to be any loners here. She had also noticed boys of five or six being breastfed: they would grow up to be good, strong men.

"It's only people alone who get taken. We have lost some that way. One woman had an argument with her lover and she went to the water's edge alone to throw stones out there. She did not want to hit her lover although she did want to. So she threw stones, and they roused the sea monster. He came up quietly to the water's edge in the shape of a small child, and he put his metal hand in hers. Before she realised he was a monster, he tugged her into the sea where she drowned. Her body was found much later, after her lover had a new lover, many more. Her body turned silver, like the metal. The monster turned her into metal."

"So no one lives alone here?"

"Just one crazy old woman. She likes herself more than anyone else."

Lillah envied loners their solitude sometimes. They didn't need to speak to anyone, or share, or sympathise. They were alone.

She watched this old woman trip along the beach.

"She's crazy. We couldn't send her as a teacher. Nobody wants her."

"Doesn't she know it's dangerous, walking alone?"

"She's not scared of the sea monster. He's taken her once before, spat her back out. She liked it."

"Is that where…" Lillah said. Her friend nodded. The woman was covered in pockmarks; Lillah had wondered how she came to be so disfigured.

"She won't even wear red to keep the bad away." This Order distrusted the sea more than any other Lillah had seen. Perhaps because people had been taken; it had actually happened here.

"Sometimes our young men will walk out, taunting the monster. They think it proves their manhood. And, to be sure, they are considered very attractive when they return."

He was so serious, Lillah felt like making him laugh. She wasn't sure how to, though.

"I have another story to tell you. A love story," said Sapin. Lillah wondered why his voice was so deep and sweet. "There were once two david-saplings which grew from the Tree. Unlike the other david-saplings, which stretched for sun and space, these two twisted together. They are still there today. You can gaze at them and see two lovers. You will see your face and that of your lover."

"Be wary of men who appear to be perfect. They may be putting on an act in order to catch you," Melia whispered to Lillah.

"These men do seem perfect! Let's just enjoy them. I think they are good men."

The ancestry was spoken. Lillah waited nervously, hoping that she and Sapin shared no grandparents. It was Tamarica, this time: her grandmother had stopped here, and therefore she could not sleep with any of the men.

Sandy-haired Sapin watched Lillah as she showed the women how to cook semolina with cardamom. She always carried the spice with her.

"Sapin! You should watch this. You're never going to find a wife so you will have to cook for yourself." The women laughed, which Lillah thought cruel. She glanced at Sapin, concerned he would cry, but he raised his eyebrows at her and gestured with his head to the door.

The women were arguing about who could do what, so Lillah wiped her hands and left with Sapin.

Lillah and Sapin stopped by the david-saplings. "I told you," he said. "You see? There is my face and there is yours." Manroots rested on the dirt in a thick carpet and she wondered at the ghosts.

There was a whispering sound. Lillah hated it. "It's the ghosts inside," she said. "Whispering about us. Wanting our bones." She shuddered.

He said, "Sometimes I whisper back. Tell them things I don't want people to know."

"I've heard other people do this. Telling the Tree secrets."

His cave was set deep in the sand, and she couldn't breathe, even looking at it.

"I can't go in there. I hate small spaces. I don't like the sand. I can't stand the thought of ghosts."

"Immerse yourself in the smell of it. Damp sand has a smell all its own. Rich with salt and minerals, it will heal you just by smelling it."

"I'm sorry. I can't go in there."

"Imagine it is huge and that you can feel fresh breeze on your face. If you feel a breeze it isn't too small." Above her fear, Lillah was curious to know what his cave looked like. Melia never cared about the walls, the pictures. "I'm too busy for that," but to Lillah it was part of the seduction. To see the images the men found sexual gave her an understanding of them. Already she felt like an expert. She had seen a cry for help and she had seen things that made her back out of the cave and choose somebody else.

She stepped into Sapin's cave. He let her go first, which meant she took in the full impact of the drawings and scratchings. She held her breath to see it; it was so beautiful. Every space filled with art. Drawings that showed the past, and the thoughts of all things.

It seemed to her that all human life was explained there, but she could not say how. Children piled onto each other in a great game, careful drawings of arms and legs, including the muscles. This was a man of great intelligence.

Sapin had gouged small alcoves into the walls of his cavern.

"Are these the stories of Sequoia?"

"They are."

"Do you record the old women who walk through? Ones who might have a talent like cooking?"

He laughed. "Old women are not such an interesting story, Lillah! Although you, you will be a fascinating old woman. Mostly I like birds," he said. He showed her one picture of an enormous Tree smothered with birds. "I like to imagine the noise they'd make. The birdsong. We don't hear enough here. Our birds are so huge and terrifying it's hard to remember some are lovely."

Lillah thought of the profusion of wildlife on the sunny side, and it occurred to her how lucky women were, that they could find a new place to live. Men were stuck with what they were born with.

"Birdsong is beautiful," she agreed. "Any music is." He shook his head. "Not the music of the angry sea." He touched another etching. "This one is from an ancient image the children found." It looked like an elongated house, with a bird's wings on either side.

"How did they find such an old thing?"

"They like to climb up as far as they are able. They like to see more than we can see, standing on the ground."

Lillah shuddered. "You're very talented."

"I am. I practise a lot. The plates were mine. Did you notice them?"

Lillah nodded. "I did. I barely concentrated on the food for looking at the story around the plate's rim."

"Sorry to be so distracting," he said. "But you are very distracting yourself."

"Not compared to the others. Erica is considered the most beautiful. Melia is the smartest. Thea was the most interesting. Tamarica is very lively."

"None of that is true," he whispered.

"Why don't you cover the doorway?" Lillah said. She hated her eagerness but sensed a tentativeness in him that would make things difficult if she didn't act.

He pulled his decorative door across. His hair looked much darker now and his eyes.

"Can you see me?" she said.

"Only just." He stepped forward until their bodies touched, stomach to stomach. He was taller by a handspread.

He stood so close and felt so firm against her Lillah could barely take a breath. He bent his head and Lillah thought, Not the forehead. If he kisses my forehead he is doing this out of duty, not terrible desire. He kissed the side of her neck, a gentle butterfly kiss she could not be sure had occurred. She expected another, the same, but this time he opened his mouth and sucked her there in a great lunging bite. Her body broke out in bumps. He kissed her mouth next and this time she could respond, drawing his tongue into her mouth and pressing him. He growled from deep in his chest. He gently pushed her backwards to the floor. There were pillows and a softness she took to be leaves. She lay back and he bent over her, kissing her neck again in his wonderful sucking biting way. He kissed one collarbone and ran his thumb over the other, then rested it in the dent between the bones. She reached her hands up to his hair and grabbed handfuls. She ran her fingers down to his neck and shoulders.

He unbuttoned her shirt and peeled it off her.

He was beautiful to fall asleep with. In a way this was a better test of compatibility. How a man slept beside her. How he felt.

She awoke to a delicate stroking of her stomach. His fingers measuring her hip width. He had a softness about his face, a dreaminess she recognised. A man thinking of his offspring.

She thought, I have no desire for it. No need for a baby. She stood up. "I'm hungry. I wonder if people are up and about and if food is coming."

She found Erica standing next to one of the sand structures, looking at the etchings. So many careful, brilliant hours of construction: depictions of the seawalk, the Tree, the long houses and the small, perfect in their detail.

"This is beautiful. I wonder how long they will last?" Erica said. She had spent the night with Sapin's brother, who was funny and light-hearted. She looked happier than Lillah had ever seen her.

Her lover waved his hands in the air. "Until the wind blows them. The water can't reach them. We know where our tide-line is." He kissed Erica, spun her around, then ran to the shore and returned with a perfect shell. "I'm going to see if breakfast is ready," he said, tossing the shell to Erica.

"I like it here," Erica said.

"So do I." Lillah wondered if she would miss her chance. She liked Sapin and would think about staying here; would Erica take her place? This was the first place Erica had been happy.

Lillah and Sapin climbed the lower limbs and sat together, talking about the sea, the Tree and knowledge. She could see Morace not too far away, building a small house from sticks and vines. He was involved, self-absorbed. Helping him was a young girl Lillah knew he was entranced by, with clear dark eyes and a lively laugh. She wondered if there was any way they could both stay here, be happy. The Order seemed less bothered by illness than others, and perhaps Morace would be safe here.

There was movement below, something odd; a flash of white and below them, a ghost stepped out.

"Morace!" Lillah whispered. "He's in the path of a ghost!"

Sapin tried to stop her jumping off the branch but merely threw her off balance so that when she landed it was awkwardly, with her ankle twisted.

The ghost walked. It did not seem interested in Morace, but Lillah ran anyway, lifted him up and carried him behind a clump of Tree undergrowth.

Morace finally saw the ghost and froze. It walked stiffly, unseeing. Sapin climbed down more carefully and stepped sideways before running so fast Lillah thought he'd disappeared.

"Is it a ghost? Or is it dead-but-walking?" Morace said. He stood up to get a better look. "The men are coming."

Lillah peered over the top of the shrub and saw Sapin with five others, carrying knives, rocks, sharp shells.

The dead-but-walking man stepped one foot after another, walking to the water.

The men raised arms and felled him. He didn't fight, but he did lift his arms to protect himself. Lillah thought, Why would a dead man do that?

The six men beat him with fists and sticks, kicked him, stoned him. Lillah ran over to them, not wanting to see but wanting to stop the violence. They seemed so much at ease with it. What do they practise on? Lillah wondered.

She pulled at Sapin. "Stop that! What are you doing?"

Sapin turned to her. His eyes were bright, his face splattered with blood. His hands covered with blood. He reached out and stroked her cheek, and she felt the blood there; he'd drawn a line on her. The tenderness of the gesture made her feel sick.

He turned back to the dead-but-walking and landed a blow that cracked the man's nose.

"We do not welcome dead-but-walking here. We don't let you walk on our sand, we don't let you put your eyes on our children, we don't let you breathe the air we breathe. We don't want you in our water, we don't want to smell your rotting flesh."

Sapin said this as he kicked, as they all kicked. The man no longer moved. His eyelids didn't flutter.

"But he just wanted to get to the water. You could let him walk to the water."

"Don't you understand, Lillah? Every person he looks at will rot from the inside. I've seen it. They cut my father open and inside was a mess of maggots, eating away at his rot. You have never smelt anything like it, Lillah. You would never eat again if you smelt such a thing."

They started to drag the body away. "I'll be back in a day or two," Sapin said. "We need to take this filth to a place in the sand where his burial will not affect any community."

"We'll bury him deep so that he can't leap back to life," one of the local children said. They all followed the lines in the sand left by the body; Lillah, the teachers and their children stayed behind.

Borag said, "I can't believe what they did to that man. Do they know who he was? He might have needed help. He might have had knowledge to share. They just destroyed him."

"He was dead-but-walking, Borag. He was worthless. He would have brought disease." Erica shook her head as if this were obvious.

"You are one to talk," Borag muttered. "You should learn to be more forgiving."

Lillah sat down by the Tree. The children covered up the blood spots with sand and leaves, and they all were silent, thinking of the violent death they had witnessed.

Erica sat by Lillah. "I had been thinking I would like to stay here," she said.

"I had been thinking the same."

They looked at each other. "Do you feel different now?" Erica asked.

"I'm not sure. I'm not sure I want Sapin to touch me again. Not now I've seen what he is willing to do."

"My lover was not part of that violence."

"Where was he?"

"He was preparing the meal."

They were quiet.

"He is the first man I thought I could love. This is the first place I have thought about staying in. I am not like you, Lillah. I am not likable. You are liked wherever we go. Mostly people do not even notice I am there. Here, they notice."

"And after what we just saw?"

"My man was not a part of it."

So it was decided. Erica would stay.

The community selected a girl named Musa to take Erica's place.

"We haven't had the chance to assess Musa. I don't even know her. I haven't spoken to her," Melia said. She knew what she'd been through to be chosen.

Erica said, "We trust each Order to provide their best. These people would not be any different."

Lillah felt so disappointed with Erica she didn't want to say goodbye. She wasn't sure she'd wanted to stay, but she hated the idea that Erica was staying instead. Two teachers stopping in one Order was not accepted. Morace sat with her.

"You like it here, don't you?"

"I like Sapin. He is the closest I have come to thinking I could spend more than three days with a man."

"You could stay. Mother wouldn't know. I'll be all right. We can tell Erica she can't stay, that you chose first."

"Morace, I can't do that to you. You are my brother, my half-brother. I have promised your mother, and you, and myself, to care for you to the best of my ability. I will do that. I knew what I was taking on. And anyway, it is Erica who is staying. Not me. And after that attack, that killing, I feel differently towards him. I would not be able to be with him without remembering it."

Sapin was not there to say goodbye.

Erica said, "Perhaps you felt love one way, after all. It does not always come back the way you want it to. He may not have wanted you, anyway."

Lillah pushed her, hard, knocking her to the ground. "You have a happy life, here. Steal my place and enjoy it."

Morace dropped his hat and didn't notice; Lillah picked it up, knowing she did not want to come back to the Order to collect it.

In her mapping, Lillah told the Tree: *Damp sand, dear man, pebble piles and piles of bones.*

Here, the Tree grows vegetables. The leaves are soft, the Bark as hard as I've seen.

Sequoia — ALGA — *Pinon*

There was a long walk to the next Order, close to a hundred days. They took it slowly, in no hurry. It was good to be alone, just the school. Lillah told Phyto about Sapin, how close she'd come to staying.

"It's not just about the man, though," Phyto said. "Most teachers choose a place for many reasons. Something they can give, something they can take. You need to feel useful."

"I could have made it work. But Erica made sure she took the place."

The sand was hot to the foot and dry.

Musa proved difficult to get to know. Prickly, agitated, she was a far cry from the sensible Erica, who, while annoying Lillah sometimes with her need to stick to the rules, had made them feel comfort in her presence.

Melia and Musa clashed early and hard. Musa had a sharp sense of humour and a cruel wit, and Melia did not like being laughed at.

Musa spoke a lot about her own achievements, but she was lazy in her walking, falling back, feet dragging. She was not unkind, but neither was she kind, nor was she gifted with brains to know when to be quiet.

When Rham, lagging behind to look at shell variations, was tangled by the rubbery, smelly seaweed on the shore, it was Tamarica who went back.

"Either keep up with the group or look after the laggers," Tamarica told Musa. "Otherwise the others will think you are not a good teacher."

Tamarica tried her best to keep the peace, because she was still so happy to be with the school, would always be happy, that she didn't want dissent. But Musa ignored her, flicked her away. She thought that Tamarica, being from Douglas, was not her worth.

"We are not concerned with where people came from. That is the whole point of the school. To realise that there is no good or bad place, there are simply different ways to live."

Musa rolled her eyes when Rubica said this. "Nonsense, rubbish boring nonsense no one believes. We think our own place is better than all else. Admit it. If you don't admit it you are lying to yourselves."

To draw Musa in, Tamarica asked her, "So what do you know about the Order we are headed for? We've heard little about them."

"I know they're figuring out a way to get drinkwater from saltwater. They can do it, but in small amounts. Though I have heard that they are not passionate. They are so concerned with their science, they forget the physicality."

"Really?" Melia said. "That will be odd for you. Your Order was passionate. My man was wilder than I imagined. You know? And he asked me to tell the story of the bad men again. More than once. I think he rather liked the idea of them, their cruelty. Their violence."

"Then Erica is welcome to that place," Lillah said quietly.

Melia put her arm around Lillah. "I'm sorry. You liked him a lot, didn't you?"

"I don't know that he felt the same way. I wasn't myself. It has thrown me, the business with Thea. It upset me a lot more than it did you, that's for sure."

Morace came up and held her hand. "Are you feeling sad, Lillah? Did you want to stay there?"

"Your timing is always perfect, Morace." She kissed him on the head. "No, I didn't want to stay. Erica stayed. I wanted to stay with you."

He seemed weaker. Paler, although he walked with high steps, pretending energy he didn't have. Tamarica collected a shell of water and sap for him, a soft, sour drink he swallowed with a grimace.

"Haven't you noticed that the children are happier without Thea here?" Melia said.

"Not true," Lillah shook her head.

"It is true, Lillah," Rham said. "She held us too hard and she got angry when we did nothing wrong. She told us off for things we hadn't done, things she had done herself. We didn't like her. You liked her but you were the only one. We thought she would kill us one day."

Musa snorted. "Don't be ridiculous. Why would a teacher kill you?"

"This teacher did kill children. You didn't know her," Morace said.

"She didn't kill those children. They drowned," Lillah said.

"She told them to swim until they could swim no more and she would swim out and save them. She tried to make me swim as well."

"And me," said Zygo.

"You're a good swimmer, Zygo."

"Not when she was around."

"How about how her cheeks went red when a baby died? Didn't you ever notice that?"

Lillah felt a coldness in her heart. An acceptance of something she had denied.

"I don't want to talk about this anymore," she said.

"There is no point avoiding the truth," Musa said.

"Shall we talk about the way the dead-but-walking was dealt with in Sequoia, then?" Melia said. When Musa said nothing, Melia nodded. "I thought not. It's all right when it's somebody else's truth."

• • •

As they approached the Order, Melia said, "I can't stand to be within a hundred steps of that Musa," and moved. She walked far in front, something they had been told never to do. "Never arrive on your own. Assess the Order as a group. Make your decisions together until you become more accomplished."

They saw a lot of people in the water, an odd sight. Lined up, moving fast, on the water's edge.

It was a muted arrival. Very soon after they got there, word went out that a messenger was arriving. Any news made Morace nervous. It made Lillah nervous too, and she wished his father would stop sending messages. It didn't do any good. She supposed he wanted to strengthen her resolve, keep her caring for Morace, and that insulted her. She cared for Morace as much as she could. She had given up her true love for him.

She wondered sometimes, if she was doing the right thing. Was it worth risking their civilisation to save one child? She wasn't even sure if she believed that he was worth saving.

He wore a garland of seaweed, they said, and the Order went quiet around the children and teachers. Will it be my mother? My father? Someone I love?

A garland of seaweed meant a death.

The messenger came at them before they had settled, even before they ate. He took water then said, "News from the Order of Ombu. There has been a passing. Rhizo, wife of Pittos, died quietly in her bed."

Lillah felt momentary relief that she had not lost her father, or Logan, Magnolia or their baby. But it was Rhizo, with all the trauma that would bring. They took Morace into embrace and stood together, letting him cry. He cried for only a few blinks; Lillah knew how prepared he was for this. Even Zygo stood with him. "Don't worry," he whispered. "We'll keep you safe."

The locals helped as they could, feeding the messenger, bringing hot sap water.

"What news of her death? How did she die? An ailment?" a local asked the messenger.

"What news of my nephew?" Lillah pushed forward. They shouldn't talk about the cause of death. The other teachers clamoured for gossip from their homes, and he told them news of Erica ("She is not yet with child") and others until he shook his head, his cheeks red.

"I know only what I'm told," he said. He turned as if to run back to his own Order. Someone grabbed his arm.

"Strange to have so little information," a local said, looking at Morace. "Illness or age or accident, we should know this."

The messenger said, "I can tell you rumour; she died in childbirth and the Order has discarded her body as a foolish waste."

Morace sobbed and Lillah knew she had failed him, letting him hear this. He threw her arm off when she went to comfort him, and glared at her as if he was the grown up and she the child.

"She's been dead for almost six months and I didn't know. I didn't know!"

"You're lucky they sent the fast messenger. You would have waited a year, otherwise."

"Who has her smoothstone, Lillah?"

"Someone will look after it."

The messenger had other news for them, small things about their families which he relayed once Morace had settled. They didn't want to discuss the ramifications of the news so revelled in gossip for a while.

A huge turtle shell, curved side up, rested near the Trunk of the Tree.

"That's beautiful."

"Don't lift it. There is a man underneath. Being punished for taking love when it was not given."

"He's under there? For how long?"

"Some time."

"It must be dark."

"He blinks when it is lifted. Weeps. He won't do such a thing again."

Rubica felt proud to hand over the metal plate in welcomefire. She received a sealed wooden bowl. "There is sweet water inside," they told her.

The teachers had to pay in words for a meal. Melia loved it; she loved to talk, loved to question and to answer questions. The words were fired at her and the other teachers: *Where do you*

go when it's stormy in your Order? Can you read the
stars? How much sun do you get? Do you like the
water? What do you use for plates? Where is your
water from?

Lillah sighed, unable to hide her weariness any
longer. Morace was lying down, not interested in
food. She had spent hours with him and she felt
drained, impatient. The Tale-teller, a grey, arrogant
man who took in everything he saw with blinking,
watery eyes, said, "I'm sorry. I question too much.
It's in my nature. I like to have something to tell
the Tree."

"Well, our Melia questions. But she stops after a
while!"

"Our early leaders had a motto of only believing
the evidence of their eyes and ears, and not of history. We have this too. The past is meaningless to
us. We only believe the answers we hear to the
questions we ask. Do you understand?"

"I guess so."

Lillah closed her eyes and let the talkfire warm
her.

"We tell stories, too. We do not only ask questions. Have you heard the story of the first
woman?"

Lillah nodded. "I've heard many versions. Yours
may be different. I've also heard versions of the first
man, and the Tree born through his ribcage."

The Tale-teller looked shocked. He said softly,
"There is only one story. The one which questions

and does not accept as truth everything that is said, just because it is said."

"Will you tell us your version?"

With fury, he rose and threw his cup onto the fire. "This is not a version! This is the story! You shall not hear it!" He stomped away, his fat buttocks jiggling under his skirt.

The teachers giggled, smothering the noise till he was out of earshot.

"How pompous!" Musa said.

"You shouldn't judge our teller. He takes his tales seriously. You do not," one of the younger locals said.

"We do! We think tales are important. But we realise that there will be different versions of every tale no matter where you go."

They nodded amongst themselves and no one seemed too bothered by the Tale-teller's mood. He came back after a while, hovering on the edges, bending his neck, stretching to hear all.

The mood livened without his central presence. The Order played music, lively and energising.

Melia began a good natured argument with a handsome man. Musa rolled her eyes and tried to interject until the man said, "Perhaps you could find some occupation in helping to prepare the next meal?"

Musa stood up. "You are welcome to the fool," she said. She was pale skinned in the afternoon light.

"Well, thank you for your permission, Musa. What a difference that makes to me."

The Order laughed as Musa stomped away.

Lillah sat alone beneath the Tree. She was tired and wanted to sleep, but the children came for her. "Morace needs you. He feels sad."

Lillah could not help but yawn. Melia joined them, her smile large on her face. "Perhaps you could see to Morace for a while, Melia. I am tired. Tired."

Melia took her into a short embrace. "I'm sorry, Lillah. I am always selfish. You should walk alone for a while. See your spiders, or touch the Tree. Feel the bark. That will bring you back to yourself again."

Lillah kissed Melia on the cheek. "You are selfish, but sometimes you surprise us all."

"I'll set them to digging. The sand here is damp and should hold well."

In a small hollow of the Tree, Lillah found a cluster of small, smoothstones, each with a rough marking indicating the death of a newborn. It chilled her to think of dead babies grouped like that, and she turned away to look out to sea, to think of elsewhere.

While she had been brought up to think that babies died easily and there was no shame in this, no sorrow, other Orders thought differently. Knowing how terrified Magnolia was of losing her child had instilled Lillah with that fear herself. She did not want that death to mourn.

"This is the placenta garden." A man with a grey beard stood beside her. "We believe the placenta is a seed to be planted."

"And what have you grown?"

"Nothing comes up. But it will. When our Order crumbles and dies, the placenta garden will fruit the next generation." Lillah realised this man was a 'watcher', someone who crouches on the low branches, protecting the Order's secrets.

These men were very wise; they saw all. Lillah thought that the Tale-teller was probably envious of this man, knowing how wise he was, and this might be a reason for his arrogance.

"I thought perhaps these were lost babies."

"We don't bury the dead here. We send them out to sea."

He shivered.

"Why is it that we fear death so greatly? Do we not believe that there is an elsewhere, a smaller island, somewhere we go to be safe and small?"

"We can try to believe that. But we cannot know. It is the unknown that frightens us."

The watcher reminded her of Tilla, though he looked older with his grey beard. Lillah reached up to touch it; it was soft. She saw very few beards.

"This is a strange colour."

"I drank from the women's pool," he said. "When I was a boy. I was trying to prove that the myth wasn't true, but instead I proved it was true."

He took her to see the drinking pools. "If you drank from the men's pool your hair would go grey. All the hair on your body. Let's rejoin the feast."

Melia and Morace sat among the others as water was brought in carved wooden cups. Melia sipped, then sipped again.

"This is delicious," she said. "What sort of rainfall is this?"

"This is not rainfall. It is sea water. We have removed the salt from it, that is all," a young, strong man said.

The Order chuckled as he said this. "He makes it sound very simple, but each jug of pure water takes many hours of work, many resources. You may have seen us on the water's edge, at work."

"Not for long. I will discover easier ways. Better ways. We are lucky here; we have a lot of land between water and Tree. We have the space to make this water." His muscles rolled and there was a twist in his cheek.

"I have never tasted water like it," Melia said softly.

"You won't taste it anywhere else. No other Order will make the sacrifices needed for the water."

"Anything is worth it for this water. How do you know what to do?"

"Many years ago a newcomer arrived. She had word of sweet water and how to make it, but she was disbelieved. I'm ashamed to say our ancestors killed her; strapped her to some wood, slit her arms and her legs, and sent her out to sea. Her words were remembered, though."

Lillah closed her eyes. She felt sad already: she knew that Melia would stay. This is where she always meant to stay.

"So you don't fear the sea monster? You are not afraid taking his water will make him angry?"

"We do not believe there is a sea monster. There is perhaps a very large fish, bigger than we can imagine. But the fish don't mind if we use their water. It would be like us minding if they used our sand. Look at it; it will never run out."

Lillah hardly knew what to say to this. She walked away to check on the children; they were by the water's edge, staring out.

"Look, Lillah, out to sea. There is something floating," Morace said.

"Pull your shoulders back," Lillah whispered to him. "Sit up straight. Look well." She said aloud, "If Thea were here we could send her out to get it."

"It will float in before too long."

On the morning tide, it rested on the shore. A raft, built with long solid, sheddings from the Tree. There was nothing tied to it; it was wood alone.

"Months ago, a long time ago, a raft came back with a body tied to it. You should have seen it. We could no longer tell if it was a man or a woman; the flesh had been picked clean and the clothing rotted away and washed off." Melia's lover told this story with a smile. "This happens sometimes. We send our dead out on a raft, and they come back changed."

"This happens on the other side of the island, too."

The watcher came down to the water, shouting and spitting with fury. In this mood he was so much like Tilla, Lillah's old friend from her Order. She stopped herself talking to him, though. He was frightening when he was angry. He seemed even angrier than Tilla was, shouting warnings of terrible gaps in the earth which suck you into the centre.

"This raft has come from the cracks in the earth. Send it away before it destroys us."

"Don't listen to him. Superstitious and nasty he is. He thinks the Tree will crack down the middle and devour us because of our evil ways," one young man said, smiling.

"It's not funny, you great fool. You waste flesh and ignore omens."

"Where did you come from, old man? Not from here."

"Is he a newcomer?" Lillah asked.

"No, we just tease him. He bothers the birthing women, begging for placenta. He wants to perform his ritual but none of us like that."

"Don't you remember? Are all of you so stupid you don't remember? We sent out that old woman who died at our campfire. She came back black-boned and covered with moss. Don't you remember? Soon after we lost eight, eight of us lost to branchfall."

"She was one of your people?" Lillah asked. She felt her skin go cold.

"No, she wasn't one of us. She was a wandering old woman, lost. She said she had no home. She said her home was a place of emptiness and fruit-fulness and that she would walk until she found a place fulfilling. She cooked for us, don't you re-member?"

"We remember! We remember the woman, old man."

"She cooked?"

"She cooked with spices we had not tasted be-fore. Delicious. She was an overly proud woman, though. And not well. Don't you remember? After a meal. We had swallowed too much fortified fruit, that much I do know. She had danced. I rather liked her. She reminded me of what it was like to be a young man. Those were my thoughts. I re-member them."

Lillah felt tears forming.

"And then?"

"And then she died. She danced, she drank, she sat by the fire, and when we went to rouse her, she was gone."

"Where did she come from?" Melia asked, be-cause Lillah couldn't speak.

"I remember that she said she came from Ombu. But she was born in Rhado. She said she might walk back to Ombu if there was nothing else for her. That I remember."

Lillah sank to the ground. Melia caught her by the shoulders.

"At least you know, Lillah. And she was happy. From what he says, she died as happy as any of us could hope to die."

Lillah nodded. "I know. I know. It's good."

But still she felt a sense of loss. It was an ending. Her search was over.

It was three nights before Lillah felt she could choose a lover. She liked the strong, muscly one with knowledge of water. "You can have him tonight, Lillah, and until you leave. After that he's mine," Melia said. Lillah watched Melia kissing the other men, caressing them one by one, as if testing out the whole Order to see if it fit. After Douglas, they felt kindly towards other men.

The sun was up late and the children wouldn't sleep. Morace remembered every now and then about his mother and his face would drop. Lillah thought he wasn't as sad as he pretended to be. It was more fear for his own survival. The school-children began to dig deep in the sand, telling the local children of the last Order, where deep sand caves had kept them cool. Rham told them, "If you dig deep enough, you find the roots of the Tree. They are powerful with magic. Some of the roots stretch all the way to the sea, and if you dig deep enough, make a tunnel, you can let the water run up the beach. You will be the ruler of the water."

The children took to the project with great delight and the adults were glad of the peace.

Lillah and her man sat together, talking quietly. They would move away soon, but she was enjoying this quiet time, this thoughtful moment. She saw his home, with its seaweed door-hanging. It smelt faintly of the sea, but it was not as overpowering as she imagined it would be.

She spoke of Rham, her great cleverness. And of Morace, who was becoming a kind boy.

"Do you only talk of the children?" he said. "Your children are better than ours." But he smiled as he spoke and kissed her so she couldn't respond.

Close to four weeks later, Melia leaned against the Tree, staring up into the leaves intently.

"Can you see the sky?" Lillah said. "Your eyesight is very good."

Melia tilted her head back and Lillah saw that she was crying.

"What is it, Melia?" This girl had never cried, in all the time Lillah known her, in all her life.

"I'm thinking about my uncle climbing the Tree."

"Very sad for your mother."

"Not that. I'm worried these people will find out and they won't take me. No Order wants the risk of someone climbing the Tree. Telling others to climb the Tree."

Lillah turned her back, partly amused and partly furious at herself for thinking that Melia would care about anyone else.

"None of us will tell them. Don't worry. We'll protect you."

"I'm sorry I couldn't protect you from knowing about your mother, Lillah. Would you prefer to think she is free somewhere?"

"I don't know. It seems she died happy, at least. Something she rarely was in life."

But then there was a terrible scream from the beach. The children came running; school children, local children, all sandy, tear stained, terrified.

"The cave fell in! It collapsed! They said it would stay up!"

"You can dig again," said one of the fathers.

"No, no, there is someone underneath!"

Morace, barely able to speak, said, "It's Rham."

They ran, all of them, the men grabbing large shells on the way, and too many people dug to get her out.

A sickening silence settled as they reached her face. Her eyes were closed and her mouth full of sand; they dug desperately to free the rest of her body and saw her fingers clutched, her fingernails torn and bloody.

The Birthman stepped up. "Bring me water and wine," he said. He cleared her throat, so full of sand, and he sat her up. The water and wine came and with these he tried to revive her, but she was gone to the spirit island.

Morace threw himself to the ground and the other children followed, all of them wailing a terrible, inconsolable sound. "She won't go to the island of the spirits! She'll be caught in the ivy."

Lillah threw herself down, too, and the other teachers, no thought of comforting the children, just allowing the grief to take them in all its passion.

For two days the Birthman and the fathers tried to revive Rham, painting her cheeks with red, opening her eyes for her. They propped her against the Tree, food in her hand. They did not want this bad thing to happen in their Order; they did not want to be thought of badly.

Lillah walked to the water's edge, looking out to the island of the spirits. She felt ill at the thought of Rham's soul being lost, drifting out to sea. If only they'd had a turtle close by, or a bird.

Morace stepped into the water nearby and fell to his knees. The other children joined him, kneeling and letting the waves slap them.

A low, rhythmic moaning from them, so low and rhythmic Lillah couldn't tell it from the sound of the waves. They stretched their hands towards the island and the sight broke Lillah.

"I saw a bird sitting on a rock over there," she said. "Did anyone else see it? It had red feathers on its shoulders, like a neck ruff. It sat there for a long time then flew up into the Tree.

"Really?" Borag said. "You saw that?"

"I did," Lillah said. She wished she was a child then, to hear a happy lie and believe it. She wished she knew that Rham's soul was safe.

Finally, Melia said quietly to Lillah, "We need to send her out to sea. She will never reach the Island of Spirits otherwise. And we don't want her bones eaten by ghosts."

"That is an odd thing to say," Melia's lover said, kissing her neck. He took her into his arms. "There are no ghosts in the Tree."

Lillah watched Melia change in that moment. She let belief go so easily, because her lover told her to. Lillah thought, Yet I still see her strength. The teachers washed Rham's little body again, weeping, pouring their salt tears onto her skin. They placed her beloved wooden puzzle in her pocket. The children sat quietly now; some already bored with it all, some so shocked still they couldn't talk.

"Another messenger is coming. With seaweed around his neck."

"No. Not more death."

It was Thea. Fallen from high in the Tree, the messenger said, but they knew that she had been murdered by the men of Douglas.

Lillah put down her washing cloth, put both her hands up in surrender, and walked up to the Tree. She found a small alcove, dry, ghost-free, and she stepped inside, wanting to be alone, without anyone, alone and not caring about those who died.

It was two days before Melia came to convince her to come out. "We need you, Lillah. You can't give up on us because of a person like Thea."

Lillah spat at Melia, "It's Rham as well. We failed her. You hated Thea, but I didn't."

"You didn't like her. You are lying to yourself. You despised her as much as the rest of us did."

Lillah stared at her. "What do you care? You'll be staying here, I imagine."

"How did you know?"

"You are so predictable. You don't care about the men. You want the water."

Melia flicked her hand, as if dismissing the importance of the men.

"The men will do," she said.

The children seemed to recover well. Lillah caught Borag tasting sugar, and Morace went swimming with some local children. The others, you could see their faces sometimes, when they thought of their schoolmate but mostly they played, and ate, and waited to move on.

"These children wouldn't care if we lived or died," Lillah said to Tamarica.

Tamarica said, "They would care, but only sometimes. Not always. They don't feel grief as an all encompassing thing like we do and that is good. Grief leaves no room for learning."

"And you," Lillah said, because that wasn't what she wanted to hear. "Your brothers have murdered my dear friend."

Tears came to Tamarica's eyes. "I am sorry for that. I'm sorry she died in my Order." The two women looked at each other, no recriminations. They stepped closer, like they would stand with a man, and for a moment it felt like the right thing to do. But Lillah did not feel that way about women: she liked men, their length, their strength. And Tamarica did not know yet what she wanted: she had come from such a bad place it would take time to know this.

The leave taking was cold. For Lillah it had to be that way; to lose Rham, Thea and Melia, and to care, was too much to bear. She felt a certain envy that Melia had found what she was looking for. That she had the freedom to do so; no brother to protect and keep from death.

"You're staying in this place of death? The place my mother died, and Rham? You care so little? The place we heard about Thea?"

"I don't care at all," Melia said.

"Then you are lucky."

Melia picked at her toenails. She said, "You don't really care about consequences, do you? About punishment, or protection. Safe keeping."

Lillah didn't speak. She didn't know if the others knew what she was doing. They didn't know

Morace was her half brother, but did they know that he was sick and she was protecting him from being treated and cured?

Melia looked at her. "I convinced Thea to stay in Douglas. I told her she should do it as punishment, to atone. So she would go to Spirit Island when she died."

Lillah was suddenly so furious she couldn't breathe. She shook with rage. "You told her to stay with those men? Who we knew would likely kill her? How could you?"

"Because I believe in guilt. You don't. You would have kept her by your side, safe. With the children around her unsafe. And you would know that but not admit it. I should have told you, but only so you would not sacrifice your beads. That was not needed."

"That is the very least of it."

Lillah's face filled with salt water, it seemed. Her whole body a sea of tears. "I can't speak to you again," she said. But she knew that Melia was right. She had to feel this way, in order to protect Morace at the risk of others.

Melia gave Lillah a smile, but Lillah ignored her.

Melia hissed, "I can't believe you put Thea before me! She is a child killer. I am your dearest friend."

Lillah turned her back.

"You're angry at me? Over Thea, who's no longer with us?"

"I'm angry because you don't care. Because you think you can tell people what to do but you don't think it's your fault when people die. I'm angry to have lost Rham when she would have been a wonderful teacher. And now you're staying and I'll never see you again."

Melia looked at her. "This is how we live, Lillah. I'll miss you too."

Melia's place was taken by Ster, someone very different, quiet and nervous. Lillah wondered who would play the role of the curious, with Melia and Rham gone.

In her mapping, Lillah told the Tree: *Alga is those who question.*

Here, the Tree grows death. The leaves are pale and dead, the Bark is dead, the ground is dead.

Alga — PINON — *Arborvitae*

Phyto was shocked to hear the news. He alone re-alised how desperate Morace was to have lost his mother, and he tried to talk to them about death, news of death, sudden death, so much of it in one place. And Lillah, too, now knew she would not see her mother again. She now knew her mother was dead.

"Why was Rham in the hole? What was she doing in there?"

Morace answered. "You know that we spent a lot of time in this community in holes. The sand was quite hard, we thought. We were taking over and showing them how clever we were, then I got out to find us some water and Rham was left behind."

He began to cry, hunched down where he stood and cried. Lillah was pleased to see the tears; pleased that Rham had been loved.

"Thea... we don't know all about that yet. We know that she is dead and we think of course that the men of Douglas killed her. We don't know though."

Tamarica covered her face. "My men are not good men. I don't know if they would kill for no reason, though."

"So you think that Thea deserved to die?"

Tamarica looked shocked. "No! No! I don't mean that at all."

Lillah touched her shoulder. "It's okay, Tamarica. It's okay."

There was a shorter walk, only twelve days, to the market, and it was lively and colourful, serving hot drinks and cold, food snacks, making it a place for people to meet. Phyto was accepted as a travelling man without much concern, and he said that already he liked the people of Pinon.

Lillah felt like a bad tempered old man, but she couldn't help it. She missed Melia terribly; Ster, the teacher who'd taken her place was dull, quiet, far too nice. She agreed with everything Lillah said, wanting to impress her, Lillah supposed. She brought out the worst in people, Lillah thought. Just being around her made Lillah want to behave badly, speak ill of people long gone, make shocking statements.

Borag and Morace quietly took her hands and walked with her. She loved them for it; supporting her in her bad mood, not expecting her to change. They talked about Rham; told the stories they knew of her, sad and funny clever, the stories they knew.

Morace coughed, tried to smother it. Even a cough could give him away as sick, though it was pimples and other growths that would cause the greatest concern.

Lillah kept some hard sap balls in her pockets; she gave Morace one to suck, to soothe his cough.

After four days walk, she began to feel calmer and more connected to the present.

The first thing they saw as they entered the outskirts of Pinon, the first thing they smelt, was a man, hanging from a Limb.

It was close to being more than Lillah could handle. She bundled the children forward, distracting them, wanting to remove them from the stink of it.

Phyto said, "Perhaps I should come with you this time." As if to answer this question, a tall man, shaven head, greeted them. They had not seen him approach. His teeth were broad and white as he smiled. He did not comment on Phyto's presence.

"We weren't sure whether to hang our treated man as you enter the Order, or as you leave. We decided entry, because we want it made very clear we do not like illness here."

"Nobody does," Lillah said. She pressed her elbows into her sides to stop from grabbing Morace, giving anything away at all. I must believe that he's not sick, she thought. They won't know he's sick unless I tell them. If I believe he is not sick, they won't know.

"That's a cruel way to kill a person, though."

"Sometimes cruelty is needed to save an entire Order."

"But what if Spikes is a myth? We have no real proof of that part of our history," Tamarica said.

"You have learnt nothing in your travels then. Proof is everywhere. In the places where the population is so low they are barely surviving. In the Trunk, where people have etched pictures of suffering. In our stories, our myths. All of this tells us Spikes is something to fear. This is what we must protect the people from."

Musa said, "You are a fear-monger. This is wrong, what we do. You know that. Spikes is in the past, and this is now. We shouldn't kill people because they might be sick. It's a terrible thing."

The argument continued. Finally Musa said, "We are tired, and the children are very hungry. Do you think we could move beyond your border?"

The tall man nodded at her. "Please excuse us. We are a philosophical people and we tend to forget the needs of children. Of course the needs of children are more important than anything else which could be discussed."

Musa and Lillah exchanged glances. Lillah thought, We must be careful of these people.

"We won't discuss then the Tree of life, the earth mother and the sky father. That we will leave, because the children are hungry."

"If you don't mind," Musa said. For the first time, Lillah was pleased she was with them. She was tough and unrelenting. She was not bothered by slights.

These people walked with a slant, always facing the Tree. As they sat for food, none of them faced the sea; always the Tree.

Borag whispered, "Do they know that Oldnew Day is coming? Do they even care?"

Zygo said, "We will ask them. See what they think."

"No, Zygo. Not everyone believes in the things we believe in. We must leave them to decide for themselves," Rubica said.

Zygo stood up. "This day is too warm to be sitting here with you. I will find some excitement." The light around his shoulders made him seem taller, larger, and the teachers and the students alike watched him, wondering what he would be like as a man.

Lillah looked at the Tree Trunk and felt disturbed by the greenness of the moss she saw there. It almost covered the ground area and, as she stopped closer, she could see that it was both slimy and furry, almost seaweedy in texture.

The women lived in groups of two or three and the men shared with them. It seemed a happy arrangement, without the rules of ownership which, when broken, can be so distressing.

None seemed concerned with Phyto, and Lillah was happy with his company.

At welcomefire, the people were not impressed with the sealed bowl of sweet water. They reluctantly gave a bag of morning-after moss. Lillah spoke quietly to her school. "We remember our lost women. Rham and Gingko and Rhizo and Thea. We remember them and eat in their honour."

Morace sat quietly, chewing slowly. He did not often talk of his mother, but Lillah knew thoughts of her sat with him most of the day. He awoke from nightmares in which he said she was dead-but-walking, making her way through the Tree towards him.

At last a messenger arrived with good news. Logan had sent Lillah a small present; a shell, carved with intricate designs. She could see the faces of her Order there, and it made her happy and homesick in one. "Was there a message with this?" she asked. She remembered their promise.

"The message is that your brother wants to know how it feels to stay the same."

"That doesn't make any sense," Zygo said. "Logan is full of nonsense."

"It does make sense to me." Lillah felt such a deep sense of loneliness she could not bear to be around people. Logan was right, of course he was. She had changed so much since leaving Ombu. All that had happened, all she had learnt; everything changed her perception of herself and the people around her.

"Sometimes it's hard to get a message from home," the messenger said. "Many teachers will cry, because if you don't have the message, you can try to forget."

"You are a smart messenger," Borag said. She looked at him sidelong and Lillah knew that she was already thinking of the time she would be a teacher. "Where do you live?"

The messenger blushed. "I am from Arborvitae."

"I'll remember that," Borag said.

The messenger, stuttering now, told them that Erica had helped to build a home and was much admired for the carving she did.

Lillah had a small woven doll she had worked on for many months; this she gave as a gift to the messenger to send forward to Logan at Ombu.

"Any words with this?"

"Yes. That his sister will soon be taller than him."

"You speak as much nonsense as Logan," Zygo said.

"He will know that I mean I am growing and changing. He is a man of deep thought, Zygo. Perhaps you should spend some time with him once you return to Ombu."

Lillah felt huge and clumsy watching these graceful women move. They were strong, lifting pots and great loads of coconuts without complaint. But they did it beautifully.

Is it the length of their arms? Lillah thought. Their necks? But she knew that physically they were similar.

They did wear their sleeves cut high across the shoulder; perhaps that was it.

Or perhaps it came from within. They were self-sacrificing. Lillah watched them take food from their own plates for the children; saw them tend each other graciously.

Their ceilings were hung with netting woven through with shells. It gave the rooms an openness, a feeling of the sea.

Morace came to breakfast pale and shaky.

"Are you all right?" Lillah asked.

His eyes widened; he filled his mouth with bread and didn't answer. Lillah did not press him. Either he had dreamt bad again of his mother, or he was feeling ill. That she did not want to discuss.

Rubica was good at reading the moon. She had told them the last few nights that the Oldnew Day was nearing. They wondered how it would be celebrated; each Order was different.

The night before Oldnew Day a woman told them, "There will be no work done tomorrow, so we need to make harvest now." The Order was frantically busy: some fishing, some cleaning, others preparing huge pots of stew that would cook all day over a low fire. There came a loud call, a shell-blowing. "Gather the moss, gather the moss," the people chanted. The teachers followed the crowd. There were comfortable places to sit.

They sat out on the seawalk enjoying the sun and the sight of the children playing. As the sun set, they gathered together and watched as the light changed.

"Look!" Morace said. "That old woman is still coming."

"Turn your head away," a local said. "Quickly. Don't look."

"It's just an old woman walking home. We've seen a few of them."

"Don't look at them! Don't talk to them! If they get their spittle on you you'll die by next Oldnew Day."

One woman with a knife stood at the Trunk of the Tree.

"This is the most important lesson you will ever learn." She scraped the moss; it came off in great flat sheets and curled over itself. Others ran in to collect the rolls and take them away.

"We must control the babies we have. With crowding comes illness, with illness comes death. The joining of bodies is unavoidable, desirable. You would never give child to an untested father. So we must have the freedom to test, to sample, without the nuisance of childbirth."

The children began to fidget, bored. "Each of you is precious, because you were chosen. There are no unwanted children."

Morace asked, "But how do you know if what the teachers do makes the babies? They do it all the time and only sometimes the baby comes."

"Rham would have known," Zygo said. "She would know that answer." Lillah nodded.

"This is where we show the importance of sharing knowledge. We know that the men of Douglas study cycles, the weather. They are the experts at making connections, drawing conclusions about cause and effect. They noted, over many years of observation, that after the sex act, often the bleeding would not come. And if the bleeding didn't come eight times, the belly grew with child.

"We heard these studies and we wondered at our teachers, who caught child very rarely. Further questioning of travelling schools led us to understand that our moss did not grow everywhere. And that we chewed our moss all day, because it soothes the mouth and makes food tastier." Lillah thought of how dull the food tasted here and could see why they would become addicted to the moss.

"We began sharing our moss with the schools and eventually enough news came back for us to show that the moss prevented a child from catching. We are in control."

Lillah looked around for Melia, knowing how

much she'd be loving this; the questioning, seeking and finding of answers.

But Melia was not there. She had stayed behind in Alga, for the fresh water.

The feeling of loss, rare to Lillah, was intense.

"I have a friend who would love to hear you talking. Hearing about when people first discovered answers. She used to wonder how we knew the love making led to children."

Phyto nodded. "Melia," he whispered. "Who was the first?"

"Observation, that's all. Every generation has one or two who will watch and remember. Remember what happened last year and many years before that. Most people aren't interested."

Lillah thought, Melia is too self-absorbed to learn that way. She wants to be told.

"What happens when the men take the moss?"

"We are not sure. Certainly they chew it for the pleasures it brings, and we have very few children here. Teachers who have never taken the moss catch more easily. The men tend to self-administer a lot, too, to keep their potency down. Nobody wants the consequences of an unneeded child."

Lillah knew people thought the longer you took the moss, the longer it would be for you to catch child when you stopped taking it. It was the reason why most of them had their children when they were older.

Lillah said, "There are some Orders that deal with their unwanted after birth. Leave them out to die. They disappear though. Perhaps the monkeys, looking for a good meal. There is no trace ever found. Not even the Tale-tellers know, or the Watchers." The listeners nodded. "Where is your Tale-teller?" Lillah asked. The men seemed quiet here; she'd seen no one with a Tale-teller's voice.

"We don't use a Tale-teller. We know stories as truth without being told." The woman seemed defensive. Lillah didn't think it was because Phyto was with them; mostly they barely noticed him. He took on the characteristics of a woman and that was how people saw him.

Three women climbed the highest limbs of the Tree they could reach. Up there the moss grew hard and needed to be scraped with stone knives to remove it. It was a hard job, but these devoted women didn't complain. They climbed down covered with bruises, their palms and fingers marked with cuts and scrapes.

"The moss is not edible in this state. Once we throw it in the fire, it burns so slow no one will need to work the fire tomorrow. And it is transformed by the heat into a sticky ash. With this we can cook a tasty bread. We mix it with water to make clay, cover the dough with it, bake it slowly. You cannot imagine the wonderful smell when we crack the case."

"But you're exhausted. How do you keep working like this when you are so tired?"

"We all need to eat, and we need the fire to burn."

Lillah wondered if she would ever be so self-sacrificing, to give up comfort, sleep, cause herself pain for others.

Lillah watched the lowfire, feeling hungry for the stew as it bubbled gently.

"And there is the stone itself. Where the timing of the year comes from," the woman said. "We will sit up tonight and wait for the moon to strike and show us the symbols we cannot see on any other day. Then until the moon strikes again, we will not speak. We will let the day decide for itself what it wishes us to do. Anything is possible on this day. The sick cured, the dead risen, the sea monsters emerged to steal our babies."

"I've never seen the ill cured. Nor the dead risen, nor any sign of the sea monster," Musa said. She was a cynic, arguing a lot against the Spikes story and other stories she considered unproven.

"Those who sleep by the stone tonight will dream their future, or their truth. Or they will dream an answer to a question," the woman said.

"I think the children can camp out by the stone tonight. I can't see why they should miss out on this opportunity to dream of the stone," Lillah said.

"There may be nothing to dream," Ster said.

"Yes, but it's worth a try," the woman said. "They won't be here again, never for the boys, many years for the girls, if at all. I must warn you, though. The stone takes an occasional sacrifice. Sucks the blood out of the victim. There will be no warning. We will not know who will be taken. But that hasn't happened for many years. It may be that the stone has taken enough, or it may be that it is very hungry and will take more than one on this night."

Morace looked pale in the moonlight. Worried.

"You should keep him indoors. Away from people who may pass judgement on him," Musa said, her back to the locals.

Ster nodded. "Keep him inside. There is only so long we can use the excuse of his mother dying to cover his lethargy."

Lillah felt worried for them all. She remembered sleeping by the stone when she passed through as a child. It was frightening; she couldn't get to sleep for a long time that night for the fear of what she might dream.

She had spent the night absorbing noises, her body moving beyond tiredness.

Just before dawn she fell into a dream of darkness: her head encased in a block of wood from the Tree.

They danced that night, once Oldnew Day was over. Lillah and the other teachers leapt about, waving arms and leaping with excitement.

In contrast, the women of Pinon danced like smoke: wispy, ethereal, so graceful they made Lillah feel like a great sea bass floundering in the sand.

This was a very promiscuous Order. The women's jaws moved all the time, and for a while the teachers thought they were talking quietly. But it was moss; they chewed moss most of the day, only stopping to eat.

The land was far less fertile here, on the shady side.

Sometimes the food made Lillah feel dulled.

The men chewed, too. It seemed obvious to the teachers that the lack of children was due to the men's lack of potency and the damage done by constant use of moss.

"Oh, My Tree Lord, we'd love to have more children here. We love their little faces, we do," one woman said, but as she spoke she sighed in irritation as the noise the children made in play reached them. Lillah wondered if they really did love children.

It was a most uncomfortable night. Again, Lillah found it hard to sleep for fear of her dreams. As a child, she'd remembered nothing but the blackness and the feeling of her head in a wooden block, and her teachers were ashamed of her. Even Pandana had said, "Surely you remember something apart from that?"

She would not be that way with these children.

The whole community slept out by the stone. They were given a sweet, hot drink to help them sleep and dream but still Lillah found it difficult. She went from child to child checking the covers, sweeping away insects.

In the morning the children compared dreams, each one bigger and better than the last. Lillah wondered if they were lying, if, perhaps, they dreamt blank and lied to cover it up.

Most people spent the day quietly.

The next night, Lillah noticed that the men were not always there, and she wondered where they went; gone quickly, back blinks later.

"Do they have a secret stash of wine?" she asked Phyto. He laughed. "They like to be able to control themselves, so they release their own seed to take away the desperate need."

Lillah knew that Phyto gave himself this privacy and she wondered if he would join them.

When Lillah finally took her lover, his penis was stretched, elongated, and she wondered if constant masturbation has an effect. The thought made her laugh until she cried, by which time he had left her alone in disgust.

He had a very deep cave, full of ghosts, he told her, haunted. The further you go in, the more ghosts. He said this in such a foolish way Lillah knew he was teasing.

"They are on you now," he said. Lillah laughed more; she had never met such a funny man. She knew there were no real ghosts there. She would smell them, she was sure. Feel them. She'd feel them in her hair and she would run so fast to the water to drown them her lover would not even see her go.

"You are very good with words. Why aren't you the Tale-teller? You could tell the Tree beautifully, I imagine."

"We have no Tale-teller. The moss-eaters don't like the idea. They say it bores the Tree and makes the Tree sleepy. A sleepy Tree will not produce moss."

"Have you never had a teller?"

"Oh, we've had them." He touched his ear. "But sometimes they disappear. There are no volunteers for the job now."

"How do they disappear? Do they leave anything behind?"

"Only blood," he said. Lillah could not tell what he thought of this; a bland look came over his face and he began to stroke her.

The old woman who had been following them finally caught them. It was not Melia's mother.

"I am heading for home," she said. She seemed very tired.

"What if it's closer the other way? Keeping the Tree to your right shoulder?"

"You have a sense of which way is closer. This way for me. This way to Bayonet." She smiled at Lillah. "You will walk one day. A long, long way."

A storm broke over Pinon and, following their nightmares, it made the children terrified. Morace was the bravest, singing songs, making them feel better.

The storm tossed up massive waves and the children, the teachers too, thought of sea monsters.

Lillah drew the map, but wrote these symbols onto the Tree as she passed through.

In her mapping, Lillah told the Tree: *Walking through the Tree does not feel natural. The Oldnew year stone is here and they are pleased with it, as pleased as they are of their moss that keeps us from child.*

Here, the Tree grows moss. Leaves moss-coloured and the Bark covered with moss.

Pinon — ARBORVITAE — *Aspen*

It was hard to leave the women of Pinon. Lillah said, "I really enjoyed being with them. Their joy in life, their humour, I think, when you get to know them, see beyond the seriousness, made them very easy to love."

Ster agreed. "I was tempted to stay," she said. "But I wanted to go with you. Help you."

"I could have stayed, too," Phyto said. "I almost felt I belonged there. But there is a deep loneliness in me. Something not met."

Borag began to cry. "I dreamed you were gone, Phyto. I dreamed you were taken by the sea monster."

"I dreamed the sea monster was made of giant Leaves," Zygo said.

"I dreamed that my mother grew Tree limbs and she held me close and the branches went up my nose," Morace said.

"I dreamed you climbed the Tree and threw

yourself off," Rubica said. "I dreamt the colours of it and I woke up feeling sick."

Musa said, "Rubica, no one is interested in your dreams. You brain isn't like everybody else's. Yours is like seaweed. You haven't been trained."

Rubica snarled. "I suppose you wish Gingko was still here. But she was so foolish she allowed herself to be killed by the Tree."

"I never knew Gingko," Musa said quietly.

The others were silent. The children touched their ears, hoping the Tree wouldn't hear Rubica and punish them all for her words.

"She died in the service of the Tree," Tamarica said. "She gave us great blessing."

"Blessings you need. There has been a lot of death, hasn't there? The child, Rham. Your lack of care for her means you have no right to instruct me."

The teachers felt under attack with this. As if there was not enough guilt already.

Phyto walked ahead of them; when they caught up with him he was pale, shaky. Too cold to speak, although the weather was not so freezing.

"I'm lonely," he told Lillah. "I'm aching with loneliness."

"We're here."

"You are very dear, but I am out of my place. I want to race ahead, be with those people."

"You should walk ahead, then. Really, we are slow. I'm surprised you haven't walked on before.

It will take us over a year to reach Osage."

"I felt like you needed me."

"I love having you around but I know you need to go."

Lillah could see that Phyto had trouble sleeping. She and Tamarica kept him company, watching the moon light the sea.

"Are you thinking so much of Osage?" Lillah asked him.

"I've placed so much expectation on the place. What if I don't like them? What if they're awful men?"

"They can't be," Tamarica said. She dusted sand off his face, rubbed red powder onto his cheekbones. Practicing for arrival in so many months.

He pushed her hand away. "I want to arrive as a man. If these are my people, they will accept me for that."

Later, he said to Lillah, "I think Tamarica is interested in me as a lover. Doesn't she realise I don't want her?"

Lillah laughed. "She has no interest in you at all, you fool. Haven't you noticed? She's like you. She doesn't want a lover on the other side. She wants a lover like her. She wants a woman."

Phyto stood at the Order's edge. "You are closer now, Phyto," Lillah said. "Closer to where you should be. I wish I could watch you arrive at Osage."

"What if they think I'm ugly and dull?"

"Not possible, Phyto. And I think you should take the shells we have carried from Ombu to give to them. I think it is best if you do it."

They hugged each other, treasuring this rare friendship.

"Stay safe, Lillah. Keep Morace safe. Perhaps he will do something great; perhaps not. But don't give him up."

"I won't. I'll get a message to you somehow."

The air felt odd; the wet season should have come but hadn't. The air felt strangely dry.

"There are people in the next Order who can't hear," Ster said to the children as they walked. "They are quite isolated and don't have a lot of communication with other Orders."

"What do you mean they can't hear?"

"Their ears don't work. There is only silence in their heads." The children were silent then, imagining.

"I wonder if it's Spikes that took their hearing," Rubica said. "Should we walk straight past?"

"No, they are born that way. They don't fall ill," Ster said.

No one had told them what to do in this situation.

They came across a wall of rock from the water to the Tree. Some large rocks but mostly small, rising higher than their heads, unstable. Sticks ranged along the base of the wall, poking up like seagrass. Light along the top reflected off the small shells stuck there.

"We can't climb that," Rubica said.

"We'll wait till the tide's out and paddle around if we can," Lillah said. "It will only be a few hours." She felt like the mother to them all, having been with the school since the start. It hurt to see the children attaching themselves to the other teachers, because she wanted them to love her, rely on her. And she hoped they remembered their departed teachers Erica, Gingko and Thea. Melia and Agara, the women she grew up with and would never see again unless they safely made it back to Ombu once their children were reared. Most believed you should let people go, let memory drift. It was easier that way.

But to forget her mother? For Morace to forget his? When both had died so wrongly, when there had been no time to say goodbye? That she didn't think was possible.

The bigness of the wall filled her, gave her that sense of vastness she sometimes experienced, a sense of every space filled with bigness. The Tree filled so much of her vision, and yet she had seen only the bark. The outside, the surface.

The children built a house with small rocks while they waited for the tide to shift. They went at it with such determination the teachers were struck quiet, watching them with great pride.

Later, they gathered their things high on their shoulders and picked their way carefully around the edge of the wall.

On the other side, a man sat in a thick wooden chair, looking out to sea.

He rose when he saw them, lifted his arms in greeting.

"Welcome to Arborvitae. You will find us a pleasant place to visit."

Lillah exchanged a look with Tamarica. Why would the man be here to greet them alone?

"I am one who uses my ears and tongue. There are more like me, many more not. We communicate differently here. You will understand. You must have patience, as will we. We only talk if we have something to say. We do not discuss the weather unless it will affect the way we spend our day. And we do not discuss our food unless it is poisoned. The silence is not caused by Spikes; you are risking nothing by entering."

"The feast is going to be fun, I can tell," Musa muttered.

"You are such a happy being. I'm so glad you took the place of my best friend Melia."

"Oh, yes, the wonderful Melia, who cares so little she stayed in a place full of death without a care for you."

Lillah realised this was true and it filled her with fury. "She deserted us, didn't she?"

"She did. You should be happy she is gone, Lillah.

I will always be a better friend to you. I will be honest and true, even if you don't like what I have to say."

"You know that one of the reasons Melia stopped at Alga was to get away from you? She hated you that much."

"That says more about her than it does about me."

Their spokesman led them towards the Tree; the limbs here were hung with broken branches, tied on with seaweed.

"No ghosts here," Tamarica said. "Plenty of protection." Around a large home, the people sat. They opened theirs mouths without sound and used their fingers as signals.

"They are happy to see you," the spokesman said.

One skipped forward and threw a pile of sticks to the ground. They squatted around the sticks, pointing and smacking their lips together.

"They are deciding what next. Feast or bathe," the spokesman said.

"I'm hot and sticky," Morace said. "I'd like a bath first."

The spokesman put his fingers over his lips. "The sticks will decide."

The sticks called bathing, so they went to the water's edge. Huge baskets appeared, with light, rough stones for scrubbing, sweet smelling oils.

They stepped into the water. Lillah swam under the surface while she could hold her breath, happy to be in her own world.

She banged into something in the water, something that rattled and she opened her eyes under water. A cage. Inside; two feet, green and white in the water, pockmarked with dissolved skin.

Lillah choked, rose to the surface.

The woman in the cage screamed, screamed, cowered away from Lillah.

"Monster! Monster!"

Her panic calmed Lillah.

"I'm not. I'm Lillah. I'm a teacher. Sorry I banged into you."

The woman kept screaming, mouth open. The spokesman swam over to say, "Don't talk to her. Her head is done with."

"Why is she jailed?"

The spokesman shook his head. "We don't discuss the crime. It gets no hearing here." But later, someone whispered, "She had love while her father was in the village. Can you imagine breaking such a taboo?"

The sticks were thrown again for the feast and to decide who would be the storyteller. It was Lillah.

Welcomefire first; the morning-after moss exchanged for a perfectly carved wheel and the coloured sand, sent by one of the mothers of Ombu, given to a grateful relative.

"The people of Parana told me the story of why they acknowledge the fire. They said their ancestor gave them great gifts. He showed them how to use hot stones for cooking. He had very hot thighs and he could warm his hands between them then heat the stone. They say he was so disgusted with his apprentices, he did not teach them the art.

"He drowned when the sea monster sucked his limbs off so he couldn't save himself. Those are the words they used. Then the lesson of the hot stones was lost for many years."

The Order nodded politely, but Lillah knew she had not told the story well. Then one of them stood up and showed her how to do it.

"There was once an island full of stones, each stone tall as a Tree. Each stone pouring out a deep well of sap because beneath the sand grew Trees, upside down, reaching into the underworld. In the underworld were men of power and hearing, noise and calm. They lived lives of taking, nothing belonging. Above ground only the stones, barren ground, no place for a child. Then one day an underground woman tired of the men there. Men there did not respect the women. They would use them, mistreat them. The woman decided to move above ground, but she did not realise that the pressure of the air up there would take her hearing. Deafened, she made sure the other women underground knew the choice they would be making if they joined her. The sacrifice they would be making. But they didn't care. They would prefer not to hear than to live with those men any longer."

• • •

"Come and look, Lillah," Morace said. "They are making a great wheel turn using fast-running water."

"What is the point in that?"

"They say the wheel could turn the spit for the meat, or a wheel to spin a pot. They say when they get it right it will mean more rest for everyone." The wheel was like the one they had been given at welcomefire and they realised its great worth.

Lillah was entranced by such cleverness, and she wished she could stay forever to observe it. They were too sickly, though. They had damaged ears, and they were weak, and they couldn't think clearly, some of them. In other Orders these people would have been treated as ill. Lillah thought of Morace, though she hated to. If he was really sick, what would she do? She couldn't bring Spikes to an Order or they would end like this one.

Their spokesman stretched up and plucked down a spider as big as his hand. He let it crawl over his arm, up to his shoulder. Then he plucked at it, pulled off the legs.

He held the spider over a flame; ate it.

The others watched in horror. "You can't eat a spider."

"They do," he said. He pointed into a cave, poked his head in there. "They eat spiders. I've heard them talking about it."

The teachers and children backed away from him, horrified. All but Morace, who stayed to ask him questions.

The main house had a veranda like the main house in Ombu. Lillah had not seen this elsewhere; other Orders thought it used too much precious wood.

But Ombu had received a great wave of planks, some coloured with flaky green, flaky red. They used the wood well.

"We receive a lot of drift-in wood. We think our inlet calls for wood," the spokesman said.

Lillah felt at home on the veranda. Nice to sit up and look out.

The sand was oily here, damp and greasy to the touch. The children moulded round balls out of it and they held together.

The wall of rocks on the other side of the Order was even higher. Here, children and young men climbed to the top. They had pressed sticks, sap and seaweed between the gaps to make it sturdy. Morace and the other children climbed up too, the effort wearying Morace so he looked pale and weak by the time he came back down. Zygo climbed up, down, up and down, shouting with his vigour, showing his power.

The teachers lost all caution when they spoke. They forgot who could hear and who couldn't, and for a while spoke freely. Then, after three days in the place, they felt a quiet peace descend. They spoke less, gestured some, but mostly they let natural teamwork take over. This had happened to those women who chose to stay in the community. Some had forgotten how to speak, others chose not to.

Lillah missed Melia again, knowing she would have loved this Order.

A great bough cracked and fell to earth. No one was hurt; a line of sticks had kept people out of the area. These people knew wood, knew the Tree, they knew when a bough would fall. They had to; they couldn't always hear it.

The spokesman told them, "It means there is a lack of purity amongst us. Don't take it to heart; a branch will often fall when we have a school to visit. It is the different way of thinking. Of behaviour."

They set up a fire and one of the young men walked along the trunk. He found dark red twigs and tossed them into a pile; Lillah picked one up and smelt it. There was a perfume, a rich scent.

"These twigs grow in that place only. They are very strong and will only snap when there is need of a purifying fire."

They built the talkfire. The smoke was thick and seemed to take the shape of a man.

"All is well," the spokesman said. "We are purified."

Lillah watched the young firemaker, and she thought he would be her lover as he took up a piece of wood and began to carve it. She marvelled at his gentle, clever hands. Many of them had huge carved bowls from one piece of fallen wood.

She stood close to him, letting her thighs touch his back.

"That's beautiful. My father makes cradles."

"He can't hear you, Lillah." The spokesman cupped his hands over his ears. "We are lucky here. The wood is drier, so the boughs drop off more easily. They are larger. We can do good work," he said.

The worker put down his tools. His cheeks were red and there was a sheen of sweat on his shoulders. His shyness, his lack of confidence, was odd. He took her hand. The spokesman walked with them.

"Do you have caves here?" Lillah said.

"We do. But the heat is too great there in the Tree. We like our huts better."

"But it's cold out here. Warmth would be good."

"That isn't warmth. It's heat. Burning fire to frizzle your hair away."

"Where does the heat come from?"

"From the eternal fire. The undousable flame. The Tree burning from within, and one day the Tree will crumble to grey ash. Only those connected to the Earth will survive. We keep our feet touching the earth. Some part of us connected to the earth at all times. We carry a sack with a pinch of dirt if we need to, so that we always touch dirt."

Lillah had noticed they were always barefoot.

"Because all was created from the Tree. A great woman stood still for so long her toenails grew and took root in the earth. We do not walk on the sea or climb the Tree."

"Why did she stand still for so long?"

"She waited for her lover to return from his bath in the sea. But the monster took him and spat out his bones."

Her lover rubbed his face against her cheek and she pulled away from its scratchiness. He laughed. Most men had soft facial hair or nothing at all.

"I'll leave you now. You seem to be communicating well enough." There was bitterness in the spokesman's voice. Always talking, never loving.

Her lover took up a knife made from sharpened shell and rubbed his chin with oil. He dragged the knife across his skin; Lillah flinched to watch it, but he didn't cut himself.

He rubbed his face into her thighs. Smooth, oh, very smooth. The silent loving was long and sweet.

The children were very disturbed by the jailed woman. They sat by the water's edge, watching. Sometimes crying. Finally Musa approached the spokesman.

"Is there chance of her release soon?"

"Release?" He shook his head. "Usually they are dead before there is any talk of release."

"It upsets the children. I know that won't and shouldn't effect your decision, but it would be good to pass along with a positive memory of Arborvitae."

"You don't feel positive?"

Musa looked at him. She had not experienced the bad men of Douglas but had heard about them many times. She knew about men wheedling and whining to be chosen, using pity, taking advantage.

She didn't care for the jailed woman but she cared that the children were distressed.

"How much power do you have here?"

"I am the one who speaks. I have power," the spokesman said.

"Then please," Musa said. She stroked his hand. Grasped his thigh. It was too easy. "Please, consider setting her free."

The sticks were thrown and it was decided: the jailed woman would be released.

They winched the cage to shore. The woman whimpered, screamed, rattled at the cage. Her skin was burnt red, peeled off, her hair a wild mess of knots and filth.

"What will she do?" Tamarica asked the spokesman.

"That's up to her. She may wish to walk home. We certainly won't stop her."

Lillah's lover opened the cage door, and they stepped back. The woman cowered in there, her feet pulled up.

Ster walked to the cage and reached out a hand. "Come on. It's all right." The woman took her hand and crawled out. She couldn't stand: her feet were rotted, her legs weak from lack of use.

"Help me," Ster said, and Tamarica helped to carry the woman to the talkfire. Someone placed a stone in her hand, not smoothstone but smooth enough.

The Order ignored them, went on with their work.

"Can you hear?" Ster said. The woman nodded. She opened her mouth to speak but her mouth was dry from the screaming. Lillah brought her fresh water and she took it greedily.

They sat with her for a while, as none of the locals would. She began to talk, when she could, and it was complaints. She said she had been jailed for ignoring the sticks, for being too loud, for talking too much. How can they lock you up for talking too much, destroy you damage you finish you end you destroy you for talking?

The teachers tired of the sound of her voice. They soothed her one last time and moved away.

The rain began, a gentle mist. The people stood out in it, palms upwards, reading it, it seemed. Looking for future in the water droplets. The whole community came out for this, including some older children the teachers had not seen before.

"There are children here ready for school," Musa said to the spokesman. He could not take his loving eyes off her. "You need to prepare."

"We can't think who should be our teachers. We can't take the leap of faith required to send the children away for so long."

"They will not survive, then. Your Order will die. Nobody will choose such a place."

"Help us, then. Help us choose our teachers."

Lillah and the other teachers discussed it and agreed to help. They already knew which women they preferred; it was not a difficult choice.

The locals gave them a pouch of dirt to take. A comfort for them; always connected to the earth.

In her mapping, Lillah told the Tree: *Jailed woman talks too much, water used to make things move, all decisions by sticks. It makes no sense the smart in one the not smart in the other.* Lillah added to her map: *Rock Wall three people high.*

Here, the Tree grows sharp, bitter apples. The leaves are crisp and the Bark soft and wet.

Arborvitae — ASPEN — *Sargassum*

Lillah told the children Phyto had moved ahead and they were all unhappy, though they had talked about it at Arborvitae and expected it. Zygo was the most upset. "He was a good man. He taught me a lot."

"He's not dead. You'll see him at Osage."

Morace said, "He was a good listener. They will be lucky to have him." He looked at Lillah and she wondered if he meant to say that she did not listen so well.

The long walk seemed even longer without Phyto.

It would be seventy days before they reached Aspen.

As the school approached Aspen the sand squeaked. It gave a sense of cleanliness, and they tidied themselves. They stopped to comb the knots from their hair and change their clothing. Borag, who had grown more serious since Rham's death, helped each teacher with her grooming.

"One day this will be you," Musa said. "You will be dressing for a lover."

"Not me. I'm going to stay home, where it's safe."

Lillah pulled her hair back into a bushy tail and said, "Right, Let's go."

The sand was dry, soft. So very different from Sapin's Order.

Lillah dawdled back from the others, thinking of her lover, how he had looked into her eyes, made them connect in a way she could never forget.

News came to them of Erica. Lillah did not want to hear it. Erica had caught child, and she was happy. She would call the child Rham. She sent message to say that she felt gifted to be there, that no other place on Botanica could be so good.

"That isn't news! Why are you telling us? That is just an opinion," Musa said, irritated.

The messenger shook his head. "That is the information I received."

They were asked to bathe on arrival. The people here walked lightly, airily. They didn't stand too close together for fear of transferring sweat. They spoke in soft voices and every word was gentle.

In preparation for the feast, shells tied on strings were draped around the Tree. Fish bones on strings hung around the doorways. They were cautious here not to damage the Trunk. They did not like to spill the sap.

One man sat on a low branch, playing the flute, making it sound like the sweetest bird you ever heard. Rubica gave them the wheel and received a wooden flute in return.

The children did not fight; they seemed to want to avoid the usual childhood arguments. Even Zygo seemed peaceful, unwilling to make his usual comments. He started up a game with the other children, a gentler version of one he'd learned along the way.

Men and women sat together weaving leaf plates. They used soft leaves so they layered them, many on top of each other, and held them together with long thorns.

Before each meal, they bathed. Chattering and laughing, all problems solved, a simple wash to cleanse the body.

"They're washing again," Lillah muttered to Morace. "Look at them."

Morace nodded. He was a kind boy, Lillah knew, and she treated him too much like an adult confidante. "My mother didn't like to wash. She said your skin shed itself naturally and that washing removed too many layers of skin at once. She said clean people got sick much more easily."

Morace seemed angry as he said this, not sad. He rolled his shoulders, as if feeling the bones.

"We don't need to bathe this time. Let's wander along the Tree Trunk. I haven't seen where the spiders are yet."

No one noticed as they walked away. Lillah felt a deep sense of peace, walking with her half-brother.

"Look!" he said. Ropes dangled down from high branches. They looked at each other.

"I'm going to climb the ropes, see where they go," Lillah said.

"Me, too." Morace jumped up, rubbing his hands together.

"No, you should go and eat. You need the food."

"I feel sick in my stomach. I don't want food."

Lillah placed her hand on his belly. She reached in her pocket and took out a small, smooth pebble.

"Suck on this. It'll stop you feeling sick."

He took it obediently and Lillah knew then that, in an emergency, he would follow her instructions without question.

"I still don't want to eat," he said.

Lillah took his hand and led him to the first rope. "Can you reach? Can you do this?"

Together they climbed up. Looked out. There was a ghost hole up there, which terrified Lillah. There were noises in there, voices. She scratched her legs in the scramble to get down.

"Don't climb down, Lillah! I want to look more!"

"You explore, Morace. I am not as keen on ghosts as you are."

Morace laughed. "Lillah, you are too frightened. Stay!"

She climbed to a lower branch, stopping to notice that the Bark there was red, dripping with sap.

"What's the matter with the Tree?" Lillah called down to a young man below.

"Nothing. That's what it looks like."

"But the rest of your Order is terrified of damaging the Tree. The Bark is stripped here."

"We don't need to follow all the Order does." He reached up and pulled a strip down which he let fall, wasted.

"You can't do that to the Tree. You're damaging it." Lillah jumped down and assessed him. Strong, with lively eyes and a smile he showed. He was good to look at and a talker, too.

"It's huge, in case you hadn't noticed. It's not going to be hurt by one small strip. My brother is digging out a tunnel. He says we need a place to run in case someone decides our place is desirable and they want it for themselves."

"You would run and hide? Not stay and fight?"

He looked at her, curious. "Of course we run and hide. Then when they are sleeping we sneak out and fill their mouths and noses with sand." From his pocket he pulled a handful, which he let spill in a stream.

"I've never heard anyone talk of stealing this place. It has barely been mentioned."

"It wouldn't be," he said, gesturing towards Arborvitae. "Hiding behind that wall as they do.

And they wouldn't there," here he pointed on to Sargassum, the next Order,. "Because they live in a beautiful place full of sun and are very happy."

Lillah knew they believed gods lived in the sun.

The young man made some love magic. A gentle touch with twigs. He laid them over the door to his cave and the magic worked. Lillah overcame her usual fear on entering a Tree cave. She did not like to be on the inside of the Tree. She felt as if she were entering its veins, swimming in its blood. Climbing through its bones. She felt as if she should not be there.

"It must be hard to be away from home." He twirled Lillah's hair in his fingers.

"It is. Don't you remember what it was like when you travelled with your school? And how it felt to reach home again?"

"I do remember. I remember thinking that I would not like to leave home again."

They sat in silence. "Where is your brother? I haven't seen him."

"He's not very sociable. Not in big groups. But he likes small gatherings. Shall I call him to us?"

Lillah felt a flutter of excitement, a rush of blood. She knew that some teachers took two lovers at once; she never had.

"Call him in," she said. "I'd like to hear about his tunnels."

The brother was a broad, muscly man with scar tissue running over both shoulders and down to his nipples. His hair was straight and long. He looked at her from under it.

"Hello, teacher," he said. She stood up. He bent down; she kissed him. His lips were soft but firm and very warm. He reached around to grab her buttocks and lifted her that way, high so that she didn't have to stretch her neck.

His brother stroked her hair as the kiss went on, and her neck, a gentle, feathery touch which made her shiver with delight.

The kiss broken, the three looked at each other and laughed.

Big brother knelt to the floor, still holding her, and between them they removed her clothes and stroked and kissed her from head to toe.

She reached for the smaller brother and bade him to lie down, then she straddled him and let him enter her. His brother knelt behind, raising bumps on her flesh.

The big brother bade her lie down and he entered her that way. He was bigger than his brother, harder, and she gasped. There seemed to be no competition between them. They were happy to work together.

Afterwards, they lay there together and the brothers spoke of their irritation with the Order – how the rest of them were weak, ready to run, would not protect their village, hurt anyone to save it.

The brothers thought the village was worth killing and dying for.

It was a very different attitude to the rest of the Order, who were so fearful of people disappearing they would not fight anything. They said they had lost three to the Tree; three disappeared inside never to be seen again.

Lillah thought of Rham, never to grow up, and of Thea and Gingko, grown and gone, never to be mothers.

She wanted to stay. She liked the Order and she liked the brothers, but they were only two Orders from Gulfweed. She thought, "I will make Morace safe. Hand him over to his relatives. Then I can come back.

Lillah and Morace held hands as they left. Another Order that hadn't made the connection between Morace and a woman dying in Ombu. Another time safe. Ster walked with them, too. She had gained strength, no longer mouthing Lillah's opinion. She took the lead more often and Lillah thought she would be welcomed in an Order where a leader was needed.

Lillah wondered, as she had many times, what she was doing. All her learning told her that if Morace was sick, he needed to be sacrificed. But she didn't believe that. She didn't believe that he could cause destruction.

• • •

"This is a beautiful place. So peaceful," Tamarica said. Lillah nodded. To Tamarica, any place where the men weren't cruel was peaceful.

In her mapping, Lillah told the Tree: *Lovely brothers go to war, lovely brothers so nice together.*

Here, the Tree grows red fruit. The leaves are small and dense and the Bark drips red sap.

Aspen — SARGASSUM — *Gulfweed*

The market between Aspen and Sargassum was lively, full of laughter. People were different away from their homes. Some became dour and complaining, others seemed free of constraints and expectations and all the better for it. With only a two week walk, people travelled there often.

It still seemed strange to be walking without Phyto. Zygo in particular seemed downhearted.

"I hope he's all right. I wish he could have walked with us all the way home."

"He has his life to follow. We were lucky to have him for as long as we did. He liked being around us, I think. He learnt a lot from you, too, Zygo."

"This is where Aquifolia's mother lives. She came from here." Lillah said as they approached Sargassum. She wondered how poor, lonely Aquifolia was. Unloved forever, not even liked particularly well. But then, no, she had married Araucari and they were happy, Lillah was sure. He was a good man even without use of his legs.

They saw the Order ahead and before it, the sand white and full of glare. It was odd; a bad omen.

Morace ran ahead. "It's fish doors. All of it! Have you ever seen such a thing?"

It was, too, the small white shell circles. Lillah had only seen scattered dozens before. Here, there were millions. Lillah and the other teachers did not remember such a thing from when they were students.

The children, amazed by the shells, ran through them. Ran their fingers through them and collected them in massive piles.

Ster and Lillah watched together. "I remember finding this Order strange," Ster said.

"In what way?"

"They seemed to know so much. They often knew what we would say and they seemed to know what would happen before it happened. They were never taken by surprise by Leaffall. Or by Spikes."

"What are you telling me?"

"I'm telling you that here we need to be careful. These people, of everywhere you or I have been, understand each other. They understand us. They are not as caught up in their own existence as most others on Botanica. They know people and remember the things they have heard."

"The messenger would not have bothered to tell them about Rhizo, surely," Lillah said. "They would

not be interested in the death of a woman they
don't know."

"They are interested in all deaths. And she is
from the next Order, don't forget. They may know
her in some way."

They spent the night near the sea doors because the
children seemed to love being around them and
they had few joys. Lillah felt nervous. She saw
them as a bad omen, as did the other teachers, but
she didn't want to share that nervousness with the
children.

The Bark here was pale, almost luminous. Green
onion shoots grew amongst the roots, so they had
a tasty meal of flavourful fish.

"In the morning we will walk into Sargassum,"
Lillah said. "I know a woman who came from
there. She settled in my Order. She is the one who
burnt me."

She showed them her arm

"Why did she burn you?"

"She didn't like me much," Lillah said. "That's
what I always believed. She said it was a message
for her Order; I guess we'll find out."

As they were settling to sleep, they heard, "Lillah!"

"Who knows you here?" Tamarica said.

"No one! Who could know me here?"

"Lillah!" they heard again. In the falling dark, a
young woman came to them under the trunk.

"Nyssa!" Lillah ran over to her childhood friend and they swung each other around joyfully.

"You look the same! I knew you straight away!"

"You, too!"

"And this is your school?"

"This is them."

"And which one is the young boy in your especial care?"

Lillah didn't speak. The teachers and students stared at Nyssa.

She said, "Sorry. Sorry. We were told…but you can find out that later. Are you going to join us tonight?"

Lillah noticed her friend had burn scars on the backs of her hands and wrists.

"Did you have an accident? Are you all right?"

"No, they burn deliberately here. They can read the scars, tell your future."

Lillah remembered dismissing this talk from Aquifolia.

"Do they really believe that?"

"They know you are coming. With him. Not your name, of course. They're not good on the details. But they saw running big and running small."

"We are not running," Lillah said.

"I'm not small, I'm almost fourteen," Morace said. Lillah pinched him to be quiet.

"You are. Of course you are. Big man," Nyssa said. "Come on, let's sit amongst the branches, Lillah. We can talk."

They held hands to help each other climb up. They talked of Nyssa's life, her husband, the child she had caught.

Then Nyssa said, "Lillah, we don't see everything. But we do see some. We don't know why you are in danger. But we see that you are."

"What should we do? Will they help us or hurt us? Should we walk on?" Lillah gave up any thought of pretence, although she didn't tell Nyssa of Rhizo's death and their fears for Morace's health.

"Don't walk on. They won't hurt you here, not tonight and not for the next while. Aquifolia's mother Maringa wants to see you. She leads us in many ways. She told me to bring you to her when you arrived."

"But will she help or hurt? Nyssa?"

"We have to trust her, Lillah."

She led them through the thick low branches of the Tree. They could hear some quiet voices, but not many.

"They're mostly on the outskirts, building a welcoming shelter for your school. They like to build. And because one of us dreamed there was someone special in your school they are taking extra care. Do you think that it is true?"

Lillah's heart gave a flip; she could feel it. Was it her? Lillah? Would she do something the whole Tree would know about?

"I don't know. We're all special, aren't we?"

"Maringa is sleeping, now. It's ash sleep she's having; sometimes we put fresh ash under our pillows and have a dream-telling in the morning. I think she is struggling to know what to do about your arrival. In the meantime, my Order will welcome you all."

The shelter was built, lined with the white fish doors. The Order welcomed them all tiredly and it was decided to have welcomefire the next day.

"Are you hungry?" Nyssa asked them. They had eaten, but it seemed like many hours earlier.

Nyssa gave them bags of dried fruit to eat. It was perfect; the sweetness, a touch of saltiness and it filled them without bloating. More of the fruit would be exchanged at welcomefire in the morning for the flute they had been given in Aspen.

They rested then, in the temporary building made for them.

"I like it here," Borag said. "It has a good smell about it. I wonder whether they use that fruit in cooking?"

They talked amongst themselves for a while, then slowly drifted off.

When Nyssa called them, Lillah rubbed at her eyes, feeling like she'd slept for blinks only.

"Maringa is awake. It's dark out. Come on." Lillah pushed Morace awake, and they followed Nyssa down to the water's edge, moonlight path for them to walk. A woman sat hunched over, way out on the seawalk, unmoving.

"Is she okay?" Lillah asked. She could hardly talk for the fear that filled her. She thought, "Run. Run. Take him home," but home was still so far away. And home may not be safe; home may still hurt them both.

"She's fine. Walk out to her."

Maringa turned as she approached. Aquifolia had warned Lillah of the disfigurement, but Lillah had imagined something like Aquifolia's own face; small patches of shiny skin on the face.

This woman had been burnt over and over again. There was no skin on her face that wasn't shiny and pink or scabby. Morace gasped in horror.

"Lillah," she said. "Step forward."

She took Lillah's arm and ran her fingers over the scar tissue. "You came from Ombu, didn't you?" Lillah nodded, not really wanted to admit this. "My daughter stopped with you. Aquifolia. She always promised to send us a gift. We haven't seen it yet." Lillah thought guiltily of the parcel she'd thrown away. She shouldn't have done that.

"She didn't send anything," Lillah said.

"Really?" Maringa closed her eyes and touched the scars on Lillah's arms. "You know my daughter then? Aquifolia? Were you kind to her?"

Lillah nodded. "She helped us prepare for school. She stopped in our Order because she felt comfortable there. She has made a lover with a very good man. I know him. He is a good man."

"And yet she didn't send a gift for me?"

Lillah felt her whole body flush with guilt. She wanted to continue with her lie, but looked into Maringa's eyes and knew she would not be able to do that.

"I have done a very bad thing with that," she said. "Your daughter sent you some sticks, but I did not want to carry them. I discarded them. I thought I would collect more sticks before we reached here and that you would not know the difference."

Maringa stared at her. Maringa's face was almost all scar tissue and she did not smile. "I would have known the difference. Better to not receive the sticks at all than to receive a false message."

Lillah shivered. She had never felt so cold. So unprotected.

The woman lifted Lillah's arm and inspected it closely, sometimes touching her nose to the skin. "My daughter has given me something to read. You see now, she knew what she was doing. Fire is cleansing. She must care very deeply for you. I hope she does not know how little you care for her."

"I was always kind to her," Lillah said.

"Yes," she said. "Yes. I see you try to be kind. And you have kept this boy safe. But now is his truest danger."

"I don't think so," Lillah said. "We are almost at the Order of his mother. They will care for him there."

The woman stroked her arm again with a tenderness that made Lillah anxious.

"There is only one direction you can take. They are coming for him, and for you, too. You must enter the Tree."

Lillah began to cry. She had come to this woman for help, and while she had not really expected to be saved, she had hoped for a hint at what to do.

Not insanity. Not an impossibility.

"You must enter through the ghost cave, and make your way to the centre of the Tree. I can't tell you more; what is inside sits beyond my imagination. It is not evil, though. They wish you no ill."

"The ghosts? I can't go to the ghosts. You are a terrible woman. You are terrible and cruel. We came to you for help."

"Are they ghosts?" Maringa ran her lips along Lillah's scar tissue. "I do not believe they are. I believe they are people living inside, not ghosts."

"Of course they are ghosts. I've seen them. We've all seen them. They mean us no well. They hate us. They want to destroy us. Everybody knows this. Everybody."

"Lillah, if you don't risk entering the Tree you will die, and Morace will die, and they will probably kill your entire school as well for hiding you. They will kill me and all of my family. They will slice you open with far more violence than any ghost will, and they will find illness inside you, and they will kill anyone you have contacted. All your lovers, all your family. You will cause the deaths of many."

"But they will do that anyway."

"They will not do it without the proof. They will not do it without looking inside Morace for Spikes."

Lillah turned away. She ran down to the water, wanting to wash herself clean, wash away the past and all she knew.

"Do you think she's right, Lillah?" Morace said. His voice was quiet. Mature. There was nothing of the child in him now.

"No, I don't. Your people will welcome you and protect you. You'll see. She is an old woman with a scarred face and we need not listen to her."

The time spent at Sargassum went quickly. The children soon grew used to the scarred skin of the people, and Lillah caught Zygo with one of the younger women, carefully preparing to scar his arm.

"Do you think all women would like to see that?" she said, stopping him.

"All the good women would," he said, grinning at her.

Nyssa and Lillah spent all their time together. Lillah found lovers and enjoyed being with them, although their rough, scarred skin took some getting used to. Nyssa tried to convince her to stay and she knew, again, that once she took Morace home, she could choose to return to Sargassum and make her life there. She would be happy with Nyssa as a companion; the men would not matter so much then.

Morace spent too much time with Maringa. Lillah avoided the woman; she had stories to tell Lillah did not want to hear.

In her mapping, Lillah wrote: *Here the Tree grows pale and luminous and there are shells so white they make your eyes hurt. Here they see too much and know the same.*

Sargassum — GULFWEED — *Chrondus*

Lillah worried, as they neared Gulfweed, that Rhizo's people would be like Rhizo had been. Self-centred, self-serving. She worried that Maringa had been right, that they would hurt Morace.

"What do you think they'll be like, Morace? Will they know you?"

"Will they know you are my sister?"

"We will see, I guess. Do you think Rhizo always had this in mind? For us to use our blood connection when we need it most?"

"I don't know what she had in her mind. I think she just wanted to keep me close. Maringa says–"

"Let's not worry about what Maringa says until we arrive, Morace."

"We should be prepared."

"I am prepared," Lillah said, although she was not.

• • •

As they left the market very early in the morning, Morace could not contain his leaping. He was excited to be seeing his family.

"Your smoothstone? Do you have that?"

"Of course I have it. I will show my family and they will know me through it."

These were his people; he would be safe there. His grandmother, his uncles, all there to take the burden of responsibility from Lillah. She knew she would miss Morace if he stayed with his family but the thought of that burden lifting made her very happy.

The air seemed clear and the light golden, as if all was right with the world and there was nothing to worry about.

Lillah tried not to show her nervousness to the others, but she was terrified of how she would handle things at Gulfweed. She had to get it right, to win them over and make them believe her.

Outwardly she was buoyant, as they were whenever they approached a family Order. But here they would ask more questions, and Lillah would have to decide if she trusted them with the truth, with Morace's life.

An old woman followed them, a fair way in the distance, for their journey to Gulfweed.

"I think it's Maringa," Morace said.

"No, she wouldn't be leaving that place. Why would she leave it? They listen to her there. If she walked anywhere else she would be outcast."

There was no one to greet them. Morace looked at the sand, blinking, trying to hide tears.

"Aspen told us they rarely greet the schools," Lillah said. "They are too pleased with themselves and their sun.

"Maybe they don't know it's you," Lillah said, squeezing him. He winced, his flesh sensitive to the touch.

They entered the central area to find the people sat on a massive hollowed out piece of wood with a whale's tooth protruding from the bow.

Lillah called, "Please excuse us. We are a school set off from Ombu."

Three people stood up and stepped out of the massive canoe.

"Greetings, of course. Welcome. Please share our meal."

Tamarica whispered to Lillah, "They won't look us in the eye."

Morace clutched Lillah's hand. "Don't tell them who I am. I don't like them."

"Morace! Don't be foolish. You haven't spoken to them."

"They don't want us here. They don't."

"We are busy preparing for the drying season," the man said. "And we are not so good with strangers."

Lillah wondered if it was simply arrogance that made them that way.

Ster said, "What's going on? Do you want us to keep moving?"

"We are hospitable. It is strangers we are difficult with."

He looked the teachers in the eye.

"We are not all strangers," Lillah said.

"Please, Lillah," Morace begged. "Please."

Zygo whispered to her, "Don't tell them, Lillah. Not yet. Wait till we know them."

Ster said, "We are all of the Tree."

The brightness of the place was almost painful and very warm. The Tree looked odd from below, and the huge piece, long since collapsed, lay on the sand. They'd carved seats into it, and it was inside this huge piece of wood that sixty of them sat. Lillah could see old sap there, traces of it in the Bark, and she wondered if sitting here gave them strength, long life.

"When did this fall?"

"Three generations ago. There was a thundering that went on for a day, and then a great tearing. Many people left, camping along the beach. But others stayed, thinking this was a message from the Tree." He lowered his voice. "Eight were killed when it fell. They lie beneath this dugout. We have never recovered them. They were sacrificed to the Tree. They gave us the great future of the sun and the worship of those around us. Many wish to stay because of the sun." Rhizo had never mentioned this.

The Order nodded, muttered, went back to their food. Someone handed Tamarica a pot with a bubbling stew in it and some beautifully carved wooden plates. The people didn't want welcome-fire. "Gifts for all," they said. Rubica gave the dried fruits they had received in Sargassum to the children.

"These plates are lovely," Tamarica said.

"We are given gifts often."

They were not invited into the canoe, so they settled by the water's edge, enjoying the sun.

Morace took Ster's hand and kissed it. "Thank you, for not telling them," he said. He said the same to Zygo, without kissing him.

Lillah snapped her head around "For what? These are your people. You should tell them so."

Ster said, "They are acting strangely. We should understand them before we tell them anything."

"Maybe they're acting strangely because they think we're keeping something from them."

Morace breathed deeply, sucking in air noisily.

Ster put her arm around him. "I don't think they should know he's sick."

"He's not sick."

"Of course he is, Lillah. You've hidden it well, looked after him beautifully. But we are not fools. You have treated him differently all along because he is your half-brother and Spikes hangs over him like a cloud."

They ate in silence.

One of the men walked toward them carrying a wooden pitcher and mugs. He smiled at them as he poured out drinks. No one spoke.

"You're a quiet group," he said. "None of you speak."

"We speak. Our mouths are full."

The man placed the jug down in the damp sand. "Which of you is Morace, son of Rhizo our sister?" He stared into the faces of the boys. "Well?" He pointed to Morace. "You? You have her features."

The head father said, "We are sad to hear the news of Rhizo and her death. Her death so far way from us. We wish there was a different circumstance for your visit."

Morace cried quietly. One of the residents comforted him, but Lillah realised the person was squeezing him, seeking the lumps that would indicate he was Spikes-ridden.

"He's fine. He is very healthy," Lillah said, pulling him away. Morace wept more loudly now, all the fear and loss shaking his body.

He's only thirteen, Lillah thought. I expect him to act like a man, but he's only thirteen.

Morace was used to hiding his coughs with noises; he clapped his hands a lot. He made jokes. Made his coughs seem like laughs.

A messenger came to them. He wore flowers around his neck and the words he formed sounded difficult in his mouth, as if he did not understand them. He said he had news from Ombu.

"The man Dickson took a child to his cave and would not let her out."

The locals, hearing this, said, "A man from your Order did this?" to Lillah.

"The man Dickson kept the child for many days and then he killed the child."

"No! No! Killing a child!"

Lillah said, "Which child was it?" Not my nephew, she prayed.

She thought of Thea, her huge great hands, and the children who had suffered. She wondered if Dickson felt a similar guilt. If there was something in their blood to make them that way... she realised she didn't know where their mother was from.

"This is the place you came from?" Morace's grandmother asked him. "You knew this person?"

"Which child died?" Lillah asked the messenger. "Why did he take a child?" She wished one of her friends was with her, one of the women who knew Dickson and his foolishness, knew Ombu.

"Dickson was always rough with us," Zygo said. "He thought he was still a child."

The sadness of this made Lillah feel tired.

The locals watched Lillah. The other teachers didn't talk to her, though Musa didn't physically move away as the others did.

"We should know the story before we judge."

"We know the story."

• • •

After the meal, Lillah and Ster ventured on to the seawalk.

"You are wrong that I treat Morace differently."

"So if the seawalk was to collapse, and all of us dumped into the sea monster's bathwater, who would you save? Morace, or one of the other children?"

Lillah didn't speak, although she knew the answer. Morace would be right beside her and he would cling to her whether she wanted to save him or not.

The Tale-teller, tall with rough skin like Bark, leaned up against the Bark, his lips pressed into a knot hole.

Lillah crept up to listen.

"We have Morace, son of Rhizo, here with Spikes. Rhizo died of it and we have no sorrow for that. She was not a good woman. We have sorrow for Morace but need to treat him regardless of pity."

Later, the Tale-teller said, "We will give him tonight because he is Rhizo's son. But we will not be the ones to break the way. In the morning his illness must be treated."

Morace started crying. "Lillah?" he said.

She took his hand. She knew that this was an important moment; she needed to do exactly the right thing or Morace would be lost.

"It's okay, Morace. They'll be gentle. We've known this was coming for a very long time." She held him to her chest to keep him quiet.

"Sleep well then. Good dreaming."

The school was left alone. No one spoke. They prepared for bed as if nothing new would happen in the morning, but Borag and the other children slept close to Morace. Lillah noticed they turned their backs to him, as if avoiding breathing his breath. As if suddenly what was in him could kill them.

Lillah wondered if they cared at all. She remembered treatments in her own Order, how the crying had been disturbing but how she had never felt she had to act.

That night, with the children asleep, the adults told terrible tales.

They told the story of a man at sea, a friend of the sea monster bringing shame to all. Lillah thought they meant her uncle Legum, but she did not say. There was reason enough for violence here.

"And now," the headfather said, "Now the treatment must begin."

"No! You said in the morning!" Lillah said.

"Now."

They walked to the place Morace slept and they gently carried him from his bed and laid him on a flat, long wooden table. He woke as they did so, feeling the salt breeze, hearing the voices.

"What? What?" he said. Lillah took his hand, tried to tug him.

"Can you run? We'll run," she said desperately, but she knew they couldn't. She knew she should have taken him before, she should not have listened to the stories but taken him and run.

"We begin tonight and we will treat this boy for ten nights. On the eleventh night we will join him with the Tree and all will be well."

The headfather took out a large, sharp shell. Morace screamed as they held him down.

Lillah threw herself on top of him. Tamarica and Ster pulled her backwards. "We must accept, Lillah. We must. This is their way."

"We must not accept!" she called, but they held her back, covered her mouth. Three men held her and she hated their smell, she vomited at their feet but they were not bothered.

"You are sick too, perhaps?" they said.

"He is not sick!"

Morace screamed, terrible, full of pain. She could not see what they were doing.

"They've sliced some flesh from his thigh. A chunk. Oh my Tree, it's bleeding."

"Let me get the webs. Let me go," Lillah snarled. They let go her arms and she ran into the branches, seeking the spiders she knew spun there. Greedily she grabbed all she could find.

They had staunched the flow with leaves. Lillah pressed the webs on top of the leaves and stroked Morace. He was pale in the moonlight and seemed sleepy.

"Rubica gave him some tea, Lillah. He is not feeling the pain now. Tomorrow, when they take more of him, he will feel great pain. With pain comes cure," the headfather said. "You may take him now. He will need rest for tomorrow."

Lillah and Ster carried Morace back to his bed. The other children murmured but didn't speak.

"I warn you again, Lillah. They will kill him and all of you."

Lillah spun at the sound of the voice. Maringa.

"You are a ghost," Lillah said to Maringa.

"No, I am not. But I will be if you don't listen to me and I will haunt you and yours for all the life of the Tree."

"Lillah, I'm scared. I wish Rham was here. She would know what to do," Morace said sleepily.

Lillah wanted to hit him, drown him. Years of care and protection and he thought Rham would be the one to know what to do.

She rose above those feelings and said, "Let's go, Morace. Now. We will run, run to Ombu. We will keep ahead of them."

"I will say goodbye to everyone then we'll go."

"No, we can't alert them. We'll see them at home. They understand. They know your life is important," Lillah said.

All they needed to do was stay ahead. That was all. If they ran for fifteen hours a day, they would manage that.

They could be home in nine months.

She felt a deep ache in her cheekbones, along her jaw line; the strain of smiling when she felt like screaming.

"Lillah," Maringa said.

"I don't know how to keep him safe any longer. I'm so sorry to put this on you. We don't know what Rhizo, his mother, died of, but she was worried he would have it, too. She wasn't going to send him to school but knew that at home, in our own Order, they would be more alert to his health. And to hers. She knew he would be killed if he stayed at home. She is not my mother. My mother went walking. Is… dead. But Morace and I share a father. I feel great responsibility for him. We've done so well, but Rhizo is dead now and it's like a power, a protection, is gone. We think Morace may be sick."

Lillah felt great relief to be telling this at last.

"Regardless of the effect on an Order? You save him at the risk of many others falling ill?"

Lillah said, "I don't believe he will infect people."

"That I can't see. But I tell you, Lillah; you must go into the Tree. I am no longer seeing the future. I am seeing the present. Now."

Morace said, "I don't want to die, Lillah. I am not going to lie down and die. Let's just go and look, at least. Just look."

"I will not."

Maringa held out her hand to Morace and they walked together to the ghost cave. Morace limping, his hand gently holding his thigh.

"Morace!" Lillah followed them. She could hardly see through her tears, and her legs provided shaky support. She felt as if her body were going to give up, that she would collapse. They were going into the Tree.

The entrance to the ghost cave rattled with hanging bones.

As they stood beneath the Tree, Maringa gave Morace a small sack of stones. "All are marked. You pull one out when you need help and you will know what to do. This one, you send to me and I will know you are well. And do not lose your smoothstones. They are part of your identity. Learn all you can. Remember all you can. One day you will be Tale-teller, Lillah; these are the stories you will tell."

Tale-teller, Lillah thought. Why not?

Lillah wished it was Musa and not her standing here. Thea, or Melia, or anyone, anyone but her. She wished she could sink into the sand and die rather than go into the ghost cave.

I remember in Aspen, how calm and peaceful they were, she thought. The brothers, with their words of war, were still gentle and filled with love not hate. I should have stayed with them. I could have been happy there.

But Morace coughed and she thought of how easily they had cut his flesh, how little they cared for his pain. How the people around him cringed away, lifted their shoulders to avoid him, and she knew that she was the only one to protect him.

He climbed into the ghost cave.

"We are just looking, Morace. We are thinking."

"We have to go in, Lillah. We have to. I am going with or without you. But I want you to come." He reached his hand out to her. "Please, Lillah. Please. You know I am not as scared of ghosts as you. I don't believe they want to hurt us. Please come with me. I will be too scared to go alone but I will have to. I don't want to die and I don't want them to slice me open. I don't want to be looked at from the inside."

He turned away, shaking.

Lillah thought, There have never been two people more scared of two different things at the same time.

Maringa put her arms around Lillah. "Listen to him, Lillah. You are the strongest women I have ever met; stronger even than I am. This is not just about Morace; this is about your future, and the future of all of Botanica. You must know that I see this with all certainty. You must do this."

"There's nothing I must do," Lillah said, standing tall.

"There is this," Maringa said, so quietly Lillah felt as if the earth had stopped spinning so her words could be heard.

"Send word back about what you find," Maringa said. "I can see black air in your future. Hard to breathe at first, but you get used to it. This is not dangerous, but there have been people go in who don't come back. You will know. There is much to ask for forgiveness for inside. We have killed their dead-but-walking and I know others have too. Take this pouch of seeds. They will be precious to those inside and worth presenting."

Morace had come out of the cave and was jumping on the balls of his feet.

"It's right, Lillah. It's what I always wanted to do."

"You wanted to do it. Not me. I don't want to go into a place like that. We don't belong in there."

"It will be all right. I know it. I really know it."

"You're a child, a sick, weak child. You know nothing but what I've taught you."

Morace laughed. "I know much more than that. If that was all there was to learn, we could have stayed safe and dull in Ombu. Met no one, experienced nothing."

"This is your destiny, Lillah. Your past; I see your brother, your father, walking with wood. Your mother with food. Leaving too soon. I know this about you, and I know you will be a greater person if you venture inside. You have the Tale-teller within you and you need to know all you can."

"You shouldn't be scared," Morace said quietly. "Imagine what Logan would think. He would want you to take this adventure."

"I think we should run."

"To what? To where?"

Lillah walked out into the water. The sea bed here was thick with broken shells and the small sharp stabs of pain took her out of herself.

Lillah thought of her true love, Sapin. And of Magnolia's brother, Ebena. Of the two brothers in Aspen.

She thought of her uncle, the one who disappeared out at sea.

She slowly walked back to Morace and Maringa.

Lillah said, "When the school wakes up, tell them we went to sea, that we have disappeared. Tell them not to wait."

She touched her wooden necklace, wondering where it would be safer. She did not want to be parted from it but she didn't want the ghosts to steal it, either. She kept it, hidden deep in her carryall.

Maringa pointed. "You go in there."

"But… the ghosts? How do we keep the ghosts away?"

"I don't think you will have to keep them away. But I will give you each a shawl, which you will soak in the salt water. Even when it's dry, they are scared of salt water. Without flesh to protect it, the soul dissolves at the very smell of salt water. And you'll take these." She handed Lillah small clay jars. "These have some seawater, enough to flick at any ghost."

"I can't take a child in there."

"You can't leave him out here. Out here he will be treated."

"They don't even know for sure if his mother died of Spikes."

"They don't care. Of course they don't care. Sickness means Spikes to them. They don't realise that not all illness kills. They see Spikes as a monster."

Maringa gave them each a bundle filled with dried fruit and strips of salted bird.

"You need to get going. The sun will be up soon. You need to be well inside the Tree by the time they all wake up."

Lillah thought of the places she hadn't visited. Focussed on them to take her mind off the idea that she was about to enter the place of the ghosts. Chrondus, Osage, where Phyto could be by now, Bayonet and Laburnum, with which Ombu traded perfume. These places perhaps she would never see. Most teachers had no idea of completing the island, of seeing it all, but Lillah felt a great desire to do so.

In her mapping, Lillah told the Tree: *Scar tissue tells a story. The family of cruel men and women I see where Rhizo came from.*

Of Gulfweed I remember nothing else.

Here, the Tree grows bitter nuts. The leaves are too soft for use and the Bark looks diseased.

PLANTAE

Lillah and Morace, clinging to their belongings, wrapped in their sea-soaked shawls, walked up to the entrance of the ghostcave. Morace squeezed through the crack and stepped inside the Tree.

Lillah tried not to think how small and dark it would be inside, how enclosing. She tried not to think of the ghosts she'd been warned about her entire life.

"Come on," Morace said. "It'll be fine. Come in."

"I'm coming," Lillah said, wanting fresh air on her back for a bit longer. The idea of stepping inside the Tree, inside it, made her want to choke.

Morace thrust his face back out, then a hand. He said, "I've always wanted so see what's inside. Come on!"

He pulled his head back in and called, "It's big in here. Hollowed out. And lighter than you'd think. There's nobody in here. There's nothing."

Lillah passed their belongings through for Morace to stack neatly inside.

"We can't leave anything behind outside," she said. She swept the dirt at her feet, covering up all traces. She was terrified, going through the small motions of preparing to cover her terror. She knew she should not be as scared as that. She knew now that not everyone believed in ghosts, or in the malevolence of ghosts. She was no longer sure ghosts would eat her bones. She thought that if she had been born elsewhere, in a community where they didn't fear the ghosts, she would not be scared now.

Lillah took a deep breath and stepped through.

Their things were piled in a mess.

"Morace! I passed you these things carefully. Why did you let them all spill out?"

"What? Oh, Lillah. I was too busy looking to bother about those things! Leave them!"

Lillah, hunched over, breathing through her mouth, repacked their clothing, food and water in the heavy weave bags. She held onto the little bag of dirt, given to her by the woman in Arborvitae, where Rham died, where Melia stayed, where they heard about Thea's death. She wanted it close by if she needed it. She also held the small container of saltwater given to her by Maringa.

The area they were in was quite light. Lillah couldn't see the source.

There was silence. No waves. It was like her heart had stopped beating, so strange and frightening was the silence. She strained to hear and she could find a faint rhythmic noise but no more.

It was much drier than she'd imagined. She'd thought of the Tree as human inside, wet, soft, red. This was dry, hard and brown. It smelt like fire, like wood burning, and she thought of the legend she heard in every place, of the great Tree burning from within, one day slowly collapsing.

The floor was covered with broken shells.

Lillah heard a whispering and wondered if they were Tale-teller words coming in from the outside or if it was the ghosts, talking about how to kill them. She backed up to the entrance, put her arm through.

"I can't stay here," she said.

"Lillah, it's all right. Come on. We'll be all right."

It was warm, at least.

They both jumped at a creaking noise, grabbing each other fearfully.

"The ghosts will be friendly," Morace said. "They won't hurt us. We should explore. Look further in."

"Why can't we stay here?" Lillah sat down and curled herself. "It's nice here. Warm. We have food and light."

"I'm bored. This is boring. I want to explore in there." Morace dug his thumb into the air and glared at her. "And the shells hurt. It's not comfortable here. And they will look in and find us, Lillah, and then what?"

Lillah sat heavily, feeling like a child but not ready to take the journey yet. "I've been forced to come in here, I won't be forced to move on unless I want to."

"So we'll rest, we'll eat and soon you'll be used to it and we'll move."

He stuck his head through the large gap further into the Tree.

"Can we just move into here, the next chamber? It's even warmer, and no one will see us. There's nobody in here. I swear. There are no ghosts. It doesn't smell of anything at all. I'm going in. You can stay by yourself if you want to." He climbed stiffly through and she remembered the terrible injury on his thigh. Being alone was more terrifying than anything else, so Lillah crawled through after him.

It was warmer in there. Smooth walled, and soft underfoot. "We'll stay here for a while," she said.

"No! Come on!" Morace said, heading towards another cave.

"Morace! You said just this room, and here we'll stay. Don't make me go any further."

Morace came back and sat beside her. "We'll stay here for a while, but promise me we'll go on soon. This is our chance to know what there is, Lillah. We can't let that go."

She slept well. The air was thicker than she had ever breathed and it made sleep deep. She awoke to Morace standing over her.

"Come on, Lillah! You should see the next room! It's full of bones! This is where the bones go!"

"The ghosts… oh Tree, the ghosts… they take the bones, Morace. Don't you understand that? We go in there and they will suck the flesh from us and add us to our collection."

"I've been in there for hours, Lillah, and nothing happened. Nothing. The bones have been there for a long time."

He pulled her until she stood. She poked her head through, thinking she would sense ghosts if they were there.

White bone. Lined up ceremonially, bones like a seawalk, lined like the slats of a seawalk. Or the wall of a house, if the house was built of drift-in wood faded by sun and worn smooth by sand and sea. Some of it was drift-in wood. Some of it was Tree roots, stripped back and pale, looking almost edible.

Morace carried their things in and set them up neatly. "You see? This is okay. We'll rest until you're ready."

They slept, ate, talked, sat in silence. Morace concealed his impatience well.

There was no way to tell without sunlight how much time had passed before one of the bones reached out and grabbed Lillah's shoulders. She screamed.

Morace held her. "No, no. That was a falling bone, but can't you see amongst the pale strips, there, can you see it?"

A face.

Mouth opened slowly, like the fish puffing out the last salty breath.

Lillah screamed, dug her fingers into Morace's arm. She pulled him backwards, towards the gap to outside. He shook her off and stepped forward to peer into the face.

"Morace! Keep back! Keep away!" She took the plug from the jar of salt water Maringa gave her.

"It's a person," Morace said. "Look. Arms, legs, stomach." He pointed. "It's a man."

Naked. Naked, pale, hairy, stepped out.

Lillah screamed and scrabbled back towards the first cave. "Ghost! Ghost! Dead-but-walking!" She dragged at Morace, tugging him, terrified.

"It's okay, Lillah," he said. "It's a man."

"It's not a man, it's a ghost." She threw the water at him.

"No. I am not a ghost." The man spoke. His voice was very quiet and he had his hands to his ears. Water dripped from his nose.

"Too loud," whispered Morace. "We need to whisper."

"That is not a man," Lillah whispered.

Naked hairless took his hands from his ears.

"Yes. Too loud." He gave a shimmy. It was an odd move, one Lillah had never seen. He didn't shiver with the cold, though she could see her breath frosting in the air.

"We've come in from Gulfweed. I'm Morace," Morace whispered.

The man nodded. "I'm Santala. Where are you from?"

"From Ombu. But we came in from Gulfweed."

He wrinkled his brow. His whole body seemed to fetch up with it. "You have travelled a long way, then."

"We should not be here," Lillah said. "We should have stayed in the other cave."

"It was covered with broken shells, the whole floor. This bone room is better," Morace said.

Santala nodded again. "Out there they leave the bones for us. From the Tree. We take these gifts when offered. The place we call Bone Table leaves the body out for us to remove and use. They are a kind people."

Lillah thought he must mean Pinon; she remembered the stone table, the ritual laying out of a child's body.

"You steal the bones from outside?"

"We don't have our own. We are held together with a framework of wood. Where else would we get them from?"

Morace looked at him, softly fleshed, languid.

"You must have bones. What's left when your flesh falls off after death?"

"We dissolve in the heat. Melt into this." He pointed at the luminescence running down the wall. "We fuel our own lights."

"We say outside that the ghosts take the bones."

He smiled at her. "I can't speak for the… ghosts. As for us, we don't waste what we are given. We use everything."

His voice was calm. Lillah reached out and touched his arm. It was soft, but definitely made of flesh.

"Are you hungry?"

"We have our own food. But we will offend you without intending to because I've almost nothing to bring to share."

"That's unimportant. We have plenty. You must be hungry."

Morace said they were. Lillah looked at him, so calm. And at Santala, this strange man, this not-ghost. She decided she would let it happen to her. She would trust the Tree. She would not fear unless she had reason to.

Lillah's guide took her hand to lead her. His hand was very soft, almost squishy. It felt like a jelly fish wrapped in cloth, and she squeezed it for the sensation.

He squeezed back, and she worried she was sending signals she didn't want to send. She had no desire for this man; not even out of curiosity.

"You have come into the Tree at a good place. We live mostly on this. The mushrooms grow well here and there is moss for us to use. It is very quiet on the other side. You might have climbed for days without finding anyone."

"We use the moss to stop us catching child."

"We have not heard that. Some of our children leave for a life outside. They seek what they can't have: a sense of place in a place they don't belong."

"We call them Newcomers. They are always treated well. Welcomed."

"As we welcome you. Where are you travelling? Do you want to walk through the Tree to return to Ombu?"

"We are not sure. We were told to head for the centre of the Tree."

"Then that is the direction we will head in."

He fed them with a cold stew of mushrooms and herbs. It was so delicious Lillah did not want to swallow each mouthful.

Then they began to walk. Morace, always pale, became almost translucent, but he didn't cough, didn't worsen. His thigh was dark red with scab tissue and Santala gave him ointments along the way. It seemed to heal well, pink around the edges rather than yellow. They travelled slowly, peacefully. Lillah enjoyed the silence.

They saw few people.

She watched Santala walk ahead, his odd sideways limp. He had lost his leg below the knee and wore a carved leg glued with sap and some of the luminous material that flowed through the internal roots of the Tree.

It meant his leg glowed; the dripping thick stuff glowed in the dark of the Tree.

"How did you lose your leg?" Morace asked. Lillah nodded. It didn't occur to her he might not want to talk about it; she was curious.

"I didn't lose the leg. I sacrificed it to the sea."

"Outside, we are fascinated by the Tree. It is like god to us. Because we don't know it or understand it; certainly not what lies within," Lillah said. "You have the same feeling about the sea. To us, we often fear the sea because of the monsters, but we also understand the way it comes and goes. We know that if it goes, it will come."

"But how do you know? How can you know such a thing?" he said.

"The same way you know the fire of the Tree. Watching, learning, understanding."

Lillah reached out and touched his wooden leg.

"Why do you find it so odd? You have men in your own Order with limbs not there."

"You know that?"

"We know Treefall. We remember every Treefall of our lives. That one, we felt the creak of it from everywhere. It was a deep line fracture which worried us. We thought the Tree would crack through the centre and we would be exposed to the bright open sky." He shivered at the thought.

"The open sky is beautiful. When it's blue you feel like you can see forever. At night, the stars reach so far you feel like you could grab hold of one and travel to some distant place, where there are no Trees and perhaps no green." Lillah sighed at the thought.

"I don't like the sound of it. It's too big. I like this closeness."

"If you know when Leaffall is about to happen, why don't you warn us? You would save lives. We lost Gingko, a good teacher, to Leaffall." Morace looked at her sidelong. He knew what she'd thought of Gingko and it was not that she was a good teacher.

"You don't know yourselves? We thought this was deliberate sacrifice."

"Not deliberate. No. But appreciated by the Tree."

"We watched your teacher's sacrifice. Felt it within us, accepted it as worthy."

"She didn't do it on purpose."

"Doesn't matter for her. She still reaps the benefit. That is good."

Lillah thought he showed impressive sensitivity.

"What else do you know?"

"What else do you want to know?"

"We hear a crackling sometimes. People say it means the end of the Tree is close. What causes it? Do you know?"

"Sometimes we will have a breaking of the limbs. When there has been a Limbfall outside, there is often debris inside as well. Everything has a reaction, a response. So we will break the Tree limbs, crack them, and that is what you hear. The echo of it. It is like music to us. One of our most beautiful songs."

"It doesn't sound good from the outside."

"You should hear some of things we have to hear. All those people confessing into the Tree. Whispering into the cracks as if no one can hear, as if the Tree won't be damaged by the poison. We knew your friend was a child killer long before you did. Before she even knew it herself, when she was still struggling with her demons."

"Thea? Those killings were an accident. Thea never meant for it to happen."

"I'm sorry. I know you want to think that. You trusted her and took her in as a friend, but she whispered into the Tree about the deaths in detail before she committed the murders." As she spoke, she thought They even see this? They see all the small things of our lives?

"You did nothing."

"We tried to give messages. We strung out bones. We cracked limbs. You didn't listen. These children and adults who stare into the ghost caves. Call in. Imagine what would happen if we responded. Our lives would be invaded. They are already trying to tunnel through in some places. These people we haunt, we terrify. We don't want them in our Tree.

"We 'crunch crunch' noise to scare them. One man, you may remember. You may have heard. He spoke into the Tree and he said, 'You will not wait long for us to come. We know you are there and we are not scared of you. What you have in there belongs to us.' We took him into the Tree and did not return him. We left a clump of his hair so they would know where he went."

"What did you do to him?"

"We involved him."

"What does that mean?"

"It means we passed him through initiation. Not all of the young men survive this. He did not. Your mysteries are our answers, of course. Your missing people, or the strangely killed? We have the answer."

This was too interesting to be annoying. "Is there nothing we know that you don't?"

"We know all of the stories of the Tree. But you know of food, fire and water. These things we aren't expert in. We use the existing fires. We will never start a fire, or move it. We can't bear to watch fire made outside or to watch it moving from place to place.

"We scare our children with stories of the fire-demon, who prowls around ready to burn the hair of bad people. He can look into your soul and find goodness or evil. We scare young mothers to care for their children because sometimes they would rather be elsewhere. We take the placenta and bury it. When the child is becoming an adult, we dig up the placenta to see its state. Sometimes it is still perfect, and those are the children who will be our leaders.

After some time (one month? two? time passed so differently inside the Tree; Lillah was never tired because her body ruled her sleeping, not the sun) as they woke up, Santala said, "We are almost at the place my mother lives. Would you like to meet her?"

Lillah didn't really want to, but Morace, desperate for other company, insisted.

They walked for a day, climbing through the Tree. The wood changed as they walked. In some places it was pale, almost colourless. Others it was dark. Sometimes there were clear markings, circles and knots. Others it was like the sky on a clear day; smooth, featureless.

Santala led them through a small tunnel into a large cave with walls almost purple.

"My boy!" Santala's mother was very small, pale and fat. She reminded Lillah of a slug, but she was lively, not sluggish at all.

"Mother, I brought some friends."

"They are very dark."

"They are from the outside."

His mother looked at them through her lashes. "What is it they want here?"

"Mother! I told you they are my friends. I have brought them to meet you."

Morace stepped forward and took her hand. "We wish you no harm. We are here to understand. To explore. We are adventurers."

Lillah smiled to herself. Such a different boy from the one who'd walked out of Ombu.

Santala's mother took Morace into her arms, then. "What has my son been feeding you? I hope he has been feeding you well."

She led them to an open area. Growths out of the floor were smooth and comfortable for sitting. In an alcove, fire glowed and there was a round pot sitting in there. Santala's mother lifted the lid and the smell wafting out made Lillah gasp.

"Ah, you enjoy the smell of my soup." That made the old woman smile.

Lillah said, "I have a student outside who would love to see this food cooking. Wouldn't she, Morace?"

He nodded.

She remembered the pouch of seeds, the offering, and pulled it out.

"We have a ceremony outside where we make an offering to ask forgiveness, for all offences. I know we have hurt some of your people; will I be able to make an offering somehow?"

Santala's brother, his arms shrivelled below the elbows, joined them. After they had eaten, wiped their mouths, he said, "You think you can atone for the murder of our people with a small bag of seeds? Why should we forgive you, all of you, for these things?"

Lillah wished she were cleverer, that she knew people, understood them.

"I'm sorry," she said.

"You have not killed. It isn't your responsibility. Others have done it," Santala said, knocking his brother on the side of the head.

"I have never seen a newcomer killed. Only the dead-but-walking."

"Those 'dead-but-walking' are the ones who have almost reached enlightenment. They moved beyond the physical needs. This takes all their lives to perfect. Their very existence means the sea stays calm and doesn't suck the souls from all of us. Every time you kill one, the danger grows. Every one of them who makes it to the water keeps us safe and helps us grow. They live on a diet of salty food. Most salt is kept for them. Salt is rare for us."

"I'm sorry."

"Every one who is killed is a great loss. You cannot imagine the sadness we feel when one of these evolved beings is murdered."

Lillah thought of Sapin, how much pleasure he had taken in the killing of the dead-but-walking. She felt small pride that she had not chosen him. That she had moved on, moved away.

"I am sorry."

"I am happy to have that regret, but it is not you, Lillah. You can say sorry for your people but you are not responsible for these actions unless you commit them yourself. That is what we believe."

Lillah reached up and drew her finger through a silky patch of liquid on the Tree. The sap here was smooth, not sticky. She loved the feel of it on her skin, smoothed it onto her arms just for the feel and the smell of it.

"We have our monsters, too. There is the Woodsman, so tall he cannot move through the tunnels but needs to chop his way through. This causes collapse, great destruction, but he barely notices or cares. He's hungry, always hungry, but he doesn't like organic food. He likes flesh. People. And his hunger is huge, his mouth very wide." Santala shuddered. "We don't like to talk about him very much. We think that words make him stronger. The more we talk, the stronger he is."

They were quiet for a while Lillah thought of the monsters of the deep they feared, and how some young men would prove themselves by taunting them. "Has anyone been close to the Woodsman? To prove their bravery? That is what they do outside sometimes."

He blinked at her. "We have nothing to prove here. We don't work that way. We are brave when we need to be. We do not admire foolish bravery such as exploring outside the Tree."

He started to play act a short story where he pretended to be a brave young man, struck down. It shouldn't be funny but it was; he captured the young man spirit so well, the arrogance, the foolishness.

His brother, still angry, said, "You can't say you don't have cruelties. To your own people as well as ours. You place babies you don't want in the Tree limbs for the white birds to peck clean."

"Not all of us," Lillah said. She remembered the revulsion she had felt in Thallo on seeing this.

"And you are the ones who give us bones to build with, piles of bones, skulls and stones. We are not the only ones to build with bones."

Sequoia, Lillah thought. They make such piles there. She wondered if there was anything these people had not observed.

The men smelt stronger here. It wasn't a smell of dirt, or an unwashed smell. It was the male smell, but it was so much stronger.

Later, around the food, Lillah looked in her bag for something to give Santala's mother. Something personal, with meaning. She felt awful, coming to each meal with nothing.

She found the small stone with sweet markings, given to her by Corma, the girl who caught child and died in Ailanthus. She realised she had missed visiting Chrondus, the girl's home, and had therefore failed to deliver this stone to them. She had forgotten to pass this on to one of the other teachers, in her rush to escape, and she felt badly that she would not complete that task. She gave it to Santala's mother.

"That is a beautiful stone. What do the markings mean?"

"They mean something only to the person it is meant for. It came from the hand of a loved one, and all thought is inside it. I wish I could give it to those in Chrondus."

Santala said, "We can leave it under the Tree, at least. If they are meant to find it and understand it, they will."

"You'd do that? Isn't that contact too close?"

"It's fine. Some contact is fine, because they don't believe we are real. They will think someone dropped it."

Lillah imagined the children of her school finding the stone. She imagined a whole story unfolding, what they would say about Lillah and Morace.

"I wonder if our school misses us. I wonder if they notice we are gone."

He shook his head, smiling at her. "Oddly enough, the world goes on when you are not there, Lillah. You remember what it's like to have teachers choose an Order. There is a space for a short while, then it is filled. That's how it should be. You are used to loss and departure."

"But they should worry for our lives. We are inside the Tree."

His smile dropped. "That is terrible, is it?"

Lillah felt her cheeks burn at her stupidity. "No, no, you know what I mean. There is a fear of inside because we don't know inside. I have no fear now. Understand me, please. Don't be hurt by my words. You know this is true."

"I'm used to it," he said. "And they think you have gone out to sea, anyway. That is what they are told and that is what they think. And you are a very fine woman. I love to spend this time with you."

Lillah felt his warmth spread through her. She closed her eyes, listening to his voice. "Tell me a story," she said. "About the people I know."

He put his arm around her. "They have reached a place with the people we call the golden folk. They never burn although they are paler, like us."

"I heard they use a lotion to protect their skin. I planned to take some of that home. I have to trust someone did it."

"You always planned to go home?"

"I did not really have a plan at all. I knew I had to keep Morace safe, that's all. Tell me, is Phyto with them? Do you know? The man who travelled with us."

Santala motioned to a young girl. "She will tell you a story. This is not exactly what happened; many of our stories come from mixtures of this and that. A name from here, a word from there. We also know what happened once and is likely to happen again."

The young girl had long white hair, smooth and shiny. Her face was a pale wood colour, unlined, and she took Lillah's hand and spoke straight into her face. The story was for her alone.

"As they approached Osage they saw the men working at the water's edge, dragging in a catch. Osage is set in a deep atoll; fish are kept as if in a bowl.

"They pulled in the net and the teachers saw many sea sponges among the flapping fish.

"The men worked in short skirts of material, their backs bare and wet with heat sweat.

"Three women plucked out the fish and cut their heads off with large knives. They scaled, gutted and tossed the fish into a large wooden bowl. They are beautiful people, the golden sand clinging to their sweaty bodies.

"The women kept gutting the fish as the men piled the sea sponges into large net bags.

"The school together walked to meet them but they continued with their work. They did not look up. 'Are we going to stand here all day? I'm hungry,' said the tallest student. He called out, 'We're here. Have you noticed?' His voice carried to the water's edge. The fishermen looked up, at last.

"The men linked arms with each other; the three women did, too.

"'Welcome to Osage. We have been told of your approach,' said the leader. They stood forward. The leader tilted his head at them. 'Is this all of you? No more? In this place we don't believe in ceremony or ritual. We believe in plain speaking, good food, and some dancing.'

"Then your friend came out of the Tree. He embraced all of your teachers and your children and there were many tears. They were very happy to see each other and he was a happy man.

"'You are welcome here, friends. All of you are welcome. It is a wonderful place. I have never been so happy in all my life. I belong.'

"The dancing that night was wild, frenzied. They could not help thinking of those in Chrondus, where they had left jail, those in confinement. They thought of those inside the Tree, the two they missed but did not mention."

The story seemed to excite the women listening, and they spoke of men, the men they liked and those they didn't.

"The men outthere are so smooth. Too smooth."

"But they are too hairy inside! I like men to be smooth," Lillah said. They all laughed.

"I think it is lucky we all like different men, or we would rip each other's eyes out," said one woman. She spoke rarely, and watched Lillah's every move. It struck Lillah that perhaps she was worried she would take Santala away. Capture his heart.

They joined Morace in a meeting place. He was smiling broadly, and Lillah wondered what had made him so happy. Earlier, Santala had told her, "We know all. You forget that. We know your fears for Morace's health."

Lillah had felt a great weight lift from her. This was not her responsibility now. She had failed, and someone else would do the job, make the choices.

She looked at Morace. He hummed to himself and fiddled with a wood puzzle, waiting for her to stop speaking.

"Lillah! You won't believe it!"

"What is it, Morace?"

A woman stepped forward. She had short hair, cut spiky. She said, "Morace said that you were worried he had Spikes. Did you know we had a test for this? An absolute?"

"I didn't know such a test existed," Lillah said. She looked at Morace. Smiling.

"And?"

"He is not sick. Perhaps his lungs are not as strong as they should be, but he does not have Spikes."

Lillah started to cry. With relief, to begin with, then with loss: all she had given to keep him safe. Her love, her chance at her own life. She had not needed to.

But he was not ill. He would not die.

She drew him to her and they held each other close together.

The healer said, "We are like you in this. Spikes is something we fear more than anything else. We are confined; illness spreads quickly inside the Tree. When one child coughs on Monday, there are five dead by Friday." Lillah had heard this saying in variations around the Tree. "The first people came here to run from a bone-deforming Spikes but we think they brought a variation with them. A Spikes body is full of odd bone peaks."

Morace said, "We say that, on the outside, too. They are very serious when they say it outside, and they nod like this when they say it." Lillah smiled at Morace's light mood. He wouldn't sink into despair.

After some celebration, Lillah and Morace discussed with Santala what they would do next. "You can rejoin the school. Or we can take you to the ghost cave at Ombu, and you can go straight home. The school will reach there in six months," Santala said.

"I'll have to take the healer with me, to tell them I'm well," Morace said.

"I can't do that," the healer said. "I don't want to reveal myself. Insiders don't do well on the outside."

"Slaughter. We are slaughtered." Santala stood up, angered.

Lillah had heard stories of this; she didn't comment. She had seen it.

"We can teach you the test, though. To show them you are healthy, and so others can test themselves. We are happy for the outside to know."

Morace's cheeks looked pink, and Lillah knew he was happy at the thought of rejoining the school.

She was not so eager. She felt as if this was an opportunity she may not have again. There was so much more to learn about inside. And about outside.

"I think I'll stay here. If someone can guide Morace to the ghost cave at Ombu, or to Bayonet, to meet the school, then I can stay to explore more."

Santala smiled at her. His eyes slitted, as if he was assessing her. She hoped he didn't think she was interested in him as a lover.

"You're not coming with me?" Morace said. He looked at her, wide-eyed. "What will my mother say?"

"Morace…"

"I had forgotten. What will our father say?"

"I will be home before long. I will not be forever. I need to go to school inside the Tree."

The next day, Morace left. She felt a great gap as he went, disappearing quickly through a tunnel. But a lightening as well, an easing. She was alone, with only herself to care for. It was freeing.

She had so much to learn. Santala explained to her the measurement of time, of names, and of the past.

"Those first people brought with them only one book. One book in eight parts. Called "Botanica". It is from here we find our names, and how we measure our time, by how the plants grow. The seasons.

Lillah was silent. Is this how simple it is? she thought.

"All of us, insiders and out, are named from that book."

Lillah said, "Why do you know of the past and we don't?"

"You don't have the books outside. And also this is the rift of so long ago. Insiders wanted to remember the past. Outsiders wanted Botanica to be all they knew.

"Why didn't they change the names?"

"I think they still believed in Botanica. Just not the bone world they came from."

They walked. Lillah missed the sun but was used to the light provided by the Tree.

They came across some musicians. They played a hollow tune, three of them squatting in the darkness. It seemed without rhythm or reason, but Santala smiled.

"You don't like this music? It is a particular sound, played on toe bones. It gives the sense of down on the earth, because of the kind of bone."

Lillah tried to smile but she found the music discordant and unsettling.

"Are you happy, you outsiders? Can you feel joy in the small things?"

"Mostly we're happy. Botanica works well; the system we have makes most people happy. There is room for loners. Those who don't fit in find work as Tale-tellers, marketers, potmakers. I would love to be a Tale-teller."

"But you know nothing of the past."

"They are not curious. But I am, Santala. I want to know."

"We came from another great island, from the sky, many, many hundreds of years ago. Those people came on a secret endeavour.

"There were four men and three women. They gave themselves names from Botanica when they arrived: Rhizo, Cynthia, Platanace, Dickson, Tilla, Logan and Capri. We have lost their birth names, all but two: Ruth and David. They were people who understand the plants, the things that grow. They gave themselves plant names, and they called all their children, their grand children, all names come from the plants. The place names come from plants.

"In this we have not grown apart. They knew of this island, this Tree and they knew it was the place for them. Legend says the Tree sprouted from their bones. Truth is, the Tree was already here.

"They thought we could always have good air to breathe. The air was worthless on the place they left behind. They brought many seeds with them. This is why we have food all over the Tree, different food in different places. These people planted everywhere, and a wild hybrid grew. Mushrooms grow thick on the side you call shady.

"If we travel further up inside the Tree, you will see strange boxes, many of them, the last remaining scraps of the belongings of the first people. We don't know what these things are. We don't know what they used them for. Some things we have used ourselves in small ways.

"They came from a place where there were few Trees remaining. From outer rings in, they read the markings, the etchings in the Tree and added more, leaving their words behind. It is etched in places inside the Tree."

All lit by the strange glowing stuff, Lillah thought.

"We know little about the birthplace, only that there were many land masses, many people, and that their bones grew smooth together. One Bone disease, which killed them.

"There came a time when the people of the Tree no longer wanted to remember the history. They wanted to begin again, untainted by the past. They call this time the Chase of the Rememberers. The Rememberers ran up the Tree, too old to climb, yet so determined not to die they couldn't stop climbing, escaping. Forced up, higher and higher, on the branches of the Tree. These stories of our past we found on the Trunk of the Tree etched and clear.

"The etchings speak of visions: all possible futures present in their dreams, all possible pasts remembered and set into the Tree. They spoke of disease and of death, of great birds carrying our ancestors to the island, metal birds with a name we don't know.

"They dug deep pit ovens as we do now, heating the stones until a dry Leaf shrivelled in an instant on contact. They ate great crabs, so large their shells could be used as a bath for a child. The flesh was sweet, and the early settlers etched stories and told tales of the intoxicating feasts they shared, sucking on crab's legs and swallowing great chunks of crab flesh until the mound of shells reached knee-high."

"Why did we never question this on the outside? Why don't we know this?" Lillah said.

"Most of you out there don't care where you came from. Most of you think it doesn't matter. But it's everything about who we are. And it's how we can change.

"We all descended from the same place. These things happened beyond memory ago, when most of us lived inside the Tree. There were many factions and we have no record of what the arguments were. This is the nature of war, the nature of conflict. The conflict is remembered, not the cause. The cause is unimportant with the passage of time.

"They fought, and there were deaths. Some small groups found safe havens in the Tree, but many others, tired of living inside the Tree, ventured out. The insiders would say they lost all sense and knowledge. Most people did this. The outsiders would say they saw sense, saw that living inside was wrong, and that outside, where there is sun and fresh air, is the only right place to live. They started eating fish. We would not eat fish.

"All communication was not lost, though. As time passed, contacts were made and conversations held. There was transfer of insiders to outsiders, breeding between the two, for a long time, then slowly, slowly, the separation became complete. We forgot how to speak to each other and the outsiders began to believe we did not exist."

They climbed out onto a branch way above the ground. Below them were people, strangers, living their fascinating lives.

"But do I tell them? Will they listen, and will it change anything at all?"

"They should at least realise there are no ghosts inside the Tree, just another Order, more Orders, living their own way."

"There are some who do believe that. They have ghost-free places."

Santala shuddered. "Some of the places... they are taboo. Places where people die of their nightmares."

"That is in Pinon. That's what they tell us. Everybody has a different belief." Lillah felt suddenly overwhelmed by all she had heard. "It's so vast, inside the Tree."

"There is more Tree than there is land."

This was too much for Lillah to absorb. Too huge, too all encompassing.

"It is a large land, so varied."

"It is very large."

As they moved through and up the Tree, there were surprising patches of dirt resting in deep impressions in the Tree, or filling hollows.

Lillah realised they were using a rib cage to dig. It provided deep, equal groves to drop seed in.

"How does anything grow in here? It's hard for us to grow food in the shade."

"This food has changed so that it no longer needs sunlight."

"Does it give you enough life when you eat it? Sun-raised food has so much life."

"We're alive, aren't we?"

Lillah thought, You are, you pale weak creatures. But not like we live.

• • •

She saw a woman she thought was perhaps a Tale-teller. The woman used a sharp bone to cut words into the Tree.

Lillah watched her. "On the outside, it's the men who have these jobs. The women leave. The men stay. So the men have these important jobs."

"We do not travel so much inside. We will meet together near the internal fire sometimes, but we like our small groups."

"Children, though. How do you make new children?"

"When we meet a lot of connections are made. And you outsiders leave your unwanted babies out. We want them."

She etched with a sharp bone tool. Lillah ran her fingers over the story and marvelled at the woman's skill.

"Clever, isn't she? Will you come to stir the beer?" Santala led Lillah through to another cavern.

The bowl was enormous; a massive stone scraped and scraped till there was room inside for food. Santala picked up a bone spoon the size of his arm and stirred.

A yeasty, fermented smell came off the mixture.

"This will be ready in some months. It draws flavour from the stone and the stone helps turn it into something that will make us all happy."

The walking was slow, which was good because that way she could acclimatise to the changing light and the heat. The closer she moved to the centre, the hotter it got.

She missed sunlight terribly. Lillah felt her hair dying, falling out, though in the half-light of their existence it was hard to tell. Her skin thickened, coarsened; she could feel the pores when she stroked her face. But the learning, the learning took all physical difficulties away.

She found the spring that ran out into Douglas. Santala warned her about this stream. He said, "It is so pure it will hurt your throat."

She sat by it, resisting the urge to swim in it, piss in it, dirty it for the murderous men of Douglas. But she drank, instead, and then lay down and let the dreams of future and past, of lovers and killers, fill her until she thought she would never wake up.

"Is that noise the leaves? Is there a wind out there? It sounds like talking."

Her guide shook his head. "It's outthere. They whisper like that all the time. It's nonsense. We can't hear the words unless we creep closer. Sometimes we do it, if we're tired of the pictures in the Bark and bored with each other."

"What do they say? Can you tell me?"

He laughed. "Sometimes shocking. Sometimes very dull. Farting in the mother's bed. Tearing away Bark not loosened or given freely by The Tree. Bad thoughts and ideas; these things we hear. Terrible killings, sometimes. Sometimes I whisper back. Tell them things I don't want people to know. We hear the planning of a killing. Terrible killings. One place they leave seaweed oil in their ghost cave."

Rhado. Lillah thought. I won't tell him my mother is from there.

"We heard them, many of them, whispering about a boy and how they would kill him. They don't like those who are flawed, do they? They don't see the strength in flaws."

"Those people should have been jailed."

Santala smiled. "Jail. It looks nice, to us. Sitting in the water and the sun. It seems warm and cool at the same time."

"You would think so. And at first it is. The prisoner thinks they have got off easy, that there is no worry at all. The water is refreshing the sun is warm, and they are not required to do any work. Most way-breakers are lazy. I don't know if that is the same inside the Tree as it is out. But they are mostly lazy, and try to get out of doing work."

Santala nodded. "They are lazy here, too."

"It may not seem to be a punishment. But it is terrible. They move ceaselessly, lifting one foot at a time out of the water, stepping and stepping."

"Their feet would begin to rot, if they are there a while," Santala said.

"The cages rise and fall with the tide, and their feet are often in the water. Once the foot starts to rot, when there are open sores, the salt water gets in and those people are in agony."

"It's hard to tell that from this far back. It looks pleasant."

"Sometimes it's not good to be close to a thing. Their feet are destroyed by it. You've seen that?"

"I've seen them crawl from the cages. Yes. But I don't remember seeing their feet. I wouldn't like your life out there. You have so few freedoms."

Lillah wondered how he could think such a thing.

Some crystals were set in the walls and Santala, using a bone tool, scraped them into a small bag.

"This is our salt," he said.

Lillah pitied him. "Our red salt can heal bruises," she said.

As they talked and long days passed, he led her through roots, tunnels and caves.

"How do you know where you're going? We understand a straight line; this seems to be circles and spirals."

"The Tree is a very complex organism. You must have noticed that from the outside. Many species merging to one heart. So my map is to follow the species. This track we're on takes us to jasmine, which is surrounded on most sides by almond. Almond leads to Rowan, and that's where we'll eat tonight."

"Is it near the centre of the Tree?"

"It will take us several more months to walk to the centre of the Tree."

• • •

They climbed and walked, dropped from branch to branch. Lillah felt warmer, uncomfortably so.

"Thirsty?" he said. He seemed to understand her physical state. He handed her a wooden bottle to drink from.

"We'll fill it at the next well."

"Is there is fresh water in here?"

"Of course. It's the source of all water you use on the outside."

"We're almost there," he said. "Through here, and we'll be there."

It was very warm. Lillah couldn't understand where the heat was coming from, but she was too tired to form the words to ask.

They stepped through a fissure and what Lillah saw there made her scream.

"What's the matter?" her guide said, his composure gone for the first time.

"Fire, the great burning fire! The stories are true. The Tree is burning from within."

Lillah sobbed. She had never really believed these tales, and never told them herself, yet here it was. The Tree being destroyed as they watched. There was a large cavern, fifty steps at least, maybe a hundred going the other way. You could not walk in there, though, because the ground burned. There were no twigs or sticks, no logs burning. The ground was the wood of the Tree and it burned at a constant red glow.

"Lillah, it's good. It's good fire. The wood here is so ancient it doesn't burn, just appears to. This flame has been alight since before I was born. One of my first memories is playing up against the burning block, because it was warm and I loved the crackle of it."

"We hear that outside sometimes," Lillah felt calmer, knowing it wasn't her responsibility to save the Tree. "There are crackles about the Tree. Sometimes an internal Limb will shatter with dryness. That crackles."

"Come and eat. This fire is a great comfort. The eternity of it gives us faith. My grandfather sat by this flame. His grandfather."

As her eyes focussed, she saw there were others in the cave.

"There are other flames burning. This is ours. This one has been burning for many years, and it is a reminder of battles that should never be fought. A battle between two good men ended with the flame going out so long ago. It was many years before it was lit again. Now we are wary of war and careful with our fire."

The cavern filled with whispering people. Mostly they were naked though some wore strips of material around their necks to wipe their fingers and noses on.

They watched Lillah, and smiled if she looked at them, but did not surround her.

"They'd love to talk to you, but don't want to

frighten you," Santala said. "They feel like they know you; we watch you all out there."

"They can talk to me. I'm not frightened," though she felt overwhelmed. There had been much interest in her travels, but this was different.

"They know less about you than others. They don't hear the whispering as much. The secrets. One young girl, the story goes, hid and listened. She knew all the secrets. She didn't use them wisely. The people killed her for knowing the secrets, but before she died, she cursed her killers. She said, 'With me dies the Tree'. But the Tree still stands, and she is long gone."

Santala handed Lillah something, twice the size of her fist, on a skewer of wood.

"What is it?"

"It's delicious," he said.

"But it's…"

"Spider. It's spider. We farm them not far from here."

"I can't eat that!" Lillah said. The insiders looked at each other.

"We've seen the terrible things you eat out there. You eat crab, which goes red when you cook it."

"Crab? Crab is good to eat. Some people don't eat crab, though. I can understand why you might be cautious. We never eat the crabs that eat people, though. We've seen them, and we've seen the bodies left, chewed and meatless. We don't eat those crabs."

"Spider is delicious."

Lillah looked around at her and knew this was an important moment. She had to eat. She had to be brave. They may not be offended but they would think her a complete fool if she starved herself to death.

"We see the spider as something to be worshipped. We don't eat the things we worship," she said.

"Anyone worthy of worship would rather be eaten than let his people die." Lillah could see the sense in that.

An old woman squatted beside them, staring at Lillah.

"We don't see you here. Not young ones."

"Old ones? Some old ones come inside?" Once, she would have been excited at the possibility her mother had walked inside. She wished for a moment this had been the truth, that Olea was alive and well and living inside. "Do they?" She spoke more loudly than usual.

The old woman winced at the noise.

"A few old women come in. The ones looking for home."

"But this is not home to an outsider. How could it be home? The old women walk, my mother walked, they walk around the Tree until they reach their birth Order."

"Yes, that's right. And most will stop there. But some... not your mother... some will feel the draw into the Tree."

They paused to collect a colony of spiders. "Not that one. See? She's got babies inside. That's next month's meal."

"So I'm the first smooth-skinned person inside? The first young person?"

The old woman seemed frustrated. "No, not the first. I didn't mean to give you something to be proud of. But very rare. That's all."

"They haven't seen too many from outthere," Santala said. "Certainly not as many as are sent outward."

"What happens to those who enter? Who survive?"

"They are absorbed into Tree life. They may live alone in a Tree cave. They may climb higher. Some become members of our small community."

The old woman leaned forward. She was toothless, and Lillah found it hard to understand her words. She touched Lillah, saying, "I thought I was cold while waiting for the sun. But here the sun has never reached. Here is never warm. We did not always eat the spider. Until one day one long time in the past, when the moss was gone, the mushrooms, the sacrifices and the findings. All gone. We were dying inside and out. It was then that the spiders began to drop, many, many spiders dropping to us, some into the fire and some beside it. It was a sign to eat the spiders, to stay alive. And this is what we did." She gave Lillah a piece of bread, mimed eating it.

"All food has a partner, an opposite. Tomato and basil. Corn and potato. The spider once had an opposite: a white bird that flew low, caught fish and like to eat on the shore. A foolish creature. The last of his kind was eaten by those outthere many generations ago. The bird and the spider worked together. Spider flew on bird's back and bit the bird. In the spit of that bite was a good thing, it kept the bird travelling. Outthere, if they knew it; they would take every last spider for themselves. The spider survived, the bird did not. We always thank the spider when we eat it." She sprinkled one grain, maybe two, of sea salt onto the spider. "This is to remember the saltiness of the bird's blood. Salt is precious inside. You don't know that out there, where you have it in abundance."

"Not everywhere. And you need to work for it."

Lillah took the skewer and sniffed the spider. It smelt like cooked bird. Charred. They'd taken all the fur off, and removed the legs, though these Lillah could see on a plate close by.

She closed her eyes and bit into the spider. She chewed. "It's not bad. It actually tastes a bit like crab!"

Lillah closed her eyes and imagined she was eating crab. The texture was nasty; much chewier than it should be. And the thought of it made her ill. But she could feel it doing her good; every bite restored energy.

• • •

"Would you like to view a baby new born?"

"How do you know there's one? Nobody has brought a message."

He cupped his hand to his ear. "Hear the quiet talking? They call out who gave birth and where the child."

They travelled to see the baby. Lillah asked Santala where the placenta would be buried, or how they cooked to eat it.

"We would not eat it. How would we know which will be our leaders?"

Lillah remembered then that he had told her; they buried the placenta, then dug it up when the child became an adult. If the placenta was still perfect, that child would be a leader.

The mother wept. The tears of the insiders were thicker than those of the outsiders; opaque. Saltier, perhaps, Lillah thought.

She did not feel inclined to lick a tear from the face of the crying mother to find out.

"Is the baby all right?" Lillah said. Her guide took her hand.

"He's all right. But she will not live to keep him."

"What do you mean? Why will she die? Who'll take him?"

"She is weeping because she knows she will not live. She has lost too much blood. But she is not worried about her son. You see he is darker? His hair thick? That means he will fit in outside. She will leave him in a Leaf cradle and someone outside will take him as their own."

"Some say my mother was found that way."

"It's possible. You may have inhere blood. You see how we send babies we think will fit in, whereas outthere they leave babies they reject. Unwanted babies they expect to die."

"They don't realise you are taking the babies. If they knew they may think about it more."

"Different blood needs to mix with different blood. We all know that. You seek it as you travel around; we seek it too. Some of ours are yours, you know."

"We thought it was the monkeys feasting on the babies when they disappeared. But we never knew what happened to the bones."

Lillah stroked the baby's head. She said, "Can I take him? Will he come to me? I have missed my chance for children outside. I am tainted now. Too different. I will go back to Ombu and be an old woman."

"You don't have to do that. You can go wherever you want to go. To your lover, to Melia, to your father and brother. Your school is no longer your concern, and Morace isn't your concern either."

She felt a wonderful sense of freedom. The baby cried and she thought, "Do I want it? Do I want someone in my care or do I want to be free from responsibility?"

"There are many who want this baby," Santala said. "Many. There is no need for you to have him, unless you can give him all the love and care he deserves. Then we might consider it."

Lillah looked at the baby and felt nothing. She shrugged and smiled. Santala frowned at her, angry. "You think you should take this child? I don't. It needs a loving mother."

"You're right. Very right. I don't have to be a mother."

"You may be. You may turn out to be. But you won't be mother to this baby."

Lillah gathered spider webs and took them to the bleeding mother. She showed them how to stop the flow.

"You've never observed this?"

"We felt wrong in doing it. But perhaps we were wrong not to do it."

They travelled long and far. Some places on the inside had a great stink about them; dead places. Cold, empty spots he pulled her back from. "Don't step into there. I will not be responsible for a cold, senseless woman. Those are the places cursed by Spikes. Your people send it into us."

"Not all. Many send it out to sea."

"I wish they would not send it in to us."

"They think it is a sacrifice, and that the Tree purifies all. What would happen if you step into the dead spot?"

He grabbed her wrist. "We will not find out."

"Aren't you curious?"

"Not like you are. We like our knowledge safely."

"I am not like you. I want to know. I want to

know it all."

To distract her, Santala said, "You don't ask after your friends. Your school. Morace."

"Are they safe? Can you tell me?"

"We can. That is safe knowledge. Your school has reached Bayonet. Morace is not with them. He will join them at the next Order. Bayonet is not a good place for him to prove his wellness. Your school does not wish to stay for too long in Bayonet. There are terrible death rites there. Those to be jailed beg not to be sent there. It is a cruel place without mercy. It is a place of terrible nightmares, and they have cruel rituals to stave them off."

"You are frightened of them too?"

"More than any other Order we observe. They seem to have a magic others don't possess. They can bring a person back to life; we have seen them do it."

"They cannot."

"We have seen them."

Santala took her to a storyteller. There were many of these women, obsessed with the tale, unable to talk of anything else. This woman smiled as she spoke, an odd smile without humour. "One of the children of Bayonet died, and they cut him into pieces. They threw the pieces high into the Tree, the limbs, the torso, the head and they fell to ground whole. The boy stood. He was missing a foot, though, so they carved him one from wood. That boy did not lead a kind life; he was known for his slow slaughter of those who are sick, those who require treatment."

Lillah felt sick about how close Morace came to be treated in this way.

"I see that this is necessary. We all do. The sick will infect the rest." She could say this, now that Morace was safe. Earlier, she denied it.

"It is mostly that. It is also the natural desire to keep the population down. Our forefathers said that the crowding lead to disease, death, great and terrible suffering for all. If we keep our numbers down this will not happen. And a lesson forgotten, as well, when Spikes took so many of us." The old woman waved her hand up and down, a boat on the waves. "They lost the art of boat building. I think deliberately; they thought that way meant safety. That ignorance would keep them safe."

The storyteller shifted from buttock to buttock. She was large, her eyes unfocussed. She drank stone beer, huge swallows of the stuff which made her eyes roll back in her head and her voice to rise in pitch. She couldn't hear questions, just said the words she wanted to say. "In a cage out at sea; the killer from Osage. They give messages to him. He cries. 'I'm so lonely. I'm so sorry.' We can see what will happen. He is there for a while but soon he'll be sent out to sea. Cast adrift. Sent in the direction of the Island of Spirits. He shouts at them, 'I will escape and go back to my people. They will forgive me.' He rattles his cage weakly; it is clear he would barely make it to shore, let alone survive the long walk back to Osage if he escapes. He thinks he will float away, run away, but in fact they will kill him, send his body out to sea. They kill like this to keep away the nightmares. If you hear someone call out in the night, be wary. If you hear two people, be prepared. If you hear three people calling out with nightmares you must leave by the next night. They will kill one of you, they will carry out the death rite to appease the god of bad dreams.

"The death rite of the murderer. Someone tells him, 'They praise the strong. You are supposed to be quiet during your ordeal; accept the pain, let it purify you. If you scream, they will give you a drug to keep you quiet.'

"'Will it stop the pain?' he asks.

"'Yes. The pain will be numb along with your tongue. Feel something nice before you start screaming. Suck something sweet, kiss someone, run the dry sand through your fingers. Once the drug is swallowed, you'll never feel anything again.'

"He holds a smoothstone in his fist. Starts screaming as soon as they begin cutting, so they keep him quiet. The stone drops as he feels no more.

"They hum around him as his flesh is removed in chunks and thrown in the fire. The smell made your teachers, your children, strangely hungry; it had been a long time since they had eaten roasted animal. The last one was an enormous bird found with its wing broken. Unwilling to let it die in vain, they killed, cooked and ate him.

"This human flesh smelled similar."

Lillah did not believe the words; she did not want to believe them. "The children? They will be terrified by this."

They were interrupted as a quiet roar began. The storyteller stood up.

"The mother has died. Her story is over."

"Your webs did not work," Santala said.

"If you use them earlier next time, they will work," Lillah said.

Santala pulled out a pot of burnished metal. Lillah ran her fingers over it, marvelling at its coolness, its smoothness.

"We found this metal at the site of the aircraft landing. You will know it."

She nodded. "Sequoia. They don't use the metal themselves. They practise sacrifice inside it."

In the pot, a coppery powder which he pinched out and began rubbing into his face.

"This is how we look for the meal after a death ritual. This dust is only found in one place in the Tree."

"What is it from?"

He didn't answer, trying to distract her from his lack of knowledge by pinching some powder out for her. He didn't like not knowing the answers; he liked to know it all.

Lillah rubbed the powder into her face. Her guide nodded. "You look like one of us, now," he said.

They joined the largest group Lillah had seen in one place, in a massive cave in the roots of the Tree.

There was food on huge leaves; dried fish in lemon juice, soft fleshy coconut, spiders.

Lillah missed hot food. They cooked very rarely here, and then the food was only warm, because they used the heat of the Tree.

They sat on great fallen branches. Santala showed her how the Tree grew in rings, each year another ring, and how some years the growth was small, if the weather had been poor or if there was illness in the Tree.

There were two caughtchild women, treated well, like goddesses. They sat closest to the warmth, and had small fires burning nearby.

"Fire is the essence of fertility," Santala said. "They need to be close to fire to keep the child. We have had times when there is no fire, and the children are born dead, cold. We need fire to keep them warm. The prescience of fire. This is why you have more babies on the outside: you have the sun to keep the babies safe."

"We lose babies there, too."

"You kill babies there."

"Not me. I have never."

"You have condoned the death of babies. You have not hated the baby killers."

"She was my friend."

Lillah sat through the grieving ritual, all the while thinking of Thea, of her mother, and of all the women she had loved.

As they walked, Santala spoke. Lillah didn't interrupt him; she barely said a word. She hoped she could remember it all. This was the history, not etched in the Tree and lost, but spoken, handed down, known.

She would tell it like this when she left the Tree.

"I can tell you about the buildings," Santala said, wanting to show off his knowledge again. "The ones built by our ancestors, the scientists." His voice was soothing, vital. "They left buildings but the locals never took to them like they did the rest of the culture."

"There were people living here? Before the scientists?"

"Not many. And not well. They were so dispersed the families didn't grow large. They liked to live alone. It was only the scientists, with their houses, their idea of family, which grew the population."

They travelled. Walked. She came to understand how he thought and to guess what he would say next.

"Why are you devoting this time to me?"

"Not just to you, Lillah. You are the first to come to us with real thirst for knowledge, the first to listen without feeling as if I am saying you are lesser because you know less. It is so important for us to have one who knows."

Some days they moved slowly. "Time is different for us," Santala told her. "We live our lives more quickly. Our women mature more quickly, and our bodies shut down sooner. I am matured, Lillah. I am on the way out."

"The sun. You need the sun. You should venture out. Find a place. There is a large stretch of land between Parana and Torreyas and the market there is rarely used. You could set up there. Build. You could start a new Order outside."

"Would you help them? Live with them?"

"I would. But you will be among them."

"How would we keep our knowledge?"

"You would tell the schools as they come through. They will tell and remember themselves."

"This is for the future, though. It won't happen in my lifetime. It will take much time. I am too tired for it."

"I think two should go out, build, then more join them as time passes. You give yourselves a name from the Botanica, and you become one of the Orders."

"So much would be lost."

"You only lose what you choose to lose. No one will take it from you."

They spoke to other insiders as they travelled. Made plans. Asked questions. Some turned their backs, others showed interest. Santala seemed some days to be full of fire and energy. Others, he seemed unwilling to walk far, or to talk with her any more.

Santala led her through the Tree and she didn't ask where they were going. She listened and learned and tried to understand.

At one point they came to a place where the luminescence flowed thickly. There was a small cave beside it; the notation told her this is where the almost-dead crawled to die.

She didn't want to see it; she avoided it. Time, she told herself. She knew it was a two day journey into the place of death and she wasn't dying.

"Lillah," Santala said. "This is where I must leave you. I am tired and I am done. The journey will take me to the end of the trail."

"No!" Her scream made him bend over with pain, and she covered her mouth. She felt more grief than ever before; more than losing her mother, Morace, any of her teachers, Rham. She couldn't bear the thought of this man gone, of life without him. He had won her; she had won him. It was time, she thought. Time together. He was like a brother and she could not bear to be without him.

"This is my place. You should continue the journey. Climb up. Find the upsiders, the Rememberers, and learn from them, if they still live."

• • •

So Lillah said goodbye.

"They'll be watching," he said, and, far from disturbing her, this gave her comfort.

"I'll listen for them," she said. "And one day I may come back. If I knew you were here I would come back."

He nodded. "Yes, you may," he said. "But I will not be here. And I am too pale and soft for you, too quiet. You will find a lover and stay with him and his brothers. A lucky man. You will not find a lover amongst us. We are not strong enough for you. You will find someone good, who will listen to you. You will tell tales and people will love you."

"I will help you set up the community outside. Send someone to collect me when you are ready."

"Lillah, people know. They will make this move if they are ready. But I– I will not be among them. You will know them, though. One will come to tell you they are ready."

Lillah looked at him. "The more I know you, the more attractive you become," she said. His skin seemed to shimmer in the green glow. She bent to him and kissed his mouth, hoping it would be good and she could be carried away with passion, be with this good man once before she went back to the sun.

It was terrible. Slack-lipped, too soft, his tongue flopping weakly into her mouth. She pulled back and smiled.

"Goodbye," she said.

• • •

There were many decisions along the way. Lillah found choosing a direction very difficult. She had walked in a line outside, followed the sway and curve of the water. Here there were always options; sometimes three or four.

She learnt to read the notations by each tunnel. Inside the Tree was well-mapped.

Upward movement became natural to her, arms and legs in a rhythm she barely noticed.

Up here were berries, and there were birds. There was water in grooves and niches; she wasn't bothered by the grit in it, the woody flavour. As she climbed, she saw evidence of past habitation.

She learnt to wrap her feet in leaves to protect them from the roughness of the Bark. Many places were smooth, as if the tougher outer layers of skin had been shed and never replaced.

She almost gave up any number of times: when a tunnel she'd been following for days ended in a solid black mass of wood; when she saw skeletons tied to branches, flapping. These times she'd take out her pouch of dirt, given to her in Arborvitae and she would smell it. It brought her great comfort; the smell of home and the point of her journey, to learn, to take back the knowledge.

There were times she was lost, the signs not telling her where to go. The Tree was like a great maze. Sometimes she found bones in a pile, skulls grinning and she thought, This person was also lost.

She used the stones Maringa gave her, truly

believing they could help her find her way. Knowing they would help her map inside the Tree and find her way home again. She gave the marked stone to a young child she met along the way and asked her to deliver it to the ghost cave of Sargassum. She knew that Maringa would receive it and understand.

Lillah felt so exhausted some days all she wanted to do was curl up into a ball and sleep forever. Pull a cover over her head, hide from reality, not face what she knew or decide what to tell.

She heard laughter and wondered how anyone could be happy.

She found caves with walls of bone, walls of skulls. These were old, she thought, brittle and cracked, and there was a smell of the sea, somehow, salty and sweet at the same time.

Lillah knew she was reaching the top when the wood was old, so old it wasn't safe. Above her the canopy began and she couldn't climb in there. It was so dense, so thick. They had told her this; she hadn't believed them. Her way was smaller; sometimes she felt she was walking through hollow branches. Other times she sense she was close to the outside; she could feel a breeze, a light, clean breeze.

She looked for a sign of the Rememberers. Something left by the men and women who had formed

the Orders, who had landed and made this a place
for them.

She had seen remnants, these last few months.
Bones. Crumbled remains of Bark, thick Bark.
Metal rusted into a heap. Cups that looked like they
were made of water but were hard. She saw bird
nests so enormous four children could sleep in
them. She saw a hugeness so vast it filled her with
a sense of blankness.

She saw emptiness and the past, scrawls and
scraps. A shrine to the great botanist who set the
place up. The books. Santala had told her that in
these books were written the names of their communities, and their own names as well.

She found boxes, many small boxes, some still
filled with seeds. She had been told that the
botanists brought thousands of seeds with them,
giving Botanica its rich diversity.

She found no Rememberers.

It was big in the canopy, so vast. She felt it filling
her, the bigness, as it had elsewhere. A momentary
understanding of the hugeness of it all.

She tried to climb higher, but for the first time
felt unsafe. She stepped inside a hollow branch,
using the roof of it to rest her hands for support,
but she had not taken more than fifteen steps when
she heard a creaking noise.

She stopped. It was not the settling sound she
had grown used to. It was a harsher, rending noise.

She took a step forward, but felt the branch tilt slightly. She stopped. It tilted more, making her lose her footing. A cracking noise forced her to action at last, and she stepped backwards, knowing that she was not far from the trunk. Seven steps, eight, the branch tilted so far forwards she was thrown to her knees and had to crawl, pushing herself backwards until her toes reached the more solid wood of the central trunk.

She wriggled through. The branch she had been walking through cracked almost all the way through and she knew that if she'd been inside it, she would have plummeted with it through the branches below.

She rested, then she began to climb down.

Lillah knew which way her Order lay because she could read the notations, but she would need help to find the ghost cave that led out. She spoke to rare people along the way; they all knew how to send her to the next junction. She missed speaking to people. She liked to talk, to learn, and to tell tales. She had enjoyed the silence as she climbed the Tree, but she would not need that silence again.

After many months she entered the ghost cave of Laburnum, just one Order from Ombu. They made perfume there; Lillah found the smell cloying. She wanted to walk home, feel the sand, get used to being outside again. She didn't want to emerge in

Ombu. Too sudden. She did not want to be seen emerging from the Tree like a ghost. Santala had told her to sleep in the inner cavern before emerging into the ghost cave and outside.

"Your eyes will settle while you're asleep, and your eyelids will filter the light. It will seem very bright to you for a while, but you'll soon be used to it."

They had given her a cloth to shade her eyes because the bright sunlight could blind her. She draped this over her head and touched the wall of the cave. Light filtered in and Lillah thought she could smell it.

She stepped out of the Tree for the first time in five years.

The light was too painful, and the noise out there bothered her. She stepped back into the ghost cave, stopped near the entrance and closed her eyes. She slept to allow her eyes, and her ears, to adjust.

She awoke and stepped out again. The light was beautiful this time. Things seen in such detail, such perfect detail.

She stood close to the trunk and watched the Order of Laburnum. In this place the roots came out of the ground, reaching up and bending over with the huge, head-like flowers. Once these turned brown, they were removed and turned into perfume.

She watched as they threw wine at the Tree, hollering, their tongues making their voices vibrate. It was a sacrifice, though nothing like that she'd seen elsewhere around the Tree.

They sat in the Tree roots and the Tale-teller told of the burning Tree, the same story Lillah had heard so many times, so many variations. She knew now that story was a telling of Spikes, that they were warnings against disease and foretelling of the end of Botanica.

All Orders had these tales.

She smelt the sap flowing and saw them rubbing it into their hair, their eyes white in their heads.

In her mapping, Lillah told the Tree: *They tell the tales we tell all over the Tree.*

Here, the Tree grows as it always did. The sap flows.

She looked at the young men and wondered if she should take the chance on one of them, take up the life she had avoided so far. She felt as if her whole life was about drastic choices. Each choice taking her up a certain path, with no forks along the way. Unlike her journey within the Tree, which was all about choices. She looked at them and thought how easily she tired of men.

Lillah waited until night, until all was quiet, then she stepped away from the trunk. She carried very little. Her wooden necklace was in her bag. Some clothing she never wanted to see again.

Stones. Small mementoes she had picked up along the way.

She walked.

She loved the feeling of air on her skin, the smell of moisture in the air. She had missed this, inside, where every day was the same.

Lillah passed the market. She had forgotten the seaweed stench of this area. It was worse, though. Thicker. Deeper. The seaweed was sludgy beneath her feet and she considered climbing into the Tree, walking through the labyrinthine tunnels and roots to get home.

It would take too long, though, and she was very anxious now to get home.

She walked.

As she rounded the rock, knowing she was almost home, her step faltered. She wondered if they would know her, or if they thought her long dead and a ghost.

She could see people working by the water and in the roots, but she didn't recognise them. Her eyes were used to close distances and she couldn't see the faces, the details. She felt suddenly desperate to see those faces and she ran, loving the strength in her legs built from climbing and walking.

She saw a young woman bent over a bench, cutting fish carefully.

It was one the children, grown. Borag.

"Borag! Borag!"

Borag put down her net and looked up, shielding her eyes. She pointed.

Lillah walked closer. "Borag! It's me! It's Lillah!"

"Teacher! Teacher! Lillah!" Borag screamed. She ran to Lillah and they embraced. She was taller than Lillah and had a deep voice, full of laughter.

"Still the cook, Borag?"

"I am! I plan to be the best cook who ever travelled the Tree."

"You will be." Lillah thought briefly of her mother, also a travelling cook, a grudging sharer. She wondered if her father would like to know the truth of his wife's death, or if she should say nothing.

"You look so skinny and pale, Lillah! Where have you been?"

Suddenly exhausted, Lillah embraced Borag again. "Let's gather the others and we can share the stories together. Where is everyone?"

Borag waved her hands. "All over. Let's walk over to your father and they will gather. Look, there's Zygo! Zygo! It's Lillah returned!"

Zygo, handsome and tall, was fishing. He carefully laid his net beyond the tide line and walked to Lillah. She was struck by his maturity, by the powerful way he held himself. He took her hands. "We thought you'd died. Morace said you disappeared in the Tree."

"Morace? He made it home?" Lillah was nervous about seeing Morace. They had been through so much together; he owed her so much, yet she didn't want to be paid back. She worried that it would affect their relationship.

"Yes, yes, he caught up with us. He is well, Lillah. Very well. I am very happy to see you alive."

"And you, Zygo. And you. You must be looking for a wife soon."

He turned away. "Not you too!"

Borag said, "Everyone asks him. He says he is not sure he wants a wife but no one will listen to him."

Lillah heard a shout and turned to see Morace running towards her. He stopped short as he reached her, and they looked at each other for a long time. She drew him to her, and they held each other, speechless.

"You're so handsome, Morace. Look at you. Strong! You look so well."

"I am well. I will always be well. I feel so much responsibility to make my life worthwhile. You saved it; I must make it worthy."

"You just need to live it, Morace. Though I would appreciate some help once I get older!"

The others began to talk at once. They seemed like children again, these young adults.

"How did it feel to come home?" Lillah said. "When you came upon Ombu. What did it feel like?"

"As we rounded the rocks, we knew we were almost home. We were on our side of the island. We told each other, 'We're nearly home.' Morace cried, didn't you, Morace?" Borag said.

"We all cried, you know. It had been five years without our families. And I knew my mother would not be there to greet me."

Zygo interrupted, saying, "But Lillah, tell us about you. You survived the ghosts. How did you? We thought the ghosts had taken you. Erica sent news that one of their men had been taken. That man Sapin. A dead-but-walking came out and took him. We said he deserved it. Don't you remember how they killed that dead-but-walking? I have never forgotten. You are lucky you didn't stay with him, Lillah. He was not a good man. He was worse than the men of Douglas."

"He was a good man. That was their way, Zygo. Didn't you learn that on the walk? That each place has their way, and their way doesn't make them bad?" Lillah turned away. Sapin dead? The dead-but-walking had never been aggressive before. Her thoughts of Sapin were ruined, now. She wondered what the real story was. If perhaps one of the other men had killed Sapin and blamed it on the dead-but-walking. She could not imagine the evolved insiders killing.

"He is worse than the ghosts on the inside."

"There are no ghosts in there. There are people like us."

There was silence. They looked at each other, wondering how she could say such a thing. She saw that she would need to tell a lot of tales for the truth to be known.

"And speaking of family," she said, suddenly breathless. "MY family! I must see them, now now now!" The children laughed at her.

She felt such joy, deep joy at the thought of seeing Logan, her dear, dear brother, her greatest friend. Unbetrayed.

She said, "My brother. I must see my brother, and Magnolia, and the baby."

Laughter at that.

"Time didn't stand still while you were gone," Morace said. "There is no longer a baby!"

Logan and his family were fishing off the seawalk. Lillah walked out to meet them and as she did it was like eight years dropped away. She remembered walking this wood, the splinters, the way the air changed as you walked to sea. She had seen so much since then, done so much.

"Logan," she said. Her voice carried away seagull-wise; a cawing, loud shouting over the top of her soft missing voice.

"Logan," louder, more excited, and he heard this time. Measured, he handed the rod to a small child. The boy she had seen born would be at school. Eight years old. This one was only five or six.

"Lillah." They embraced. Both knew this was a rare moment. So few siblings shared this.

"Lillah." It was Magnolia, so happy, her face the same with a few lines, so like her brother.

Logan said, "We thought you were one of those old women, as you approached. The walking women."

"No, I'm not that old, thank you! Is that all you can say to me?"

He punched her lightly on the arm. "Still a fussy little sister, I see. That hasn't changed."

She embraced him again, and this time they held each other until tears came.

"Come on," Magnolia said. "Let's go to your father. And you must be hungry. Let's eat something."

The little girl at her feet tugged her skirt. "I'm hungry." She picked her up.

"This is your niece, Aralia. Her brother is off at school, isn't he, Aralia?"

Aralia hid behind her mother's legs. "She will be over being shy soon and you will not be able to get rid of her!" Magnolia said.

"She's beautiful," Lillah said.

Magnolia put her hand on Lillah's belly. "No child there?"

"I am without child. I'll be an outcast here."

Magnolia shook her head. "You'll live with us. We have a big house now, and room for plenty.

"What about Morace? Where does he live? I didn't ask him."

"He's with your father."

"Not his own father?"

"The Birthman became bitter and difficult after his wife died. He wants nothing to do with Morace and could not see the miracle of his return."

"And our father doesn't mind?"

"Why should he mind? Morace is a pleasant and amusing young man. At the same time, he is training to be the next Birthman, so Rhizo's husband must have contact with him. Come on, let's go see your father."

"He'll be so happy, Lillah," Logan said. As they walked, he said quietly, "Did you get my message?"

"I did. You wanted to know how it felt to stay the same. By which you meant, I know you have changed. And of course you were right. We are all changed by even the smallest experience. We cannot stay the same no matter how hard we try. Did you get my message?"

"I got yours, too. You made me very proud."

Her father stood quietly, building a sturdy chair.

"Father!" she called. He looked only a year or two older, not an old man at all.

"Lillah! Oh, Lillah!" He carefully put down his tools – he would never drop them – and held out his arms.

To be held by her father was the most comforting, safest feeling she had ever had.

As they ate, Lillah said, "I know what happened to my mother."

She waited. Her father looked at the high branches of the Tree, as if seeking comfort. "What can you tell me?"

"She didn't stop at Rhado. They were unpleasant there. Unwelcoming. She walked on." She touched her ear. "Walked on. Until she reached Alga. Do you remember walking through there as a child?"

He shook his head.

"They are good people." She touched her ear again. "Here, she was happy. For a short while. And in her happiness, she died. Of that I am certain."

Myrist nodded again, staring unblinking at the Tree. "I am glad to hear that she was happy. That someone could make her happy."

"She was happy with us, Father. But she needed more. Some of us do. We need more than the small life we are given."

Morace joined them, standing happily, quietly, nearby.

"And your brother Legum. He is legendary. He is known as the man who travelled away on a raft and was never seen again. Some say he is living on Spirit Island. Some say he found some new place and has started a family there. One community said he came back."

"To them?"

Lillah looked away. "They say he came back, his bones picked clean by the birds."

"How like him," Myrist said, though he did not say how.

After the meal, Lillah wandered around the home she never thought she would see again. She saw the wooden doll she had carved while walking with the school. Up high, pride of place. Looking at it, she felt as if a stranger had carved it.

Myrist said, "You and Morace should go to see Pittos. He is lonely."

"He only sees me to pass on instruction. He doesn't talk to me like he used to," Morace said.

"What about when you came home? Wasn't he happy to see you?" Lillah asked.

"He was, at first. But somehow he has become more and more angry."

They went together to Pittos.

"Lillah. I heard you were back. Thank you for keeping Morace safe."

"It took some doing. I am pleased to have done it, though. Are you happy to have him?" When he didn't respond, Lillah put her hand on the man's shoulder. "Do you miss Rhizo? Are you lost without her?"

"She was not a good woman. Yet she was mine."

"You are whole without her. And Morace misses you."

"Morace is busy."

"He misses you."

The Birthman turned his back. "I will see him at the birth of Dickson's child. He will assist me then."

"Dickson! I haven't seen him yet."

"You go. I am busy."

"We heard some terrible news when we travelled. About Dickson and a child. How he kept her in a cave until she died."

The Birthman turned to face her again. "Strange. What strange news. We did have a terrible tragedy here, but Dickson did all he could. It was a student, only fourteen years old. It seems that one of the men of Laburnum took her. That's what they said. The child came to us, without her school. She had caught child. Dickson cared for her in one of the Tree caves, bringing her food and making her feel safe. From all accounts she was cared for well. But she died in childbirth, and the child did as well. We were all there. We all saw it. He did all he could and so did I. Messengers can not always be believed."

Lillah felt great relief to hear this, though also anger at the message they had received which had caused them grief in Gulfweed.

Morace said, "That is not what we heard."

"Perhaps your ears are at fault, then," Pittos said. He did not look at Morace as he spoke.

"You see?" Morace said as they walked away. "He doesn't care about me."

"I'm sure he does care. I think he cares too much," Lillah said. "You remind him of Rhizo and that Rhizo was not only with him. That must be hard."

"But how can he not love me enough to get over that?"

"Because he loved her more. That is how men are. They love the women in their lives more than they love the children. That's how it should be.

You'll feel that way about a woman one day."

"Maybe. Dickson does."

"Let's go see him. I'm so happy to learn he is not guilty of killing a child."

They were at home, sitting to a meal.

"Lillah!" Dickson jumped up. He looked fatter around the cheeks; he liked to eat. "My dear girl."

His wife put her spoon down and stood up. "Lillah. The explorer. I'm Capri. Mother of his four children. All four!"

She took Lillah's hand. She was tall, with strong features. Around her neck, a beautiful shell necklace.

"Did we meet along the way?" Lillah asked.

"I remember your school as you passed through. I remember thinking how clever you were, and thinking your community would be a good one."

"Where are you from?"

"Douglas. I left for school soon after you left."

"We were distracted in Douglas. I'm sorry I don't remember you. I'm glad they let a school group go."

"It was Thea, mostly. She inspired us. She told us of the other people, other places. Before she died."

"I'm glad she did some good."

"She really did. Clever sister," Dickson said. He seemed genuinely happy and in love. Lillah did not talk to him about the young woman he had tried to save. She would do that another time.

His children seemed healthy and happy.

• • •

Smoothstones lined a shelf on the Tree, those gone, those returned, those dead, those settled in new Orders. There were the stones for Rham and Thea; the dead remembered. The others weren't there and it seemed odd to Lillah that here they didn't know Gingko, Rubica, Tamarica, Musa, Ster or Phyto.

As she touched all these stones, an older woman joined her.

Lillah stared too hard, barely recognising her.

"It's me. Aquifolia. You see the lives of the girls I've turned into teachers. Written in the lines on my face."

"In other places, they just gather together and go. They don't have someone to look after them like we do. The girls here are very lucky. We are very lucky." Lillah blinked at her, thinking of Maringa, Aquifolia's scarred mother. "Your mother saved us. She is an amazing woman. Slightly terrifying. She understood the message you sent. She saved my life, Aquifolia. And Morace's."

Lillah stroked the burn scar on her forearm. Maringa had seen black air, hard to breathe. She wondered if she was looking back, not forward. Seeing the place they came from, not the world they were making here.

"We heard about you and what you did. You cursed us. Cursed us all. You have cursed the womb of every woman here by not choosing to have a child," Aquifolia said.

"And yet I see the bellies full around me," Lillah said, wondering why Aquifolia hated her so much.

"And your friends. A bad bunch from what we've heard. Thea a killer by all accounts, and your Melia so unpopular with the children."

"Melia did fine," Lillah, unwilling to talk about the many betrayals. She had realised that her expectations of Melia were too great. Lillah had needed more than Melia could give. It was always going to end badly.

"I am married now, you know. You haven't congratulated me or told me I am fortunate."

"We heard on the school. Araucari is a good man."

"Don't you talk of him. Don't you go near him. He is my man, not yours."

"I don't want him, Aquifolia."

"That's not what he says," the woman muttered. Lillah took her arm.

"He is your man, Aquifolia. He married you. Not me. I have no desire for him. He is a good man, but he is yours."

Aquifolia shook her arm off. "I know that. And you know that. But does he?"

Next, Lillah went to see Annan, the Tale-teller. "Lillah! My greatest listener!" He was older and so full of stories the day passed and night fell before Lillah said goodbye to him.

"You are the best Tale-teller of the Tree, without comparison," she told him. "They should learn from you."

"Ah, I'm too old for that. You have done well, Lillah, as have your companions. Ster, Tamarica, Musa and Rubica are settled happily, we are told. Tamarica stayed with Phyto at Osage and she is very happy. Melia is a mother and happy with it." Though Melia's father told her afterwards that while Melia had three babies, she had lost a fourth to drowning. Lillah didn't talk of the irony of Melia, the great protector of children, having one die in her care.

"I am so pleased for all of them. I miss them."

"That is the nature of the Tree, Lillah. We must let go, bud out. There is no other way."

He scrabbled in his belongings. "Here. This is from Tilla. He left you a message. We buried him at sea not two years ago."

It was a smoothstone, carved with a beautiful bird. "He means to say that he was wrong. He means that he now accepts that the school is not dangerous and that you are safe."

She wished she had said goodbye to Tilla.

That evening, at the feast, Lillah sat while her Order celebrated around her. The younger children didn't know who she was, but they brought her small gifts, showed off smoothstones, if they were old enough. Borag, red-faced but unflustered, cooked a wonderful feast of crabs, fish and greens.

They sat and reminisced about the school, and only mention of Rham made them silent. The thought of a great teacher killed before she became one.

Annan said, "We are thinking of your punishment, Lillah."

"My punishment?"

"You concealed an illness. Morace's. You kept him safe by endangering life all around the Tree."

"But he wasn't sick!" Lillah said.

They nodded. "True. True enough. We will let you know."

Lillah knew it would be all right. If they threatened to jail her she would run into the Tree and find her insiders.

Lillah watched the young women prepare for testing. It was a great thing, the school. It kept the island whole and living with understanding. One of the things Lillah realised is how they needed each other to continue. Each element of life different to another but vital to it.

She shared what she knew with her people, told them the things she'd learned inside the Tree. The history, the background. Why they were there. It did not find a good audience: she was saying that all creation myths were false. Also that they came from a diseased place. Lillah saw the flaws in her own community after she had been away from it. It wasn't the perfect place she thought it was.

But she liked the way they listened to her when

she talked of her experiences. When they felt she wasn't trying to give them a lesson. She liked playing the role of Tale-teller.

Santala had said, "All else in this world are dead. They may be small enclaves, or large Orders like ours on other islands. Maybe they keep to themselves like we do. Maybe they have laws passed down, don't cross the water. Keep the island pure from deep sea footprints."

The child-adults told her of the Orders she'd missed:

Chrondus they spoke very little of. "They believe in punishment there," Zygo said, and his eyes slitted. His lips turned down. If even Zygo found it disturbing, Lillah did not want to know.

Osage, full of beautiful golden skinned men. Phyto waited for them there and he was happy, but not blissfully. "He realised that life is never perfect," Borag said. "They made nice food there."

Bayonet where the old woman who'd walked behind them for so long belonged. They were very fearful of illness.

Laburnum, of course, which Lillah had seen and smelt but not experienced. "They were good, there. You didn't meet your replacement, of course, but she stopped there. I think she was nervous of reaching home with us. She thought we never thought she was as good as you."

Zygo brought Lillah a bowl of coconut milk.

"I'm not an old woman, you know. Nor am I crippled."

"No, you're not." His voice was deep but his face still boyish.

"Tell me more about Phyto. Do you remember? How was it when you got to Osage?"

Zygo laughed. "Happy. Very, very happy. He had that look you teachers get sometimes, when you see the men and they see you. He said they were cautious at first. They told us some schools couldn't understand. That the men had to pretend, or the teachers got angry. Most teachers are happy to form brotherly friendships, though."

"I was," Lillah said. "I wish I'd seen him settled."

"We'll send him a message that you've come home. He will want to hear."

They ate some fried coconut.

"Part of me wanted to stay with him. With them," Zygo said.

"You feel that way?"

"I don't know. I'm attracted to women, but I like men as well. I like Morace."

"You will have to see how life plays out."

Lillah wondered if Zygo was meant for something great. And Morace too. Any justification she had that she was saving him for something great may well be proven wrong. She had saved him for no other reason than individual survival.

• • •

Later, she asked them if they still have nightmares about the rituals they witnessed. They did; every one of them dreamt bad, and Lillah felt furious that the other teachers had allowed them to witness it.

Zygo said, "Have you explored enough? Or would you be willing to take on more?"

"Such as?"

"Spirit Island. Just to see. As you've seen inside. New land."

"They told you why we shouldn't travel."

"Not a long way. Just to Spirit Island. To take away the fear."

"We'll be killed on return. Banished, at least. We won't be welcome back."

"Perhaps."

Morace said, "Me, too. I want to come."

Lillah knew that Zygo had spent a lot of time with Logan. "He's a thoughtful young man now," Logan told her. "He questions, and makes connections. It's been wonderful to see him grow."

The Birthman approached her. "Lillah, are you here to stay?"

She had not spoken to him since their first conversation. She couldn't speak of Rhizo; it made her angry.

"Yes. I will not seek children."

"Then perhaps you will agree to be our Tale-teller once Annan passes. You have the skills beyond any other. And the knowledge."

Lillah had been hoping to hear this question. She had been hoping to hear it for many years; hoping that she would not have children, that she could tell the tales.

"Oh, Pittos, thank you. To be the Tale-teller would be my greatest dream. But Zygo is right; there is so much more to see. So much more for me to learn. I want to know all that before I become the Tale-teller."

"You don't imagine Annan will die tomorrow! He has many years. You should do what you need to do, Lillah. You will make our community great with knowledge."

And I have promised Santala, she thought. The day would come when his insiders came out, and she would need to join them. She did not know how she could do it, knowing that he was dead.

"What about your son, Pittos? What about Morace? He is in pain every day. He did not ask for any of that to happen. He is the same boy as when he left, except he knows so much more. He needs you."

"I know, Lillah. Every morning I wake up hating myself, and every night I go to sleep with the same thoughts. I will come to love him for himself, not as my son. But it can't happen so quickly."

"Maybe a little more quickly," Lillah said, smiling.

Rutu, the trader, returned from visiting Laburnum. "I can't believe you've returned!" she said.

"What things you've learnt and seen!" Lillah knew that in Rutu she would always have someone to talk to. Someone who found pleasure in the new and the mysterious.

Morace told Lillah, "I want to be the market holder. They have told me I must be the Birthman, but I want to be the market holder. I can't be both. Can you talk to them? Tell them that I must be happy?"

"I will try, Morace. But who will be the Birthman in your place? And why do you imagine Rutu would give up her position?"

"There are many who want to be Birthman, Lillah. Many young people you don't know. It is a great glory, to be Birthman."

"I don't know what I can do, Morace. You are old enough now to sort these things out for yourself. You must talk to Rutu first. See if she will be happy to share the job."

"She likes to walk but she does not like to stay at the market and sell. I can stay there."

"Then that is what you'll suggest to her. You are not scared of the ghosts?" Lillah smiled as she said this.

"Lillah, my own people sliced half of my thigh away and would have sliced the rest if you had not saved me. I have no fear of anything after that. You and I know about the ghosts, Lillah. I intend to trade with them as well. You know that I can do it."

"I know, Morace. You will change the world."

• • •

Lillah showed the potmakers how to use ground-up seaweed to bind the clay.

"They have a lot of knowledge in there," the pot-maker said. Lillah had a worry. Would the outsiders think they could take what the insiders had? Would they even believe her when she told them of how the insiders lived, of their intelligence and love, of their rituals and beliefs? She resolved not to talk about it yet. She did try to convince people there was no such thing as ghosts. This was important; to lay the groundwork for when the insiders were ready to come out.

The last thing Lillah did each night was to place a pouch of salt inside the ghost cave, for those inside to spice their food. She hoped it helped.

While she was there she told the Tree all she had heard in the day, all she had seen, all she had learned.

She told the Tree the truth.

Dramatis Personae
(in order of appearance)

Lillah	Main teacher
Morace	Main student
Logan	Lillah's brother
Magnolia	Logan's wife
Melia	Lillah's best friend
Thea	Teacher
Dickson	Thea's brother
Tax	Thea's brother
Pandana	Lillah's favourite teacher
Olea	Lillah's mother
Rhizo	Morace's mother
Erica	Teacher
Tilla	Old man in Ombu
Sapin	Lillah's true love
Cynthia	Melia's mother
Gingko	Teacher who replaces Agara
Ruth	First female botanist

Tamarica	Teacher who replaces Thea
Rubica	Teacher who replaces Gingko
Musa	Teacher who replaces Erica
Agara	Teacher
Ster	Teacher who replaces Melia
Aquifolia	Woman who organises the teachers
Araucari	Aquifolia's husband
Santala	Guide inside the Tree
Borag	Student who loves to cook
Rham	Smart student
Zygo	Student
Corma	Pregnant girl
Hippocast	Corma's husband
David	Original male botanist
Annan	Tale-teller at Ombu
Bursen	Lillah's first lover
Gutt	Aquifolia's lover
Pittos	Morace's father, Ombu's birthman
Simarou	Lillah's Aunt, Olea's sister
Ebena	Magnolia's brother
Capri	Dickson's wife
Ulma	Melia's sister
Legum	Lillah's uncle, Myrist's brother
Ruta	Ombu's trader

RECORD 18779/ddgrf/c(i)/9032

The Formation of the Island of Botanica

The rising tide swallowed many islands as the third millennium closed. By then, humankind had returned to basic survival. Hand to mouth subsistence farming. The Spikes epidemic, which took ninety percent of the population in the years between 2107 and 2212, had died with its last victim, but the rise of the animals and insects made human life precarious. Plant life was at risk through disease and the needs of the food chain. Plagues of locusts, intent on survival, roared through food crops. Domesticated cattle chewed grass to the ground and tore out the roots with their flat teeth.

In some areas, volcanic mud spewed for centuries, and in others new land masses were thrown up by the shifting plates.

In 2519 a group of scientists, the last existing perhaps, set sail for what they had identified as the highest point in the Pacific, an island perhaps five hundred years old and approximately 800,000 km², the size of Turkey, filled with a legendary, ancient Tree. They were botanists and plant biologists and they took with them a Noah's Ark of seeds. They did not bother with animals, wanting to avoid the virulent nature of breeding and the future temptation to farm animals for food. Spikes had come from abusive animal consumption and other manipulations.

The island of Botanica was only sparsely inhabited; most of the area's people believing it to be filled with spirits.

The cause of fear was the massive Tree which almost filled the island. Such a monstrous thing in nature must have grown on the spirits of man; most people would not step foot on the land, or even sail close to shore.

Rainfall was adequate on the island and the Tree itself grew year by year.

The inhabitants were an undeveloped, disparate group living at far extremes in small communities. With the Tree filling most of the island, there was no cross-country travel and very little circumnavigation.

When the colonists arrived, life changed.

About the Author

Kaaron Warren's award-winning short fiction has appeared in *Year's Best Horror & Fantasy*, *Fantasy* magazine, *Paper Cities*, and many other places in Australia, Europe and the US. She has stories in Ellen Datlow's *Poe* and *Haunted Legends* anthologies.

Her short story "A Positive" has been made into a short film called *Patience*, and her first published story, "White Bed", has been dramatised for the stage in Australia, where she lives. Her stunning first novel, the Ditmar Award-winning *Slights*, is also available from Angry Robot, who will also be publishing her modern-day fantasy about immortal magicians, *Mistification*.

kaaronwarren.wordpress.com

Author's Notes

THREADS

Keeping track of all of the different communities was one of the key challenges I faced in writing *Walking the Tree*. As a result, I have an exercise book where I kept notes about what they ate, how the spoke, whether or not they had a platform out over the sea, what their relationship with the Tree was. I added to, changed, referred back to this constantly.

The other thing I had to keep straight was something I called *Threads*. These were my many, many thoughts on the things I wanted to say. Character traits, actions, plot developments, philosophical thoughts, language; everything. These appeared throughout the first couple of drafts in square brackets, but I realised I couldn't keep them all in my head that way, so I pulled them all out, categorised them, and labelled them Threads.

The fourth draft was all about lacing these threads through the novel. Some of them didn't work; others became irrelevant. This lacing helped to determine some of the story line. Part of writing is to use your threads as part of the story, rather than as a download of info.

So if my thread says "the bachelor house", I didn't want to write a paragraph about how the bachelors all lived together in one house, I wanted to have that bachelor house as part of the story. Either moving the story forward, or building the mood in a particular community, and/or developing character. I used the bachelor house in the community of Douglas (or Bad Men, as I nicknamed it). Douglas was an important community because it is where we realise just how filled with self-hatred Thea is. It also shows the women in control, as they leave early rather than "put up with" the men of Douglas.

Part of my inspiration came from stories of habitual rape on Pitcairn Island. Abuse as an accepted part of a society is horrifying. I also had at the back of my mind a small story told to me years ago, about an innocent young girl and a group of men who teased her about wearing a "pearl necklace". They didn't do anything about it, but they mocked her and to me the intent was very strong. A "pearl necklace" is something you probably don't want to google. This was the sort of man I wanted to inhabit Douglas.

We thought you might find it interesting to see this in action, so what follows here are just a few pages of my Threads. I had about forty of these pages – that fourth draft took a long time!

House

Back home; what is organiser doing? Does Lillah lie or tell the truth about what happened to the parcel organ. Sent? She could easily get away with the lie.

Living arrangements; girls will live with an auntie between 13-18 years old.

Need to talk about variety of living arrangements. Not just male/female.

Need to think about the dwellings. This will be part of who the people are.

Now here's a thought; when the children come back from school, they don't live with their parents. They are sent in groups to the homes. So the family unit could be two carers and three 11 year-old girls, or two carers and two 10 year-old boys etc. This way the children are not physically reliant on one set of adults; the kid groups are never broken up, but they move about to different homes together. So Lillah, Melia and Thea have been together like sisters.

Or perhaps not in this community, but it other communities.

The bachelor house.

Details of the homes, the things they have – all wooden, or from the sea. Lots of shells large shells for bowls etc. Coral for scrubbing. Sea sponges, sea weed, etc. Add to existing descriptions.

Do most houses have 360 degree veranda, all made of wood from the tree and driftwood? In words.

Enough about houses? Distinguishing feature? More metal used here?

Furniture. What sort of rooms do they have Some of this will depend on how/when the sun is there. They sleep more if there's less sun. Rooms will change depending on how their life is.

I think the houses are simple. Four rooms. Perhaps they all like a little privacy. Covered?

What is slightly different about their houses? The distinguishing feature.

History

Tall women. "So long ago that no one remembers, the people who lived here were as tall as ten women." (ALL THESE KINDS OF REFERENCES TO WOMEN.)

Birth

Are there more males born than females?

Babies born with longer fingernails to catch onto the mothers insides so they don't slip out.

Deformities left hanging off branches instead? This as an underlying tale; beauty/great ugliness.

Discovery of malformed babies. Here, in community 6, so we see it afterwards on the journey?

Have they heard the rumours before? Will need to add that in.

From *New Scientist*: In societies where women are promiscuous, sperm competition is greater; bigger testes, higher sperm count, more viscous sperm to prevent later partners; sperm reaching egg. Higher rates of protein evolution. Sexual selection drives changes in the protein.

So the people of the tree are highly developed. Examples of.

Losing a child. The younger the child, the less actual life he lived, but more imaginary life. A child who dies a little older has more actual life, less possible life. And his possible life is more confined because of the character developed. So a newborn who dies had an entire possible life. An entire perfect life.

Mention placenta in a couple of communities. Inside the tree as well.

Pregnancy called "catching a child".

Re: pregnancy. Realisation that a virgin is never pregnant.

She stretched in the sunlight. Lillah saw her belly as her shirt lifted up; broad, white, stretched, it looked uncomfortable.

Behind her an elder appeared. "It's well past time. It will take you too long to reach Ailanthus if you don't leave soon. You don't want to birth it in the sand, do you?"

"She is testing her resolve," Melia said. "What is the point?" Lillah said. She learns why as she travels; thinking/realisation that superstition for superstition's sake can be dangerous.

Where do the people with no new babies live?

Death

Death seen as failure.

Is a baby who's mother dies thought less of? Does someone say, it only ever happens with the boy babies.

Mourning; how is it approached: physically ie shave heads etc? or will great acceptance? Or with a sense of denial. They believe a body lives forever, will look to a bird, a baby, a turtle, as the vessel for the soul. Will not kill a turtle if they think it has a human soul.

Names of different suicides.

Death. Ongoing responses to deaths of Rham, Gingko (residual response: nightmares?), Thea, Rhizo

Some will prop a corpse up, pretending it is still alive.

When does kid die? Or does lilla keep them all safe?

When does teacher die? Bad men, i think.

When the tree sheds leaves, it can be natural disaster. Houses crushed sometimes. People killed under the weight. Standing right next to the trunk is the safest place.

X 2 story told of insiders 'dead but walking' and slaughtered.

Plague

One thing all the communities share: distrusts of deformity/illness.

Any ill person is killed. Hung from a limb. They don't want disease to spread after the lesson of the plague. Each community has a special hanging limb. It is done with respect. It is like a sacrifice to the community.

Does their fear of disease make them repel any sailors?

From 11. Thread pushing forward here is Morace: news of his mother makes him nervous.

He is weakening himself.

Discuss her dilemma; does she risk civilisation to save one child? Does she disbelieve the plague myth? Does someone talk to her about this, convince her that fear of plague is misguided now?

Mention how carefully Lillah looks out for Morace never lets him get cold. Always has honey or something for his throat, so he never has to cough.

Is it, though? I think that's too contrived. I think he lives, survives. Enough. Shows that all illness is not plague.

Maybe the plague killed so many their evolution was set back 1000 years. So they don't travel over the ocean. They don't have the big boats to do it.

One community; knows the names of those who died in the plague.

Plague kills ¾ of the population a hundreds years of more in the past. This is when the school started, this killing of sick people and the swapping of women. Her grandma tells her this.

The plague was a deforming one. First sign was lumps growing out of the shoulder blades. Spurs (Spikes) mark II.

Bonsai

Bonsai (or miniature tree? Need to decide what the language will be; her terminology from our place and time remaining in theirs?). Clear?

Research. Complete in more detail once researched a little about bonsai:

How they are grown?

What soil works best?

Community

Are there other communities which have an adversarial relationship with the tree?

Communities close by, the next door neighbours, have some effect on Lillah's birth community. Mention them.

Life on the Amazon is a little like tree world. Maybe some research for details.

Family. I'm wondering if there would be monogamy or not. With the transient life of some of them, maybe there would be more moving around, not the traditional family we think of??? Lillah discusses this with hubby.

Organiser lives in the community next to the one which knows about the morning after bark. Therefore she knows about it and tells the girls.

People. The people are not unhappy. It is utopian, really, with a system which is acceptable to make it work.

Markets – amongst the roots of the tree.

Fire

Fire is cleansing.

Need a scene earlier before 15, where Lillah burns herself, or is deliberately burnt by the organiser. We think its an act of malice, but realise she is laying scar tissue for her mother to read.

Not so much a fear of fire. More a caution. Respect. They need fire, the need the burning of wood to survive.

Check at end. Use this in description of house. In words.

Respect of fire here: they listen, perhaps. They know the sound a fire makes at ever level. This would be similar around the tree.

Like the Inuit have dozens of names for snow, these people have dozens of names for fire, all the variations;

Warmth of fire (hot, warm, too hot)

Cooking fire (bake, slow back, fast grill, variations in between)

Fire going out, needs attending

Fire too hot

Dangerous fire

Fire gone, too late

Fire left to go out, done with

Names for all these.

Fire/respect a few more times throughout. Insert later if needed.

Maybe the cookhouses are made of tin, so they can use fire.

They would be fearful of fire because everything is made of wood. So how would they heat their houses? Heavily insulated. Perhaps hot coals in a pit below the house.

Not so much a fear of fire. More a caution. Respect. They need fire, the need the burning of wood to survive

Check at end. Use this in description of house. In words.

Sun

Ask: Who would know this stuff, be able to figure it out? An astromer, perhaps.

When would it be dark?
When would it be light?
How often would the sun reach each place?

Food

Alcohol. Any or none? Alcohol produced from wood products. Methanol is wood alcohol, wood spirit. Drinking or inhaling it can cause blindness or death. This could be a feature.

Research. It would be fairly barren ground. All sustenance would go to the tree. Or does the tree help the ground? Research this? And would the air be highly oxygenated?

Disgust at the thought of eating spiders. Clear?

Every part of tree edible if you work hard enough. Clear?

Have they connected food with life? Clear?

I guess they would eat insects – certainly the insiders would.

Giant spiders from Venezuela taste like crab. Outsider/insider, sea/tree, crab/spider.

Spiders have more protein than beef does.

Think about the food. Research. Describe some of the dishes. Research.

Usually would surround the house of a newborn and have a shared feast, food passed around the circle/metaphor for the tree/community, so don't disturb but do display support, etc. Covered?

What happens when stormy? Long house.

Uses for leaves; plates, already mentioned. Clear?

Usually would surround the house of a new-born and have a shared feast, food passed around the circle/metaphor for the tree/community, so don't disturb but do display support etc. Covered?

Wheat flour? What sort of flour? What would grow in this environment? I need a botanist! Check.

Would wheat grow?

How could they grow it?

Most things would have to grow hydroponic.

Research hydroponics.

Answer this by the end.

Smell

Bad smells buried.

They know a bad smell means something unhealthy to the human body. Enough?

They trust their noses. Are trained to follow nasal instinct. Enough?

Men

Dickson is making a necklace for his bride in A, and asks Lillah to spread the word. DOES SHE SEND A TEACHER HIS WAY? ONE WHO SHE THINKS COULD LOVE HIM.

NEWS COMES OF DICKSON. Done?

In this society, males crying is accepted, expected. Check and add.

Lillah was curious to know what his cave looked like. Melia never cared about the walls, the pictures. "I'm too busy for that," but to Lillah it was part of the seduction. To see the images the men found sexual gave her an understanding of them. Already she felt like an expert. She had seen a cry for help (SOMETHING DRAWN INTO THE TRUNK THAT FRIGHTENS HER in community 9) and she had seen things which made her back out of the cave and choose somebody else. (This is community 4.) Done?

Lillah has moments of resentment towards Morace – what she's given up for him. What she's risking. But sees him innocently wandering and knows she could never survive the guilt if she let him be killed. Clear?

So while women have the power because of their experience and knowledge, men have the steady jobs. Women have husbands and kids and freedom eventually, men have their jobs and security. They have to stay still forever.

After finishing Walking the Tree, *Kaaron took the unusual step of revisiting the story through the eyes of Morace, in a new novella.*

Here is the opening to his story – and see at the end how you can download the whole thing.

Morace

Laburnun — OMBU — *Aloes*
We call it Our Place.
I am ten years old.

I hope Mother lets me go to school this year. I'm bored being home with her. School may be hard, and it may be scary and tiring, but at least it will be different. I can't think of what to do to convince her to let me. I don't want to be too useful or kind in case she can't bear to part with me. I don't want to be bad because she might punish me.

I'll have to talk to Dad. He might be on my side, see that I have to go to school and he might be able to think of what to do.

School takes five years. We leave our village and we walk around Botanica. Around the Tree, the island. We walk quickly, and we stay in other villages and we will walk back into Ombu five years from now.

The other children have no doubt they are going. They don't have crazy people deciding for them.

Every time a school comes through here, I am jealous. I want to disguise myself and go with them. They are tired, often, but they are so confident, so full of knowledge and information, so easy with each other and with all of us. I want that. I really want that.

Rham came by to ask me to go swimming. She's younger than me but taller. With her, it doesn't matter. The others tease me because I'm skinny and short, but she doesn't care.

"Mother won't let me go." I kicked a rock as I spoke and hurt my toe.

"She won't know if you dry off before you get home." Rham bounced around me. She always had good arguments.

"She knows everything, and if she finds out she won't let me go to school," I said.

"Come and watch then." I let her drag me along. I could collect shells along the shore at least, to trade with the older boys for sweet berries or for small carved tools. If I save enough shells, I might get a fish spear. Then I'll be popular on the school walk. I'll be useful.

Once I go to school, I'll swim so far, so hard. The teachers will let me. I will follow my mother's rules until I am out of her sight, then no longer.

I collected two scoops of shells, piling them onto

a smooth, flat piece of drift-in wood. Carrying them back home, I planned what I would say to Dad when I found him alone.

He was readying his things in a basket and I knew what that meant. I tried, anyhow.

"Dad?" I said.

"Morace, I can't talk. Magnolia's started to have her baby."

Mum hates it when another woman has a baby. She doesn't like to share Dad yet she has to. He's Birthman and the women want him with them.

Mum's awful when Dad's away. Shouts at me, as if it's my fault, until I want to hide under my bed and pretend her voice is the Tree screaming in the wind.

I walked with him to Magnolia's house, knowing I could get a few points in while he was distracted.

"So, Dad, you know Rham is going to school this year? She's so smart, don't you think?"

"Yes, yes she is."

"And it would be a shame if I wasn't around that cleverness for five years, don't you think?"

"You're very clever yourself, Morace. So you don't need to convince me about school. I know you should go. But it's hard for your mother to let go."

"Every other mother does it."

He stopped walking and put down his basket. "You know your mother is not like others. I can't talk about this now, Morace. Magnolia needs me.

Come along and help. We'll think of a way to convince your mother."

When we got to Magnolia's, he was greeted with great welcome. I waited for a while, but it took too long for the baby to come and I felt useless. I went to the trunk and explored the caves there. Some people are scared of ghosts inside the Tree but I know what to say if I ever met one. I'll say, "Can you show me what's inside?" I went back to Magnolia's a few hours later with some coconut and fish for Dad to eat, because sometimes he forgets and he comes home so hungry he can't swallow. When I got there the baby had arrived and there were all sorts of people crowded around. Logan, Magnolia's husband, looked very tired but happy. Dad looked okay; I think they must have fed him.

A crabby girl shoved us out of the room. Lillah. She's Logan's sister. She wants to be a teacher but she seems very mean. I hope she doesn't get picked. I hope Melia does. She is very funny and likes to talk to us.

I didn't want to go home and see Mother because all I could think about was school and I didn't want to say the wrong thing. So I went back and sat by the Tree Trunk, at the place where stories are told, and I dreamt of people telling stories about me and my adventures. I waited for Dad there and when he walked past, tired but happy, I ran to take his hand. Mum doesn't like him happy, but I do.

Sometimes Mum moves stiffly, as if her bones hurt. But sometimes she forgets, and moves like the rest of us.

When Dad came home she did this thing where she moves, but smiles bravely as if she is hiding her pain. I can't stand it when she does it, trying to make us do what she wants, but Dad doesn't seem to mind. He sat down and drew me onto his lap, held me tight and said, "You are my precious son. There is no question of how much I love you." That started to get embarrassing. Mum yelped with pain and he put me aside. He was exhausted. He said, "I'll rest for a short time, but I still need to get back to Magnolia. Her baby is glorious, Rhizo. What a beautiful child."

She nodded, my mother did, but with her eyes closed.

"Are you feeling pain?"

"Just a little," she said, but so quiet, as if she couldn't bear to talk. So instead of resting, he looked after Mum. I don't know if I will be so kind when I'm grown-up.

Children love my Dad. He's big as a bush and strong. Other men get annoyed with kids, but not my Dad. He thinks we're funny and says adults can learn a lot from children. Smart man!

He rubbed Mum's legs and gave her a drink of warm lemon. He stroked her head and murmured to her. I hoped he was saying, "Let Morace go to school. Let him go."

• • •

The noise rose outside. "Baby celebration!" Dad said, and he and I grasped hands and smiled at each other. The community is so happy at a baby celebration. We have a lot of fun, once the boring talking is over.

Mother squeezed her fingers to the side of her head. "I'll come. I should come," she said, but she stood up and let her knees wobble. "You go on. I'll come soon," she said, holding my arm so tight it hurt. I went, even though I knew she wanted me to stay with her. Dad wanted me to go.

Lots of people were there already, including Dickson, one of the grown-ups. He is so awful. He teases us kids. Hides in the branches to frighten us and he takes our food sometimes because he's bigger. We were eating food and talking at the celebration and he peed on people. I couldn't believe it. I wouldn't do that. The grown-ups laughed as if it was funny.

Later he picked up one of the other children, not me. If he'd picked me up I would have screamed. But Zygo loved it. Loved being spun around so fast he was nearly sick. The grown-ups said stop, but Zygo said keep going. He is young. He's wilder than I am and makes fun of me. He's not brave, though. When I look into the ghost cave, he screams with the rest of them.

I like the emptiness of the ghost cave. The fact no one else goes in there, looks in there. The fact it is mine alone.

Sometimes I feel this hard nut of something in my stomach. I think it's hate. I feel like I hate Dickson, hate Zygo. Sometimes I even hate my mother. And I hate being told what to do.

I was bored, listening to the grown-up talk. I sat there, though, because they want you to and sometimes it's easier doing what the grown-ups say.

You don't just get to eat and play when there's a celebration. You have to listen to stories and rules and future plans.

"The Tale teller makes a good story boring," I said to the other children later. "Come with me and I'll tell you the real story of the Tree and the noise inside it. If you are scared you should stay with the adults. You don't belong with the children." Most of them followed me up to the base of the Tree. I made them press into the thick leaves. I like it in there.

"There is a massive insect inside, a giant termite, nibbling away at the flesh of the Tree. They say if you scrape your shin on the bark, leave any skerrick of yourself behind, the insect will come for you. Once he's had a taste of you he'll come to gobble you up."

They ran screaming from the Tree down to the safety of the water. They are not used to hearing bad things; in our community children are never hungry and we are treated well. We are not beaten. Our sins are punished with discussions, long, dull discussions about what should and shouldn't be.

Every time I looked at Dad I pleaded with my eyes. "Ask her! Talk to her!" He did start talking to Mother about school, and about how my life would be if I didn't go. He whispered other things, too. Grown-up things which made her smile.

They announced the teachers and crabby Lillah is one of them. She actually smiled and didn't seem crabby while we celebrated. Rham said to me and Zygo, "She might be fun." They are both going, of course, and Borag too, and three or four others. The teachers are Lillah, Melia, Thea, Erica and Agara.

I wanted to be happy for them, but I couldn't do it. I didn't think I was going.

Lillah saw me sitting alone and walked over. "Morace, I'm sure you'll be coming with us. Your father talks a lot about it." My mother hates my father talking to the young women.

"It's her that's the problem," I said.

"I'll talk to her. It can't hurt me if she hates me; I'll probably never see her again."

That's the thing with the teachers. They don't come back. They find a new village to live in and they stay there.

"Yes, please!" I said. "If I have to wait for the next school to leave, the children will be even younger. I can't be friends with children who still need help to wipe their bottoms."

She laughed. She is turning out to be not so bad after all. Most of them wouldn't even know I was worried about it, so I think she might be all right.

Mother welcomed Lillah in her tight-faced way. She spoke so quietly Lillah couldn't hear her, until finally Lillah sent me away to find a smoothstone so my mother would be able to speak normally, not try to keep me from hearing.

I hid under the window. My friend Rham saw me outside and came over and stood with me. I didn't want her to hear any of my secrets. She is too smart. I caused an argument with her and she threw her hair back in anger and walked away. So she didn't hear what I heard. Mother played her foolish talking, lying game and I listened outside the window, wanting to run in and push her over. The words were muffled by our window coverings. Oh, Mother and her secrets. I thought I knew them all. But here were two. Two things I didn't know. She said "Can I trust you, Lillah?" then she said she was very sick.

I felt so bad about it. It meant that she might die and I couldn't bear the thought of that. Plus, what about me? What if people thought I was sick with Spikes and decided to treat me? I didn't want to die. I was too young and I had not even been to school yet. How could she do this to me?

She said she didn't want me to know, but how would she think I wouldn't?

And then she told the next secret. A terrible, wonderful thing.

My father is not my father. I don't understand. Myrist is. Lillah's father Myrist is my father also. So Lillah is my sister, my half-sister. Such a wonderful thing. And then so is Logan half my brother! And then so is that baby half my nephew, or is he quarter my nephew? He's mine, anyway. I belong.

But my father is not my father.

After all that, she said yes. I'm going to school.

Lillah's turning out to be really good. She took me to see Aracauri. He hasn't got legs that work but he's got the strongest arms you've ever seen.

He gave me a great hat with flaps on the side so I only had to look ahead. It was to keep the world small, he said. I like small places. I hate looking along the beach, out to sea. It's endless. I want to know when something will stop.

The hat blocks a lot of view off and I like that. Aracauri told us a story which made me think he was like me; he said he used to wear it because he used to hate open spaces but now he didn't. He might have been lying but he seemed to be truthful.

I can't believe Mum is letting me go to school. I thought she'd say no, and I'd be left here with the babies and the old people. The other children see the sand and the beach as places to explore. They don't think ahead. I do. I see sharp rocks, spiny fish, poison food. If I think about it, everything ahead is danger. I want to be like them. Fearless. Not like my mother.

I can't believe I'm about to go. Leave home to walk around the Tree. I can't believe she's letting me go.

I look at my father. The one I've always thought of as my father. I will miss him. I feel bad leaving him behind. I'll miss him. They say you barely recognise your parents when you get back.

I have his smoothstone. He gave it to me. I never thought I'd own this; I thought it would sit on the shelf, forever. Or until Mum and Dad died, but it would be too late for me to go anywhere, then. I'd be grown-up. An old man.

The one who really is my father? I don't care about him. I am too scared to talk to him in case he finds me weak.

Is it bad I feel so happy to be leaving Mum behind? Even ten steps away I feel better. My nostrils are clear, and I smell salt air, the Tree. The smell of Mum's illness has gone. I stink, though. No wonder the other children keep away from me. It was so clear away from home. I can fix that, easy. They'll like me soon enough.

Hopefully.

Ombu — ALOES — *Ailanthus*
We call it Jasmine Place.

The further away from home, the more I only wanted to look at my feet. The water was so big away from our community and I didn't know if around any corner, behind any rock, a huge sea monster lay in wait to swipe me out to sea with his tail. Break my legs, my back, and I lie face down and can't breathe.

I tried to hold Lillah's hand but she was too busy being excited. I felt like running back to the fathers and saying, "You've chosen the wrong one. This one is mean and doesn't care for the children."

I felt like saying, "Hey, sister." But Mum had warned me I had to keep the secret, not let anyone else know. Lillah made Mum tell me in person, which was good, because then I didn't have to pretend not to know. But Mum said never to tell anyone or I would put my life in danger.

She always thinks of the worst thing.

We feel tired. We have never walked for so many days before. We sleep out and we have to build a fire to cook our food every day.

Rham took my hand. She's the smartest person I've ever met. Smarter than all the adults put together.

"Can you believe how foolish the teachers are? We are going to have to look after them."

We were close to the next community and the teachers were sitting in the sand rubbing the grains on their legs to make the skin smooth.

"They are crazy. We're all going to die with them looking after us," I told the other students. "Look at them. Don't they realise we're hungry? Well, at least they die smooth."

The children laughed at that. I like it when they think I'm funny. Back home, mostly they didn't notice me. Out here it's different.

Going into a new village for the first time was really strange. It looked like Ombu from the edges; the houses there were the same, and they had a seawalk to take you over the water to fish and to feel the sun if the Tree's shadow filled the island.

But they were strangers. All new faces. They knew each other but not us.

I let the people of Aloes put seaweed on my face. The things I'll do for a laugh. It felt bad when it was on, but my cheeks felt tingly and good when they washed it off.

Many things are different. In Ombu, we wash in a pool of collected sea water, letting the water soak off the dirt. Here, washing yourself hurts. You go out into the water (Lillah had to walk beside me because I still felt worried about being deep in water) and using scratchy seaweed, you scrub and scrub.

The ones I feel really sorry for are the oil-makers. They make oil here from the jasmine flowers, and the oil-makers have to wash themselves so hard their skin bleeds. They hit themselves, too. It seems as if they like the sight of blood here. I don't like it when things hurt me. These people actually scrub till they bleed.

This place stinks so bad of flowers we feel sick.

It was hard to enjoy the feast when they fed us, because the smell is quite strong. It was quite good food and then they made us go to bed, but none of us could sleep because of the noise the teachers made. Drinking fermented tea makes you screech, it seems. The men watched them. The teachers danced around and they looked okay but silly. The teachers and the men started to like each other. In Ombu when that happens no one notices what the children do, so it's our chance to run around and do the things we want to do. I don't do very much. I feel worried about the water, the sand, the rocks, the Tree.

I feel braver with Rham nearby. She is smart but not scared. She has sayings. She says, "If you think quickly, you can get out of trouble."

Finally, we ran around and played so much were so exhausted and we fell asleep. It was nice to be in a comfortable bed and under shelter.

We awoke to more shouting; the local children. Rham went to have a look. She came running back.

"Thea's boyfriend has Spikes and they're going to treat him." Spikes is the disease you get which turns your insides smooth. I hope my mother doesn't have it, but they will say she has and say I have, too.

We dressed and ran to see. Thea stood by herself crying but none of us wanted to go near her. Some adults you do not want to be alone with. They hurt you. Thea doesn't hurt you but she looks as if she wants to. Rham says she drowned her own sister, but who knows.

We know two children drowned when Thea was supposed to be looking after them. The adults say, "Oh, poor Thea, it must have been terrible," but I know Thea doesn't think it's terrible at all.

The local kids said, "You brought Spikes with you. We didn't have it before." I thought they stared at me; how could they know that my mother was sick? But Lillah said, "This man was infected long before we arrived. We are the ones in danger." The children backed away and I hoped none of their fathers would be angry with Lillah.

We couldn't believe what they did to the man they said had Spikes. The teachers tried to cover our eyes, but hearing his screams was worse. They beat

him with sticks until he bled. Borag was sick in the
bushes, then she went to her bed. Rham couldn't
believe it. Zygo and I watched until the end. I don't
know why it didn't make him sick. I know I never
want to be beaten like that, though. Zygo fidgeted,
jumped around. He seemed almost excited. I pretended I wasn't sick but I hated it.

Our time to leave came and we weren't too sorry.
   Partly I wanted to go home because I didn't
know what would be next. But I couldn't go back.
This was my only chance in all my life to explore.
When I get back from school I'll be a village boy,
man, old man. I'll marry a teacher who comes
through, hopefully one like Melia, and our children
will go to school, and on it will go.

Aloes — AILANTHUS — *Cedrelas*
We call it Nut Fish Place.

I didn't want to walk so far again so soon, but you have to walk with school. That's what you do. We had two extra people with us. One was a lady who was having a baby but she had to have it in Ailanthus. Her name was Corma. Her husband was here, too. I liked him. His name was Hippocast. We all liked having him with us. He was shy, nervous of walking, but I liked hearing his deep voice. He carried us when we were tired.

We took it in turns to be tired.

We stopped at the market. I've never seen anything like it before. There was a man running it and he hardly had to see people at all, only when they came to the market. He had his room all to himself and he ate what he wanted to eat. He didn't have to worry about anyone else.

The market was so good. I really liked it. It made me want to stay there and help. It made me think

I wanted to be a market holder.

The teachers were happy to spend time at the market, touching things they hadn't seen before. We ate a lot of fruit.

I could feel a cool breeze and wondered where it was coming from. The rest of the market was so hot, we didn't even want to cross the sand to get into the water.

Thea tried to make us swim out with her but none of us will do that. We told the local children not to, either. She plays bad games in the water. Grabs your ankles and pulls you under for too long. Only lets go if someone else tells her to.

We never go swimming with Thea. Well, I never go swimming anyway. Not yet. I like to paddle. I like the feel of the water up to my ankles. I have even walked in until it reaches my thighs. But I will swim one day. Before too long.

Before we get back to Ombu.

I walked along the Trunk, the cool breeze sometimes disappearing, then it would come back. It smelled a bit like the leaves which are not cleared away in the alcoves of the Tree.

Then I found where the breeze was coming from; a dark, deep ghost cave. I stared into it. I could smell inside the Tree. No one else can smell it, only me. It smells cool, and like some kind of food cooking. Wood at night time. I like it. It freaks them out though; they're so scared of ghosts.

I actually do not believe that ghosts will harm us. I think they are the same as us, only ghosts.

When I put my head in, the cave was like my eyes were shut, it was so dark. But I could feel air on my eyeballs. I would have stayed like that but the others found me and pulled me back.

"You can't go in there!" Borag said. She looked like she was about to cry.

Zygo sneered. "He's blood different. That's why he looks in. He was swapped as a child. He is really a ghost."

"Quiet, Zygo," Melia said. "You don't call anyone a ghost."

Everyone is scared of the ghost caves but I like them because they are so enclosed. You can feel the walls so you know where the ending is. Inside might be a person you once knew or loved. How can that be bad?

They always stop me from stepping inside, though. As if I'll disappear forever. I'd like to know what's inside. It might be better than outside…

To read or download the entire novella for free, go to the following URL and use the username & password *morace*

http://extras.angryrobotbooks.com

Winner of the Ditmar Award and the
Shadows Award.

"Powerful stuff. So powerful, in fact, that my throat
was hurting with my attempts to keep my emotions
under control. I was completely drawn in, totally
immersed. I felt ill much of the time."

— Russell Kirkpatrick, bestselling author of
ACROSS THE FACE OF THE WORLD

SLIGHTS

KAARON WARREN

ISBN 978-0-85766-007-7

"SLIGHTS is a rusted blade of a book, cutting
away at the reader's comfortable expectations
until only bitter bones are left."

JAY LAKE

**ANGRY
ROBOT**

Teenage serial killers
Zombie detectives
The grim reaper in love
Howling axes **Vampire
hordes** Dead men's
clones The Black Hand
Death by cellphone
Gangster shamen
Steampunk anarchists
Sex-crazed bloodsuckers
Murderous gods
Riots **Quests** Discovery
Death

Prepare
to welcome
your new
Robot overlords.

angryrobotbooks.com

LAVIE TIDHAR
THE
BOOKMAN

J. ROBERT
KING
ANGEL
OF
DEATH

"King does everything well – characters, prose, plot, humour, drama." – Locus

SLIGHTS
KAARON WARREN

ANDY REMIC
KELL'S
LEGEND

Triumff
HER MAJESTY'S HERO

Mr. DAN ABNETT

TIM WAGGONER

Introducing
Matt Richter
Private Eye
Zombie

NEKROPOLIS

> MOXYLAND
> Lauren Beukes

KING MAKER

THE
CROWN
OF THE
BLOOD
CA THORTH